the
'idiot spy'
(the series)
book eleven

us against the world

c. benjamin lattimore

us against the world
Published: April 2024
Printed in the United States of America
ISBN: 979-8-9889509-1-2

DISCLAIMER: This is a work of fiction. Names, characters, businesses,
places, events, and incidents are either the products of the author's
imagination or used in a fictitious manner. Any resemblance to actual
persons, living or dead, or actual events is purely coincidental.

a lattidreamer™ publication
© C. Benjamin Lattimore, 2024

To Marisa,
thanks for your tireless dedication to my obsession.
I value all that you do to help me with my
endeavors!

ACKNOWLEDGEMENTS

to my children, Christopher, Monica, and Courtney, as well as my grandchildren, Isaiah, and Desmond for just being extraordinary. An exceptional and heartfelt expression of love to my sister Mary E. and my brother Darryl A. Yet again, esteem regards to Maurice Cheeks and Reggie Wilkes.

lots of love ethereally to my mom, Mary Alice, my dad, Walthro M., my little sister, Barbara Ann, and my big brother, Walter E. Also, to my friends, Gordon Gant, Joseph Bongiavanni III, Monique Gorham, Rahsaan Stevens, and my guardian angel, Mrs. Marjorie C. Cheeks.

CHAPTER ONE

On an amazingly beautiful, sunny, and calm day, the clan came together to send members of their group to the great void. Ava and Carlos, Mike, and Carla, were laid to rest on a part of the two hundred acres designated by Jilkes and John Lee as the burial site for their members and families. Contracted security was everywhere, and were coordinated by Dempsey and Hood.

As Clyde officiated the send-off services for their fallen comrades, it was Courtney who was occupied with the question; "who, and why now?" As she considered the group's enemies near and far, she thought that most had been eradicated. As she cried about the group's losses, she smiled when she thought of Carla and her straight up-up and away, takeoffs. As she viewed the four caskets in the front of the makeshift cathedral, she said a little prayer for each of its occupants. At Ava's casket, she began to cry more intensely because she truly learned to love and respect Ava and the way she conducted herself around her husband, Ben "The Sarge" Beckmire.

Courtney placed a kiss on each casket. She was followed by Monica and her two children who began to ask questions about death, and the nature of the work that their mom and dad were involved in.

It was an extremely sad occasion, and each member of the team felt the emotional pain derived from their people being assassinated. John Lee, with his inimitable self, said to Jilkes, "I be hoping this ain't one of those tontine things someone be trying to play with our group."

Jilkes looked at him, started to castigate John Lee, but thought about it for a moment, and replied, "Damn, I hope you're right, but it appears to me that our brethren are well off, but not like Ava, the leadership, and the original 10 + 2. However, as we slept late into the day, and meandered around doing house chores for months, someone took the time to figure out how to penetrate and destroy members of our group. Like the economic theory of LIFO—Last In—First Out."

John Lee loudly exclaimed, "What the hell that means?"

"John Lee, lower your voice, or I will deck your country ass." Jilkes looked at him, and said, "It means that the last members included in our group are the first to be terminated, and then they work towards the core—10+2," Jilkes stated.

John Lee replied, "That don't make a pig's ass worth of sense. You been smoking some new shit or something?" Jilkes ignored him, paid reverence to the four departed comrades that laid before him in caskets, and who were cowardly murdered by an unknown foe.

Ben Beckmire was overcome with grief on so many distinct levels yet concerned himself with the security of the group as opposed to the question that Courtney was privately asking. Carla and Mike's children became the children of the clan and were comforted by each member.

Zanthius was a complete wreck, as was Asiram, and the children. Ava was the mother, the mother-in-law, the grandmother, and the friend. Her impact on her child, her daughter-in-law, and grandbabies would be greatly appreciated, and missed. To Asiram, Ava was the mother that she never had, and the teacher about life that was missing for an incredible amount of her existence. Although suspicious at first of everyone, Asiram began to feel the love, and share it with the group.

# # #

Once the services were concluded, at the repass, the Sarge said, "People, I would like to board our plane, and head to the Northern Territory. Is there anyone here who has a better idea, or place where we can regroup and focus upon who this unknown foe is, and why now?"

John Lee stood up, and said, "I sure hope this ain't about that tontine mess that people talked about a while back. If so, I be having a real problem with the so-called architect of that mess."

The Sarge looked at John Lee, smiled, and said, "I pray to God, that none of us are that retarded to participate in a scheme that pits us against each other. I would rather place a weapon to my head and execute myself before acknowledging that kind of association. We all have been in battle, some of us more than others, we are all dirty, and we can't be absolved of our sins because they are many, and many of them await our arrival in hell. Your mentioning such a thing stains our relationship with each other, and creates a great divide that is not mentally healthy.

We have been together for a long time, some of us, and well, we're all wealthy. If my understanding of the tontine is correct, then it would mean that someone is interested in controlling all that we have amassed. What else can we buy individually or collectively? I must honor your comment, yet look at all that we have accomplished, gained, and those we have helped. Think about it, we have removed more veterans from the bottom of the sewers, brought them into the light, provided them with a skill, a manner to pay child support, and helped with other issues they may have. No, John Lee, I don't think that we're in the middle of a tontine, but I do believe that we have been compromised, and that is the notion that I am sticking with. We buried four people that we loved and depended on. I won't confess it in front of my wife, but I lost the mother of my first child. Regardless of where the two of us were in life, she is still the mother of my son, Zanthius Beckmire De Lombardo."

The Sarge immediately began to weep, and turned his back to the group. Courtney, who is always there to help and comfort, hugged her husband, and whispered in his ear, "I loved your ex-because she was a woman of stature, beauty, intelligence, and was once the lover of my husband. Let's move this group forward, honey, leave the personal stuff in that cabinet drawer, move us forward my love."

"Always by my side, and helping move things along, my wife, my love, my everything, as well as my butt kicker when I make mistakes, Dr. Beckmire. Thanks baby," the Sarge stated.

The Sarge continued, "Okay people, I am not feeling safe here in my own back yard. I want to grab my to go bag, and be on our plane in the next two hours. Some of you may have other feelings about my concerns, but let me say this, we lost four of ours on the same day. That to me is not an accidental or random assignment people, that was strategic, and planned. In my backyard in the outback, I would like to study the facts, and try to discern who got that close to us and was able to assassinate four members of our group. I will personally and individually, decapitate the person or persons responsible for those murders. I will not rest until I have the culprits before me, and know the reasons why such a dastardly act was committed, and everyone who was complicit in it. My family, this is my promise to you. As I have often stated, we are so vulnerable when we are not as a group. I beg of you to be present and accounted for when our plane leaves the ground."

Jilkes stood up, and stated, "My leader, the action is happening here in America, why are we traversing the world to lay in safety in order to figure out who our new enemy is?"

John Lee stood up, and asked, "What that big word mean?"

Jilkes responded, "It means crossing."

"Why in pigs' heaven didn't you just say that? Why you got to use those foreign words all the time?"

Jilkes responded, "Sarge please forgive him. He is still a work in progress after all these years."

John Lee stated, "If that crossing word means to head to Australia, then I be wanting to know the same answer. Why we be crossing if they be killing our friends here, and in Spain? And Mr. Smarty pants talked about some mess called Lifer."

Jilkes looked at John Lee, and said, "I did not say any such thing. I spoke to you about a process called LIFO—Last In—First Out."

John Lee replied, "Yes sir, that be what he talked about."

# # #

A call was made from Los Angeles to New York. The two parties talked about the departure of Mr. Utz, but as far as they were concerned, his demise did not interrupt the plans they made for achieving the goals that they articulated when they were together. The beginning indicators of who Beckmire's new nemesis is, was illustrated when one of the individuals, said, "That son-of-a-bitch blew my home up, and thought that I was still in it. He helped send my only child to prison, and he loves what he gets in the rear. I will never forgive him for that."

The other party stated, "Well, he never did such a thing to me, and I guess my only consideration is that the first objective that we agreed upon, is kept in our sights. As you know, this is a most despicable plot, and at the fruition of eliminating strategically all parties involved, our road to achieving objective number one will be closer than we could have imagined. With the money earned in Venezuela, that turns $2 plus billon into $5 plus billion plus an insurmountable number in house assets. The two men discussed the potential pitfalls, however, both confirmed and agreed that every living person including infants and children had to be concluded, or the plan would be dead in the water, as goes an old navy saying.

CHAPTER TWO

John Lee said to Jilkes, "You know things are clearer when we are in the outback, plus we have all kinds of protection, and it don't be likely this villain can sneak up and commit assassinations on the group." Jilkes looked at him, and asked, "Is there ever a clear thought in that head of yours?"

John Lee responded, "Let me think about that for a minute, and remember all the times I saved your ass from those people in the jungle. However, I be having another clear thought, and that is why is the 'idiot spy', so quick on the draw?"

Jilkes looked long and hard at John Lee, looked around the room, and whispered, "This is too damn scary you country bumpkin. I have been wondering the same damn thing. On several occasions, when a key captive was being questioned, certain words were like a trigger to him, and would send him in a conclusive mindset. You heard what Mr. Utz said, before he was shot in the head, "family ain't always family." And what happened next, the 'idiot spy' put a round in his head. You remember when Asiram was questioning a captive, and he was about to tell who was involved, well, our boy pulled his weapon and shot the man in the head, and said, "Anyone who comes to harm this group is subject to immediate dispatching." The one thing I do know is that there boy loved his momma. I can't see him assassinating her, under any circumstances."

John Lee stated, "I know it all seems suspicious, but I do not want to go getting that Pope mess in my head, where he has all the answers, and believes that everyone is against his stance in that *between heaven & hell* document. That there fella has showed up a couple of times in my dreams lately. I think I am going to need a deeper cleansing than the one I had in the belly of that mountain. That is why I pushed to go to the outback. So far, the dreams are little, not like before when it was clear when I cut your black ass head off. Naw, they be creating suspicion about everyone."

John Lee paused, and was on the brink of crying. Jilkes immediately confirmed, "Big Country, I am here for you until the day I die. I will never let you get suckered into that evil shit again. Please, tell me everything that has happened in your dreams so that together we can present a clear picture to Wajickee and the elders."

# # #

At the airport, everyone was accounted for. Captain Carla's co-captain requested that everyone make sure that their seat belts were snuggly fastened around their midsection and that their tray-tables were firmly locked into place. He announced, "Captain Carla was a long time personal and special friend of mine, and in her honor, I would like to blast this lady into the clouds in memory of our late captain."

#

In New Zealand, as the plane took on fuel, John Lee asked Jilkes to look over his right shoulder, and see if he recognized the person in the blue jeans and white Polo shirt? Jilkes asked, "Is this a part of what is troubling you, or are we truly trying to figure out if this person has been in our circle before?"

John Lee responded, "Boy, my dumbest pig would say, "stop the horseshit and pay attention to the pigshit". Do you or do you not recognize that guy?" Jilkes smiled at him, and then focused on the person in the outfit that John Lee described. Jilkes looked intently at the person, and said, "That's the FBI agent. Is he following us?"

John Lee saw Dempsey and Hood and beckoned them over. Once they were in his midst, he said, "I need you guys to quietly suggest to that fella in the blue jeans and white Polo shirt that he meet me in the men's room. If he refuses, then let it be. Don't ya'll start no ruckus in this here airport. Just let him be, and let him know that we be watching his ass." As the Sarge came close to the group, he asked, "What's all the secrecy about?"

John Lee exclaimed, "The FBI agent that came to *The Sanctuary*, is in the airport!"

Hood and Dempsey walked over to the person in the pre-described outfit, and indicated that John Lee Jones Jr, wanted to have a conversation with him in the men's room." The guy looked at Hood and Dempsey, turned his head to the left, and saw John Lee. He smiled at him, and then told Hood and Dempsey, "Back the fuck up."

#

In the men's room, Jelani Latinmire exclaimed, "How coincidental! I guess you guys are on your way to the outback." John Lee responded, "That there information be correct. However, I don't believe in coincidences. Are you on official business or what?"

"Naw, I was terminated for insubordination. I am on my way to Sydney to see my grandmother."

Jilkes replied, "Bullshit."

Jelani Latinmire looked at him, and said, "Mr. Jilkes, this is the last place you want to have a confrontation. Check my ticket, and you will see where it terminates. Plus, you people are going to my country of origin. Unless this conversation turns to a much more cordial tone and atmosphere, then I am out of here."

The Sarge came in, sought confirmation, and asked, "You are the young fella that came to *The Sanctuary* inquiring about the deaths of drug dealers on St. John, aren't you? John Lee tried to impersonate me."

"Yes sir, that is correct."

"Latinmire, doesn't sound Australian," the Sarge stated.

"Neither does Beckmire," Jelani fired back.

Beckmire said, "We could do this all day, and never get anywhere. I am just going to ask you straight up, are we under investigation by you?"

"Mr. Beckmire, I am going to respond straight up, no. I am going to see my grandmother in Sydney, and I am no longer employed by the FBI. I am unemployed."

John Lee asked, "Are you looking for employment, and you must admit, this is really coincidental, meeting here after that event in St. Thomas."

"Coincidental for you, but I missed my Pop Pop's funeral because the bureau would not allow me to travel for some odd reason or another. Therefore, I resigned, on the spot. There was some idea that I was in cahoots with you people because I broke ranks and informed you that Mr. Utz was waiting to blow you out of the sky with two stolen heat seeking missiles."

Jilkes said, "As a spy, you're supposed to be able to make up stories on the spot to justify any conditions or circumstances that you find yourself in. Am I not, right?"

"You are so right, that I am honored to know that you think out of the box. However, shit happens!" He exclaimed. You think that I am working for the FBI, and they think that you guys secretly employ me. Therefore, I don't give a shit what either of you think. I'm going to spend my time in Sydney, enjoy the sights, and hopefully meet a wonderful woman. My grandmother wants me to meet a nice and respectful Aboriginal woman and then, she would be ready to go, and meet my grandpa in the afterlife."

Jilkes asked, "So, are you an Abo?"

Jelani started towards Jilkes, who surrendered by holding his hands in the air. In the interim, John Lee announced to Mr. Latinmire that he needed to relax. Jilkes with the Sarge watching, said to Mr. Latinmire, "We have been managed by all kinds of individuals, agencies, churches, and governments. My calling you an Abo was to measure your commitment and your resolve. I apologize, and deeply state that I was only measuring the tea in the cup, not the cup." Jilkes bowed low and slow.

The Sarge said, "As you can imagine, we're on edge. Several members of our group have been assassinated."

Mr. Latinmire said, "I am sorry to hear that. If I can be of assistance, please, don't hesitate to contact me. John Lee allegedly committed my phone number to memory. I'm not sure of your mission and vision statement, but if it concerns the betterment of people and societies, then I am available. I don't do random murders."

John Lee asked, "What if someone was trying to kill me? What would your response be, wait until he shoots me, or would you shoot him first?"

"John Lee, of course I would blast him or her into a new dimension prior to him or her shooting you. I just don't go out and shoot people without a strong reason."

The Sarge looked at Mr. Latinmire, and asked, "Are you a believing man? Are you trustworthy? Will you swear on your grandmother's life that you are not a conspirator or a traitor trying to infiltrate a group of people who are trying to figure out who is trying to kill them and why?"

Mr. Latinmire looked at the Sarge, then at Jilkes, and scowled. He looked at John Lee, and said, "Not sure of your plans, but if you have time to stop in Sydney, I would like to introduce you to my grandma, and she will tell me if you people are righteous or evil. Things are different there, and if you're not a believing person, then she will discount you immediately."

"How did we get from identifying you, to being invited to your grandma's place for evaluation. Why don't you get on our plane, and meet a real seer?" The Sarge asked.

"Mr. Beckmire, my grandma is over ninety years old. When you say Monday, and a time, that is what she expects. The question behind all of this is baffling to me. I am going to see my family. You're going somewhere in the outback. Why is anything else important?"

John Lee, cut the Sarge off, and said, "If you be wanting to, we may have a job available for you. We be trying to figure out that FBI shit. Are you a plant, a snitch, a stooge, or what."

"I am going to see my grandma. Guys, nice talking to you, and I wish you well."

The Sarge said, "Before you go, if you would like us to contact you, please make sure you give us accurate contact information."

Mr. Latinmire stated, "I am not sure this is what I'm looking for.   Guys, nice to have this dysfunctional conversation, I'm off to see my grandma."

John Lee asked, "Do you like the new Pope?"

"There was no announcement of a new Pope. What are you talking about?" Jelani asked.

"I just wanted to know if you are a follower of that religion."'

"John Lee, I follow no man who is appointed to represent a religion, who was chosen by other men. My grandpa always said, "Men are men—God is God, and the two shall never be equal, and the one shall never correctly interpret the true meaning of the 'word'.""

Beckmire appearing mesmerized, asked, "Would you be interested in having a more detailed conversation with us about a way in which you may potentially provide us with some modicum of service?"

"Mr. Beckmire, I will entertain that thought if, and only if, you make a stopover in Sydney, and let my grandma assess whether you people are legitimate or not."

The Sarge looked at him, and thought, "Is this guy crazy or am I a nut for listening to one?"

Jilkes said, "How about you give us your ticket, we search you from head to toe, and I do mean search, and we take a detour for a few hours into the city?"

"Mr. Jilkes, when you say search, do you mean into cavities?"

"That seems like a reasonable compromise for us to bring you on our plane, knowing that you were a part of an organization that would like to bury us."

"Oh, I see!" Mr. Latinmire proclaimed. "How about I meet you in Sydney, and then we can see what my family thinks about yours?"

"No deal!" Jilkes vehemently exclaimed. "By the time we get there, if we get there, you will have the ability to hide any contraband, gather forces to create negative circumstances for us, and put our children in harm's way."

"Mr. Jilkes, I am no longer employed because I searched documents and discovered information that stated your entire clan was sanctioned to be erased. This was in a file authorized by a person named Walter Lassiter. Those documents also stated emphatically, anyone able to breathe who was connected to your group, was to be concluded. I was searching for a connection between what happened to our soldiers on St. John, and someone who was connected to the Vatican. Mr. Jilkes, this is all classified information, but I feel compelled to share it with you. There was a picture of a nun that appeared in several situations, including events in Minnesota, St. John, Poughkeepsie, and a few other places that had your signature on a series of activities."

Jelani scowled again at Jilkes, and said, "Forget all of that, the fact that people had a file that had not been completely evaluated that had a hit order on you and your people, well, I just said that this place is as crooked as those it should be investigating. I knew from the layout of the situation on St. John, that it had a professional design to it. In other words, those people didn't kill each other, someone, or some group with the ability to successfully terminate, and disappear, was responsible for that event. My analysis of the tire that was shot led me to a third party. In my evaluation and learning that the round that blew out the tire was a round consistently found in bodies from your ranch, your farm, and from a lot of other places where people were terminated. You see, I know you people do dreadful things to people who are bad, but no one should be above the law. Please, don't worry about me, I approve of those who have been terminated, and applaud you for the fortitude to kill the scum of the earth. I just can't work for an organization, the FBI, that is unable to put 2 + 2 together, and can't seem to arrest those involved unless those of concern were bartered to do dastardly things or suffer some consequences. Listen, I am not getting on your plane, and you aren't going to be assessed by my grandma—sounds like a wash to me. Good day gentleman, and may we never meet again."

The Sarge said, "On the contrary. I think there is some synergy that is possible here as long as you understand that you don't make decisions, and that you follow the hierarchy of the group."

Mr. Latinmire looked long and hard at the Sarge, and said, "I have your contact information, and if there is still a need for someone like me in a few months, then let's revisit the notion. Have a wonderful day."

Jilkes said to the Sarge, "I like his style and resolve. I think he would fit well in our group. A little overconfident, but that ain't all that bad, is it?"

"The man has principles, and that means a lot," the Sarge stated.

# # #

Unknowingly, the celebrated success derived from the deaths of Carlos, Ava, Mike, and Carla, gave the new conspirators a sense of bravado. They knew that the attempt in Alabama was a bit extreme, since it included some of Beckmire's group most seasoned and experienced members. However, the feeling was that a strong and you'd better be on your toes message was sent.

Mr. East and Mr. West, the fictitious names that they assigned to each other, discussed the next pair of victims to be culled from the group. It was decided that next pair had to be ranking members of the group.

A lottery was held to select the next assassinations. From the East coast, it was stated that the selection would create an immediate search of all previous foes, but more than likely it would leave them searching high and low for ghosts.

The West Coast conspirator thought that it should be Mallory, Monica, Chakes, and Luana. The East Coast partner inquired, "How about John Lee, Jilkes, Yeshida, and Somara. John Lee and Jilkes would cripple the resolve of the rest since they were the ones who successfully got them out of jungle each time, they ventured in it."

Mr. West said, "You are aiming for the core of that group. Why not just take out Mallory, Monica, Courtney, and the Sarge?"

"Let me think about that. That action would surely gut the group, and send them into a tailspin," Mr. East stated. There was a long silence when Mr. East said, "Killing at that level may provide immediate obstacles to our achieving the goals we established. Not Mallory or Monica, but I think if we terminate the Sarge too soon, it may complicate our access to their war chest. The Sarge is key to our obtaining our objectives. Another option we should consider is to just wipe out everyone except the Sarge, Mallory, and Jong because Jong knows where the treasures are hidden and how to access all those accounts."

Mr. West solemnly asked, "What about the children?"

Mr. East replied, "They grow up to be adults at some point, don't they? Listen for this to work, all lives, little, medium, and large must be sent to the great void. I thought we agreed that was the only option available. Why are you raising that issue again?"

"I am just not comfortable with that notion. That doesn't mean that I won't advance it to the conclusion," Mr. West replied.

# # #

John Lee saw Jilkes, and stated, "You are too busy for me. Did I say or do something wrong?"

Jilkes looked at him, smiled, and said, "No my brother, you have said and done everything that you can to annoy the heck out of me. My only problem is that I still love you, and will love you until the day I die. My current funk is that I am forgetting a lot of simple things, and when I can't remember what they are, I get into a mood. Now, don't your country ass go and tell a soul what I have entrusted to you. I haven't been sleeping well either. When I do, I think of dying. I guess those collective souls in Hades are calling for me."

"Hold up one damn minute. Did that there Holy or Evil Father by chance touch your black ass?"

"How stupid do you want to make this conversation? Hell no, I haven't been around him, and he's long gone to some place that I am sure we'll meet him eventually."

"I be saying that because what you just drew a picture of is exactly how my mind got scrambled up, and I be wanting to kill everybody important to me."

Jilkes looked at John Lee, and said, "Listen, don't mess with me on this one."

John Lee, with his eyes swelling with tears, said, "I tell you that's how my nightmares started. I started forgetting pig shit, and then that there messaging began. It was like all the hog stuff I knew, began to slip away, and was replaced with violent acts towards my family and you, my friend. I be asking you again, did that there Evil or Holy Father ever touch you? I need you to really be thinking about this because if he be done touched you or caught you in a weak moment, that be all the time with your black ass him needs. Then I be thinking that he done compromise your ass, and we have to go down in that there mountain in Minnesota and have them friends of ours get his ass out of your mind and body."

Jilkes vehemently stated, "Not a single word to anyone. You hear me you pig loving abomination?"

John Lee astutely replied, "You see where that there silence got my smart pig loving ass."

Jilkes looked at him, and said, "Give me a couple of hours to reflect on things, then you and I will go to the Sarge and ask him to place me under house arrest away from my friends and family. If I have ever meant anything to you other than a pain in your ass, I need you always close and around me. Please don't let them sink me in a cave by myself." Both men were crying and trying to figure out the next step.

Yeshida appeared on the scene, and asked, "What is going on, and why is there so much testosterone in the air, as demonstrated by tears of sorrow." Before either man could respond, Yeshida inadvertently asked John Lee, "Oh, did he tell you what happened last night?"

Jilkes, was amazed by her acknowledgment of their intimate evening, and said, "I don't think we should go public with what happens in our bedroom." Yeshida removed the scarf from around her neck, and said, "I slept with the devil last night, and he marked me all over."

When Mr. Latinmire arrived in Sydney, he was met by his grandmother, and Aunt Jessie. His grandmother anxiously asked, "Did you talk with foreigners?" He responded, "Hello grandmother, how are you? Hi Aunt Jessie, you're looking fit as ever."

"Son, my nights have been restless, please answer my question." Jelani looked at her, and recognized the exaggerated stressful look on her face, and said, "Grandmother, I talked with a Sergeant Ben Beckmire and his crew who were on their way to the Northern Territory."

Stridently, his grandmother asked, "What did you talk about?" Jelani looked at her long and hard, and stated, "Grandma, that information is classified." His grandmother looked at him and emphatically stated, "You will answer my questions, here and now." Seeing the look on her face, Jelani said, "Grandmother, they wanted me to go the Northern

Territory with them, and I wanted them to come here to meet you, and see if you approve of their group."

His grandmother broke into tears, and announced, "That Mr. Beckmire is a member of our family, and son, you will do honorable deeds with them, and not with that crooked ass government organization you worked for. I watched all of this unfold in my dream state, but I needed confirmation from you. Please forgive an old lady who is set in her ways, and who believes in spirits and our ancestors. I thought that FBI group would turn you into a demon, and I am so grateful that you chose to announce the possibility of an alignment with the Beckmire Clan, a powerful institution in this country, even if they are unheard of. Come, give me a kiss, and let me tell you about what your next pathway in life will be. I want you to reach out to Mr. Beckmire and announce that you would like him and his group to visit you and your grandmother in four days, in Sydney proper."

# # #

After the Sarge was made aware of what happened to Yeshida, he, Mallory, and John Lee caught up with Jilkes. The Sarge asked, "Would you like to talk about what's going on with you?"

Jilkes responded, "What happens in my fucking bedroom is not your concern." John Lee approached him, Jilkes swung at him, and the Sarge caught the wild swing, twisted his body under Jilkes arm, and eventually placed Jilkes in a full nelson. In the interim, John Lee slipped triple wire ties on his Jilkes wrists. Mallory kicked his feet from under him, and John Lee placed wire ties on his ankles. The three men carried him into a nearby hut and watched as their friend's eyes rolled back in his head as if he were having a stroke or something.

Wajickee appeared on the scene, and told the group that they should take Jilkes into the cave with the history in it.

Once the group entered the cave, Jilkes began to respond differently as though he was okay. He asked John Lee, "What the hell is going on? Why am I in these restraints? Whose great idea is this?

John Lee responded, "I think that there Holy Father or Evil landlord has taken up residency in your black ass. You be done marked up your woman, and tried to sucker punch me, and that is when the Boss, placed your ass under submission. How the hell he be done got to you?"

Jilkes replied, "Cut these restraints off me, right now, or when I get free, I will beat you to death."

A surprised John Lee said, "Why you be wanting to kill me? I thought you loved me." Wajickee placed his hands on Jilkes's chest, and the man fell to the cave floor, and was out like a light. Wajickee said, "Let him rest for a little while, and then we will interview his proprietor."

Yeshida in the meantime is livid because someone or something drove her man into submission, and into providing pain, and hurt to her. She told Courtney that it was as if she was a part of his world because she only felt pleasure. When I woke up, and prepared to bathe, I saw that my body had marks and scars all over it. I don't remember any notion of pain, and as you can see, these are not love bites." Courtney continued to apply native solutions, and asked, "Has he ever deviated from the norm before?"

"If you mean has, he ever hurt me or played rough, the answer is no. We were both in a fog, and everything was simply magnificent. Wajickee appeared and startled both ladies after Yeshida had donned a robe. He said, "Pardon my interruption, but did you and your wonderful husband happen to mix the well water with your drink, and did you procure it, or did an Aborigine get it for you?"

Yeshida thought for a moment, and said, "I didn't personally get water, and I'm not sure if he went straight to the well without any guidance. Why do you ask?"

Wajickee smiled, and said, "Certain elements rise to the top of well water and create a powerful euphoric and erotic response in most humans. Initially, the effects are formidable with people who are truly in love with each other. As the impact begins to wane, the effects can become abusive because the elements have both good and bad influences on people who are not accustomed to consuming the well water freely without having the first layer skimmed away. In other words, your enraptured state was self-fulling, but then the bill came, and it was more than what you wanted to pay.

In your husband's case, he just became rebellious and belligerent. Once he wakes up, he will be so full of apologies that it will begin to annoy you. Early on, I reminded you people to have the Aboriginal people procure your water. Those marks on your neck and other places will heal fast with the herbs Dr. Beckmire is applying. Sometimes, the good comes with the bad. Your man is not a mean-spirited person, but the water consumed you both, and you both suffered an outcome that is different with every person who drinks the water freely and without native intervention. Again, be gentle with him because he is so fragile after trying to hit his best friend and being subdued by the Sarge. Please be delicate."

# # #

Three days later, the Sarge told Wajickee about the young lad he encountered, who wanted him to go to Sydney to meet his grandmother. The Sarge then said, "Something is compelling me to visit Sydney, and I can't seem to get my arms around this one."

"You my friend are considered a powerful person in this part of the world, and by people who do not know you, or what you represent to the Aboriginal people as well as the people of the world. I will not bore you with the stories about your forefathers. However, I will tell you that I am aware of this lad, and his grandmother. His name is Jelani Latinmire. He is a clone of Darryl, your nephew, when he is here on the continent. His grandmother is a doozy. It is said that she bids for the spirits in that part of Australia. I have had visions of her, and I had a spirit zoom meeting with her before there was ever such a thing.

Initially, we clashed over minor issues because we were trying to estimate the power of each other. I recall saying to her, that the people in my charge, while in Australia, were good people, and not the vagabonds that she portrayed you people to be. She was so consumed with the notion that you people were drug dealers, and you used your product as well. That bit of insight was a result of watching so many people return to America from Viet Nam who were strung out of drugs. It was only when I mentioned that you were a direct descendant of the Great Saltie that she begged me for forgiveness. This was prior to your first trip to your father's, and his fathers' land. She now knows that you people are good people, and she would like you to actively engage her grandson. Also, she is coming up on a political crisis, much like the one I faced when the elders wanted to replace me with a modern-day spirit. Her concern is immediate, because if she is removed, there will be no trace or memory of her existence, and that would leave the lad in a weird place," Wajickee stated.

"Are you telling me that she is on par with you?" Beckmire asked.

"I'm saying, with a lot of ego, that I am supreme. Listen, I have the responsibility of being the Great Saltie's great, great, great, great, great grandson's protector and counselor," Wajickee affirmatively stated.

"Wait a minute Mr. Supreme, didn't you tell me that a Beckmire does not have a counselor and, therefore, never needs counsel?" Beckmire bellowed out.

Wajickee looked at him, and asked, "Do you have further need of me? I must go and remind myself that you are, and will forever be, a challenge." As soon as he said that he was gone.

# # #

Mr. East said to Mr. West, "According to results of the random assignment, it looks as if Mr. Chakes and Mr. Mallory are the unlucky winners. I don't think it makes sense for us to have our people enter the outback and try to accomplish that mission. Intel says that somehow, the animals collaborated with them to eliminate their foes. I know you're thinking that's a bunch of bullshit, but nevertheless, Australia is not where I prefer to engage them at any time. There is something that happens there that makes me reluctant, scared, and cautious of going to where they have all kinds of alleged protection. Some stories should not be ignored."

"How do you know so much about that place?" Mr. West inquired.

"My intel indicates that large legions on several occasions, have attempted to terminate those people, and the results were the same—no survivors. Much like the intel that got the US into the war in Viet Nam—poor military intel. They didn't account for the fact that the smiling faces during the day, were the back shooting people of the night. Tactics, and often egos supersede smart military, and economic decision making."

Mr. West said, "It's going to be hard to get them on US soil. They will not separate and, therefore, more than likely, our timetable for achieving our goals will be further held in abeyance. However, I trust your decision making, and I realize that rushing this equation won't net what we have in mind. Perhaps making some incredible long-distance shots or attempts, might work to our advantage."

"Now that is exactly what I'm thinking about. The more we demonstrate our resolve, as well as our ability to make a hit, the more discombobulated they become, and will probably make both personal and environmental mistakes. As an example, we know that they rely heavily on a mechanized shooting scenario in some places. Obviously, it is not a hard-wired set of circumstances, and it depends on internet or a Bluetooth type connection which also makes hacking their systems less complicated. I had people drive down by their farm and measure signal strength, distances from towers, as well as known carriers. It so happens that those people believe in supporting local initiatives and individuals. Their carrier, as of last month, is partially owned by you and me. In a haste to expand services in the area, they failed to activate certain FCC documents that so happen to be in our control through one of our shell companies. When I found out about that, I realized that what we are planning to do, is sanctioned by the Gods. Picking up that local license, under a dummy non-profit, created a lot of good will for us. We had to be inclusive and as such, bring in minority and small business types to be a part of our network/organization through well-crafted MOUs. You don't like diving into the details, do you?" Mr. East inquired.

"I normally stay in my lane. You understand all that technical stuff, and I understand how to network nefarious individuals with like-minded aspirations. Listen, we share an unusual common bond, and that is to own all the assets of that group, to make sure there are no surviving members, and that we through simple oversight, waltz in and completely share in billions, if not trillions, of dollars in assets. Who in their right mind would want to read the small print when the bullseye is in that range? I just want to make sure I understand what you're planning. Are you thinking about corrupting their gun control system, and turning it surprisingly, on them?"

"Now, Mr. West, that sounds like a cold-blooded, premediated way of terminating an enemy. I am not going to admit to that scenario, but I must astutely say, you are as perspicacious as anyone that I know. That idea is first and foremost in my mind, and I have friends evaluating the possibility of such a corruptive and terminal event."

# # #

When Jilkes woke up, he asked John Lee, "Why am I being restrained?"

John Lee smiled, and said, "Your black ass tried to sucker punch me, and the Sarge caught your swing, and put a full nelson hold on your ass."

Jilkes looked at him, and bellowed, "Yeah, yeah, yeah! Why would I want to hit your crazy country ass?"

"We all be thinking that there Holy Father or Evil Landlord, somehow got into your mind. You marked up your woman, and hopefully you'll survive the ass whupping she's going to give you. Come to find out, you be done mixed the raw well water with your drinks, and that is what sent you to hell and back."

"John Lee, cut the damn straps off me."

"You see, that's exactly what I would expect a suppressed person to say. Naw, that's not the word, I mean a fanatical demon to say to me. Get me going along with the conversation, and then ask me to release his ass. Naw, I be keeping your black ass in restraints until you apologize for all the mean-spirited things you have said about and to me. How about that?"

"John Lee, cut these straps off me, or I am going to beat the shit out of you."

John Lee looked at Jilkes, and said, "You look obsessed."

"Does your dumb ass mean possessed?"

"Well, you see now, that is the kind of answer I would expect from your mean-spirited black ass. They both mean about the same thing." John Lee reached behind Jilkes and cut the three straps restraining him off. He then cut the straps off his ankles. He said, "You come at me in the wrong manner, and I will have to raise some mixed-race kids. Don't you be messing with me!" John Lee proclaimed.

Jilkes asked, "Please, tell me what I did to my wife?"

"You be done marked her up pretty bad."

John Lee without hesitating said, "I didn't actually see your woman. I just be hearing stuff about her condition. Dr. Courtney saw her, and applied local shit all over her body. Listen here, any deviation from what you normally do, be done defined itself as hurting your wife. The women be looking after her, and my ass be looking after you. I think everyone is going to be pissed at me for setting you free, but I swear to God, it don't be natural to see you with straps on your wrists and ankles. So, I need your black ass to tell me, are you planning on trying to hurt someone, other than me?"

As if a volcano erupted, Jilkes broke into tears. He put his head in his lap, and cried like a baby. It would be three minutes later before he was able to clearly address his friend. He said, "I am so embarrassed. I hurt my woman, and I tried to hit you. I am so ashamed, and I hope you can forgive me. I don't remember anything. All I remember is telling the Sarge that what went on in my bedroom was not his fucking business. I've never spoken to the man like that. I hope he too, can forgive me."

John Lee teared up, and said, "No one will hold that against you. It ain't like your black ass planned this abominable event. You just be like my dumbest pig, you just don't see the sign that says, not safe for piglets."

# # #

A contingency of the group boarded their plane for the ride to Sydney to meet with a woman and her grandson. No one understood the importance of the visit, but all functioned as if they were in a trance when the conversation about the person in Sydney came up. Mallory said to the Sarge, "I am perplexed as hell as to the importance of this trip. We met a lad in the airport, he was a former FBI agent, and now we're on our way to visit his grandmother. Does that make any sense to you?"

The Sarge looked at Mallory, and stated, "I am as confused as you are about this trip. Wajickee acknowledged that she is a spirit of some type, and suggested that I make the journey. Listen, I almost feel naked because we left John Lee, Jilkes and our regular group behind. I'll need the two new guys to open their curious senses, and be as sharp as possible. I hope I'm not walking into another Four Seasons kind of event."

# # #

As the plane began its approach to the airport, a huge gust of wind began to take control of the flight pattern. The co-captain began to speak fast and loudly, until the new captain expressed in no uncertain terms, "Do your fucking job, or this will be your last fucking flight!"

The man calmed down, and the approach of the aircraft was deja vu. The plane approached the runway with its port side directly lined up to the landing strip until the captain engaged the starboard engine, reduced the thrust on the port engine, and the plane hit the runway hard, but with its nose pointed in the correct direction. Everyone breathed a sigh of relief and applauded the skillful manner in which the new captain managed the plane. After coming to a complete stop at a terminal, the Sarge got out of his seat, opened the cockpit door, and said, "Damn that was thrilling and perfect. You are officially, our new captain!"

#

As the group entered the terminal, a familiar person appeared before them, and said, "Sergeant Beckmire, I know how you people travel, and once we exit the airport, you each will be presented with a welcome package from my grandmother. It will have a weapon and two extra clips in each box. Welcome to Sydney, and I must admit, I can't imagine what is propelling this conversation so powerfully forward that you and your people are here to meet my grandmother. Am I missing something?"

"Mr. Latinmire, do you believe in spirits?"

"Now that's a strange question coming from someone who allegedly is from the loins of a spirit. I don't, and I believe the stories about your ancestors are significantly exaggerated and make for a complete fairy tale."

Mallory cleared his throat, and asked, "Will we be able to have the meeting, and be on our way within the next six or so hours?"

Mr. Latinmire responded, "I don't see why not. This whole thing is out of whack. I never imagined you people would be that interested in me to come here to meet with my grandmother."

Beckmire cut him off, and said, "This is not about you my friend, you are just a consequence. And don't you think it's strange that your grandmother questioned you about strangers when you got off the plane?"

Mr. Latinmire stared at the Sarge, and said, "Come, let's leave this place and venture to her home. Nothing appears strange to me about my grandmother because before my mother passed away, she referred to her, as a bruja."

#

Overlooking Manley Bay, in a little house with an epic view of Sydney harbor, two little old ladies greeted Beckmire, and his contingency. All that was communicated was, "Sergeant Beckmire, this is my grandmother and aunt."

It was a beautiful day in Sydney, and three chairs made a circle near the edge of the cliff. Dempsey and Hood never entered the house, but checked out every possible hiding place for an aggressor. When the Sarge and the ladies started toward the cliff, he waved the pair off, and told them to relax.

The grandmother, from a cooler, handed the Sarge a can of piss, and one to her sister. The conversation would last for hours and was only interrupted when someone had to use the loo or food was being served. No one knew the nature of the conversation except the three attendees. After four hours of talk, the grandmother could be seen kissing the hand of the Sarge.

While the Sarge, the grandmother, and the aunt talked, Jelani entertained the other members of the group. As the conversation turned to who the potential assassins were, Jelani asked, "Did anyone physically see the body of the man who lived in the house on stilts in New York?" It was announced by Mallory that the individual in question had a body double on ice in his place. Jelani asked, "So, is it possible that he's still alive? I mean is there any way he could have escaped prior to your detonating ordnances to destroy his home?"

Mallory said, "Listen, we placed enough C4 around that place to open a portal to Hades. There is no way in hell, he could have survived that explosion and the subsequent fire. Plus, he was hog tied to that damn chair. Could there have been someone else besides the target in the building, to possibly free him from his bondage?"

There was no fanfare or revelations about the conversation other than the grandmother exclaiming, "What a spiritual day it has been! There is a lot to be talked about, and there is a lot not to be said. Jelani, come over here boy." When Jelani approached where his grandmother was sitting, she said, "There is a lot I must tell you, and most of it is going to be unbelievable. Over time, you will begin to piece together the facts, and realize how the world separates bad people from good ones. I shall not see this epiphany come to fruition, but you will know that deep in my heart, I tried to do what was best for you, my grandson. May God and the spirits keep you, bless you, and protect you on this quest you will embark on."

As the Sarge kneeled in front of Jelani's grandmother, he whispered, "There are two spirits that I will always listen to and obey—Wajickee and now you. This world is so small, and the connectivity of people is beyond reproach and understanding. My final public question is, why was he so adamant about us meeting you, when the factual information was unknown to all?"

"Mr. Sarge, in my world, the things that make no sense are the things that are relevant. It is unlikely that I'll have another appointment so, I expect you to do what you agreed to do, and make sure that he understands the full scope of why he, you, me, and now Zanthius and Asiram, are connected at the hip."

CHAPTER THREE

On the way back to the outback, the Sarge begged his
people for an opportunity to be alone and undisturbed to
understand all that was told to him in Sydney proper. He asked
them to do their thing, but to allow him to try to fathom all that
was presented to him.

In his normal seat on the group's plane, the Sarge, in his
mind examined every scenario that was presented to him,
repeatedly. Strategically, he tried to discern the benefit
equation for each issue. He realized that Wajickee was aware
of this person, and knew that he could place his life in his
hands. The facts were uncomfortable for even Ben Beckmire
to comprehend. He affirmed to himself that he would not
mention a word of his conversation with the grandmother until
he had spoken to Courtney and Wajickee.

# # #

Once in the village, everyone was preparing for a feast for
kings and queens. The host for the evening was the one and
only, Wajickee. He began the evening by retelling repeatedly,
"If you are of little faith, then I need you to go down by the
billabong, and rest your mind and your soul. Tonight is the
beginning of a new chapter for this group, and by the spirits
that support me, and this clan, if thou is of little faith or none,

thou will pass through the gateway to what is known as Hades. I demand you to search your soul, and if it's not pure, then please head to the billabong and rest.

John Lee stood up, and everyone was surprised, especially after his bout with demons that ordered him to kill his family, and sever the head of his best friend. The universal sound that was heard was, "Oh, my God." John Lee looked at those gasping, and responded, "I just be having one question, and that is what if I don't recognize that there faith you're speaking about as a result of having that fight with demons that demanded wicked things of me?" Wajickee smiled at first, and then demanded that John Lee sit his narrow rear on the ground, and behave. Being an obedient soul, John Lee quickly sat down and saw the scowl on Jilkes's face.

Feeding off this early victory, Wajickee boldly announced, "Demons and spirits are everywhere. If you don't believe me, then ask John Lee Jones Jr. Any smart demon would know that John Lee Jones Jr., is one of the strongest and smartest people in this group. He is the epitome of a friend, lover, family man, and if you happen to be on the other side of his blade, then you're an enemy. He was captured because some demons are plain stupid. Although sounding stranger than most of us here in the outback, his wisdom is always a teaching moment, you must disaggregate the words he uses and attempt to place them in a logical order. Now, Jilkes, oh yeah, Mr. Jilkes, well, he and his lovely wife decided to fetch their own water from the well, a thing that I strongly suggested that you not do when here. Without skimming the unidentifiable by-products of the first layer, then what you consume when added to our locally developed alcoholic drink becomes a strong aphrodisiac initially, and then it turns to a mind-suppressive downer. I single these two brigands out because one without the other is total chaos. This group without them, will be no more!" He exclaimed.

He paused for a few seconds, and then said, "I know you smell that John Dory cooking over there, but you will have to hold those appetites in check until I am finished." He smiled at Ms. Viola, and then said, "As stories go, this one will bring you people full circle. Ben Beckmire and his crew made a visit to Sydney, you people know about that, but what you don't know is the topic of his discussion. I'm going to try to make this story short."

Wajickee, looked to the heavens, and then said, "Years and years ago, an Aboriginal woman gave birth to a mixed-race child. After the birth of the child, it was immediately taken away from her by her father. The child spent its formative years in America, its middle years in Europe, and high school years in South Africa. As a senior in high school, she became pregnant by a South African native who he and his family were sadistically murdered during a raid. Her father did not believe in abortions and, therefore, the mother carried the baby to term. The baby was gorgeous with bronze coloring. That was the first and only time the mother held, and saw her child. Her father told her that she was just like her mother, useless, and that she would never see this child again.

From her bedroom window, the mother, who was tied tight to the bed, could see her father make the sign of the cross over something under a blanket, as he began to violently destroy, what was thought to be her child."

Wajickee paused, and asked, do you people want to eat or hear the rest of this story?" There was strong signs from the women to finish the story. Asiram rose from her seat, and asked, "Is this fact or fiction, Wajickee?"

Wajickee stared at Asiram for about thirty seconds, before he replied, "This is more than fact, and little if any fiction." His demeanor leveled a new quiet, and respect for his words. He said, "Asiram, I am sorry to stare at you like that, but you so much remind me of the first Mrs. Beckmire from too many years to remember."

"To continue, the mother would never see the child again or her father. To completely conclude the embarrassment, the father threw gasoline in the house, and started a fire. He entered his Land Rover, and never looked back. In the meantime, from the back of the bed post, the daughter secured a razor blade, cut her restraints off, threw a chair through a window, and dove out of it."

To make a short story long, that child is Mr. Jelani Latinmire. His grandmother is the mother of the one and only, Helga Spengatsenburg, or Sister Mary to some. Therefore, Zanthius and Asiram, he is blood to little Ben."

# # #

Mr. West and Mr. East decided that they would send a suicide squad to the outback with specific targets in mind. They decided that Jilkes without John Lee was like the Sarge without Mallory. Therefore, the two intended targets would be John Lee and Mallory, and that the would-be assassins would be women of color who could blend in and not look as obvious as white males.

# # #

Ten days later, a Quintus Airline plane landed in Sydney and a mixed group of women from a small school in London, exited the plane to connect to their ultimate destination, the Northern territory. There were twelve college age women of all races in the group. The two assassins were new to the school, and used the trip to attempt to accomplish their tasks.

Entering the connecting flight was Jelani Latinmire, who sat in a row on the plane between the twelve women. The women, at least ten of them flirted directly and indirectly with him until he informed them that he was going to take a nap. He noticed the other two women, but never considered them to be assassins, and felt that they were a little estranged from the rest of the group.

As the plane began to make its final approach to the airport, Jelani woke up to find both women looking at him. The bronze one made a sucking sound with her mouth, and said to the other lady, "If we didn't have work to do, I would probably teach him a thing or two, as she circled her lips with her tongue."

Jelani, as an FBI agent, was taught to listen, learn, and make mental notes of people who for one reason or another caught his eye. The plane landed, Jelani gathered his bags, and watched the beehive of activity to go nowhere because the steps were not in place to exit the plane. As he gazed out of the window, he saw the baggage handlers unloading the plane. What caught his eye were the two black professional cases that marksmen carry their finest bows and arrows in, with a lot of fragile stickers on them. He looked around the plane trying to discern who might the archers be, at first viewing, he saw no one who could pull and fire that kind of weapon.

As he looked more intently at the ladies, he confirmed that five out of twelve looked capable of firing it, and two out of five looked more capable than the rest. He said to himself, "you're not in the FBI anymore, stop acting as if you're on an active investigation." He smiled and chalked his curiosity to the FBI training.

After the steps were locked in place, and the door was opened, he once again looked throughout the cabin to see who the potential archers were. Not being satisfied, he wished the main group of women a safe and productive time in the outback, and cautioned them that, "most spiders are deadly, the animals are dangerous, don't go swimming in billabongs unless a native is around, and stay away from native herbs." They laughed and he said, "I heard that from my grandmother before I left. Have fun ladies."

# # #

Once in the terminal, it became apparent who the high-end archers were. The two members of the group who were a little alienated, had medium size bags as if they weren't planning on being around a long time. Jelani moved behind them, and asked, "Are you two archers?"

The bronzed skinned one replied, "Who wants to know?"

Jelani bellowed, "The FBI." Both ladies turned their heads, and the quiet one said, "Oh, it's you. The sleeping young man."

Jelani replied, "Sleep is good for the body and the brain. I just want to know if you guys are any good at archery?"

"The talkative lady said, "I probably could hit and kill you from fifteen to sixteen hundred feet away."

"No way!" Exclaimed Jelani. "That's like close to four hundred yards or four football fields."

The quiet one said, "Would you like to make a bet on it?"

"You want me to bet that you can kill me with an arrow from up to five hundred yards away? Even if I were a betting man, my grandmother told me don't be stupid, and that bet sounds a little obtuse to me. If you could hit me, and I can't see it, then I am the loser all around—my money plus being shot by an arrow. No thanks."

Jelani saw two ladies in front of a few of the other women, and asked, "Can those two really hit a target with an arrow from four hundred or so yards?"

A little lady replied, "They just enrolled last week, and have missed every class except this one."

Jelani said, "Oh, I see." To himself he cogitated, "now I wonder what those two are really up to." He smiled, and muttered, "FBI training—everyone is crooked!" He exclaimed.

As he ventured out of the airport, and as though he were on a case, he watched as ten young women got into a van, and two got into an open-air jeep. He asked himself aloud, "Could there be a connection? I must pray to be purged of this suspicion that everyone I meet, is crooked.

# # #

As the sole occupant on the school bus, Jelani sat in the seat reserved for Ben Beckmire. The driver kindly said, "Please find another seat. That seat is reserved."

"Are you expecting other passengers?" Jelani asked.

"Sir, please select another seat." The driver responded.

"I like sitting here. What's the big deal?" Jelani asked.

"The big deal is that seat is reserved for royalty, and as I see it, you're not even close, so get your arse out of that seat, and select another."

Jelani looked at the driver, and replied, "I am a guest and, therefore, I will honor your request. My name is Jelani Latinmire, what is your name?"

"I am called Wajickee."

# # #

When the bus arrived in the village, Ben Beckmire was the first one to meet it. He patiently waited until Jelani gathered his belongings, and when he alighted from the bus, Ben Beckmire greeted him with one of his manly hugs. The Sarge asked, "How was your trip?"

"It was uneventful, but the plane was loaded with some great looking young ladies, who came here to study Aborigine life. At least most of them did. I think a couple of them have something else on their minds," Jelani said.

"Something else like what?" Ben Beckmire inquired.

"Oh, I don't know. It's just that the cases they were carrying, allegedly had bows that could precisely fire an arrow four hundred yards or better, and hit its target." Jelani announced.

"Come, let's get you settled, and then we will meet some people that are curious about you, your relationship to their son, and I'm sure, other things as well."

On the way to his hut, the two men encountered Ms. Viola, who asked, "Who is this handsome young fellow?"

The Sarge smiled, and said, "This handsome young man is the brother of Ben Beckmire De Lombardo Jr.

Ms. Viola responded, "Yeah right, Mr. Sarge."

Jelani smiled at her, and said, "This thing that he states is as real as I am. I am his older brother."

Ms. Viola stared at the two men to see if they were pulling her leg, and decided that there must be some truth in what both men had stated. She then said, "We will all celebrate your arrival in the village at dinner. Until then, I offer my simple welcome, and look forward to watching how this tale is spun to the group."

The Sarge said, "Only you, my son, and Asiram know about this relationship. It is in everyone's best interest if you kept this a secret. No one else needs to know until the appointed time.

In front of their hut, Asiram waited patiently to meet the alleged brother of Ben. She, and 'the idiot spy', had several lengthy conversations about this unknown brother to one of their children. When the Sarge and Jelani reached Zanthius and Asiram's hut, Jelani said, "Asiram my name is Jelani Latinmire, and it is said that I am the older brother of your child by another mother, Ben. Let me say, I come seeking absolutely nothing except love, and hopefully acceptance. I bring nothing and I seek only an understanding of the facts."

Surprisingly, Asiram embraced Jelani, and as Zanthius came out of the hut, she said, "Honey, in this strange place with spirits and demons, I want you to meet your stepson, Jelani Latinmire."

No one considered the role of Zanthius except Asiram who said, "Honey, let this be the last surprise in our marriage." Everyone laughed, and running full steam ahead, Ben exited the hut, and stopped at the feet of the stranger. He admired his boots and pants, and as he gazed at the stranger's face, he turned and ran to his mother. Asiram said, "For now, we are going to recognize you as a new member of our tribe. Until we can figure out all of the dynamics, this is one of my requests. There are other concerns, however immediately, let's slowly and methodically enter this new arena. I only ask that you never discuss your mother, or your relationship with my son, and in not doing so, we will strategize as to how to make you a member of our immediate family, and acknowledge that you are the brother of my son. Do you have any questions?"

"Ms. Asiram and Mr. Zanthius, this is all new to me. My grandmother, who I think is a bruja, summoned Mr. Beckmire to Sydney. The next thing I hear is all the things that my mother has done, is doing, being of a split-personality, hiring people to kill other people including the father of her child as well as the woman who has cared for him, her relationship with the 'idiot spy', and a power struggle between two spirits. I was an FBI agent, who came to your Sanctuary to inform Mr. Beckmire that a former federal agent had absconded with two heat seeking missiles, and a few Laws rockets. I showed up in New Zealand, where I was literally and verbally harassed by Jilkes and John Lee, because they thought I was following them, on of all things, a commercial airline—wow, how brilliant! I finally got beyond those two guys, and kept getting messages from my grandmother about having people come to her so that she could determine if you people were good and decent or downright evil. Well, hells bells, I don't buy all that mess. However, Mr. Beckmire showed up in Sydney to meet her. Listen, I don't understand this matter at all, but I look forward to the journey, officially meeting my little brother, enjoying a trusting and lifelong relationship with him, his mother and father, and understanding the nature of those two anomalies—Jilkes and John Lee."

The Sarge broke into laughter, and said, "Welcome to that mission, because I have been around them since they were new recruits, fighting each other, but to this day, I can't tell you a damn thing about what makes them who they are. I'll tell you this, they are the best at what they do, and we all love and respect their discombobulated relationship."

# # #

Jelani socialized with his younger brother for about an hour with his parents diligently watching every minute. He said, "He is so articulate, smart, and friendly. He asked me, "If I were a family member, and if not, then why not? He also said he liked me a lot!"

Asiram replied, "Jelani, when here, everything is possible. The kids aren't pretentious, however, they are not your normal three, four, five, six, seven, and eight-year-olds. You will find all the kids in this tribe are above grade level in every aspect of measurable educational documentation. Ben is just Ben, friendly, trusting, and outgoing. As time passes, we will seek the opportune time to tell him that you are his older brother along with other critical information that he should know. Your being here, requires me and Zanthius to accentuate our timetable for telling him the truth about me."

Jelani interrupted her, and said, "My being here has nothing to do with any admissions. He may consider me a friend of the family until the day I die. I don't want to upset the wholesomeness that this family exudes. Keep me as the friend. I don't need to be exposed as a brother, I know it, you will eventually believe it, and, therefore, titles are superfluous. Love and awareness are safe for me. You, Ms. Asiram raised him, fed him, and I guess suckled him, so his lifeline is not mine, it is yours."

As Asiram began to weep, Zanthius said, "Welcome Jelani, and my family, is your family!"

## CHAPTER FOUR

There was noise surfacing in DC that a once high-powered government official, who was presumed consumed in a fire in his house had been spotted in Maryland. A secretary who once worked for him, saw him from ten feet away in Baltimore, and knew it was him because of his distinctive walk, his propensity to always stop, and look behind himself. She said to her ex-husband as he picked up their children, "You know, I believe I saw my ex-employer today. I guess that's impossible because he was burned beyond recognition in that fire in his house on the stilts in Poughkeepsie. When I was exiting the Starbucks near the Polish War Memorial, I saw a man standing very still as if he were praying, and when he concluded whatever, he was doing, he kissed his folded thumb, a thing my ex-employer used to do."

Her ex-husband looked at her, and asked, "Did he see you?"

"Naw, he turned to walk towards the Marriott, and I never thought anymore about it until you drove up." Her ex, looked at her, and asked, "My driving up made you think of your old boss?"

"No, silly man. The fact that he was as secretive as you were and are, reminded me of him and you."

Her ex laughed, and said, "If you would like to have dinner sometime, to discuss the growth of our children, I think that would be a good thing unless you're in a committed relationship."

"Okay, listen. Cut the bullshit. If you want to know if I am dating, then ask the question. Don't blow smoke up my culo."

Her ex smiled, and asked, "Actually, I want to talk to you about someone that I've met."

As the children began to tug on their dad, she said, "I'm sorry, that is not a conversation that I would be objective or civil about."

She turned to walk away, and he said, "I almost reached out to touch you and pull you close to me. I also realized that would have been a deal breaker in terms of fulfilling the edicts of our divorce. Just so that you know, I will love you until the day I die. Have an enjoyable day."

As he and his children entered the vehicle, he could see her crying at the door. He said to the children, "Give me a second. I want to say something to your mom."

He walked to the door, and said, "I really would like to have dinner sometime to discuss us. Please, don't tell me about the divorce decree. I'm just saying as a man who screwed up, I think I can manage what drove us apart. See you later."

As he turned to walk away, she said, "I want to show you something, come in for a minute." He walked in, and she jumped his 'jones', throwing her tongue down his throat, and saying, "I cry every night because we are no longer together. I want to have that dinner, and soon. Go before the children start to make faces."

When he entered the car, he made a call to a resident of the sewer and indicated that the man on stilts may have been seen once again. Talk to you as soon as I return my kids home.

He turned to his kids, and said, "This is our day out without supervision, so let's have some fun."

# # #

Word of a possible second or third sighting of the person of interest, made its way to one of the active boards in the underground world. A text was sent to Ben Beckmire that stated, "possible sighting of the stilts."

When the Sarge finally received the text message, he said to himself, "must be a triple because we killed the primary, secondary, and perhaps there is a lookalike out there. That guy was tied as tight as hell, and that inferno occurred three minutes after we vacated the premises." He tried to text back, "stilts was barbequed—impossible," but it failed to deliver."

# # #

That night at dinner, Wajickee performed his magic, and entertained the group with stories of yesteryear, and the Beckmire clan. He said, "I know some of you are still wondering what makes for tales like the ones I tell, to have relevance, and not seem incredibly impossible. Let me recount an encounter for you. In your place on the islands at *The Sanctuary*, a young man came seeking Ben Beckmire. A charlatan, John Lee Jones Jr, pretended to be Ben Beckmire. The young man immediately knew who the pretender was, but nevertheless, continued with his story. The story was that a certain person had stolen heat seeking missiles with the intent of eradicating you people from the face of the earth. I say all of that to say, that God and spirits come in all sizes, colors, and shapes. That young man is sitting over there with Asiram, Zanthius, and their gang."

Wajickee paused, bowed to Jelani, and then said, "The real Ben Beckmire, and a small contingency of associates flew to Sydney, and had a lengthy conversation with that young lad's grandmother who wanted to know prior to any information whatsoever being talked about, or a relationship considered, she wanted to know, were you people good people. I know the answer, she knows the answer, he knows the answer, and the spirits know the answer. You people are good people, and are applauded by spirits all over the world. Mr. Jelani Latinmire is a good person and I fully endorse him as a new member of your group, prior to your voting on his membership. Does that seem fair? I don't think so, nor do I care. He has helped and will help Darryl here and stateside as your group continues its path of righteousness. People, for this special occasion, John Dory is the main course for tonight. Enjoy your meal, each other, and make sure you all get to meet your newest member, Jelani Latinmire."

During the meal, the Sarge continued to focus on the text message he received and decided to share the information with Mallory. He moseyed over to where Mallory was, and showed him text messages referring to a certain nemesis. Mallory looked at the communication, and said, "No way in hell, he or his body double could have survived that inferno. The blast alone shook the foundation where we were. We placed explosives all around his seat. No way in hell, Sarge."

"Do you think it's possible that he had an escape plan, or a partner in play? I mean that chair was centrally located, and looking outside of the box, Larry, who has a nose like John Lee and Jilkes, fell down a trap door. I'm just wondering if that chair was there just in case there was a breach in his plan. I mean we saw the look alike body, and why on earth would we interrogate a man in a bedroom where there was white powder residue all over the place. I think we got played on that one."

"Sarge, we blew the man's house off the stilts, with him tied three separate ways to an old Victorian chair, and into a fiery conclusion at the bottom of the hill. We all saw that shit."

"What if that chair was his escape tunnel transport? Come now, it's not like that shit ain't impossible. Look, they wrote on my boy's intestines. After seeing that shit, I am convinced that there ain't nothing that's impossible."

Mallory slowly lowered his head, as if taking refuge from it, and said, "Yeah, that plus that thing in the billabong equals, screw scientific theory."

# # #

Jelani sat by the billabong, and stared at the night sky, and began to cry. Asiram, who was curious about this new addition to their tribe, followed him. As she approached him, he tried to hide the fact that he was crying. She boldly and without any consideration for his tears, asked, "Are you here to create a problem for me, my child, or this tribe?" Jelani's head fell deeper into his lap, and he began to hyperventilate from crying. Asiram showed no concern for what the nature of the tears were.

He looked at her, and said, "I don't want to be here, but I now have nowhere to be or to go. My grandmother and aunt have passed on to another dimension. I am funeralizing them from this billabong, and hoping that they will forever watch over me, my brother, and this group. I have no malice in my heart. I feel that I am a failure on so many different fronts. I didn't know any of the issues that concerned my mother, you, my brother, this group, and I certainly didn't want to know that all of this was my doing, and that I no longer have any living family except a brother who must never know that I am his blood relative."

Asiram sat down beside him, and began to cry. Jelani fell into her arms, and the two of them cried without words for a while. He broke the silence by saying, "I have no family, friends, and I feel terribly alone and at risk."

Asiram began to squeeze his hand, and finally acknowledged, "I know exactly how you feel because prior to this group, I was alone and sad."

Asiram paused, and then exclaimed, "I murdered my family. They abused me repeatedly, and I am overly suspicious of everyone who I come in contact with that is not a member of this group. Your showing up and proclaiming to be my son's older brother, was a little unsettling as well as unbelievable. I pray to God and the spirits that you are not here with any malicious intent and that you are who you say you are. Can you assure me of this, and will you make sure that I am dead before you hurt my children if you are evil?"

Asiram began to cry uncontrollably, and suddenly, it was Jelani who was comforting her. He muttered between hyperventilating, "I have no one! My mother was a good person and a bad person at the same time. Her mother, my grandmother is no longer, and her sister, my aunt, have moved on to the spiritual world. I am flesh and blood, I have meaning, but I don't have substance because I don't have a family that I can publicly claim. I am not like my mother, sharing a

Christian name, and a birth name, and switching conveniently between them based upon what domain was dominating her mind and body. I am Jelani Latinmire and my only living relatives have moved on to another dimension. I am currently lost. I have no malice in my heart for you, or any member of this tribe. I need to be made whole or I will have to resolve my circumstances in the only way that I know how. My grandmother is crying and praying for my survival. I didn't plan this rendezvous, it was planned for me. Please believe me, I am a lost soul with a desire to be welcomed and loved by a wholesome group such as this one."

Zanthius, who is never far from his bride, walked to where the two were sitting, and acknowledged, "I watched my wife somewhat secretly leave our hut, and follow you here. I heard every word, and I want you to embrace your brother, my wife, me, and the tribe soon." Immediately after making that statement, a moon lit silhouette of the Great Saltie appeared. Jelani jumped up, grabbed Asiram, and began to drag her from the water's edge. Zanthius said, "Jelani, that is the Great Saltie, welcoming you into our tribe."

"Oh, my God! Did you see that?" Jelani exclaimed.

Zanthius responded, "I did, and each time I see it, my heart realizes that this group is doing excellent work by 'helping people help themselves'. That occurrence will happen only when there are two events being evaluated—good versus evil! When it is evil being evaluated, it is consumed. When it is good being evaluated, it is sanctioned, and that is exactly what happened just now, you were sanctioned by the Great Saltie, and it was witnessed by Asiram and me. Your path is clear, and your family will officially welcome you tomorrow at the celebration of life and inclusion. We never know what we do sometimes, but I was commanded to show up and watch this miraculous event. Listen, I will never think that I've seen it all. When I am here, and when Wajickee is around, you won't believe half of the things that you will see and/or experience. Although your granny was a spirit of sorts, she led us all to this moment."

Wajickee appeared next to Jelani, who yelled, "Whoa, where the hell did you come from? You're that arrogant driver who wouldn't let me sit in that special seat. Who are you really?"

"I am Wajickee, and your grandmother and aunt are proud of the way you acknowledged their ascent into another universe. I challenged you on the bus, because I wanted you to be prepared for this night, the night when your only remaining relatives, save one, transitioned to the great void. The people here will guide you into their group. Listen to them, recognize their presence, enjoy their humor, gingerly get to know your brother, believe that when here, anything is possible, but most of all, boldly go and meet each member of this group, for they are your lifeline, and you are theirs.

# # #

Later, Wajickee said to Ben Beckmire, "There is something mysterious about this lad, every time I try to do a deep dive into his aura, his past, his presence, and his future, something or someone attempts to block me. Each time I try, I get additional information about him. It is nothing violent or malicious, but someone or something is trying to keep critical information from me."

"My liege, is that something that I should be worrying about, or is it a battle between those in the world where you exist?"

"That is a fantastic question, Ben Beckmire. My take is that someone or something is desperately gathering like forces to keep me sidetracked and away from finding out basic information. I will go on walkabout, solicit elders, and others to see if this is an anomaly, or if there is a message that is being blocked. As an example, my last focus on him concluded with his grandmother and aunt. When I attempt to expand my view into the family, it is as though there is no lineage beyond, and before the grandmother and aunt, if that makes any sense to you. We know that the grandmother is the mother of Helga Spengatsenburg or Sister Mary, and you would think that I would have a route to the other aspects of the family heritage." Beckmire started to reply, but was unable to do so because Wajickee was on his way to where spirits go.

In the meantime, Jelani was engaged in conversation with John Lee and Jilkes. He asked John Lee, "When you had your issue in Minnesota, how did it feel, and do you remember anything about it?"

Jilkes jumped right in, and asked, "Why the hell are you talking about that mess?"

Jelani looked at both men, sighed, and then said, "Lately, I have been having visions of a woman that I really don't know. Each time she appears in my dreams, she seems to be pointing at something that I never get to see. I was just wondering if you guys could help me figure this mess out. Sorry to bother you, that seems what I do best."

John Lee immediately asked, "What is that?"

Jelani looked at him, and asked, "What is what?" Jilkes replied, "What is it that you seem to do best?" As he began to walk away, he muttered, "Bother people."

John Lee yelled, "Hold up a minute. Bring your fancy ass back here, and talk to us. That is not how we interact in this here tribe. Let's begin this here dance again, but this time, let's play like we be trying to help each other understand what the heck is going on in that there mind of yours."

The men in detail, began to tell Jelani some of the craziness that they had witnessed besides that beast in the billabong. The most fascinating story was that of Zanthius having writings on his intestines. John Lee told how they were outnumbered by mercs, and the animals put a hurting on all but two guys, and how they became a part of our tribe.

Jelani said, "Holdup, you mean to tell me that two men who came to kill you are now members of your tribe?"

John Lee said, "Some people are just damn bad, inside, and out. These two thought that we were going to kill them, and they just begged for a soldiers death—a bullet to the head."

Jelani asked, "Then what happened if you didn't kill them."

Jilkes smiled, and said, "We put them in the mines to work for the very thing that they would never possess."

Jelani said, "You put them to work in the mines, now that is what I call sweat equity, but the equity was a chance to live. How did they become so valuable to the group?"

John Lee said, "That's a story for another day, and I will tell you tomorrow about our Native American friends who have land that is worth hundreds of billions of dollars, they too are a part of our group. They came to survey how to destroy us, because they were some of the best in Viet Nam in terms of finding the enemy and figuring out how to destroy them. Their families were being held hostage until they completed the job. Anyway, I have to attend to my bride and my small tribe."

# # #

The Sarge and the Doc finished a marathon session, and her comments were déjà vu. "Young man, if you're going to play in this game, you need to get that body and mind back in shape. We all have retrenched, after the burial of four of our very own. Anyway, I need this hulk of a man of mine to get his act together and lose some of the new handles and begin a conditioning campaign for us all."

The Sarge looked at her, made a muscle, and then exclaimed, "Oh boy, I see flab under the arm! Today is the day, plus I am going to lose fifteen pounds in the next two weeks."

# # #

Jelani saw Chakes, Luana, and Beatrice, and formally introduced himself to them. He whispered to Luana, "Your daughter is absolutely beautiful."

Beatrice asked, "Are you the new guy that everyone is talking about?"

Jelani paused, and replied, "I guess that would be me. Nice to meet you and your family." Beatrice smiled, and asked, "Have you met my granny?"

"I'm not sure," Jelani responded."

Suddenly, Ms. Beatrice asked, "Are you going to find out who murdered the members of our family?" This caught Jelani off guard, and Luana interrupted the conversation, and said, "Beatrice, that is an adult conversation, and one that children should not be involved in. Am I clear?"

After a brief moment of reflection, Beatrice said, "Yes mother, but may I ask him another question about a dream that

I had?" Luana looked at her sternly, and said, "You are forbidden to ask any more adult questions." As Luana, Chakes, Ms. Beatrice, and her baby brother started to walk away, Ms. Beatrice pulled on her dad's hand. She told him that she wanted to tell him a secret. Luana looked at her, and said, "Are you trying to get an ally behind my back?"

"No, ma'am. I have to tell you both about a dream that I had that he was in." With her back to Jelani, she told her parents about a dream where bad people hurt two people with arrows."

At that very moment, Ms. Viola appeared, and asked, "What's this pow-wow about?" Luana told her, and Ms. Viola asked if she could speak privately with her great granddaughter.

After listening to Ms. Beatrice, Ms. Viola asked Jelani, if he would join in the conversation. He nodded affirmatively, and that is when Ms. Beatrice said, "My dream was about more bad people hurting us." Jelani asked if he could ask Ms. Beatrice a question, and was given consent to do so. He smiled at her, and asked, "In your dream, did you see how they were going to hurt us?"

Ms. Beatrice smiled, and said, "You know how silly man, you were in the dream."

#

The Sarge was seen having some piss with Mallory. He said, "Tomorrow, we start a new regimen, and that is to get the hell back in shape. After the tragedies, we have just sat around, ate, and drank. It's time to get that warrior look about us again, and realize that someone is planning on our demise, and we don't have a damn clue as to who it is."

Mallory said, "If an enemy showed up in camp right now, it would be a slaughterhouse for us because we are still so engulfed in sorrow that we couldn't and wouldn't hear them coming. Let's put the group on notice tonight. We have to leave this paradise and hunt down the people who are so good at killing us. As an example, did they kill Carla's father and then stage the entire funeral, and its conclusion. This all seems too easy for them, and we don't have a clue as to who is pulling the strings.

The Sarge asked, "Did I show you the text about the man who had the house on stilts in New York? Anyway, our friends in the sewers sent me a text indicating that the man we tied to that nice Victorian chair, was seen in Maryland, by the ex-wife of one of our guys. Interestingly, she worked for him and knew about his abnormal walk and head movement. Our guy downplayed it, but was smart enough to send the information to his command."

"Sarge, for the last time, we blew that house off its stilts, and into a fiery conclusion of everything and everybody in it. We overkilled that son-of-a-bitch."

"Mallory, unless he has a triple, you know, we had the double in the house with him, and now if he is being seen again, then it's a triple. If he is alive, then he has every right for vengeance against us. We had his only son incarcerated, and he became the bell of the balls, we blew his house to hell, and with him in it we thought," the Sarge stated.

Mallory saw Jelani, and beckoned him over to where they were having a beer. Mallory asked, "Do you have any way of gathering intelligence on the house that was blown up in Poughkeepsie, with the owner in it?"

Jelani laughed, and said, "Now I see the true meaning of my being here. You want me to pimp my associates at the bureau for information." After witnessing the reactions of the two men, Jelani said, "I was just acting out. Listen gentlemen, I just had an interaction with Ms. Beatrice, and she happened to have a dream that I was in, and it was about people trying to hurt more of you, or us at this point. After listening to her, she indirectly said that people with arrows are going to try to hurt you, or us. Mr. Beckmire, you remember when I spoke to you about arrows and bows, well it was confirmed if in fact Ms. Beatrice is a credible soothsayer."

The Sarge asked, "What is your real opinion of what you two discussed?"

After a long pause, Jelani said, "I believe that Ms. Beatrice and I are connected, and that the potential threat is not to be placed on the back burner, or someone might suffer a deadly wound."

The Sarge was about to respond, when Wajickee appeared, and announced, "I now know why I was being blocked from ascertaining your true essence, Mr. Latinmire. Your grandmother's only daughter was Helga Spengatsenburg, or in other circles, Sister Mary. You were conceived in South Africa, and your mother abandoned you because of your coloring. You were left at a prestigious orphanage with a promise to pay forward and beyond if they would take you, and provide for you. Your father, unbeknownst to you, was a priest, who eventually became a cardinal, and subsequently, a bishop. Beyond his wildest imagination, he evolved to become the Pope, the Holy Father of the Roman Catholic Church, and maintained your mother as his concubine. This Jelani Latinmire is the missing aspects of your life. Although never involved in your life, they kept eyes on you from afar, and from every perspective. Your father is the Pope that went missing, and who collaborated with this group, and who was once here in this village, and participated in the remarrying of Mr. & Mrs. Beckmire. He personally fetched a sack that was flung from the mouth of the Great Saltie, and presented it to Ben Beckmire that contained Mrs. Beckmire's new wedding ring. Now, how about that craziness!" Wajickee proclaimed.

Jelani stared long and hard at Wajickee, and asked, "Have you consumed too much of your native version of alcohol?"

Wajickee was initially in front of Jelani when he first spoke. After Jelani made his remark, Wajickee appeared on his left side, placed his hand on Jelani's chest, he fell to the ground, and Wajickee announced, "That is the second time you have challenged me. There will not be a third that you will remember."

Beckmire, who was slow to react because things happen fast in the dimension that spirits operate in that he couldn't comprehend what had just occurred, stated, "I need everyone near and far to remain still and silent." He then asked Wajickee, "When was the first time he challenged you?"

Wajickee turned, and said, "When I gave him a ride from the airport. He seemed a little sassy towards me." Jelani formed his mouth to say something, and Beckmire adamantly said, "When in Wajickee's company, only speak when asked. Now, there seems to be some tension between you two, and I don't quite understand why and how it developed."

Wajickee stirred, and admittedly said, "The bus and seat thing was my concoction, but in the scheme of things, his grandmother and aunt were strong seers, and I was measuring him and trying to figure out his fabric. He had a veil around him that I could not penetrate. My antennae stood high because of my inability to assess him. I am no longer interested in his challenges. I overreacted when he suggested that I had consumed too much of the native brew. I must go on walkabout and relate to spirits that understand my need to protect all that is this group." No sooner said, than he was no longer in their locus.

The Sarge said, "Damn, young fella, you pissed off a spirit, and survived. I like that in a person. We're still learning you, temper your responses to him or he will not be gentle in your next encounter. I think this is all my fault because I did not tell you who he is, and who he was to my great, great, great, great grandfathers. Listen, are you a fan of piss?"

"I occasionally like to indulge in it." Jelani looked away, but finally said, Mr. Beckmire, on a serious note, I had no idea who he was. I thought he was the bus driver. How was I to know that I was jousting with a spirit? If he appears before me again, I will humbly acknowledge that I am the court jester who desires to become a servant of all who are in this group."

The Sarge said, "You are a fast learner. By all means, plead to be on his good side, and it will make all of us happy. If he finds issue with you, then the die is cast. He is all consuming and powerful."

# # #

Wajickee appeared in the village, and was hell bent on defusing the situation with Jelani. He said to him, "There are things that still trouble me about you and, therefore, I have a simple request of you. Will you oblige?"

Jelani asked, "May I speak freely without retribution?"

"Of course, you can," Wajickee replied.

Jelani considered his responses, and said, "Although I did not know who you were, and/or your status, I thought you were the bus driver that was diverting my analysis of a potentially threatening situation against our group. My FBI training had me locked on two women carrying bows that could precisely send an arrow four football fields, and fell its target. I never engaged you, but you created such a negative aura about that seat that I forgot about the important issue that confronted me. Those women are hired assassins. I didn't mean to offend anyone, but I put them through my washer, dryer, and hung them out on the line until you chastised me about sitting in a seat reserved for royalty. I will do any lowly task that you demand, but I need you to conspire with me when there are those out there who will hurt us."

Wajickee who normally is quick to respond sighed, and said, "I too am sorry for the way we interacted. I assumed a human response because of your grandmother and aunt. I was blocked from being provided the unknown information about your mother and your father. I felt proud of my action because it empowered me. I am internalizing everything, and realized that history does not always portray who we are or our ability to transform from our DNA. I, therefore, apologize to you here and now, and will do the same at dinner this evening. It was such a discombobulating feeling to focus on you, your grandmother, and aunt, and have every effort blocked. I have concluded this issue internally, and will never broach it again with you."

After, staring in space, Wajickee announced, "The drums are sending us a message that is not good. I must find Ben Beckmire, and alert him of an impending danger, that you my friend, was astute enough to at least ask questions about certain containers." In a nano-second, Wajickee was gone. Jelani said to himself, "What a skill set."

As the message from the drums became louder and louder, it was clear to some that danger was near. Wajickee, after interrupting a conversation between Mallory and Ben Beckmire said, "That young Mr. Jelani, and Ms. Beatrice were correct. Those two women are targeting you Mallory, and John Lee. They think without a Mallory there is no Sarge, and without a John Lee, there is no Jilkes. How would you like to deal with those two?" Wajickee asked.

Beckmire said, "I want to deal with them alive. Whatever you have to do, place a veil around them so that not even a mosquito can penetrate it. I want them here in this camp, and before a group of dingoes. I need to know who is financing these events that have us as targets." As Ben Beckmire completed his sentence, Wajickee disappeared, and was on task to direct his new protégé to assist in the apprehension of the two would be assassins.

On the fringes of the village, four hundred yards away, Wajickee and Jelani, watched two females dressed in black, unpack sighting scopes, wind, and temperature gauges, and finally, two hand-crafted high-tension bows. Jelani said admiringly, "I like those bows, they look like they were custom-made for those ladies."

As the ladies from their sighting scopes looked for their targets, Mallory was sighted entering his hut and John Lee was sitting outside of his hut with one of his children. One of the ladies said, "I got the farmer, you take the perpetual corporal. I'll bet you $500 my shot is more fatal than yours."

The other would-be assassin said, "Listen my sister, we make the shots, and we get out of here like a cloud. No time for bullshit. I've heard about these guys, and they are not to be played around with. I want my target dead on impact, and before he hits the ground, me and my bow are going to be making our way to that jeep. If I get there, and you're waiting to collect on a simple ass bet, then I will say, it was nice knowing you. I am going to deliver and disappear. You feel me?" The mood changed, and as they settled in, Mallory came out of his hut. One of the women said, "Your target is ready, and so is mine. Let's do this, and be gone. Okay, we got windage, distance, tension, and pull. Let's put these arrows through those bastards, and get out of this backwards ass country. At the count of five."

At the count of three, Wajickee asked, "Are you people hunting animals, and if so, that is not allowed out here?"

"Where in the hell did you come from?"

Jelani from the bush in front of them said, "Oh, don't worry about him, he's just a spirit, he comes and goes as he pleases. What are you people sighting, or better still, who are you targeting? I know you think that you can fire that thing and hit me, but that guy will let those dingoes and snakes, that have surrounded you, have a go at you. Listen, as I said on the plane, as I admired what I considered cases for your custom-made bows, oh, by the way, the longer you caress those weapons, the more you create a feeding frenzy for those animals. Listen, this is my first time here, but I must warn you, if you don't put those weapons down, you will get to watch your arses get eaten alive—and that ain't no metaphor."

Both women complied, and Jelani said, "Now that was easy, what are your names? Now before you give me some bullshit names, we got your entire manifest from our friends in customs. So, Ms. Bronze and Beautiful, what are your names?" The first woman announced that I am Anel, and my sister is Angel. Jelani jokingly asked, "Did your parents send you two to assassin's school?"

Angel replied, our parents died early on, our aunt taught us to do what we do."

Jelani smiled, and said, "She must be a wonderful person. What's her name?" Anel smiled, and said, "Her name is Aunt Que."

"Okay, now that we have been properly introduced, the rest of this session occurs unfortunately for you, outside of our village, but in front of those critters who have not been fed in three days. This is what I recommend to you. Don't go and try to be macho, don't protect anyone, but each other, and when asked a question, go straight at it. You pull that bullshit amongst these people, then that is exactly what you're going to get. They will smile, act as though they believe you, and then gut you from that mid-section to your brain, and make sure you watch them take a bite out of your heart before you die."

Angel replied, "Then why are you feeding us bullshit. No one can shank a person from their midsection to their brain, and then take a bite out of their heart before they die."

Wajickee smiled, and said, "Hold that thought as you answer questions presented to you. You're in Australia, many unbelievable things can occur here. I suggest you gently pack your belongings and prepare your life-or-death testimony."

# # #

An hour later, back in the camp, everyone was amazed that the two gorgeous women captives, were hired assassins. Courtney asked, "Jelani, why are these women in bondage?"

"Mrs. Beckmire, I have not had the opportunity to interrogate them, but the skinny of this situation is that they had several people in their sights as targets," Jelani stated.

Courtney said, "No way. They don't look like assassins."

"Mrs. Beckmire, what does an assassin look like?" Jelani nonchalantly asked.

Courtney smiled at him, and said, "We learn about human nature each day, forgive my naivety."

The two ladies were escorted out of the village to the border where anything that is there without sanction is fair game, and an easy meal. On this adventure, Dempsey and Hood assisted Jelani and Wajickee with the captives. As they approached the point of no return, Hood said to Anel, "It's a damn shame that you're going to be eaten alive by those massive jaws on those dog look a likes. Plead for mercy, ask for **deific intermediation**, because I would hate to see that fine ass body of yours be eaten by some damn animals. I would at least like the opportunity to try to seduce you. You and your sister are off the charts. Seek community service, mine work, or anything. Listen, because you're two beautiful ladies that do dirty, the penalty is the same. That country looking guy over there with those wild looking children, is an expert at gutting and tasting hearts before the subject dies."

Anel asked, "Why are you so concerned about what happens to me and my sister, and why are you giving me this information?"

Hood laughed, and said, "Me and Dempsey, came here to steal diamonds and gold, but we were captured, and our sentences were to work in the gold and diamond mines."

Anel cracked a smile, and asked, "What is so terrible about working in mines that can make you rich."

"You are not working for yourself or by yourself, you're surrounded by snakes and spiders all day long. If you were to place nugget or a diamond in your pocket and leave the mines, then your death would be immediate and painful. Snakes, spiders, and spirits protect the mines. If you have no faith in anything, then ask to be summarily executed. The things that happen here will leave you with faith in the alternative world, or dead. The choices here are simple, confess all that you know, or die a violent death." Dempsey stated.

Wajickee came to a stop, and said, "From this point on, you're on your own. The animals will track, and devour you. Is it not better to divulge information about people who conspire to murder other people, than to die attempting to protect them?" Neither lady said a word until they heard the roar of a wild animal. Anel asked, "What was that?" Wajickee announced that it was the wild inviting members of its pack for a human feast. Ladies, fare thee well."

Anel looked at Angel, and said, "Are those people worth our lives?"

Angel responded, "Not to me." She then looked at Wajickee, and said, "Is there any way we can discuss this matter further before you turn us out into this desolate place?" We didn't kill anyone although we had specific targets."

Wajickee, knowing and seeing all, said, "You had Mallory and John Lee as your targets." Both women looked at him with astonishment.

Wajickee asked, "Were you two involved in the assassination of Ava, Carlos, Mike, and Carla, former members of the group?"

Anel said, "We picked this job up on the dark web, and it promised partial payment up front. Our other work was in Panama, Mexico City, and the Dominican Republic. In those places our targets were all in the drug trade, a thing that we deplore. Our parents died of over-doses from laced drugs. We love doing drug dealers—high-level ones at that."

"My problem is that you people came here to kill some of us. A thing that someone has succeeded in accomplishing. It is highly unlikely the group will find you innocent and/or pardon you from prosecution and execution. Their grief is over-bearing, and I doubt that they will just say, "pack up your fancy bows and arrows, go home, and play with dolls."

Anel admitted, "It was my idea. How about letting my sister live, and I will freely walk into that barren area, and seek penitence. She is, and has always been, a follower. My idea, so take everything out on me, but let my sister live." Wajickee looked at the billabong in search of a sign from the Great Saltie, but none was presented.

Angel in the interim stated, "My sister couldn't plan her own death, let alone the intricacies of carrying out a proposed hit. In other words, it was my idea, and my fault for providing Mr. Smarty pants too much information about what we were carrying and how far we could impact a target. When he said FBI, I should have just smiled, and walked away, as opposed to engaging in conversation about the range of these medieval weaponry."

Jelani asked Wajickee if he could speak to him privately. The two stepped away from the others, and began to dialogue. Wajickee proposed, "I can speak with the leaders of the group and perhaps suggest the same kind of treatment that those two brigands guarding them were sentenced to."

Jelani said, "I'm not sure what happened, and what led Mr. Beckmire to sentence them to the mines, and then welcome them into their group. If you think, I'm sorry, using your wisdom, I agree we should attempt to clean these ladies up from being assassins, and perhaps, there is a legitimate role they can play in our group."

# # #

Later in camp, Jelani looked for Wajickee to express their desire to find an alternative to having the two ladies killed by animals. Mallory saw Jelani talking with little Ben, and asked, "What did you come up with for saving those two ladies. I thought you were going to leave them in no man's land, and let the animals feast upon them."

Nervously, Jelani said, "I believe that I have consensus with Wajickee, and that is, we should put them in the mines around snakes and spiders. There is a role they can play in the group. I mean, you guys lost Carlos and Mike, not to mention their wives. If nothing else, we can charge them with raising Carla and Mike's children, plus a stint in the mines with hideous creatures." Mallory looked at him intently, and said, "There is merit in what you say. Have you spoken with the Sarge about this?"

"I have not, I was hoping Wajickee would do the honors."

Mallory asked, "Why can't you talk to him?" Without knowing anything about it, Ben Beckmire was headed their way, Mallory smiled, and said, "Here's your chance. He's on his way over here."

When the Sarge arrived, he asked, "What are you two scheming about?" Mallory laughed, and said, "Jelani here wants to suggest an alternative route to killing those two women who had as targets, me and John Lee."

The Sarge looked at him, and asked, "Well, what's your alternative?"

Jelani said, "Mr. Beckmire, your presence intimidates me. Anyway, I was hoping Wajickee would be here to help me with my presentation. I suggest that we attempt to improve upon the model that you developed when you sent Dempsey and

Hood to the mines, gave them shit jobs, latrine work, and surprisingly, made them trusted members of your organization. In the case of the two sisters, I would like to give them a stint in the mines with all of its trappings, you know, the snakes and spiders. I would give them latrine work, and then I would see if they can become parents or proteges to Mike and Carla's two children." Beckmire looked long at Jelani, smiled, walked a short distance away, returned, and asked, "Who do you propose to oversee them?"

Jelani laughed, and said, "Who else is there except Dempsey and Hood who have the hots for the two sisters."

Everyone laughed, and the Sarge asked, "How do you know that they are interested in those two?"

Jelani responded, "Hood without pulling punches pleaded with one of the ladies to cop a plea because he was interested in trying to seduce her."

"No, he didn't. I don't believe you," the Sarge said. Jelani let out a loud whistle that got Hood and Dempsey's attention, and he beckoned the two men over. When they arrived Dempsey asked, "What's up people?"

The Sarge asked, "Did you or Hood indicate to the captives that you were interested in seducing them."

Dempsey scowled at Hood, and said, "His dumb ass keeps me in trouble because he is always with me. However, Sarge, I can't throw him completely under the bus. He stated it, but I thought it. They are two extremely beautiful sisters."

"What happened to your two friends from Minnesota?"

"Oh, Sarge, we stay in contact with them, and they are profoundly good friends. We respected and honored them when they visited us at *The Sanctuary*. They both have boyfriends of sorts and their visiting us with a chaperone strengthened their positions and their importance. They control their relationships at the moment, and we are going to be in a wedding this coming summer," Dempsey stated.

Mallory said, "Why you two old semi-saints. I thought you guys got what you wanted, and flew them away. I have a different respect for you two." He looked at each man, and asked, "Suppose we put you in charge of the two assassins, would you put them through the ringer or play for the booty?"

The men were silent for a few seconds, and Hood said, "They came to kill you and John Lee. Now, I know it's sometimes all about business. They are fine specimens of women, and yes, I do like one of them. I don't know them, but they are pleasing to my eyesight. Now, on the other hand, they are killers!" Hood exclaimed.

"Yeah, and so were you guys!" the Sarge proclaimed. "Is it possible to change? I would have to say yes because you two are high ranking members of our group. Okay, enough of the "bs". You two will sentence them to the mines for forty-five days. They will also do the latrines, clean, and prepare to become potential overseers to two motherless and fatherless children. Now, let me be noticeably clear! No intimacy of any kind with prisoners or captives. No physical contact such as hugging, kissing, or touching. You will treat them like shit, or I will terminate our relationship with you two."

Beckmire stared at both ladies, and was impressed by their knowledge of his group and their resolve to destabilize it. Ben Beckmire yelled, "Screw it! I'm going to kill you both by making you work in a place where there is wealth beyond your wildest imagination that you can only handle, but never own. That is my sentence, be gone!" Angel started to say something, when Beckmire screamed, "Be silent, be gone, or be dead!"

"Sarge, that's a little harsh. Suppose I fall in love with one of them?" Hood asked.

"Excommunicated from the group," the Sarge announced.

Jelani saw an opportunity to engage him, and said, "Mr. Beckmire, since there is a stated potential set of feelings, between these two and the captives, it would be better if I assumed a supervisor role for the two ladies. I too think that they are easy on the eyes, but they considered me the sleeping little boy on the plane."

"There you have it. You two will stay away from the captives unless approved by me, Mallory, or Jelani. Are we clear people about what is expected?" There was a consensus and the meeting ended. The two female assassins were granted life, subject to the terms of their captivity.

# # #

Two weeks later, Jelani informed the two sisters that he wanted to meet with them. When they appeared before him with native guards, he said, "I want to know about that dark web site that you allegedly accessed to accept the job of killing two members of this group."

Anel quietly asked, "Are we in trouble?" Jelani looked at her, and replied, "Absolutely not. I want to hopefully, close in on your former employer."

Anel responded, "If you have internet, I can in thirty seconds get you to a place where a mother can sell her babies, and a man or a woman can acquire any fantasy that interests them. I am going to speak freely Mr. FBI man, we have been doing shit jobs, working around those nasty snakes and spiders, and we are still alive. This is a gift for you, I know who one of the persons who hired us is. Listen, Angel is a tech genius, and I can hold my own."

Jelani said, "Hold up, time out. I need the boss man here. Will that alter this speak freely mindset of yours?"

Anel responded, "Absolutely not, we're still alive."

Fifteen or so minutes later, Mallory, John Lee, Jilkes, and Ben Beckmire appeared where Jelani was speaking with the two sisters. Jelani said, "Thanks for coming because I didn't want to lose anything in translation. The sisters say that they are tech savvy, and know the dark web. Anel indicated that she knows who one of the purchasers of their services is. I don't want to interpret, so Anel, take over the show."

Anel meekly stated that she has been deemed brilliant when it comes to computer science. She admitted, Angel was equally as smart, and that we know how to unpack messages that are encrypted, sequenced, and in partial form. She said, "When you take a job on the dark web, you can't go by faith that a crook will decide to be honest and pay you. No, no, you have to unpack, place socks in shoes, underwear in pants, shirts on skin, connect ears, eyes, handwriting, any voice, or text messages, in order to find out who owes you money, and when you'll get paid. We've bankrupt people mathematically until they paid us. In unpacking this guy who wants you, Mr. Mallory, and you, Mr. John Lee dead, we uncovered a series of distinct messages aimed at a group, and at a particular sergeant and corporal.

Okay, we got travel to Australia, hotel accommodations, a per diem, and a bonus for head shots. We knew the kill radius, and had you two gentlemen completely compromised, until Mr. FBI, and a very mysterious guy appeared, and showed us a pack of dog looking things that were ready for a meal. Our motto is to fight to the last breath. When we saw all of the snakes near us and those dog-like looking things showing their massive teeth, we gave up with the hope of living another day." She began to tear up, and yelled, "I will do anything to keep my sister alive."

After a two-minute break, John Lee asked, "How come you decided on me, rather than my African American friend?"

Angel replied, "Here's our marching orders; Beckmire without a Mallory, and Jilkes without a John Lee, is a what? It's a wrap! She exclaimed. "However, let me say, those calculations were dumb. Jilkes or John Lee could run this operation, from what we have seen. After studying your group and the roles, we mathematically concluded, "kill the money man and you kill the group--Jong."

Ben Beckmire stated, "Since the consensus is to keep you alive, tell me more about the person who you suspect hired you to kill my people."

Anel softly said, "When I go looking for the guy who paid us, I investigate his filter systems, or the process of floating money through different channels and sources until they think it's impossible to trace. Not so with me and my sister, and as such, everything that relates to this job began in California, and found roots in Poughkeepsie, New York, and the Washington DC area to be exact. Did you and your people complete work there?"

Beckmire angrily looked at Anel, and said, "Everyone knows that we had a beef in Poughkeepsie." Anel softly said, "Not everyone Mr. Beckmire. We traced funds and chatter that came along with each station the money passed. The person indirectly hiring us is the same person who you thought you blew off the face of the earth. The media had a field day because you blew the house off the stilts, and showed before and after pictures. Your problem is that the person you thought you terminated, may still be alive, and is hunting you along with someone from the New York to the DC corridor."

The Sarge replied, "You're giving me community information. Everyone who can read knows about this situation." Angel hesitated for a minute, and interjected, "You're right, but he didn't die in that blast, and that is why you have four less people in your group."

Ben Beckmire sighed, and admitted, "You can be sure that we won't leave matters like this undone in the future. Can you get any information on the person in the DC area that is allegedly partnering with the man who didn't die?"

Anel smiled, and indicated that the DC person had no footprint. Ben Beckmire swelled up, and demanded to know what that meant. Anel said, "If there is no footprint then there is no history of this person being involved on the dark web or that this person has ever dabbled in chicanery. If you allow us to use the internet and have our computers, we can track the other person down."

Ben Beckmire said, "Thanks for your help, and I'll consider your request about the use of the internet. My problem is that I'm not sure you're free of your past life, and you may see an opportunity to maximize your profits."

Anel immediately responded by saying, "Perfectly understandable. Listen, it is just my sister and me. No husbands, children, or significant others, just us. We'll do whatever you need us to do, and we appreciate the fact that you did not feed us to those hideous dog like looking things."

The Sarge thanked both women, and dismissed them. He said to Mallory, John Lee, Jilkes, and Jelani, "I think it's a bit too early to start giving them access to the internet. Let's keep them on the same regimen, but increase the outside cleaning and latrine work. Have those two numbskulls see to it, and make sure they're not trying to get off on those ladies."

#

Darryl saw his uncle, and asked if he had heard anything from Hutang. The Sarge stated that he had not and wanted to know why the interest. Darryl replied, "Usually when I send him a list of requested supplies, he acknowledges the fact. It has been two weeks, and I haven't heard a word from him." Beckmire looked at his nephew and suggested that he keep reaching out to him.

John Lee and Jilkes met with Chakes, Gladstone, Whitmore, and Jong to figure out how to endow Carla and Mike's children. The two children were currently being cared for by Mr. & Mrs. Benjamin Beckmire. Jong with his inimitable self said, "Each body has insurance. Carla, Mike, Ava and Carlos, everyone has insurance plus the earnings from our group. No one is poor in this group except the new people."

John Lee asked, "Is this insurance thing like that tontine mess?"

Jong looked at him, and replied, "I not put funds in casino. All monies in reputable firms, no piggy banks." Jilkes interjected, "Play nice people."

Jong asked, "I play nice, how did I insult him? When I say piggy bank, I mean money not under mattresses." John Lee laughed, and said, "I don't know why my African American friend feels like he has to protect me from my friends. Jong, I knew what you were referring to. I am still concerned that the assassinations of our friends was not the result of one of us trying to get all of the wealth we be done run into."

Chakes asked, "This insurance for the children, how is that going to be handled. Would it go to the caretaker for keeping until they reach a certain age?"

Jong said, "In this case, the Sarge, and Dr. Courtney, would be responsible for managing their funds until the children are of age." John Lee said, "This here thing beginning to look like a tontine, and I think we need to have a meeting to make sure that we all be reading from the same book. Seems to me, that someone done been bitten by the greed snake. I'm just saying. Ever since my smart friend brought that there tontine thing up, seems like someone done got poison and be looking to get all that we done got as a group. I'm just saying."

Jilkes looked at John Lee, and said, "If I didn't know any better, I'd think that you were trying to place a suspicious eye on me."

John Lee responded, "I know you be smart and all, but you ain't that damn smart to arrange and carry out assassinations of our group members, but you know if you be feeling a little singled out, then I think I be watching your ass a little closer." Jilkes looked at him and shook his head, as Larry walked up, and inquired as to what was going on. Jilkes immediately answered by saying, "John Lee thinks that I am the leader of a tontine."

Larry exclaimed, "How ridiculous is that! You have to be an institution to manage and arrange for implementation of the program. You just can't decide one day when you wake up to start a tontine. Guys, it is a business arrangement that is mired in a lot of detail and complicated considerations." Larry began to laugh, and said in parting, "John Lee, if I were to accuse anyone, it would be Jong. Okay guys, catch you later."

# # #

Anel said to Hood, "Is there any way you can get us an audience with Mr. Beckmire and Mr. Mallory? Oh, and the snakes became extremely aggressive when we were leaving." Hood looked at Anel and saw a small stone lodged in her hair twist. He summoned Darryl who was nearby, and pointed to Anel's hair wrap. Hood told him that the ladies indicated that the reptiles became aggressive when they were leaving. Darryl stated, "We must go back into the mine and return that small, but noticeable stone. The reptile's aggression was a warning that if you proceed beyond the boundaries of the mine, you will die, in other words, they gave you a pass."

The two ladies, Darryl, and Hood entered the mine. Anel slowly fondled her hair until a small stone fell from it. She shook her head and the group proceeded to leave the mine. Once topside, Darryl was greeted by his uncle who asked why the group was leaving the mine so late. It was Anel who responded by saying, "Mr. Beckmire, a ridiculously small stone got lodged in my hair and the snakes became aggressive, but did not bite. I and the others went back into the mine to return the stone. If I were to steal a stone and die for it, by all means it would have to be as big as the Hope Diamond."

As the Sarge started to walk away, Angel said, "Mr. Beckmire, we may have a way to figure out if your original New York person is alive, or if someone is using his accounts." The Sarge stopped in his tracks, slowly turned around, and asked, "Does this mean allowing you the opportunity to utilize our internet services?"

Angel responded, "I am afraid it does." She smiled, and said, "No one is going to come here to help us, so there is no alarm that I can engage that will save me and Anel. We are like slaves, but that's okay. We came here on a mission, we failed, and now we have to do the grunt work."

The Sarge asked, "Are you guys free for dinner? I would like to have you meet me for dinner by the billabong. Don't worry, I love my wife, and I surely don't want to tangle with two guys who admire and adore you two ladies." Both women looked a little perplexed by his statement. Beckmire said, "Don't worry, in time, all will be made clear."

# # #

At dinner, John Lee made it extremely clear when he announced, "Anyone in this village involved in that there tontine thing will be dispatched by me and my African American friend immediately. That's all we got to say for the moment."

Jilkes looked at him, and said, "Next time you include me in your insanity, give me a heads up, okay?"

# # #

As the entire group had dinner by the billabong, Beckmire gave Hood and Dempsey the okay to bring in the two would be assassins. As they entered the locus of the dinner, a compassionless quiet could be felt that was un-nerving for the two sisters. Hood and Dempsey led the two, loosely bound, near the fire. The two men cut the restraints off the ladies, and disappeared into the night. Anel said to Angel, "Don't you say a fucking thing. I am going to accept all responsibility and, therefore, beg for your life. Angel, if you screw this up, I'll jump into that fire." From nowhere, Wajickee appeared, and said, "That is so honorable, but so unnecessary. Be a guest, be quiet, be humble, and be honest."

As the drums began to beat again and the didgeridoos began to make their harmonious sounds, Beckmire announced, "I have a plan for the two people who came here to kill two of us. Should we consider an eye for an eye? Should we give them discounts for not accomplishing their tasks? How about we simply dispatch both of them for the notion of their intent?" Beckmire yelled, "I need Hood and Dempsey here now!"

Two or three minutes later, as the two men approached the massive fire, Dempsey said to Hood, "If you screwed this relationship up for us, never fucking speak to me again, and stay away from me, for I will kill you for killing us both by doing stupid." Without anyone seeing him, Wajickee said to both men, "Relax and confirm your faith?"

Ben Beckmire walked to where the two ladies were sitting, and said, "Here and now, tell me the honest truth as to why you want to have internet access? If in fact you make the smallest inconsistency of truth, you will be escorted into the billabong where your fate and your life will end in the belly of my humongous ancestor. Now, tell me why do you want to be granted access to the internet?" Anel looked at Angel and whispered, "Don't mess this up."

Beckmire in turn asked, "What did you mutter to your sister?"

"I told her not to mess this up." Beckmire loudly inquired, "What does that mean?"

"That means that I love my sister more than life, and it's my fault that she joined me on this path, and I beg for her life, but offer mine willingly and without resistance."

Beckmire asked, "Why do you want internet access? Is it to inform people of your capture and send other messages about our group?" The woman began to cry, and exclaimed, "I just want to make sure my sister lives beyond my demise! I know it doesn't matter to you, but we think we know how to track all those involved with or without footprints."

Beckmire smiled, and announced, "I believe we have two new members of our group, if in fact they are willing to accept the base nature of our group." Angel looked a little disconcerted, Anel looked extremely confused, until Wajickee said to them both, "You have now just become a part of royalty. Be quiet, be honest, and be humble. Offer your services, never double dip, and never deceive. Now, I want you both to look at the billabong, for now you will see the Great Saltie, and your faith with be restored and your commitment will be forever."

Majestically, the Great Saltie rose from the depths of the billabong and sprang effortlessly into the air, exposing his massive size and girth. The sisters sat in disbelief of what they saw breach the waters. Wajickee said, "That was not a mirage, that was Ben Beckmire's great, great, great, great, grandfather."

Anel said, "I just want to do what is right. I don't want to focus on that which I saw, for I will dream myself into harm's way by seeking stimulants that minimize my reality."

When Ben Beckmire appeared, he said, "You saw who we are in my relative in the billabong. Don't deceive, be honest and begin to learn parenting for you will be entrusted with two children whose parents were assassinated. Is this a function, among many that you two can agree to partake in?"

Angel with tears flowing from her eyes, hugged her sister tightly, and whispered softly, but so that all could hear, "I love you with all of my heart." Anel, crying hard said, "I know, I know." She looked at Mr. Beckmire and stated, "We are honest, faithful, and loyal. We will make you proud through our information gathering skills, as well as our ability to take on that parenting job. We don't know much about kids, other than liking them. Once we have achieved a level of trust, I would like to tell you a story that drove us to this line of work. More importantly, I thank God and that thing in the water that you did not hurt my sister, the only person on earth that I love, at this moment." She looked in the direction of Dempsey and Hood, and smiled.

CHAPTER FIVE

John Lee was sitting by the billabong in a fog, with his kids when his phone rang. The alleged caller said, "I failed you and me. Can we try it again?" John Lee hung up the phone, and loudly demanded that his kids follow him. He ran to where the Sarge, Mallory, Jilkes, and Jelani were talking. He screamed, "Sarge, that there Holy Father person just called my phone again!" Jilkes asked him to calm down, and explain what he was talking about. John Lee stated, "I was sitting by the billabong with my kids when the phone rang, and the person on the other end said, "I failed you and me, can we try it again?"

The Sarge said, give me your phone, and why on earth are you carrying this relic around here?"

"It be a habit. That there Holy Father, I know it was his voice, and that is why I am concerned. I don't like that person, he is pure evil, commanding me to kill my family and my friend." Jilkes embraced him, and said, "This battle, I will fight for you. Don't you worry about this, I got you on this one."

The Sarge looked at John Lee's phone, turned it on, searched for incoming calls, and found that the last one that he received was made three months ago, and it was from Jilkes. He touched John Lee and realized that he was running a fever. The Sarge summoned Darryl over, and when he looked at John

Lee he asked, "John Lee, have you been eating unsanctioned foods?"

"Well, now what might that be? I mean I been eating the berries that everyone else be done liked." Darryl touched his arm, and said, "John Lee, can you show me where you got those berries that you like?" The two men walked away from the group and John Lee pointed to a bush. Darryl asked, "John Lee, are those the berries that you've been eating?" John Lee authoritatively announced, "Them there be the berries that people told me were okay to eat." Darryl smiled, and asked, "John Lee, which billabong was sanctioned to swim and bathe in?" John Lee entered a soliloquy, and finally asked, "Am I at the wrong billabong?"

Darryl smiled, and said, "John Lee, you are safe at either billabong because you are connected to my uncle. However, the trees, bushes, berries, and other appetizing fruits, don't know that. You've been eating from the wrong area, and you manifested that call. Your last call was three months or so ago. The Holy Father or whoever he is, or was, did not call you. You ate from an unsanctioned bush of berries because you got east and west confused. John Lee, I am going to prepare a concoction for you that will put you out for twenty-four or more hours. I will need to talk to the Sarge, and he has to broach this action with your wife. However, before moving forward, are you willing to follow my instructions?" John Lee scratched his tangled hair, and asked, "Are you saying that I made up that call from the Holy Father?"

"John Lee, I am saying that, and the fact that you ate from the wrong bush. Listen, all I can tell you is that the bush you pulled berries from causes epic psychedelic trips into the unknown. The result of eating from that bush is like eating laced mind-altering stimulants that focus on everything that is negative. It focuses on that part of the brain that stimulates violent, abusive, and suicidal tendencies. How did you find yourself at this billabong?"

"Sometimes, I just be trying to figure out that thing called life. I wake up early sometimes, and I get out of bed and take walks around the village." John Lee was about to continue his conversation, when Darryl asked, "Do you see the same people when you go on these walks?" John Lee paused for a few moments, and said, "Well, yeah. I see the old man over there by the tree offering me an open invitation to try the fruit." Darryl pulled out his weapon and fired five rounds into the air. Every member of the group except the new ladies came out of their huts loaded for bear. Darryl yelled, "demons have infiltrated Us! John Lee is a vessel for a new enemy. People, we will all sleep near the fire that is burning high."

Wajickee appeared, and stated unequivocally, "Demons have permeated our very fiber. Ben Beckmire, someone is trying to call you out, and punish you and your people for past deeds. He turned violently around, and screamed, "Where is Zanthius? Where is Asiram?"

Still not sure of what was happening, Ben Beckmire asked, "Why are you calling out my son and daughter-in-law?"

"I only call out those who are missing. I need everyone here, including all the children. The messaging is that a person near and dear to you and the group is conspiring with others to eliminate the entire group. We are under attack by one of our own who is so caught up in witchcraft that I can't decipher who it is."

Courtney said to the Sarge, "You know I am all about science and this mumbo jumbo stuff is beyond my reasoning and acceptance except when I am here. Honey, we need to feed you some of those berries to try to figure out who amongst us is conspiring to kill us all. I find all of this so hard to believe because everyone except the new girls are set for life. Maybe John Lee was right when he mentioned that he thought someone was involved in a tontine event." He rubbed her hand, and then said to Wajickee, "What would be the benefit of killing us all?"

"Ben Beckmire, there are gold and diamond mines that you have not ventured into. Darryl is aware of them, and soon, Jelani will assume a role for the new places. You, this group, as well as the Aboriginal people, have a lot of work to do to bring my people into the 21st Century. Opening mines on some of the Aborigine lands would be a disservice because foreigners would set upon those areas like the plague. They have no systems except their ancient ways of doing business, they are ripe for the taking, and their lands are unmarked, not recorded in such a way that could be defended in the white man's court of law. We just got this area under our control by using the talented lawyers, but in the other areas, it would be a free for all. My people's land are marked by the ridge to the south, the billabong to the east, the mountain range to the west, and the boab trees to the north. In other words, there is no defense and, therefore, the lands are up for grabs."

"Who is the person or persons that want us dead so that they can have more of the same riches beyond their wildest imagination?" Wajickee stared at the two newcomers and realized that if their skill sets were as cunning as they stated, maybe there is a way to discover who is sending and receiving messages. He said, "As you know, this internet thing is light years ahead of my comprehension, which was one of the reasons the elders wanted to retire me. Perhaps their arrival is spiritual in that I can have them share their expertise with me and, therefore, I can visit, with their assistance, places on the dark web, and learn how it works."

Ben Beckmire looked at him, and asked, "My liege, are you having earthly considerations about those ladies?" Wajickee shot back, "The idea is enticing, the reality conceivable, but that act would send me into retirement. No, Ben Beckmire, my interest is purely, how do you say it, academic."

# # #

That night everyone slept outside around a massive fire that was tended to by members of the village. John Lee asked Jilkes, "Do you think I'm losing my mind?"

Jilkes smirked, and asked, "What might that thing you call a mind, be?"

"I be serious brother." Jilkes looked long and hard at John Lee, and stated, "You called me brother. You have never called me brother. You only call me your African American friend, you never call me brother."

John Lee started to cry, his wife noticed him crying, and asked, "Did Jilkes offend you again?" John Lee made a few sniffling sounds, and replied, "No, my brother just be caring about me, that's all."

Somara responded, "You called him brother. Are you not feeling, okay? You never call him brother. Is all good inside of my pig farmer's domain?" John Lee smiled, reached over, and kissed her, and mumbled, "I just used him to get close to you. I need to feel special in your heart if'n you are still in love with me. We don't be doing a lot of talking here lately, and I be worried that you don't love me anymore." Somara swelled up, and screamed, "I'm pregnant again, and ran off into the bush."

John Lee, slow to get up, asked Jilkes, "Did she say she be pregnant again?" Jilkes stood up, and said, "Listen you pig farming baby making machine, go get her now, kiss the ground she walks on, tell her how much you love her, and how beautiful she is."

When Somara reached the artificial boundaries where the animals were able to consume anything or anybody that was in that domain, she saw a mauled, but alive dingo. As she approached the animal, it growled at her as well as others who were planning on feasting on their wounded brethren. As she moved towards the animal, Wajickee appeared, and said, "Your concern and effort will endow you in this land forever." She commanded John Lee to fetch Dr. Beckmire. John Lee was reluctant to leave his wife until she said, "John Lee Jones Jr. please fetch the Doc. Wajickee and I are good, ain't that right Wajickee?"

When Courtney appeared on the scene with her medical bag, she exclaimed, "Oh, my goodness, I've never worked on an animal." Wajickee reminded her, "We're all animals Dr. Beckmire." She looked at him and approached Somara who was calming the animal by stroking it softly. Courtney said, "John Lee, I need you to place a double wire tie around the animals mouth so that when I inject it, it won't react defensively, and bite the you know what out of one of us." The animal was on its last leg, and Wajickee watched the humans try to save a badly mauled animal. Courtney said, if I can put it to sleep, I can fix and perhaps heal those bite marks.

Needless to say, the actions of the two women, spread throughout the camp, and before the drama was concluded, everyone except the children were in attendance watching Dr.

Beckmire and Somara attempt to save a dingo. With her final stitch, Wajickee announced, that the two women would be enshrined on the walls of the caves, and that they would be known forever more as the healers of the dingoes, a title that will allow them passage anywhere in the outback with protection of the dingoes because the one being healed, is the Alpha." Wajickee then instructed John Lee to take the binders off the animals mouth. When he did, the animal licked the hands of Courtney and Somara. Wajickee announced, "This is a great day in the outback and for this group—no one heals dingoes' this is a first, and must be enshrined in the cave of history."

Anel and Angel were sitting near the billabong when Wajickee appeared suddenly, and said, "I need you two to show me the ways of the internet. I am a fast learner and my tenure in this sphere is contingent upon how I process and disseminate my knowledge to those who are my elders."

Anel asked, "Have you ever been on the internet?" Wajickee smiled and announced, "I don't even know what it is. Show me this Trojan Horse so that I can see why so many are mesmerized and addicted to that medium." Angel thought to herself, if the rumors are almost accurate about this guy, then I should open a simple platform and let him diagnose and learn all that there is."

When the ladies turned on their laptops, Wajickee asked, "Is this tour for beginners?"

"It has to be since we don't have access to the internet because we don't have Wi-Fi."

Anel, smiled, and said, "I was just going to show you how the computer operates." He frowned, and said, "I don't need to know how to operate that thing, because it would take me less than five-minutes to figure it out, compose a message and send it to you. Remember, I am a fast learner.

# # #

Four hours later, Anel, Angel, and Wajickee were surfing the internet and tracking how the South African diamond is handled, marketed, and sold. Wajickee grunted, "Our diamonds are much clearer, without blood, and they are reasonably priced."

Angel looked at her sister, smiled, and said, "This guy is playing games with us. He's able to access sites, multi-task portals, and cause my unit to stall because it does not have enough ram to load the information that he is adding at an incredible speed."

Wajickee looked away, and said, "You guys have just let the Genie out of the bottle. I now know how this works, and I can see how easy it is to become addicted to information flowing at your command. You two must eat, I will join you later. Your personal information is what it is, I will not enter your encrypted domain in search of your history. In the few hours that I have been with you people, unless you are a demon, I have seen another dimension that offers good. I know you're concerned about your personal information, how can I assure you that I will never enter your domain without your being with me. I hope you two will continue to show me how to master this medium, and I will show you how to do even more than you can imagine from my experimenting with the world wide web. I love this thing and being who I am, I can assimilate information at an incredible speed that will allow you to use short cuts to find and trace the footprints of those who are financing the effort to terminate this group."

Anel asked, "May I ask you a question?"

"Absolutely."

"Who are you, and how can you be that knowledgeable about the internet after allegedly having never been on it before. Who are you?"

Wajickee slowed his momentum, and replied, "I have been involved with the Beckmire clan for a long time. I am the liege to Ben Beckmire, and I was the same to his great, great, great, great grandfather, who is behind you, and has been monitoring your every move and sanctioning your inclusion into group." As Angel and Anel turned around, they witnessed the largest saltwater crocodile ever seen by a human. Angel fainted, but was caught by a marauding Dempsey. When she came to, she asked, "Are you real or an aberration?"

Dempsey smiled, and said, "I am as real as they come. You will find that when you are here, nothing is impossible, if you are a person of faith. I was summoned here, and when I got here, you were in the process of fainting. Listen, I am new as new can be to this kind of place and the people." He asked Wajickee for permission to escort the two ladies to the village for the evening meal. Wajickee lowered his head signaling his approval.

Anel looked long at Wajickee, and asked, "Are you going to delve into our personal matters?"

Wajickee smiled, and said, "I knew who you were before you came to kill members of the group. Listen, this is Australia, this the outback, that was the Great Saltie, I am Wajickee and, therefore, when here, there are no secrets from me or the other spirits." Anel began to cry, but was comforted by Wajickee when he announced, "I know all there is to know about you. Your past is your past, your future is bright, rewarding, no more monetizing from terminations, just a blissful, prefab family, and then your own. This information is for the moment, and you will not remember any of this in the morning.

# # #

At dinner, the Sarge welcomed the two ladies into their group, and said, "I hope you two ladies will consider joining our tribe, and working for the good of humanity, and not money." He took a sip of a beverage, and said, "I know this is going to be a good thing for you, and for us." The Sarge started to say something else when Michael stood up, made the time out sign, and beckoned the Sarge. The Sarge said to the group, "Hold that thought for a moment. I am aggressively being called about a message."

When the Sarge reached the area where Michael was standing, Michael pointed to Jilkes, John Lee, and Mallory to join them.

When the group assembled, Michael said to the Sarge, "From the sewers, I received a message and a link to a website that reads as follow: "Looking for coldblooded mercs who can help the rightful owners of a fortune claim it. Will reward loyal and committed associates who help and deliver an end result (US $100k maximum for 3-days work + per diem, plus all of the natural resources you can carry in a knapsack)."

The Sarge said, "Michael, that sounds like a dictator trying to be restored."

Michael responded, "Sarge, in Australia?" The Sarge frowned, and asked, "Are you trying to be funny?"

"Sarge, I never mince words with you. I got this out of the sewers, and they thought it might apply to you since, and I quote, "you're the only dictator in Australia." Those aren't my words, but the words of the people we support. That was the first advertisement. Here is the second ad, and it reads as follows, "Management is happy about the response, and is considering the applications from the first day of this notice going public, of two hundred dedicated comrades. In order to make sure that there is a seamless response by the other side, we are looking for another two hundred to provide support and actual ground engagement.""

The Sarge was about to vehemently respond when Wajickee appeared on the scene, and announced, "There is an advertisement for four hundred people to help remove a dictator, that I just scanned on the web. As a result of our two new ladies, I have learned to enter sites that should be banned from viewing. The extremely wicked sexual scenes, and conclusions are not only beyond belief, but they have enormous followings that total in the millions. How can perverted behaviors be sought after by the masses? Is there not a limit on subscriptions to watch dastardly acts being performed on people? Anyway, my friend, someone has enough funds to recruit an army to conclude your reign."

Ben Beckmire stared at Wajickee, and envisioned each stronghold's advantages and disadvantages. He knew that the outback was the best place to defend from those numbers.

"I hear that your ranch and your farm utilizes mechanized weapons, but your topography is available online. No, Ben Beckmire, this land is the best, but it requires you to summon all of your friends and allies. Hutang for one is a warrior of unparalleled skills and needs a last battle before heading to that great void. Also, you could use those people in the sewers that you speak of so often and support. I believe the people at the ranch will be able to help as well. Clyde and his crew are anxious to come here and lend a hand. I'm sure you're about to ask me how I know all these people are willing to help out. I know Ben Beckmire, because I sent them all a group email with an SOS at the top. I told them for further information, to contact Darryl." Ben Beckmire laughed, and said, "So you're now a computer expert and you know how to send emails, eh?"

"Thanks to Anel and Angel, I am not only able to send emails, but I have also begun, with their assistance to track the digital footprint of those involved in the assassinations and attempted assassinations." Beckmire began to walk away, but muttered, "miracles never cease." Wajickee announced, "I heard that remark, Ben Beckmire."

"Tell me my liege, did you really reach out to those people?"

"Indeed, I did," Wajickee commented. "As soon as me and my new staff got wind of a lot of passengers coming this way, we started planning. We will make sure that your people are here and ready. Up to four hundred people is an expensive undertaking, wouldn't you agree? I mean, I don't have to use an abacus to tell me that the amount is nearly $40 million. However, if you know that two-thirds are going to perish from this event, then your downside is roughly $13 million, when the stakes are in excess of a trillion dollars when you add the diamond and gold mines as well as your groups' assets. Not a bad three-day adventure if you ask me."

Beckmire sighed, and asked, "Are you looking forward to this potential epic clash?" As if he was ignoring Beckmire's question, Wajickee garbled a thick outback rendition of slang. He articulately stated, "I am indeed looking to prepare for the onslaught of foreigners for the wrong purpose which allows me to dedicate my full attention to this matter. Not to mention, the tremendous amount of information I am gleaming from that world wide web that gives me examples of epic battles fought and won by the underdog."

Mr. West placed a call to Mr. East, and asked if everything were in a go position, and was informed that in six days, all the manpower and resources would be on point. Mr. West indicated to Mr. East that he was concerned about committing up to $40 million to conclude this aspect of their arrangement. Mr. East flatly stated, "I'm expecting that our maximum payout will not exceed $13 million. I expect that group to display a larger-than-life response, and that will mean at least two-thirds or more of those breaching the village won't be coming home. Now, that is on the high side, that group may be old, but if you look at their history in battle, those people don't give up, and don't quit. I am high siding the $13 million, and I frankly don't believe that eighty to ninety percent of them will return. I have that kind of faith in that group, as I have studied them over time, and they rarely fail."

"So, you're saying we can gain control, eliminate our obstacles, and knowingly, send men to their death, and at a cost of less than $2 million?" Mr. West summarized.

"That is exactly what I am saying. Listen, when you are a merc, you do this kind of work for pay, the glory, and if you're not successful, you don't get paid. I'm not the bad guy here, my degree is in business, not in combat," Mr. East stated. There was a long pause, and Mr. East said, "You seem to have a problem with eliminating people to obtain those glorious personal goals that we agreed upon."

"Naw, I don't have a problem. I do have a conscience, and sometimes, momentarily, it gets in the way of me embracing the consequences of our actions. I'll be alright, but I must admit, I am a little anxious to get this over and done with, and piss down that assholes throat for blowing up my house. Listen, catch you later, by the way do you ever talk to those people?"

CHAPTER SIX

Wajickee and his new associates, agreed that one of the perpetrators of the assassinations and attempts was indeed the man who lived on the hill in Poughkeepsie, and whose son was incarcerated and having the time of his life. They identified him from his use of an old gasoline credit card. With all of the precautions that he took to make sure that everyone thought that he was dead, some habits don't die easily. Anel showed Wajickee how to hack into camera systems, and that is how he was identified. At a local gasoline station in Compton, California, Mr. West was openly filmed filling his Ford Bronco. Wajickee did analysis, after analysis, and announced to Anel and Angel that he had found one of the men responsible for the assassinations of Ava, Carlos, Mike, and Carla.

Angel, Anel, and Wajickee looked at other aspects of the individual to make sure that it was the person of interest. The trio concluded that the person of interest's new name is Spencer Bruhaven. Anel showed Wajickee how to hack and track everything relative to Mr. Bruhaven, even though most of his elaborate channels were secure, fake, and changed on a daily basis. Yes, Mr. Bruhaven knew how to disappear, reappear, and used a number of fictious names to manage his finances, and depended upon a lot of cash to stay hidden.

In the meantime, Angel discovered one of his frequently utilized passwords, both digital and verbal. She uncovered a significant deposit into an anonymous account that used the name Sterling Broadus, another bogus name used by Mr. Bruhaven to advance his counterfeit organization.

Anel asked Angel, "How come Mr. East Coast is hard to gather information on? We know they talk, and they probably use an encrypted medium like WhatsApp, but that can even be infiltrated. However, I believe our person on the East Coast is one smart tech savvy individual. As a matter of fact, I am uncertain if it is a man or a woman. No footprint of any kind."

Anel responded, "Let's not divide our efforts, I suggest that we focus on that person on the West Coast and attempt to track his finances, and then turn completely to the East Coast person. The kind of money they're talking about, you just don't store under your pillow. We have to search harder and see where the source of his funds emanate, and then I'm sure somewhere along the line, the two men have traded coin at some point in time, and that's the kind of thing we should be trying to find. Listen, as fast as that Wajickee is at deciphering information, we should let him focus on the East Coast person. We might be looking for the obvious, but he may perhaps investigate it from another perspective."

CHAPTER SEVEN

After returning his children to their mother, the associate from the sewer announced, "Me and the kids had a wonderful time, perhaps next time, do you think you might want to join us? Anyway, did you consider my last request?"

"I thought about it, but I didn't get anywhere with my thoughts."

"Oh, I see!" He exclaimed.

"I don't think I'm at the place where I can discuss your potential lover."

"Girl, are you crazy? I was just kidding because I felt awkward asking you out, knowing full well having that conversation with you was a no-no. He stared at her, and said, "I've not been a good person to you or our children. I know we both suffered a lot, but I don't care about anything other than you and the children."

"Okay, listen, I will have dinner with you. However, you had better make it real soon before I change my mind about dealing with you again. Oh, and by the way, I was in the Mac gym yesterday, riding the bike by the window. I saw the person I thought was my ex-employer, and I took a picture of him from the window, and I am damn sure that it's him. I will send it to you later, but you had better send me a text in the next twenty-four hours confirming a date, a time, and a place for dinner and drinks."

# # #

When her ex-finally received the photo, he sent it directly to his sewer buddies, and they forwarded it to Michael, who passed it on to Ben Beckmire. When Ben Beckmire received it, he muttered, "no way in hell is this guy still alive. Oh, my goodness, no damn way!" He proclaimed.

Ben Beckmire saw Zanthius talking to Jilkes and John Lee and decided to let them know who one of the potential funders of the assassinations was. He said to the trio, guess who is still alive, and determined to see our demise?" John Lee immediately responded, "That there Holy Father." The Sarge shook his head indicating that was the wrong choice. Everyone else chose not to guess, and waited intelligently for the Sarge to state the answer. The Sarge put on his glasses, found the text message on his phone, and showed the guys a picture of the person who owned the house that used to be situated on stilts in Poughkeepsie, New York. Everyone was shocked to see who was in the picture. John Lee exclaimed, "Well I'll be a pig's uncle. That there fella must be like that there Holy Father, you know able to get away when his ass is about to be discovered."

Jilkes said, "At least now we know who one of the persons we are dealing with definitely is. Once we find out who his partner is, then I think we can go and whip their asses permanently."

Zanthius studied the photo long and hard, and said, "Someone else was in that house, and that guy must have had an escape plan that probably ended up where Larry came to rest after falling through a trap door. His desire for revenge is monumental, and I think we should really focus on his ass first despite the fact that we believe that he has a partner. Dad, do you think his partner could be my uncle Walter, the bionic man?"

Beckmire looked at Zanthius, and said, "I really hadn't considered Walter, but it is not outside of his purview. However, I think that it is someone else pulling the strings for our termination. Somehow, I think it's all about money, but if we're all dead, how can anyone benefit from our demise, unless it is purely about the diamond and gold mines, but even they are locked down in a safe made by the devil himself. I am perplexed about who the other partner could be, but I am not naive enough to not try to calculate all of the people that we have put a hurting on, including family members. I don't know, but Walter is traceable and easy to find. Let's keep thinking about the possible suspects.

# # #

Franco called the Sarge on December 20th, and proudly announced that the reconstruction of the farmhouse was complete. He indicated that the requested upgrades for both the farmhouse and the guesthouse had been installed. The Sarge asked, "So, Franco, what is all that noise I hear in the background?"

Franco responded, "Oh, Sarge I ordered a special color caulk, and I drove up to the hardware store to pick it up." The Sarge thought to himself "why would he do that when he has a lot of laborers there to assist him." He asked Franco, "With all of the people we have helping you, why didn't you have one of them pick it up for you?"

Franco, not sure of where this inquiry was coming from said, "Oh, Sarge if you're worrying about me, no one in this town knows me." At that moment in time, the Sarge heard "puff, puff, puff, puff, puff, and what sounded like a phone being dropped." He asked, "Franco what was that noise?" There was no immediate answer. The Sarge asked again, "Franco what was that noise?" The Sarge then yelled, "Franco, are you alright?"

Franco was felled by two assassins, and died immediately. In the meantime, the Sarge is screaming Franco's name into the phone trying to find out what had happened. The phone was picked up by someone who said, "Kennedy, King, Kennedy, guess whose next motherfucker?" The Sarge screamed at the top of his lungs and Courtney came running to him only to find him sobbing his heart out. Between sniffling, he said, "I think someone just assassinated Franco in Virginia."

# # #

A week later after Franco's funeral, the Sarge announced, "That is the last member of our clan that we will lose to assassins. From this moment forward, we will work together, never alone, never in areas that are not secure and protected by members of our clan. I want the two new ladies, Dempsey, Hood, and Wajickee when he has time to assist, to focus completely on locating the two assumed partners."

The Sarge continued, "I am moving on to another matter, what is the status of Mike and Carla's children?"

Anel replied, "We have begun to entertain them, dine with them, swim, read, write, talk, and play with them. They seem to enjoy us, and both of them say they like being around us. They wake up in the morning, and the first thing they want to know is, where we are. I think we are on the right foot, we might ask them to spend an evening with us, and soon a night, and hopefully we can move into a full relationship."

Beckmire asked, "What does a full relationship mean?" Both ladies paused, and Anel said, "We are looking for a long-term commitment with the children." The Sarge walked closer to Anel, cocked his head sideways, and said, "I think I'm going to really like not terminating you two. The very idea that you're planning a long and hopefully fruitful relationship with those two kids is sweet music to my ears. They need consistency at this point, and I'm going to pray that you two can provide them with it. I am so happy we found roles for you guys."

Anel said, "Your mandate for us to be caretakers is so, not necessary. I think I speak for the two of us, we love those children, and have daily discussions as to how to make things happen, and to make sure that whatever we do, we consider the short-and long-term implications of our actions and decisions."

# # #

Wajickee woke Angel and Anel up at four in the morning. He said, "I know where Mr. West keeps his money, and I have access to his encrypted accounts." Both ladies feeling a little bewildered didn't act surprised.

On the contrary, Anel anxiously stated, "What took you so long my genius friend?" Not sure how to take the words and the tone, Wajickee asked, "Well, are you ready to help me find out who is targeting our people slowly, but surely?"

Angel hesitantly stated, "We had a sleep over last night with Stella and Leonardus. Is there any way we can do this much later, we had planned on swimming with them, and doing some math work." Wajickee, looking a little defeated, announced, "Perhaps I am too excited about what I'm able to do on the world wide web, and just want to impress you two. For now, your current mission is the absolute one. Teach them, console, and love them, and you will find happiness beyond your wildest imagination."

Anel stated, "That sounds like a cliché that I have heard a thousand times. Are you using it colloquially, or are you seeing into the future?"

Wajickee smiled, and said, "I am too old to be trifled with. Tend to the children, bring them to the billabong, and I will ensure everyone's faith."

Wajickee was prepared to disappear immediately, but decided to say to the sisters, "Since encountering you two, and the world wide web, I have found a new passion and pursuit. I owe it to you two ladies, and I just ask that you not consider doing dumb or stupid. If, speaking from a spirits' vantage point you attend to this mission with sincerity, then all of your earthly desires will be consummated as well as you guys earning more than you could ever earn from shooting arrows at people." Before they could respond, Wajickee was gone.

# # #

At eight in the morning, two pleasantly rambunctious kids, woke up to two weary and tired young women. This was the first night that the siblings had slept through the night without waking up and crying. As the two women attempted to gather themselves and make a natural presentation of themselves, Leonardus, the oldest announced, "Last night was the first time in a long time that I, or we, have been able to sleep throughout the night." With tears in his eyes, he said, "I hope we can do this all the time. I like you guys, and Stella likes you." The kids ran out of the hut, leaving the sisters with an important decision to make.

Although they were fulfilling a condition of survival, their hearts were deep in sorrow because they both cared for and loved the siblings. Angel said to Anel, "We have got to set some boundaries, or they are going to be jilted, and so are we. We have to talk to Wajickee and Monica to try to figure out how to handle these emotions, without setting everyone up for a disastrous conclusion."

Anel looked towards the billabong and said, "Before we do anything, we have got to get buy-in from the Sarge, Courtney, Wajickee, Monica, and everyone else involved in helping out with the children.

# # #

Ava's lawyer sent a message to Zanthius indicating that he was needed in Spain to attend to estate papers, insurance policies, and a bunch of other documents that needed his signature. He spoke to Asiram about the issue who told him that he needed to consult with his dad.

Around midday, Zanthius saw Mallory, and asked him if he had seen his dad, and was informed that he was taking a hike with Jilkes, John Lee, Gladstone, Chakes, and Montomie. Zanthius asked, where are they hiking to?"

Mallory smiled, and said, "Aren't you from here? How in the heck would I know where they go when they go a wandering? I've learned to stay close and be humble when I'm here." Zanthius smiled, and said, "You and my dad are some real characters. I wish I could have known you guys when you were in your prime."

Mallory looked Zanthius up and down, and asked, "What's that prime shit you be talking about? Would you like to set a quarter of a mile indicator, and see who arrives first?" Zanthius smiled, knowing full well that Mallory couldn't beat him in a quarter mile-sprint. He said, "Mallory, I have not really exercised since my mom was cut down. The reason I want to see my dad is because there are some legal issues that I have to take care of in Spain, and prior to considering going there, I am going to get back into shape so that I can beat those who participated in my mother's death, with my bare hands. That is a promise I made to her long ago. I told her before she had to rescue me from myself, that if anyone ever raised a hand to her, I would beat them unmercifully to death with my hands."

Mallory looked long and hard at Zanthius, and said, "I doubt if your mother would condone such an act by you. She loved you more than any human being should be loved. She took you away from your father because she didn't want to share your love. I'm going to tell you this and you had better never mention it to anyone. When your mother left your dad without notice, that man almost made the ultimate sacrifice in that he was suicidal. He loved Ava De Lombardo so much that I traveled to Spain in search of your mother when Ben couldn't locate her. I spent months trying to follow every lead that I could steal, buy, or intimidate people to obtain. I love Monica, but your dad loved your mother in some kind of magical way. When they first met, and how they first met was incredible and fairy-tale like. It was as though they placed competing spells on each other. All he did was talk about Ava De Lombardo, and I knew so much from his conversations about her that I thought I had met her and knew her well. No, Zanthius, his love was and is like your love for Asiram, dedicated, attentive, amusing, faithful, and everlasting."

Zanthius with tears in his eyes, asked, "You really love that guy, don't you?"

Mallory teared up, turned around, and said, "Here comes that pirate of a father of yours. Catch you later."

Ben Beckmire and his group walked up to Zanthius, and he immediately knew that something was out of place. He asked, "Son, are you okay, and why did Mallory turn tail and get out of dodge?"

"Dad, he didn't turn tail and run off, he had something he was doing when I interrupted him. So, anyway, I have to head to Spain, and get a lot of legal stuff completed soon. I was wondering what your thoughts are on that one?"

Ben Beckmire looked at Jilkes and John Lee, and said, "Is my son from another planet or something? Does he realize that we are under attack? Oh, can someone tell him that we just lost another one of our compatriots. Would someone tell him that I'm not liking that scenario unless we are all there and loaded for bear."

Zanthius exclaimed, "Dad, dah! Why on earth would I ask you unless I wanted to know about a strategy for keeping me and mine safe?"

Beckmire backed down, and said, "Hi Son, how's your day going so far? Me and the guys found a stream that is intermittently flowing with gold nuggets."

Zanthius asked, "Dad, where is that stream, and how come Darryl and Wajickee don't know anything about it?"

"Smart ass children, always drawing on higher powers. Back to your first question, I wasn't going to broach the subject of Spain with you until you brought it to me. Me and my guys want to find the four assassins and perform some dastardly work on their bodies. I instructed the entire camp to not approach you or mention anything about Spain. Now that you have placed it on the table, let's bring it up to the group, set a get back in shape date, and a head to Spain date. Damn I love you boy. I was going to mention Spain, and here you go bringing it to me. You don't have to believe me, ask John Lee, you know he don't do no lying for me." Everyone laughed, and realized that laughter was now okay once again because a special person, mother, and friend had been publicly acknowledged by her precious son.

Ben Beckmire said, "Tonight let's have a feast honoring the spirits, and our fallen comrades."

# # #

Stella and Leonardus were sitting outside of Anel and Angel's hut, as if they were abandoned. Courtney saw them, and to herself, exclaimed, "Oh, hell no! No way in hell that's acceptable." She dead reckoned towards the hut. Leonardus saw her coming, jumped up, and asked, "Are you going to wake them up?"

Courtney calmed down a little, and beckoned the children away from the hut. She asked Leonardus, why they were sitting outside of the hut, and looking sad? Leonardus responded, "We were protecting them like they do us. I don't think a warrior smiles when they go into battle."

Courtney embraced both children, and instructed, "Go back and protect your mates. I'm so proud of the both of you. By the way, do you like Anel and Angel?"

Stella replied, "I love Anel and I love Angel."

Courtney announced, "God is good, and Spirits are as well. You two make my heart flutter with the sound of love. How long have they been asleep?"

Leonardus said, "Not long, they told us that Wajickee woke them up at four in the morning, and they just wanted a nap." Just then, Anel walked out of their hut, and said, "Hi, Dr. Beckmire, what brings you around here?"

Courtney wanting to stay away from the official title said, "I was going to visit with Monica, and the children were sitting outside of your hut looking what I considered sad. Leonardus told me that he was protecting you and your sister."

Anel, who was a little confused asked, "Guys, weren't you supposed to be with Ms. Viola until we came to get you?"

Leonardus replied, "Ms. Viola thinks that we're in school. We decided to protect those who protect us from evil, and decided to come here rather than go to school."

Anel asked, "Did you two skip school to make sure that we were okay?"

Stella indicated, "We wanted to make sure that everyone was okay, but we decided to be extra careful when it came to you guys since you guys are new, and came with some bad baggage."

Anel asked, "Stella, do you still think we have bad baggage?"

Stella leaned on Leonardus, and said, "That is why we were protecting you to make sure that the bad baggage was gone, and that no one wanted to hurt you guys because, we love you." At this time Anel is crying her heart out. Angel exits the hut, and states that she heard everything, and that she had never heard an expression of love greater than what was stated by the two children. Angel then said, "If you will have us, then we will champion to have you as our very own, throughout eternity?"

Stella asked, "What's an eternity?"

Everyone broke into laughter, as the Sarge who was watching and listening from a distance, walked closer to Stella, got on his knees, and said, "That means, during dinner, we will ask the clan to vote on endowing these two ladies with you and Leonardus. In other words, you won't have to protect them when they sleep, because all of you will be in the same hut, and they will become your new parents if you so wish."

Leonardus whispered to Stella, "They will be our new parents."

# # #

At dinner, several issues were discussed, and the group voted on each. Of particular interest was the idea of leaving the children behind when they attended to the business in Spain. Rashida kept uttering, "Never in a thousand years. Never in a thousand years." The Sarge walked closer to her, and asked, "Why do you keep repeating that statement?"

"Never in a thousand years!" Rashida proclaimed. Carlos took up the thought, and exclaimed, "Never in ten thousand years!" Rashida turned to the group, and said, "People want our children dead as much as they want the adults dead. I personally will never leave my children behind, especially since I know that those who want us terminated, want to inflict pain on the total meaning of 'us', and that is everyone who breathes this precious air, and who is a member of this clan. Remember, children grow up to be adults."

As the Sarge was about to ask Ms. Viola and Mary Alice to take the children for a walk, he noticed that Stella was crying. He walked over to her, and asked, "Why are you crying?"

Between a lot of sniffling, and almost hyperventilating, she said, "Leonardus and I just got new parents, and now people want to leave us behind."

The Sarge hugged her, and said, "That will never happen. Sometimes adults speak in ways that children don't understand, and often they hear key words that make them think that they are going to be abandoned. I assure you, where I go, you go, and Anel and Angel go as well. How about that?"

Stella hugged the Sarge and said, "I just got new parents, and I don't want them leaving me and Leonardus."

The Sarge said, "When we go to Spain, you will be the first ones on the plane. How about that?"

The Sarge continued, once all young ears were out of hearing distance, said, "I don't want to send the children away, because they may think that is another sign of being left behind. Moving forward, sensitive issues will be discussed in private prior to our convening. Now, it appears that my son, you know the guy, Zanthius Beckmire De Lombardo, must present himself in Spain to sign some legal documents and probably inherit a ton of money and property. Also, today was the first time my son mentioned his mother and her husband, and agreed to going to handle her estate. He also has some notion of finding those who were hired to do that dastardly act on our friends. Therefore, tomorrow, we will begin to do two training sessions per day for the next two weeks. In the meantime, the two new parents will be given footage of those who committed that final act. Anel and Angel, I need you guys along with your liege, to study the film, and find me those 'mf's', and let us prepare to send them in pieces to their final resting place."

Zanthius said, "Dad, I want first dibs on those four. Please, don't complicate my desire to address those who were a part of my mother's demise. Please dad, let's not discuss, let's prepare to provide the dastardliest demise that I can think of."

Monica stood up, raised her hand, and when acknowledged, said, "Zanthius, we are about salvation, not revenge. I share in your desires, but I don't want that to be the focus of this group. We treat it like any other threat. Like Walter, Mr. Utz, the man in the house on the stilts, and lots of others. I am afraid if we look at what is happening to our brethren, and decide on how to conclude those who committed the act, then we have just entered another domain. Listen, I want to die in the midst of this group. I don't want to target individuals as we did in the past. We use technology and others to do the finding, all we do is the concluding, but not in an announced manner. We're not going to beat anyone to death with our bare hands, and if so, me and mine are going to retreat to Minnesota." There was a loud muttering of disassociated sounds and words when the Sarge loudly exclaimed, "Order! I said order."

A few moments after things calmed down, the Sarge eloquently stated, "We will treat this matter no different than any other issues we have faced. Yes, we will find those who pulled the trigger, those who paid to have the triggers pulled, and we will be done with them. I unfortunately set the revenge stage when I implemented a plan to do historical things to them that was done by my first grandfather. Zanthius, I know your pain and your desires, but trust me, a myopic approach to this problem will lead us bleeding internally, emotionally, and permanently. We have done some despicable things to people. We have been manipulated and handled by some of the best.

Yes, I want those responsible for assassinating Ava, Carlos, Carla, Mike, and Franco. I want to do horrible things to their bodies, but I am not going to go to sleep fixated on revenge, we are better than that. Now, since we know we have a few weeks of training and conditioning to do, I want to get started in the morning."

The Sarge looked into the crowd, and found Anel and Angel. He said, "I have a more important matter to discuss with this group. As you know, Mike and Carla left behind two children, Stella and Leonardus. The two have been spending quality and monitored time with our two new converts, Angel, and Anel. Earlier today, my wife saw the kids sitting outside of Angel and Anel's hut, and my wife also indicated that the two kids looked sad. Ya'll know Mrs. Beckmire, she can charge like a bull in a China shop. She engaged the children to ascertain why they were sitting outside and looking sad, and was told that they were protecting the inhabitants while they slept. She questioned the children, and determined that they love Anel and Angel, and that they wanted to be with them. In the interim, I talked with Ms. Viola, and she had nothing, but high praise for the two ladies, and their immediate attention to the needs of the children. That brings me to the point where I need to have a vote as to how we proceed with this matter. We have never had a situation like this one, and that is why I need everyone to verbally say yay or nay to make the two children wards of Angel and Anel."

Ms. Viola appeared, and walked over to Anel and Angel, and embraced them. She whispered something to them, and then kissed them on their cheeks. She turned around and said, "I know these people are righteous, and will do great by these children, even though their introduction to this wild group wasn't what I would consider positive. However, I believe in miracles, and me and that wizard guy endorse these two ladies wholeheartedly."

Darryl looked at Sue Lyn, smiled at her, and said, "You guys know when I am here, I get a little more respect than when I'm in Alabama with John Lee, Jilkes, and the rest of you. I have consorted with the elders, and they too endorse Anel and Angel as caretakers of Stella and Leonardus. I give you this hocus pocus version because I need all the votes to be 'yay'."

As the Sarge prepared to ask for a vote, Wajickee appeared, and said, "These two ladies, Anel, and Angel, will make great parents. They also have found out where one of your enemies is resting consistently, and where you can find the people who actually did the field work on our fallen brethren. Therefore, I vote 'yay', and so should the rest of you. After all, this is my domain." He smiled, and said, "I am just jousting with you guys, vote your conscience."

Exactly two weeks later, a fit looking group exited their school bus, and entered customs. The first thing to be uttered by the customs officials was, "Sorry for your loss." The Sarge replied, "Thanks guys and gals, we appreciate your acknowledgements."

All the passports were systematically stamped except Anel and Angel's. The agent then started asking them about their purpose in the outback, and Anel responded, "We sought opportunity, and found a family." The agent looked towards Ms. Viola, who said, "They be good girls now. Trust me, they be done got religion."

###

Captain Franco Harris, who was Carla's co-captain, welcomed the group aboard the aircraft. John Lee asked him, "What happens when a plane ain't been flown for a while? Do you have to change the oil and inflate the tires?"

Captain Franco laughed, and said, "My friend we watch, wash, check, evaluate, and start this lady three times a week, and let her engines scream for about thirty minutes. We then shut her down, and run the tapes to make sure that she is performing at the level she was designed to achieve."

John Lee replied, "I just be interested because we ain't been out of the outback in months, and I just want our first flight to be sweet and smooth."

Ben Beckmire spoke to Captain Harris, and said, "I didn't know your first name was Franco. We lost a good friend not too long ago named Franco. Anyway, are we all stocked and ready to travel abroad?"

Captain Harris said, "Mr. Beckmire, we are loaded, the plane has been fueled, provisions are on board, and they are ready to be consumed. Also, I would like to thank you for allowing me to take over where my friend and colleague left off. I will try to make your travels as safe and smooth as possible. Once again, thanks Sir."

"Captain Franco, do me a favor. Call me Sarge. Thanks."

###

The long flight was essentially that, just a long flight. When the plane landed, and the group went through customs, on the other side of the wall was Franco's old crew. They had people placed inside of the airport as well as on the outside.

When the group exited the airport, waiting outside was a red school bus. The Sarge asked, "Where on earth did you get that relic?"

Benito replied, "Franco had this bus made to usher you around when you are here."

The Sarge replied, "What on earth did he want us to do— be shot on sight?"

Benito smiled, and said, "It is made like the one you have at the ranch. It is fortified, bullet proof, and armor plated. I wish he were on it when they assassinated him and left his body lying in the streets. Me, Giuseppe, and Michele, are staying in the same place with a lot of people watching our backs. Since we became legitimate businessmen, we have done a lot for people, and the bad guys are now good guys that have found ways to make money without embarrassing their families and friends."

The Sarge said, "We are feeling a little naked. Anyway, can you get us some metal?"

Benito smiled, and responded, "Oh, Mr. Sarge, on the bus there is a box of new 9 millimeters, and a couple of sleeves for each one, and one round is in each chamber. The .45s and .40s are particularly loud, and if you're caught with one, well, they tend to forget your case number."

The Sarge looked as if he was tearing up, and asked, "Did you send my friend off like the king he was?"

Benito responded, "We had to keep his box closed because those who did that deed focused on his head and face. Mr. Sarge, you would not have realized that the person you were viewing was your friend."

#

On the bus, little Ms. Beatrice asked her granny, "Are we going to make the people who hurt Ms. Ava and Mr. Carlos pay."

Ms. Viola turned to her, and asked, "Child where on earth you be getting these questions from?" She then yelled, "Luana, can you come back here for a minute?"

When Luana arrived at the back of the bus, she asked, "What's going on with you two?"

Ms. Viola said, "This here child wants to know if we are going to make those people who hurt our friends pay."

Luana responded, "Lord Jesus, my child is as grown as anyone on this bus. Did you answer her?"

Ms. Viola responded, "That's an answer her momma or her daddy should be trying to figure out where it originated, and then try to talk her down." Chakes walked to the back of the bus, and asked, "What's going on back here? What are you three scheming about?" Luana whispered in his ear, and he responded, "That's all my fault. I sometimes forget that she don't miss a thing, and when I was talking to Montomie, Jong, Bernstein, Brown, and Whitmore, I believe she must have heard me say that we need to make those people pay for what they did to our people. Listen, this is all my doing and I will talk her down and remind her that she is a child and shouldn't be so concerned about adult conversations when she is near. My fault, but I love my little lady so very much, give me a big hug and kiss."

Ms. Viola muttered, "Some kind of dad you be, having conversations like that around that baby."

Chakes stated, "Ms. Viola, let's hope that's the only mistake I make trying to raise my children."

Ms. Viola laughed, and said, "Scoundrel, despite a few hick ups here and there, you be done made me a believer, and I am admitting that I love you. Don't ask me to say it again."

When the group arrived at *The View*, everyone was impressed by its new façade, and remembered what it was like when it was crumbling to the ground. Mary Alice said, "Look at this place. We do good work, and we never ask for payment. I am so happy I chose Jong." Everyone broke into laughter. Jong said, "I am so happy with my selection, and look at those beautiful and smart children that I gave her. Oh, and by the way, her little business in Virginia will net her $13 million, and a lifetime 20% payment. Seems like somebody made a magic doughnut that is fortified with vitamins and minerals, and is a best seller to schools across the country and the military absolutely loves it. It was developed based upon a formula that Mary Alice created, and they added the other healthy stuff. My family and wife are the best."

John Lee retorted, "Why you always bragging about them there kids of yours?"

Jilkes jumped in, and said, "Ask him where him and his family live?" John Lee, considered the input, broke into laughter, and said, "Jong, all the kids in this here village are smart, good looking, rich, and personable. I be happy that you and the misses made some money from a doughnut, but what would be more impressive is if you would pull out that there dry rotted check book, and at least pay the electric bill." The entire group broke into stitches as John Lee eloquently cut the legs from under Jong.

After the laughter terminated, Jong said, "I apologize for minimizing the group and focusing on my family. It will never happen again, and for once, I understood everything you said. John Lee, you and Jilkes are our lucky pieces because what most don't know, when we were over in that jungle, and afraid as little kittens, we all gathered strength and resolve from you two who were always out-front smelling, looking, and keeping us alive. I sincerely meant no disrespect to the rest of the children. I apologize, and I bow low to you my brother for making me keep it real." Uncharacteristically, Jong walked over to John Lee, and kissed him on the cheek. John Lee responded, "You shouldn't do that in front of my other friend, him be a really jealous person."

The Sarge said, "Now that we have had a lot of catharsis, can we get down to the real reason why we are here. You people won't believe that our friends here are very aware of our needs, both physically and environmentally. The floor that we're staying on is vaulted, bullet proof, and armor plated. When they built this place, they had us in mind, and our need for security. Okay people, you have one hour to take a shower, brush your teeth, and be in the dining room for a testament to Ava, Carlos, Carla, Franco, and Michael. Please, don't be late."

# # #

At dinner, a magnificent tribute to those who had met an untimely death was illustrated in music and video. The children were excluded from the tribute and were locked safely away in another part of the hotel. Zanthius rose from his seat, and exclaimed, "Before my mother intuitively came to see me as I was about to commit suicide! That's right. I was full of alcohol, and grief, when my mother showed up at my door, and saved me from myself. I didn't know who I was, but I remembered all of those who I had hurt and tormented. I destroyed families, marriages, relationships, jobs, and people that I loved. I was at the end of my misery, with a loaded gun in my hand, when there was a hard bang upon my door. My place was a disaster, and my mother said, "I will not let my only child who I love so much destroy himself because of his failures in life. If you do that, which you are planning to do, then save a round in that weapon because I am coming with you where that bullet takes you. I will not live another day without my son, who I gave up the most gentle and loving man for. Give me the gun, I'll go first, and then you can follow." Zanthius began to weep, and Asiram moved slowly towards him, and said, "Honey, you don't have to do this."

Zanthius fired back, "To my mother, I must acknowledge all that I've done to others, to you, and my father who I didn't know. Listen mother, you were a saint to me until I found out how you disassociated yourself from my father. We talked about her love for me, and how she did not want to share our love with anyone. I have loved many and I have hurt as many. My mother's death was an acknowledgement that I perhaps was the cause of her demise. Anyway, I will miss my mother, but I will cherish my father, and love all of you. I was a terrible person until I was saved by the woman who rules me, and my family. Asiram is my light at the end of the tunnel, and I promised my dad that I will not act impetuously when it comes to those who have or who are attempting to cause us grief. My friends, I was a mess, and my mom's demise had increased my notion of vengeance, a thing that my father says, is unacceptable for members of this group."

John Lee stood up, and said, "Maybe if you perform that purging mess, you might feel better. What you should do is write a book about all of them there bad things you have done. I be a buyer of it."

Courtney stood, and exhaled. She said, "If there is someone here who has never hurt another person, please stand." No one stood, and she said, "You're all in denial. I don't expect you to confess all of your under-mining activities, but my stepson did, because his mother and a few other members of our group have gone to the great beyond, a place that we all must visit, but not willingly."

The Sarge announced, "I want to talk about life. We all know what happened, so, let's move forward and try to honor those who were taken from us too soon. Insofar as the businesses are concerned, Benito, are we good with the ones we rejuvenated, and the new ones that you people drew us into?"

"Mr. Sarge, I have an inventory of everything that you have invested in. If I were a betting man, I would have to say that you have turned crooks into priests, avarice, and sadness, into sharing and happiness. You will see, every penny is accounted for and there is no greed amongst those involved. Let's break bread together at this point, discuss our future, and our past in the morning. We are here to honor those who have been taken away from us, not what we have earned, or what we want to do it. No, tonight is a night for those who have been taken away from us."

As Benito announced, that night was for them to collectively remember their fallen comrades. A picture show was provided of the group doing silly, being trivial, and enjoying each other and life. It was a fifteen-minute portrayal of the life of the members who were assassinated. Obviously, the children were not in attendance.

Later that night, Anel and Angel were shown around the hotel including the escape tunnels and supplies by Leonardus. Anel asked Leonardus, "How on earth do you know about these places, and its intricacies?"

He laughed, and said, "I saw the plans that my dad had, and asked him questions about the meaning of the symbols on the plans. One night we went through the entire building plans, and talked about what he or I would do differently if it were up to us." Leonardus began to tear up when he began to remember the things he and his dad talked about, and did.

Angel said, "I would like to make one of you all mine, and the other one of you, all Anel's. As I have seen the interactions, I think Leonardus likes being around Anel the most and Stella likes being around me the most. Is that correct?" Stella with her two front teeth missing said, "I like being around both of you, but I think I like Anel just a little bit more because my brother really likes talking to you." Sometimes adults know how to navigate intricate events when dealing with children. Angel knew that Leonardus enjoyed talking to her, and that Stella loved being with Anel, and just used a little child psychology.

It was close to midnight and the children were tucked in bed and sound asleep. Anel watched the video of Ava and Carlos being assassinated. She played the video back and forth until she came across a perplexing scene. However, her first concern was how did the assassins know to be there at that time when the couple were leaving. Did they stay in that car all night long, without anyone noticing them, including Ava's security force? She then noticed that as one of the assassins turned to enter the vehicle after unloading his weapon on Carlos and Ava, he violently banged into the mirror in a strange and confusing manner. It was like he didn't see the mirror or couldn't see it.

Around one in the morning, Anel asked Angel to look at a couple of frames that she was stuck on. Angel, after watching the movement of one of the assassins, said, "That guy with the sandy hair and long green coat must be blind. He walked into the car mirror, and hit it hard as if he didn't know it was there."

After watching the replay for fifteen or twenty more minutes, Anel said, "That asshole is blind in one eye. Look how he turns, panics, and then walks directly into the mirror on the vehicle." Angel said, "Sis, that is some massive detective work. In the morning, we should discuss our findings with the Sarge, and then take it to the next level, and that is, we need some people to do a day job for serious dollars. As she thought about it, she said, "Do you think it would be alright to approach Benito without going to the Sarge first?"

"Girl, we ain't doing no dumb shit. We are alive by the grace of God, and a Spirit. We don't know all the protocols of the group yet and, therefore, I am not going to get so far out there that it instills a question about our motives. Let's just do this by the book and get clearance for everything we do. Oh, shit, I didn't get clearance to view the assassinations," Anel announced. As she pondered her next moves, she said to Angel, "We can always blame it on Wajickee and his curiosity as well as his influence on us to use our technical skills to isolate places, people, and things. And, Sis, what did we just do? Well, we just figured out that one of the assassins may be as blind as Jose, Stevie, and Ray. Okay, I'm going to go to bed before the children get up, wanting to eat, swim, talk, and do math. Gnite my love!"

#

At breakfast, Anel and Angel approached the Sarge, and could tell by his demeanor that it might be an inopportune time to talk to him. When they got to the point of no return, the Sarge said, "Wow, sisters, how are you this morning. I was just considering how to expand your level of involvement in our affairs, and here you are. What can I do for you?"

Anel passively said, "We are concerned about the protocols of the group, and don't know how far we can go and do things that may be of benefit to the group."

The Sarge cocked his head to the side, and asked, "What did you two ladies do that might draw my ire side?"

Anel, who saw that Angel was going to leave her hanging said, "Well, we did our own investigation of the assassinations of your people here, and came up with some startling potentially accurate information."

The Sarge lowered his head, and asked, "Who asked you to look at that information?"

Angel stood tall, and said, "That is why we are asking you how and what we can do without getting your seal of approval. You told us to look into the matter. I guess you forgot."

The Sarge stood up, towering over the two ladies, and asked, "Do I look like or act like a dictator? Okay, don't you dare answer that. Listen, you two are new, and will always be new until someone comes behind you. Tell me what you got if anything from reviewing the footage of my people being slaughtered."

Anel took a deep breath, and then said, "We are convinced that one of the assassins is as blind as a bat in one eye. And more perplexing is how did the assassins know to be in that spot, at that time, when the couple were leaving? Someone on the inside gave your people up. Now Mr. Beckmire, this is all conjecture, but we don't believe in coincidences. No, Sir, we believe that anything that happens is because someone wants it to happen. Someone on her staff sold her and her husband out."

The Sarge turned away for a minute to consider his next statement. While in the process of turning around, he asked, "Do you people know anything about Ms. De Lombardo?"

Angel responded, "No, only that she was a member of this group, and was Zanthius's mother."

The Sarge quickly stated, "You do know that Zanthius is my son, don't you?"

Anel looked spooked, and said, "Oh, my goodness. I didn't know that you two were an item, and how could we have known since all we were trying to do was to stay alive." The Sarge smiled, and said, "Years ago, I met Ms. Ava De Lombardo in London, and fell madly in love with her. I'm telling you two this story because I don't want you to hear the bastardized version of it. I loved her, and she loved me. She also loved the notion that she was pregnant, and that she was not going to share her baby with anyone, including its father."

The Sarge paused, and then said, "Between you guys and me, I want those sons-a-bitches under my knife soon. Do whatever you have to do to find these people, but don't expose yourself or find yourselves in foreign places without backup. Do me this one favor, and I will be your champion forever. I need to have those sons-a-bitches under my knife. I also need complete silence and secrecy for this mission. Am I clear?" Both ladies shook their heads in the affirmative motion, but the Sarge said, "I can't hear your brains rattle. Yes or no ladies?"

CHAPTER EIGHT

A week later, and essentially following no rules, the sisters were deep into identifying common characteristics of those who terminated the members of their group. After viewing the tapes from the entry gate at the cemetery where Mike and Carla were blown to bits, Anel reviewed the footage from the funeral home that was in charge of the services. Two days prior to their deaths, a man and a woman appeared to inquire about pyro vs. earth funerals. It was the man who wore dark glasses, and was possibly blind in one eye. Anel yelled, "I got you asshole! My boss and savior has a fitting conclusion for your ass. It's just a matter of time."

#

That evening prior to dinner, Dempsey and Hood walked over to the Sarge, and Hood exclaimed, "We don't think it's fair that you decide who we can talk to, and who we can't. We want to have conversations with the sisters." The Sarge in one of his calmer mindsets, said, "Guys, that was when they were captives. I can't control your testosterone. Do what you want, but don't blame me for your lack of impressing those two gorgeous women. You guys need a tutor. You do shit all backwards."

Hood said, "I feel like a fool. I've been wanting to talk to one of the sisters, and that is exactly what you said, "they were captives at that point." Mr. Sarge, I will never come to you again about moments when I listen to my dumb ass friend. I am assuming that any forward movement towards the sisters is okay with you." The Sarge growled, and said, "How much more articulate can I be. If you see someone who is not attached, and you like them, go for it. I am not a dictator, and I can't tell you what to do when it comes to matters of the heart unless, it is inappropriate."

# # #

Angel and Anel asked the Sarge for a moment of his time, and were granted a thirty-minute session after lunch. Anel said, "Mr. Sarge, a family that has served the De Lombardo's for years has a weak link in its chain. A niece that cleans the house is associated with one of the assassins. Therefore, she was aware of when Carlos and Ava were going into town. To further complicate her involvement, her brother was in prison with the one-eyed person, was targeted for termination unless his sister did exactly what she was instructed to do. The one-eyed person was her brother's forced lover, who talked about his family's association with the De Lombardo's.

Now here comes the kicker, a cousin of the man who lived in the house on stilts in Poughkeepsie, was doing time in the same prison for drug trafficking, as the one-eyed guy. The one-eyed person corrupted anyone who was assigned to him as a cellmate. As we think that family is the most powerful ally on earth, these guys looked for an advantage. The man whose house was on the stilts, offered the one-eyed man a significant amount of money, or the termination of his girlfriend and his two daughters. Obviously, a notion of little debate. With inside knowledge of time and events in the De Lombardo residence, the connection was clear, the timing was precise, and the outcome was conclusive."

The Sarge asked, "Are you guys writing a fictional narrative, or has any of this been substantiated?"

Angel responded, "Mr. Sarge, we have video of the one-eyed person entering the funeral home where the services for Carla and Mike were held. How many connections can one person have?"

The Sarge said, "I gave you no limits, and you came back with a shitload of possibilities. What's your margin of error?"

Anel aggressively stated, "There is no error and, therefore, no margin. It is as conclusive as your DNA."

"That's a strong statement, and it seems like you're willing to bet the house on the information you've gleaned. In the future, please allow for miscalculations because we take information, and act on it. Any mistakes could cause an innocent individual his or her life. Don't get me wrong, I want perfection, but I want it based upon our acts, and not the actions of others where there could be a lot of false interpretations. So, where do we start in the process?" The Sarge asked.

Angel, a little hesitant to be aggressive with a prescription said, "I think we gather the niece first, and shake her tree until it drops the information that we are seeking. I'm thinking the child probably didn't know that her information would lead to the termination of her employer. Therefore, I believe if we can aggressively pick her up, she'll provide us with as much information as possible."

The Sarge slyly asked, "I'm sure that you've calculated everything involved in this action down to who would assist you. Haven't you?"

Anel looked away, and said, "You're absolutely correct. We can't bring a plan to you unless it's complete." The Sarge waited for a complete answer, and when he did not get it, he pushed forward by asking, "Who do you two have in mind to support this plan?"

Anel responded, "I think that Hood and Dempsey would be primary actors, with Jilkes and John Lee being seniors."

The Sarge smiled, and said, "How did I know you two were going to pick those pirates. Anyway, sounds like a good plan, and when will this take place?"

Angel looked at her watch, and replied, "At 3:15 pm when she leaves for her second job." The Sarge jerked around, and asked, "How do you know she has a second job?"

Angel said, "We tapped into Mrs. De Lombardo's camera and sign-in information, and each day she would say, I have to get ready for my other job?" Thinking he found a hole in their information, the Sarge remarked confidently, "I guess you know where that second job is, don't you?"

Anel smiled, and said, "She bathes and makes an older gentleman feel clean and satisfied, three days a week." The Sarge looked at her, and asked, "Exactly what does that mean?" Anel looked at the Sarge, and asked, "Mr. Beckmire, are you saying that you don't know what I'm saying or are you trying to make sure that I am saying what it is you think I am saying?"

The Sarge replied, "That's a lot of saying, and I haven't gotten the answer or definition that clears my mind." Angel whispered, "She cleans him through and through, and he goes to sleep with a smile on his face." The Sarge said, "I'm going to leave it alone because you two seem a little embarrassed to discuss her second job."

The Sarge continued by asking, "Why did you two pick Hood and Dempsey to be primary, and please don't give me an elongated answer."

Without hesitation, Angel said, "We like them, and want to get to know them on several levels. Is that okay with you?"

The Sarge smiled, and asked, "Do I look like cupid? Okay, don't answer that.   My initial reluctance to them meeting you guys was that I didn't know if you were going to be around long enough to get to know them.   However, here we are preparing to implement a plan to uncover the weak link that destroyed several members of our tribe. Ladies, this has been a blast. Oh, and ladies, we're all adults here, don't shuck and jive me on details, respond to me in basics, not all that highfalutin nonsense."

# # #

After canvasing the area outside of Mrs. De Lombardo's villa, Hood and Angel were near the entrance to the cul-de-sac looking at a map and pointing in different directions, when a young lady fitting the description of the niece exited the De Lombardo villa. In poor Spanish, Angel said, "Excuse me."

As Angel pointed to places on the map, Hood placed one finger on his lips with one hand, and with the other he exposed his weapon and gave the young lady an evil look. He pointed to their vehicle, and said, *"Si te resistes, te disparare en las calles como lo hicieron tus amigos, la Sra. Ava y su marido* (If you resist, I will shoot you down in the streets just like your friends did Ms. Ava and her husband.)

Once in the vehicle, Anel asked, "Do you speak English?" The young lady responded, "Poquito." Anel said, "I know you're scared, but you did some bad things, and we want to know who made you do what you did."

Without threatening or any aggressive behavior, the woman began to spill information as if she was a newscaster. She said, "If I didn't give them the schedule, they were going to kill my brother. I thought they just wanted to rob Ms. De Lombardo I didn't know that they were going to kill her. I haven't slept a wink, and I know that I did a bad thing."

Anel paused, and asked, "What is your name?"

"I am called Geneva."

"How did they contact you?"

Geneva lowered her head, and mumbled, "They knew about my other job."

Anel quickly asked, "What other job?"

Geneva slouched in the chair, and said, "I service a gentleman three times a week, and the contact person is his nephew. The old man prohibits me from servicing the nephew because he thinks he is worse than a puta."

Anel said, "I need you to tell me where I can find the nephew. Everyone connected to Mrs. De Lombardo and her husband's demise will be executed in the worse possible way. I need you to make sure that you're telling me the truth about everything. If you are, then I will see that you get out of town with a ticket, money in your pocket, and a new place to live. I will send you to America where you will work for the good of the Native Americans. No more servicing older gentlemen, unless you are comfortable with doing that."

Geneva was taken back to *The View,* given a room, and introduced to Ms. Viola and Luana. Her phone was confiscated, and she was instructed to lay low and to check with Ms. Viola or Luana if she needed anything.

# # #

In the meantime, the older gentleman's nephew was cornered in a rest room of a local restaurant, and was told that this was his last piss. Dempsey said, "I am only going to ask you once, and if I'm not convinced by your answer, that big country looking guy is going to cut your penis off."

Jilkes immediately gagged the man, and whispered, "You make any noise, and I will put a bullet through your heart. Don't think, just answer the questions."

Hood faced the man, and said, "I know you didn't pull the trigger, but you were instrumental in setting the stage. I want the four people who assassinated five members of our clan. I want names, phone numbers, addresses, and anything else that will lead us to those people."

The bandana was released from the man's mouth, and he asked, "Do you people know who you're fucking with?" Not more than seven seconds later, Jilkes replaced the bandana around his mouth tightly, and John Lee, lightly, sliced his leg close to his penis.

John Lee replied, "Now that I be done got your attention, my next incision will be at your shaft going east and west, and not north and south. You want to restate that there question of yours?"

The man looking at his blood covered leg mumbled, "Listen, I didn't do anything. Why are you torturing me?"

Hood looked at John Lee, and said, "Let's end this. Cut that thing off."

The guy exclaimed, go to La Lattina at seven, and four of them will be there! Ask for Claire, and that will mean you are sanctioned and referred by an associate." Hood asked, do you know who we are?"

The man replied, "I know not to be coy with you. Listen, I am just a pass through, please don't hurt me."

Hood stated, "If there is any indication of a double-cross, you will watch my man cut your penis off. Don't play with us, give us what we want, and we'll let you live with only your leg scarred, and everything else in place, and not detached."

## CHAPTER NINE

At 6:30 pm, a reinforced group scoped out the restaurant named La Lattina, that was a few kilometers from *The View.* The Sarge asked Angel, "How will we recognize the one-eye guy?"

Hesitantly, she said, "I'm hoping he wears sunglasses." The Sarge said to Mallory, "I want three people sleeping in the alley behind this place, and I want Angel, Anel, Hood, and Dempsey inside. I want to see how they handle themselves, but I want us to be ready to crash that place like a bowling ball. The moment that guy is discovered, I want him alive, and his associates near dead if not totally. I personally am going to cut that asshole into six parts."

Mallory quipped, "What happened to that no revenge shit?"

"Ah, I was just joking. Maybe I'll cut that guy into twelfths. How about that."

At 6:50 pm, the doors opened, and Anel knew from the movement of the head and body, that the second person through the door, was blind in one eye. She said to Hood, "I am going to slap the shit out of you, and then leave the table."

Hood asked, "Why don't you slap Dempsey?"

"I like you, not Dempsey."

Two minutes later, Anel exclaimed loudly, "I ain't no ten-cent whore!" After making that statement, she slapped Hood as hard as she possibly could. He yelled, "That's what you say. You try that shit again, you bruja, and I'll slit your fucking throat."

The first guy through the door said, "Boss, too much drama here. You want to go somewhere else?"

He smiled, and said, "Hell no, I want to get with that woman who slapped the shit out of that gringo. Order me some champagne, and I'll do the rest."

As the man with vision in only one-eye looked around the room, he saw that Anel had left the gringo, and was sitting alone stewing. He whispered to his man, "Ask the young lady if she would like a drink that does not come with violence or insults?"

The one-eye guy watched as his man delivered his message. He saw the woman smile, look over at him, and say to his man, "Tell your associate that I would like to buy him a drink, and a drink and conversation is all that he's going to get."

The man smiled, and said, "At least you didn't close the door. I'll be right back."

After much to do about nothing, Anel met Jack Long, the one-eye man. Angel, who was flirting with Dempsey said, "You two guys are the slowest men I've ever met. Anel talks about how kind you are Hood, and I reflect upon that first smile you gave me Dempsey. I think that after tonight perhaps we should set up a dinner where we can find out who you guys are, and we'll entertain any questions about who we are. It seems that you guys got into this group through the same backdoor that we did. Is that correct?"

Hood always first to expose himself, said, "We along with many others went to the outback to rob the mines. The rest of our group was eaten by dingoes, bitten by snakes and spiders, and their bones crushed by something called a wombat. We confessed to wanting to rob the mines, but we did not come to kill anyone in the process. It was a true statement and Mr. Beckmire took pity on us after we both asked for a soldier's way out—a bullet to the head. Next thing we know, Dr. Beckmire is attending to our wounds, and eventually, we were sent to work in the mines surrounded by snakes and spiders. We thought about trying to steal a few rocks and run, but we had nowhere to run to. That outback is an amazing place with hard to believe things happening around you all the time. Oh, did you get wind of that thing in the billabong? Now that is some kind of beast, and they say it is hundreds of years old. Sometimes a lot of embellishing goes on, but who am I to say. However, I will say, I don't like the way your sister is flirting with that guy."

"Relax Romeo, she just spiked his drink. We should be out of here in five minutes. Alert Jilkes and John Lee that we should be moving in about five. I am assuming that you two can handle the other three without a lot of drama."

In the back of the hotel, and on the loading dock, four men were ushered out of a van, locators and amplifiers were slipped into various pockets, without their knowledge. Jack Long, who was disoriented, was swearing that he was going to kill people for kidnapping him. Anel stated, "You seem to be good at killing people. How about you tell us who paid you to kill Ava De Lombardo?"

Jack Long paused, and said, "I don't know no Ava whoever."

John Lee eased up beside Jack Long, and said, "I bet you I can make you squeal like a pig, and then you'll tell us everything you know as you wipe the tears from your eyes. How about that? I mean, you tell us, and I'll make it fast, but depending on who you give up, you might earn a pass out of here."

"Listen, cracker, I don't know no Ava whoever," the guy professed.

Anel asked, "Do you want to know how we found you? Anyway, the people who hired you are cleaning out their closets as they review their endgame, and you and your associates are not a part of it."

Jack Long looked at Angel, started to spit in front of her, realized that John Lee was in striking distance, and said, "My employer is the same one that hired you two treacherous sisters. Yeah, smarty pants, I know who you are because I was asked if you were any good. Apparently, you weren't successful and, therefore, you got picked up by the other side. Listen, what is this about, are you people the law? I don't think so because you drugged me and kidnapped my men. If anything happens to me, the law and my other associates will know where to begin their search. You people didn't see the bracelet that I'm wearing on my ankle, did you?"

Anel said, "Oh, boy, I guess you got one-up on us except, while you were entertaining me, my capable sister, moved you all the way to Casa de Campo, in the Dominican Republic. Therefore, no one knows where the hell you are, and they certainly won't find any remains because that person you called cracker, well, he is the expert at cutting people into little pieces." Angel looked at Hood and Dempsey who had searched and bound the guy's hands.

Jack Long asked, "So how do we bargain this thing away from us. We don't know our employers they reach out with plans of who is next on their hit list."

Jilkes stated, "You said they, so there is more than one employer." Jack Long replied, I'm just talking and looking for common ground to discuss how we can just walk away from this matter."

John Lee replied, "I don't know about walking, but you might be able to nub your way around after I finish with you. And you be right, I am a cracker, but when I finish with you, you're going to be crumbs." John Lee pulled out his massive blade, and announced, "This blade has cut, stabbed, decapitated, and gutted a lot of people. I almost don't think that you deserve my skills, but shooting your assassin ass is too quick. Naw boy, your ass is going to see me cut you up, and this cracker is going to let you watch me take a bite out of your heart before you die."

John Lee sliced both arms of Jack Long, and said, "I bet I be getting your attention now." Jack Long tried to say something, but John Lee ran the blade lightly across both thighs. Jack Long realized that someone had snitched on him, and decided to try to save his life. He yelled, "I only know one of the partners, the same one that you thought you murdered. He owned that house in New York that you blew off the stilts." John Lee flashed in front of him, and lightly ran the blade across the cheek of Jack Long. Mr. Long, panicking because all he was seeing is blood, his blood, decided to confess something everyone knew. He screamed, "I along with my associates, murdered Ava De Lombardo and her pimp, Carlos."

The back door to the loading dock opened, and to everyone's surprise, it was Zanthius De Lombardo. Jilkes exclaimed, "Zanthius, no repeat performances!"

Zanthius looked at Jack Long, and said, "I should just put a bullet in your head and feel good about it. You killed my mother and her husband for money. Listen, when we were kids, I hit a baseball in the air, you misjudged it, and it hit your dumb ass in the eye, thus rendering it useless for the rest of your pathetic life. I never played baseball again because I hurt you. When you were in prison you corrupted everyone that was assigned to your cell, got privileged information on my mom, and murdered her in cold blood in the streets. Usually, I pull out a weapon and just shoot people like you in the head. I promised my father that I would no longer do that. No one knew you couldn't see out of that eye. I see you've met our creative butcher, enjoy your trip to hell." Zanthius turned, and walked away.

John Lee saw that Angel was feeling a little sick from his actions, and exacerbated the situation by asking, "Hey Angel, you want to slice this guy up a little bit? This is a lot different from shooting someone from hundreds of yards away. This here be up close and really personal. How about you Anel? Do you want to try your hand?

Anel responded, "Haven't had dinner yet, but you seem to be enjoying your work so, go forth maestro."

Jack Long who was bleeding from minor cuts, asked, "What can I do to stop this torture?"

A quiet came over the loading dock, when Jilkes, leaned close to him, and said, "Tell us where we can find those who hire people to do their dirty work."

Jack Long looked dazed, but responded, "I hear some of the dirty work is being done from within." Jack Long became quiet, started breathing heavily, slouched in the chair, after suffering from cardiac arrest.

John Lee asked, "What the hell does that mean?" After receiving no answer, he said, "Hey, what does that mean." John Lee shook Jack Long, and watched him fall to the floor. He was a heart patient who tried to heal his issues by doing natural remedies, and the outcome was death."

Jilkes yelled, "I told your country ass about making deep cuts, now look what you've done."

John Lee looked at Jack Long, and then at Jilkes, and said, "This here boy be done have some bad things working against him. My cuts were supernatural, or is it superficial? Anyway, I just sliced that boy, I didn't cut him deep or near a vein. He be done have some problems going into this dance. I ain't the cause of his death."

Angel looked at the other captives, and asked, "Did he have heart issues prior to our capturing you people?" One of the guys responded, "He was on that heart medicine called Lasator, but he rarely took it because it made him sick."

John Lee responded, "I'd rather be sick, than dead like he be. Oh, well, the question now is what do we do with you guys? We have pictures of those who participated in the demise of our people. I'm going to give you a chance to fess up!"

After several minutes, John Lee announced, "If and when I look at that there film of the assassinations of our friends, and I find you people on it, Lord have mercy on your souls because I'm going to cut shit off you that no one should die without. Somebody had better tell me where I can find his other associate that performed that daytime massacre of my friends. Somebody had better say something or I'm going to go down the line, and decapitate every man in front of me, and I ain't going to give any warning. I'm just going to watch heads roll down the loading dock." A voice rang out, and said, "He was just a gunman. You want the real perpetrators, then look within your organization, and find the man aka, "the expediter."

John Lee welcomed the Sarge on the loading dock, and the Sarge asked, "Is that the one-eye person of interest?"

Angel responded, "That is he, and John Lee cut him to death." She paused for a few seconds, smiled, and said, "John Lee didn't kill him Mr. Beckmire, he died from a heart attack we think. He all but confessed that he was one of the gunmen, these guys are not confessing so, we have to hold them until we can look at the video of the assassinations and see if these guys remotely look responsible. The guy in the blue shirt looks awfully familiar to me, and that could only happen because of seeing him somewhere. The only place I believe that is possible is in the video. I want to be wrong, but I'm sure I've seen your sneaky ass somewhere."

Anel pulled the video up on her phone, and began to view it, frame by frame. At the point where the deceased one-eye man violently walked into the car mirror, there was a blip in the video where there is a full view of the driver—the guy in the blue shirt. Anel said, "John Lee, I rarely forget a face when I am on a job. The guy in the blue shirt was not only the driver, but he was one of the shooters."

Everyone focused on the guy in the blue shirt, and the Sarge asked, "Wasn't that an overkill? I mean you guys must have fired in excess of two hundred rounds into their bodies. Was the job to terminate and make a statement?" The guy in the blue shirt said nothing, and actually, ignored the Sarge. The Sarge looked at John Lee, and asked, "Is that person hearing impaired?"

John Lee responded, give me a moment, and I'll make sure he's heard in London. John Lee pulled his knife, walked behind the man, and said, "You're not going to remember this here moment because, a rookie is going to inflict your first incision." John Lee flipped the blade over to Jilkes, who threw the knife at the man's foot and missed. John Lee said, "I almost be through with your African American ass. How you be done missed that there foot three feet from you?" Jilkes replied, "Next time your simple mind thinks of a plan, let those involved in your one-sided version of life know what the hell you're planning. Okay, you country bumpkin?"

The Sarge walked in front of the man in the blue shirt, and asked, "Do you have anything to say?" The man lowered his head, and said, "When I do a job, I make sure each round meets the target, and with the expanded clip I had in my weapon, I shot those molesters until it was beyond something Hollywood could create." The Sarge looked at him, and stated, "You know you just signed your death certificate."

The guy smiled, and said, "I don't give a shit about living or dying. All I know is I did what I was paid to do, and that was to kill Carlos and his woman. Listen, Carlos recruited my sister to work for Ms. De Lombardo's deranged father. He and Carlos abused my sister continuously until she jumped off an overpass, and into oncoming traffic. When Jack Long said to me that he knew about the things that happened to my sister at the hands of Carlos and old man De Lombardo, I jumped at the opportunity to kill them both. I would have executed them for free, but Jack Long was paying plenty of coin. So, whatever you do to me, it don't fucking matter. I think I avenged my sister, and eliminated the surviving procurer who placed my sister at the feet of an old, nasty, predator who did evil things to her."

The Sarge jumped in by asking "Why did you kill Ava?" The man frowned at the Sarge, and said, "Kill the seed, and you eliminate the virus. Sir, Ms. De Lombardo suspected the abuse, but was probably glad it wasn't her servicing her despicable ass father."

Ben Beckmire jilted by the response asked, "Do you know who the expediter is?"

"Sir, I don't have that kind of clearance, but I have heard that someone in your organization is the expediter. If I'm not mistaken, the name of the person just surfaced recently as a result of west coast-east coast unencrypted conversations. I wish you luck, but that's all I know. The other two people involved in the hit are in the states, these two guys were nowhere near the crime scene. Do me justice, and place a round in my head."

The Sarge walked towards the door to exit the loading dock, turned around, and asked, "Did you know that I was once in love with Ms. De Lombardo? And did you know that we share a child?"

The guy in the blue shirt said, "Had I known that I would have tried to erase any DNA of De Lombardo's."

The Sarge responded, "You want to die, don't you. Never have I met an adversary so willing to die for a false cause. What is driving this almost demonic desire to be killed? By the way, what is your name?" The contentious man in the blue shirt asked, "What's important about knowing my name. Kill me and be on your own journey."

The Sarge looked at the three men, and replied, "I don't feel right killing you even though you murdered the mother of my son, as well as a really good friend of mine. I think we all have angels and demons that dictate a lot of our actions, but I'm not going to kill you. I have a fate worse than death, rewarding when it is consummated, and invigorating when you see the byproducts of your efforts. I am going to give you a chance to live, and help people help themselves. If my son were still here, he might systematically eliminate you. I am trying to soften his response even though you murdered his mother, my ex-lover. However, something tells me not to execute you because in the scheme of things, we are all unholy. I am going to send you people to Florida, where you will meet the most impressive, rambunctious, loving, hearing and sight impaired, individuals in the world. You will learn sign language, and how to care for the blind, or you will be shipped to the outback where you will become food for one of my ancestors."

The man in the blue shirt stated, "My name is Crosby Harris. Why would you want us to work with kids that are blind and can't hear? I mean that don't seem like a terrible job if one can get a job with as little education as we have. I mean, how bad can it be?"

The Sarge smiled, and said, "It ain't bad at all. It's righteous my friend, and you and crew will work for our group, but doing good work. If we find the need to eliminate someone unholy, we might consider offering you those tasks. My immediate task is to soften my son's resolve when he realizes that you murdered his mother, and now we're trying to keep you alive. For now, let's find out some basic things. Are you people married?"

Crosby indicated that they were all single. The Sarge then asked, "Is there anything or reason you people wouldn't leave Spain for a legitimate employment opportunity, and are any of you predators, meaning do the children have to be afraid of some hidden proclivities of yours?"

"I speak for the three of us, we don't be messing with kids, we've never worked with them, but it ain't rocket science. Not sure how fast we can learn that signing language, but any opportunity to live, and do good we'll take. I wanted to die for the reasons I stated earlier. These guys are rookies, and we had them doing odd jobs, hassling people, and doing petty things like fencing wheels, catalytic converters, and stuff like that. I am the only hardcore member in your presence."

The Sarge said, "You don't know hardcore until you've had to fight in a jungle."

Crosby smiled, and asked, "Does the desert count?"

# # #

In the meantime, Anel and Angel were interrogating the new recruits over dinner, in search of any leads as to who the east-coast conspirator was, and who perhaps from the inside of the group had a loose tongue.

Ms. Beatrice in the meantime, was being Ms. Beatrice, helping Anel and Angel with Leonardus and Stella. When the ladies were busy, Ms. Beatrice became the unofficial sitter along with some of the other children in the group. One of the younger children asked Leonardus if he missed his parents. Ms. Beatrice placed him in an unofficial timeout for two days, which excluded him from all of the fun activities.

On the third day, Leonardus responded to the boy, "Of course I miss my parents, wouldn't you? However, my sister and I didn't get placed in the Window of Adoption, like my uncle did, and we thank Anel and Angel for taking us in and being parents to us. Your question was wrong, but I forgive you. Let's be better friends and help each other."

Watching the interaction from afar, Ms. Viola scoped the action and wanted to know how it was handled. When Stella told Ms. Viola what Leonardus said, it brought tears to her eyes, and she muttered, "That kid is going to be a leader one day."

# # #

After dinner, Anel said to Angel, "Do you feel confident enough to go and relate to Mr. Beckmire our assumptions?"

Angel said, "Mr. Beckmire makes me a little nervous. I like it better when he and Mallory are together because Mallory is calming and rational. Mr. Beckmire can be a tyrant when he wants to be."

Unaware of his presence outside of their room, the Sarge overhearing the conversation said, "Ladies, if you have a moment, can you meet me in the bar in five or so minutes?" From within, there was dead silence, until Anel responded, "We'll be there in five."

In approximately six minutes, the sisters showed up in the bar and saw the Sarge and Mallory sitting in a booth. Both men stood up and welcomed the sisters, and asked them to have a seat for a few minutes.

The Sarge said, "It seems as though every time we get to catch a conspirator against us, they all say that there is an inside cancer that is leading this overt assault against us. I've asked you here because I don't want you focusing on trying to find out where our main conspirators are, but I need you to carefully exam the possibility that a member, or members of our group have ulterior motives that requires the death of members. I know this sounds absurd, but someone keeps floating the notion that one of us is planning the demise of all of us."

Angel with a shaky voice said, "This is definitely a moment of de ja vu. Prior to your knocking on our door, Anel and I were discussing coming to you to discuss the definition of that statement, you know, inside job, and that was when we decided to come knock on your door, as you knocked on ours. Getting down to business, if this is a common statement that you keep hearing at key times from informed or uninformed individuals, then I would not take it lightly. I know that when we are in the outback, things are made simple, and concerns are easy to reckon with. Wajickee is incredible, but when we are away from the outback, minor issues become complex because we don't have him forcing us to push the envelope. In other words, somehow that inner sanctum notion from Mr. Harris, haunts us." She looked at Anel, and said, "Are you going to stay asleep, or are you going to join the conversation?"

Anel looked at both men, and said, "Naw, sis, you're doing a perfect job, please continue." Angel looked at Anel and gave her the bird.

Before she could resume, Mallory asked, "Did you just give your sister the bird?"

"Not sure how to answer the question, Angel responded, "I gave her more than the bird, I gave her a pterodactyl which means she can't speak to me for twenty-four hours."

Mallory responded, "Not sure what that means, I just wanted to know if you guys were having a free exchange, and are not intimidated by our Lord and master, Mr. Benjamin Beckmire."

Anel took this opportunity to state, "My sister is intimidated by Mr. Beckmire, and so am I." The Sarge saw the waiter, and ordered a Mahou, a beer that allegedly allows a person to experience the essence of Spain. He asked if anyone else would like one. Everyone agreed and he placed an order for four. Other members of the group saw that the Sarge was buying, and they all descended to his table. Chakes said, "My wife overheard you ask if anyone wanted a beer, and knowing that you don't pay tabs or buy rounds, we thought that we would take advantage of this rare moment in time."

"Whatever, have a beer on me," the Sarge replied.

#

Later, Mallory saw the Sarge and Courtney, he approached them, and asked, "Courtney may I have a word with your husband in private? It will only take a minute."

The two men veered off the beaten path and found a bench that was situated on the hill that provided a magnificent view of the city. Mallory said, "Franco and his raggedy crew, Windom and Earther, Hood and Dempsey, Angel, Anel, now Crosby and his crew. How many more pardons are you going to give out, and what is driving this new Beckmire model? I mean those people came to kill us in most cases. Crosby killed a few of us. Was it the plight of his sister that led you to turn a blind eye, no pun intended?"

The Sarge smiled, but didn't respond. Mallory asked, "Are you going to give me an answer, or what?" The Sarge continued to look out over the wonderful city below and thought about how grand this whole matter had been. He studied Mallory for a few, and then asked, "Do you know that we're going to die?"

Mallory replied, "DAH!"

The Sarge looked at him, and asked, "How many people have you and I personally killed? I bet you can't give me an answer because you know that we hurt a lot of people who had family and friends. Come on, take a shot at it. I know you're afraid to go down that road but do make an estimate."

Mallory, not interested in entering that rabbit hole, said, "Sarge, I asked you about all of the recent pardons, and that has nothing to do with the baggage I carry."

"That's exactly what I'm trying to get over to you. Listen, you my friend have probably killed in excess of one hundred fifty people. I on the other hand am responsible for nearly two hundred and fifty. I count each occasion, incident, person, and outcome. I have now begun to dream about faceless individuals that are no longer because I acted for someone else or that person or persons provided a direct threat to me or my people. Listen, think about it, you remember when I emptied four cannisters of .50 caliber rounds on that charging group over in the Nam? I don't count them because they were trying to make us a memory. How about when I fired that rocket into the enemy's camp where seventy-five men and women were enjoying their lunch, and I luckily hit that ammo dump that decimated those people. I am sure you remember this one. Do you remember when that plane went down, and we saved that young pilot? Do you also remember that you got in his seat and fired his cannons, machine guns and rockets that tore through an entire battalion of enemy soldiers? Mallory, I am just trying to ease into the underworld with some semblance of a conscience. You and I killed a shit load of people, and so did the other members of our squad. We are all well over the four hundred mark. We killed a shitload of people."

Mallory, with tears running down his face said, "You know what saddens me? Let me tell you, my friend. I was devastated when we returned and the first thing the reentry people asked me was do I need to enter drug rehabilitation. Yes, we did our so-called job, but no one asked me how many people I murdered in that police action, no my friend, the only thing that they were concerned about was if I had a damn drug problem."

The two men sat on the bench crying their hearts out when Courtney walked over to see what was going on. When she saw the two men in disrepair, she said, "I will give you two a few minutes to recompose yourselves. Whatever it is, remember, you have a clan that depends on you two for directions and strength. Get your shit together and put your big boy underwear on, and don't let anyone else see you two like this. We've lost some great friends, don't muck this up. We need leadership, and I selfishly need my husband to be at the top of his game especially since people are killing us off. Gentlemen, I'm not jumping in that hole you are in, but you had better quickly get your asses out of there and back into the leadership booth."

# # #

At dinner, the Sarge said, "People, I am the unappointed leader of this group, which by the way makes me a dictator of sorts, and I want to share with you a story. Mary Alice, can you take the kids for a walk?"

Ms. Beatrice said, "One day, Mr. Sarge, I'm going to ask if someone can take the adults for a walk." Ms. Viola said, "Hush child, don't grow up too fast." Ms. Beatrice responded, "Yes Grandma!"

The Sarge said, "Today, I had a short talk with Mallory that led us to recognize that we have been the messengers of death for a lot of people, and so have many of you. We broke down after realizing that between us, there are approximately four hundred fifty family and friends that will never see a loved one because of our actions. In most cases, we did what our uncle wanted us to do; kill the enemy. I'm not proud of that number and neither is Mallory, but the reality is simple, we have been widow-makers for a long time. Also, my Viet Nam team has a record number of kills as well. I bring this up because I was asked about the number of pardons I have made and the number of newcomers to our group. I am dog-tired of killing people. Some really deserved our resolve, but when you hear the whole story, you ask yourself, how can you unequivocally end lives that are juxtaposed with information that you're not aware of.

Since coming to Spain, so many things have come to light. Some good, some bad, and some of those perpetrating actions against us, in the scheme of things, had every right to do so, I guess. I am perplexed about how humans can be so many different things, but yet the same. Mallory is, and my guys from Nam are the greatest human beings that I've ever met. However, we all have a dark history and today, Mallory and I cried together knowing that we have made many families suffer the loneliness of a partner or parent, gone forever. I raise my glass to all of the fallen that me, my crew, and many of you are responsible for. I salute saving lives, and creating partnerships, no matter their past or desire to conclude our existence. Salute!"

#

Zanthius and Asiram spent an hour talking to Crosby. He told them about the abuse that his grandfather and stepfather did to his sister. He told them about how his sister died after throwing herself off a bridge to be repeatedly run over by oncoming traffic. He told how Ava was aware of the abuse, and how she kept Zanthius away from his grandfather because he liked little boys as well. Carlos was the person who recruited the young men and women for your grandfather. Zanthius asked, "Are you sure my mother was aware of what her father was doing?"

Crosby shot back, "Do you ever remember spending a Saturday or anytime alone with your grandfather?" Zanthius thought about it, and couldn't come up with a single time that he and his grandfather bonded alone. He did recall that when he asked his mother if he could go and see his grandfather, she would always insist that she accompany him. Crosby said, "My sister wrote a letter detailing the things that she was forced to do with your grandfather and with whomever he selected her to entertain. If Mr. Beckmire's offer is honorable, before I leave Spain, I will give you a copy of that letter. She also sent it to your mother, her suicide note that is."

Asiram crying her heart out remembered how her own family abused her. She said to her husband, "There is nothing to be done here. Let's go back and thank God that we don't have to face any potential devious activities with our children. Mr. Crosby, is that it? Thanks for the information. I don't think we will want to see any notes or letters detailing the self-inflicted death of your sister. We are sorry for our loss, and we are sorry for your loss. I see no good coming from more discussions about what has transpired between our two families. We hold no grudges. Isn't that right honey?"

Zanthius looked at the man, and stated, "It is done, it is over, and hopefully, we won't have to ever see each other to remind each other of the pain that was caused and shared by our families. Good day, Sir!"

The Sarge witnessed the conversation, and was happy that Zanthius did not blow the man's head off. He said to Zanthius, "Never have I been as proud of you, my son. That man murdered your mother, and to him he feels he had every reason to do so, and to you, those sentiments are acceptable. However, if all that he says is correct, there is and will be pain on both sides of the equation, yours and his. I am proud of you Zanthius, and boy, it restores my faith in the fact that you're not a hot head who has to conclude people without knowing all of the facts. Proud of you boy, give me a Beckmire/De Lombardo hug, better still, let's have a group hug. Get in here Asiram. Come on girl, get in here."

# # #

Crosby Harris and his two associates walked out of *The View,* and were happy to be alive. The three co-conspirators sat on the same bench that the Sarge and Mallory had acknowledged their part in the termination of hundreds of people. Crosby said, "Look at this view, and just think, we don't have to look over our shoulders because we're going to be legitimately employed. How about that? We make a hit, we clean up some old family issues, we get offered a job to work with some mentally challenged people, I mean how hard can that be, and my sister, sleeps well in heaven after me making a revenge killing on all those involved. Nothing is as good as this outcome. Maybe we should consider moving up in that group, quickly. Okay, let's go and get a drink, and talk about what we do next."

Ten or so blocks away from *The View*, Crosby said, I think we can manipulate this thing to our advantage. Damn, we played the right notes tonight. Those pansies didn't have the balls to kill us. They all seemed a little effeminate, didn't they? I gave that guy the story about my sister, and he bought it lock, stock, and barrel. I barely knew my sister, and besides, my daddy had lots of children. This is what we should do, we beg to help the mentally challenge kids, take over that operation, and then move into the big house by eliminating those guys. Oh, and by the way, did you see De Lombardo's woman? I would like to put some wood in that thing. Boy, I got just what she needs. There's the car, I would like to go back there, and take that big ass knife and shove it up everyone's ass. Those people are the kind of people who step on little people like us and make us clean their toilets. Fuck them, we just have to come up with the best plan to take over their operation. Let's go down by the water and have a few drinks."

Once in the car, Crosby announced, "After looking at the De Lombardo woman, I need to drop a load somewhere. That dive near the water, the women are pretty clean, and not too bad to look at. Let's go down there."

As the group was driving, a phone started to ring, and everyone searched their possessions to see who had a phone in their pocket. From under the front seat, a phone was retrieved, and Zanthius said, "We heard your conversation, and decided that since you're in an area where there are no residences, we bid you adieu!"

Crosby asked, "Who is this?" Three seconds later, there was a horrific explosion that rocked the area, shattered a few windows, but left everyone safe, except those in the car that Dempsey, Hood, Anel, and Angel strategically, placed ordinances and timers to reduce the impact on the environment. Hood said, "If you have larceny in your heart, this group will know it, and deal with it."

#

Later that night, when everyone convened, Stella and Leonardus were sitting in the hallway with papier mâché weapons. Dempsey and Hood veered off to the right, and whispered, G'nite to the ladies. Hood asked, "Do you think we can meet for breakfast, and see if there are some mutual things that we can do to convince the children that we are on a good path to be wholesome and accountable to them and you?"

Anel turned, approached Hood, and whispered in his ear, "If this is about sex, I can understand, and perhaps play that role. I am in love with the children. I need a permanent partner, don't bother me with bullshit. If all you want to do is screw me, then so be it. Don't play with my heart. Not a good way to grow old." Anel moved closer to Hood who was still in awe by the fact that she indicated that she liked him, and he said, "You are too committed to the principle that all men are dogs. I am a beast, I am no dog, but if given the opportunity, I will be a dream come true. I feel it, I feel you, and I want to talk to you until every single issue has been brought to the forefront. We were forbidden to have conversations of the heart with you when you were first captured for obvious reasons. We have been cleared or at least allowed to have conversations with you guys. Listen, I like you and what you're doing with those children. I would love to be a part of that decision moving forward if you think that I am worthy of your time, and their attention."

After hearing Hood's opening salvo, Anel said, "I've never known a man that announces, creates, and demonstrates, his desires in words like you. We just might have something to laugh and talk about moving forward. Sincerely, I need you to think about our commitment to the children. Don't bring me "bs", if sex is what you need and want, I can be your lady, but I don't want to send a mixed message to Stella and Leonardus. Do you understand?"

Hood smiled, and said, "Not only do I understand, but I am also prepared to make a commitment to you that will not include any conversation about physical contact for any amount of time you want. Listen, I am so much into you, and it is not because you slapped the shit out of me. It is because I had decided that if they were going to kill you, I would attempt to help in your escape and come with you if you would have me. Dempsey and I talk all the time about you and your sister. The fact that a part of your penitence was to become parents, made his chest and mine expand. We are like you guys. They captured us, made us work in the mines alongside snakes and spiders. We proved that we were capable of being rehabilitated, and they gave us an assignment in Minnesota that we did well, I would like to think."

There was a lull in the conversation when Anel stated, "You are an upfront kind of person, and I like that in a man, not that I am a worldly advisor on men's behavior. Listen, I am going to say goodnight, and I look forward to meeting for breakfast, in which case you will meet the children and they will put you through the ringer. Your choice, but eventually, they are going to dissect you." Anel smiled, and said, "I am glad we had this discussion and I thank you for being man enough to express your feelings and your desires to me." She moved extremely close to Hood, and asked, "May I kiss you on your cheek?"

Hood responded, "Please, by all means, touch me for I am so enamored with you presence." Anel with her right hand rubbed the left side of his face, and with her left hand, she maneuvered his lips until they were facing hers. She said, "Don't make me regret this." She placed her lips on his, and pressed her body oh, so close to his until both of them realized that the moment of passion was being held in abeyance, but the notion of closeness and comfort, portrayed a genuine desire for human and spiritual interaction.

After the kiss, Hood said, "I know that if you have me, I will make you an incredibly happy woman in so many different ways. I don't want to use any adjectives, but I just want to say, you will not be disappointed in me. I may not be the best-looking man in this group, but my commitment and devotion will overshadow any physical abnormalities. Listen, I am going to walk away while I am on cloud nine, and say, that was the most stimulating, and intoxicating kiss that I have ever had. I am not a virgin, and your hello kiss to me almost caused me to pass out. That was an amazing introduction to Anel, and I hope my response was as inviting. Goodnight my love. I look so forward to seeing you in the morning, and working through the nuisances that people deal with, but that are not all-encompassing."

# # #

The next evening, Angel and Dempsey completely ignored each other at the cocktail hour prior to dinner. Both acted as if they were so superior that the other would run over and beg for an audience. After an hour of sneaking indirect looks at each other, Dempsey, being the more leveled headed of the two, walked over to where Angel was sitting, and asked, "Would you like a little company for a few minutes?" Angel, expressionlessly, replied, "What's on your mind?" Dempsey wasn't pleased with that response, and stated, "I just thought we could talk about nothing for a few minutes, that's all. Sorry to bother you."

He turned to walk away, when Angel said, "I didn't mean to sound so cocky. If you allow me, I would like to buy you an apology drink. Sometimes, I scare myself, please forgive me." Noticing the sincerity on her face, Dempsey said, "I would like that drink very much. I am not a galivanting Romeo, rather, I am more of a home body who pretty much stays to himself or my friend, Hood."

Two hours later, the two were talking about all kinds of issues. Their time was interrupted when Leonardus and Stella, followed by Ms. Viola, came into the restaurant. Stella saw Anel and walked over to her, and asked, "Are you going to be late coming to the room? I am feeling lonely, and I've been crying a lot." Anel got up from the table, dropped to her knees, and said, "I am going to escort you to the room, and we can talk about what is troubling you. I thought you agreed that we could stay out until nine. Did we make a mistake?" Leonardus responded, "We get lonely lately, and Stella cries, and she makes me cry as well." Anel's eyes began to water up when Angel walked in, and said, "I went to the room looking for you guys. What's going on?" Anel said, "They were lonely and crying, and Ms. Viola talked to them, but they wanted to talk to us."

Anel said, "Come my children, we are going to go the room, put on our pjs and talk until you guys fall asleep. I am feeling like I am not doing too well on my first attempt at being a parent. We must discuss what you expect of us and what we expect of you. I am feeling really sad because I think we did something wrong in your eyes. Ms. Viola, thanks for watching them for us. We are so new at this, but we're also having issues of the heart called Dempsey and Hood, if you know what I mean."

Once in the room, Angel said, "I'm going to take a quick shower, then Anel can take one, and we'll put on our pjs hug and cuddle in our bed and talk about what we need to do to make you guys secure and know that we love you. Listen, once we get to a place where we can go through the adoption process, consider it done."

Later after all of the showers had been completed, when Anel exited the shower ready for a deep discussion, she found Stella under one, and Leonardus under the other arm of Angel. She mused, "I guess they couldn't wait on me. Now I'm sad."

In the morning when they woke up, Stella was laying across the back of Anel, and Leonardus was at the feet of Angel. Stella announced, "I'm hungry. Can we go to breakfast soon?" A groggy Angel asked, "Would you like to go in your pjs, or would you like to take a shower first?"

"Pjs," she responded. Angel and Leonardus laughed, and Anel said, "I can't go into a restaurant with pjs on. They would call the police on me." A serious Stella asked, "Why would they do that?"

"Because they would say that I am not appropriately dressed to be in a restaurant."

"Okay, I'll take a quick shower first. Anel, would you like to join me?" Catching Angel off guard, she responded, "Stella, you hurry up and do a quick wash, then you Leonardus, then Angel, and finally me. How about that?"

Later at breakfast, Anel asked, "What would you guys like to do today while we are in Spain?" Unequivocally, the response was go to a museum. Anel said, "I'll have to check with Mr. Beckmire to figure out how we do that. Perhaps, we can take the entire group to the museum."

Leonardus shouted out, "That would be really cool." We rarely get a chance to do group things because bad guys are always trying to hurt us like they did my mom, dad, Ms. Ava, Mr. Carlos, and Mr. Franco." Anel dropped her head, and said, "There is Mr. Beckmire. I am going to go over and ask him to support your suggestion."

Courtney and the Sarge were enjoying their breakfast when Anel said, "Good morning Mr. & Mrs. Beckmire. Hope your day is going well. Leonardus and Stella would like to go to the museum. How do I make that happen?"

Between bites, the Sarge replied, "You don't."

Courtney hit him on the arm, and said, "Do you need a shot of something big boy? That is not the correct answer for the people you have placed in charge of those children."

The Sarge whispered, "Listen, it's like an unwritten rule, when I am having breakfast with my wife, people typically allow us to bond because we are always in the midst of something. I just want to have breakfast with my wife, and after I take the last swig of coffee, I'll come over and let you crucify me."

Thirty minutes later, the Sarge with his tail curled temporarily up his butt from the verbal assault that Courtney gave him, appeared at the table that housed Anel, Angel, Leonardus, and Stella. He began by saying, "I am limping because my wife placed her foot so far up my ah, whatever, listen, is this a group event or just you guys?"

Leonardus responded, "We want all of the children to go because we are always under pressure. This Mr. Sarge would be a good time for the children to have some fun and learn some things as well." He looked at Leonardus, and said, "You're growing tall. I will make it happen. When do you want to go?" Stella responded right after breakfast."

"Oh, I see. Can you guys give me a moment while I check on a few things?"

Thirty minutes later the Sarge reappeared, and said, "Our bus will begin the loading process in forty-five minutes. Is that okay with you Stella, and with you Leonardus?" The two kids screamed, and said, "We love you Mr. Sarge."

# # #

The sudden notion of visiting a museum caught everyone off guard. All of the adults were assigned to a number of children to watch over. No one was ever to be left alone under any circumstances. The Sarge announced on the bus to the adults, "This is our most important mission people, let's enjoy, keep it animated, and watch our babies. Now, my babies, I love you all so very much. Whatever you do, don't go wandering off without a parent or one of us with you at all times. Now, do I have your word that you will all be responsible for each other, and make this a great trip, and one that we can plan more of in the future?" There was a rousing sound of joy and excitement.

The Sarge walked back to where Anel and Angel were sitting, and whispered, "You guys had better be on guard for every one of us. You do know how to use that weapon under

your jacket, right?" Angel smugly responded, "We would
rather use the bow and arrow, but we'll make these things
count if there is an issue, and we won't hesitate, boss."

"Wow, boss. I prefer Mr. Beckmire or Sarge, for the last
time."

# # #

Later at the museum, the children were mindful of their
pledge to stay together, look out for each other, and always
have an adult in eyesight. It was a marvelous outing, and
everyone enjoyed themselves. On the way back, they saw the
sign of the Golden Arches, the same one that Ben Beckmire
took Ava De Lombardo to lunch, many years ago. The kids
starting yelling in unison, McDonald's, McDonald's, and
McDonald's. The Sarge told the driver to pull in front of the
place. Anel said to the Sarge, "I guess you've lost another
battle today. I am going to go in there, and see if they have a
party room that this group can occupy for an hour or so. Is
that okay with you?" The Sarge thinking how he had been
manipulated by a bunch of kids, responded, "Do whatever so
that we can get back to the hotel."

The kids played on the slides and other contraptions and
just had a great time after consuming burgers, McNuggets,
French fries, and lots of soda. Anel said to Angel, the next
time we have an idea, I'm sure Mr. Beckmire is going to look
for a reason to not indulge us. Let's make sure the kids, clean
up their space, get in line and board the bus." Anel looked out
of the window and saw that three young guys were hassling
the bus driver. She pointed to Hood, Dempsey, and Angel, and
said, "Check out that bothersome trio messing with our bus."
When the trio approached the three young men, Hood said,

"Hey guys, we're going to leave in a minute. Please stop harassing our driver."

The biggest one turned his head to the side, and spit in front of Hood. Dempsey asked, "Do you have parents, and apparently if you do, they must be as ignorant as you are." The kid in the middle pulled out a knife, and said, "I'll cut you into little pieces." Angel backed up, placed her hand on her pistol, as did Dempsey and Hood. Dempsey said, "Put that tooth pick down or I will place a round into your kneecap. I won't ask again." The guy immediately dropped his knife and Hood asked the other two if they had a weapon. They responded that they didn't, but Dempsey insisted that they empty their pockets. As he searched each one by hand, the big guy had a .22 pistol tucked in his back. Hood said, "So you do have a weapon, eh? Tell you what I'm going to do. I am going to give my friend my weapon, and I'm going to fight each of you separately. Without warning, he slapped the biggest guy as hard as he could, and said, "Now that should make you want to kick my ass." The guy looked at him, Hood slapped him again, and the guy began to cry. Hood said, take your punk ass home, and don't you ever let me catch you hanging around here again."

As the trio walked back into the McDonald's, he gave Anel the okay sign. When the Sarge walked down the steps, he asked, "Was it necessary to punish that kid like that?"

"Sarge, that kid had a .22 automatic weapon on him. We are targets, if I'm not mistaken, and because they look young, doesn't mean that they can't and won't hurt us. In the desert, we let a kid like that go, and he ran off a little bit, and then threw a grenade at us. No, Sarge, no matter how you look, if you're confronting us, we either have to hope you won't do stupid, or we make sure that you can't do dumb."

The Sarge said, "Listen, I just asked the question. After those people walked up on us in that Four Seasons hotel that time, I want everyone to be as thorough as you guys just were. Thanks for securing us, and you're right, age has nothing to do with doing stupid."

# # #

That evening, dinner was served buffet style, and most of the adults and their wards took food to go, and spent the time in their rooms napping and watching television. Leonardus walked over to Angel, and said, "I want to whisper something in your ear." Angel bent down, and Leonardus kissed her on the cheek, and thanked her for letting them have a lot of fun today. Stella did the same thing to Anel.

# # #

After leaving the lawyer's office, Zanthius said to Asiram, "What on earth are we going to do with all of that money and property, and he only got through half of the book. As it stands, we are rich beyond our wildest imaginations, and now this has just quadrupled our wealth, if not more. We need to create more avenues to endow people to help themselves. I don't remember the last time that I physically spent a paper bill or for that matter, charged a bill on an account. Everything we do is always paid for, and we rarely need actual money."

Asiram smiled, and said, "Boyfriend, there are a million different ways that we can make a difference, and I don't think we need to focus on it at this moment. Let's get a bottle of champagne, toast to our good fortune, and helping people help themselves." Zanthius hugged her and proclaimed, "You're the best thing that ever happened to me!"

CHAPTER TEN

The group made unannounced stops in Virginia, Minnesota, and Middle America. In Virginia, the group was astonished by the work completed by their former compatriot, Franco. The main house was twenty-five hundred square feet larger, and the guest house was fifteen hundred square feet larger. Both structures were fortified, with bullet proof glass and remodeled tunnels.

After leaving the farmhouse, Asiram began to cry on the way to the airport. Zanthius, ever so attentive, inquired as to the nature of the tears, and Asiram said, "Somehow, I feel that I may never see this place again. I just have a very demonic feeling that all is not right, nor will it ever be. We keep doing things, hurting people along the way, destroying people, and somehow benefiting financially from our dastardly deeds. Honey, I really want to have a talk with your father once we're in the outback. I just feel that something terrible is going to happen to us." The tears began to flow until one of their children came over, and asked, "Mommy, is daddy getting on your nerves again?"

#

Michael got a text message indicating that someone was gathering the strength of a battalion for some out-of-town work. The sender suggested that the group might want to begin circling their wagons. If this is correct, then I can only think of one group that could demand that kind of attention and, therefore, I am sending you this text. Damn shame about our colleague, I want those mfs for myself, he was a good and dedicated brother. Michael saw that the Sarge was deep in sleepy land, and decided to wake Mallory instead. He walked up to where Mallory was stretched out, and nudged him hard. Mallory asked, "Have you lost your damn mind?"

Sorry Boss, "But I am afraid to wait until we land to pass this message on. I need you, Jilkes, John Lee and the Sarge in the belly of this beast, as soon as possible."

"Are you telling me this can't wait until we land?"

"That might be too late." Mallory saw his expression, and decided to go and get cursed at by the Sarge, John Lee, and Jilkes.

In the belly of the plane, the men unfolded their assigned seats. When the Sarge came down, he said, "I am going to appoint someone else in charge. You guys won't let me sleep, is this your way of getting rid of me?"

Mallory pointed to Michael, and said, "It's his show. He's the culprit." Michael slowly began to step on his words, but finally began to discuss his concerns. As he attempted to read the text message, he realized that his phone had died. In the meantime, the Sarge is staring at him, and shaking his head. He finally bellowed out, "The hell with the phone, what is the gist of the message?"

Michael smiled, and said, "Dad, you do remember telling me that I could call you that, don't you? Anyway, I got a message that said we should begin circling our wagons because someone was recruiting a battalion size troupe to do some out-of-town work against a want to be dictator. Who else gathers that kind of attention, other than us?"

The Sarge jumped out of his seat, walked around to where Michael was standing, held out his hand, and said, "I am sorry son for acting belligerent. Now, what is really scaring me is that I was in the midst of a dream where we were being decimated by people in masks. When Mallory shook me, I felt a coldness about me when I got up. Get Montomie, Gladstone, Brown, Bernstein, Jong, Chakes, McArthur, Whitmore, as well as Hood, Dempsey, Anel, and Angel. I don't care if they're naked, I need them here now."

Less than five minutes later, the elevator descended to the belly of the plane, and the sisters got out of it. Two minutes later, Hood and Dempsey exited the elevator, and then the rest of the team came down in groups. The Sarge said, "People, Michael got a message indicating that we should circle our wagons because someone has hired a battalion size group to do some out-of-town work on a would-be dictator. Have any of you had any bad dreams tonight about the group's demise?"

Angel slowly raised her hand followed by Anel who said, "My eyes are red because I dreamt that men in masks took Leonardus and Stella, and I couldn't do anything except watch."

There was silence for a few seconds, and the Sarge said, "Dreams are what they are, dreams. However, in this group, when we dream like dreams, that means the devil is coming to pay us a visit, and he ain't sparing nobody. Listen, there is nothing we can do up here on this damn plane except try to hide, and not go to the outback. If we go to other areas, the innocent may get hurt. We have approximately four more hours of flight time, let's try to get some rest, and then reset once we hit the ground. Once we get through customs, I want that bus bringing us our heavy artillery. Every living soul will be armed to the teeth until we can figure how to overcome what I expect is our Armageddon!"

"That there word be awfully scary Sarge, but we done been there before, and as long as we do good, them there bad fellas are going to keep coming until we be too old to push a broom. This thing here ain't new, it's just getting old, and we just be getting tired. Me and Jilkes will plan our response to anything and anybody that brings their asses to the outback. Ain't that right, Jilkes?"

"You called me Jilkes, twice. I didn't think you knew my name, you country pig farmer. You called my name two times, what's wrong with you? Did you get a final diagnosis of your mental illness? Damn, and I've got all these people to witness your calling me by my name."

John Lee smiled, paused for a few seconds, and said, "Once again I think you be hearing things. These people didn't hear me call you anything, and I ain't going to get them involved in such a trivial matter. What be of concern is how we prepare for a battalion of people coming to the outback to kill everyone that we hold dear. You always want to make every conversation about you. There are higher concerns than that there name of yours."

Jilkes laughed at him, and asked, "Did you get rid of your country dictionary, and get a new one? Your use of the English language seems to be getting better. I'm proud of you, my brother."

The Sarge said, "Enough bullshit, let's get some sleep, and hope that Wajickee has some news and ideas for us to implement."

# # #

After landing in Sydney to take on fuel, the weary group walked around the airport to stretch their legs, and to get some circulation going in their bodies. Stella asked, Anel, "Why are we walking around in circles?" Anel laughed, and said, "One day Stella, when you get as old as some of us, you'll do the same thing to keep the body functioning and the legs mobile."

Once back on the plane for the ride to the outback, Michael received a text indicating that the battalion size convention was in full swing with a target date of ten days from then. Michael made his way to the front of the plane where the Sarge was sitting, and showed him the text from the sewers.

The Sarge, after carefully reading the text said, "We could always just keep this plane of ours in the air stopping at random places. What do you think about that?" Michael laughed, and said, "As brilliant as you are, I know you're joking. We can only run for so long before we become weary, and then decide to face the devil, and make a mockery of ourselves. No Sir, we'll figure this one out just like we've done on every other occasion. This time we might need a little more deific intermediation, however. I certainly wish that Pope hadn't gone left on us."

The Sarge said, "Thanks Michael, no need to bother the others on this short flight with that information. Let's let everyone have peace of mind until we land, and then we go at planning full force."

# # #

On the school bus heading for the village, Darryl said to his uncle, "There is an ill wind blowing here in the outback." The Sarge looked at him, and said, "Nephew, let's get to the village, and then we'll discuss your feelings as well as the information from the sewers. Let's just enjoy this peaceful ride and reflect upon all of the good things that God and the Spirits have bestowed upon us as a people, and as a clan. Just hold it in abeyance for a few, Nephew. Thanks."

When the school bus arrived in the village, everyone was perplexed by the beehive of activity that was taking place. The door to the bus opened, and as if by magic, Wajickee appeared, and said, "Ben Beckmire, what took you people so long to get here. Everyone is here for a grand celebration of life tonight. Hurry, get off the bus, and come meet your guests."

As the Sarge stepped off of the bus, he was amazed at what he was seeing. Hutang and his warriors were stretching and doing martial arts. His late partner Franco's crew was there with people who helped rebuild the places in Spain and America. Clyde and Gilda were present with twenty-five of their neighbors and friends, Earther and Windom had forty well-built members of their community, the new commandant of the sewers sent forty former soldiers, Mrs. Carter was there in person with fifteen members of *The Sanctuary*, and last but not least, friends of Ben Hackney and former members of the Pope's Swiss Guard, were also in the village. The same ship that brought and returned Hutang and his group to the outback to terminate the Sarge, was used to smuggle enough weapons to outfit several full battalions.

The Sarge, first thinking that he was hallucinating, took three steps away from the bus, and fell to his knees. He looked

towards the heavens, and began to mutter to himself prayers
of thanks, prayers of friendship and a prayer for safety. He
stood up, and screamed, "God and the Spirits know that we are
righteous people, that we help people help themselves, and
that those who confront us are not always those who should
feel our wrath. With every ounce of life in my body, I give it
to all of you and say, as long as I breathe air, I will be there for
you, when you need me, and not when I think it's convenient.
Love you all. Let's have a grand feast, and plan for the next
few days."

The Sarge took time to talk to each person that was there
to lend assistance. He asked Hutang, "Who on earth contacted
you?" Hutang responded, "I don't know who it was, but they
signed their name with a "W". The Sarge looked around camp
and saw Wajickee, and asked him to join him, and Hutang.
Upon arrival, Wajickee said, "They should have never
introduced me to that World Wide Web. There are more people
I can contact, but I felt that might be over-kill if I might say
so." The Sarge asked, "Hutang, do you believe in spirits?"

Hutang looked at the Sarge, moved his hands in a full
circle, and said, "The last time I was here, I came to kill you
because others had convinced me that you people stole our
children, and placed them into a nefarious service. After
finding out the truth, and watching how your people honored
the agreement about funding aspects of my culture that money
would have destroyed, I knew then that you were, what's those
words, ah, righteous and honorable. You sent us back to our
country, you made us whole and rich. You even gave us a
smuggling ship that we used to bring elicit weapons here to

support you and your tribe. You could have killed me and my people on our last adventure here. No, you with your righteous self, gave us life, a way home, materials that would not interrupt our economy, and accounts that we control from afar. No, my brother, when I got the email, I said to my wife, my friend is in need, and he is in need of me and my Samurai." The Sarge bowed low, and said, "After dinner, it would be my honor if you and some of your warriors join me and some of mine in a night of drinking."

The following morning, the camp evolved as if it had been involved in a drinking contest. Wajickee said to Ben Beckmire, "We are completely out of our high energy drink. It will take a few days to make, cure, and produce that high quality drink. Your friend from Asia, and his people really enjoy it, and the preacher man from middle America is also reeling from the impact of our hooch."

Ben Beckmire said, "It is good that we consumed it all last night, now we can begin preparing for as many as one thousand mercs coming to take the mines, kill our people, and conclude all that we are. Last night was a celebration of life and death, for I believe that there will be sorrow on both sides of this equation, and hopefully, more on their side than the side of who I consider, the righteous. Let's get this process in play and begin to figure out our strengths and our weaknesses. All the people who came to help looked fit, strong, and mentally capable of being assigned strategic points and defending them to the end."

Courtney walked over to her husband, and said, "The next time you don't share things with me, will be the last time that you see me, Ben Beckmire."

"Honey, I just got confirmation of this on the flight here. Was I supposed to wake you from a peaceful sleep, and tell you that we all might be dead in ten days? No, I would not do that. Listen, you are all that I have. I have a lot of friends, but I only love you, Dr. Beckmire. We had this discussion a long time ago, and I told you then that you are the source of my heartbeat. Please, baby, sometimes when I get information, I need to process it. Wajickee and his new friends, Anel, and Angel, and the world wide web, is who made this happen. This was not my doing, and as a matter of fact, there he is." The Sarge yelled, "Hey, Mr. Wizard, can you come over here and plead with my wife not to leave me because of your newfound hobby?"

As Wajickee internalized all that was said, he realized that his surprise was not Ben Beckmire's doing, but his. He said to Courtney, "Is it possible for you and me to take a walk away from these ordinary humans, and have an ethereal discussion of sorts?" Prior to Courtney responding, her next vision was that of a billabong, and the Great Saltie. Wajickee said, "All that was done, was done by me without any buy-in or approval from those earthly types. Your man is as solid as your beliefs, and at this point in time, he needs your support and encouragement. This upcoming encounter will test even your faith and commitment to the group. You may have to operate on the fly because those who are coming are not taking any prisoners, including the children. Ben Beckmire has a lot to contend with, help him, don't give him adverse things to consider, such as your leaving him. The devil himself is coming to the outback!"

#

As the morning went on, people began to leave their huts, create spots on the ground, and make their way to the billabongs that were sanctioned for swimming and bathing. Anel and the kids saw Hood bathing under a waterfall, and Leonardus said, "That looks like a lot of fun, letting the cool water run all over your body."

As they approached the waterfall, Hood said, "The morning only gets better when I see you and the kids. Perhaps one day, we'll do this together, it would make a lot of sense to me, and that's what I want to do. It's natural, and you know that I'm honored by your very presence. Think about it and let's try some community projects, you know me, you, and your wards."

Anel smiled, and said, "Hey guys, you remember Mr. Hood, don't you? I hope we aren't disturbing your morning routine, as she admired his perfectly sculptured body.

Hood feeling a bit naked said, "I don't mind sharing my space with you guys, I'm finishing up anyway. I would like to talk to you during breakfast for a moment if you have time."

In the meantime, in another place and time, Angel and Dempsey are providing each other with a sense of commitment and pleasure. As Angel experienced motivating orgasms, and as she fell deeper into an abyss, Dempsey announced, "The first time I laid eyes on you, I wanted to be with, in, and around you for the balance of my days. This bliss is so rewarding, satisfying, and complicated that I never want to move from this position."

#

The Sarge saw Hutang, walked over to where he was sharpening one of his many blades, and asked, "My dear friend, how on earth did you get that big ship back here?"

Hutang laughed, and said, "Mr. Sarge, I no kill people quickly anymore, a thing that I learned from you and your benevolence. I made the previous crew wards of the state, and in return they showed me and some of my men how to work every aspect of that monster. That precious lady can do 28 knots easily. I learned where all of the hidden compartments are, how to submerge illicit contraband, and motor quietly into a port. In other words, I am the new captain of that beauty."

The Sarge asked, "You're kidding right?"

"No, Mr. Sarge. I am a licensed captain as I took classes online, and learned all of the answers to manipulating that big beauty with those powerful thrusters both aft and stern, that makes it so easy. I must admit that I did drop the load a bit too early as I was looking at the screen that multiplies the environment and was not an actual picture of where I wanted to drop the goodies for you and your people into those sealed containers and submerge them. Anyway, I docked her perfectly against current and wind, and my men were very thankful for the safe journey. The beauty of this beast is that I can smuggle things in and out of my country that are for the good of the people."

The Sarge began to tear up, walked over to Hutang, hugged him, and said, "I can't think of any outsider I would rather have beside me during this impending action, than you. Thanks, my friend, I will never forget this act of support."

Hutang smiled, and said, "You could have killed me years ago, but you saw that I was not the real enemy and you supported me and my people. The booty we extracted from that pirate comes to me and my people in different forms whenever we need it. Currency and other negotiable items would have destroyed my civilization with greed and thievery. You are a friend to me, and to my people, and I will always be available to support you, Mr. Sarge."

After breakfast, Anel and the kids saw Angel, and Stella ran up to her, and said, "You missed breakfast and shower time. Where did you go?" As Angel was preparing to make a statement, Dempsey came out of his hut with a new sense of swagger and confidence. Anel looked at Angel, and muttered, "Slut!"

Later in the day, the Sarge held a meeting of the entire village and newcomers. He explained and cautioned people about wandering away from camp, eating berries that are not sanctioned, playing with animals that look cuddly and friendly, spiders and snakes that have no anti-venom, and swimming in the wrong billabong. He indicated that the natives would show them how to make a latrine, where to wash, where to drink water, and a whole list of other things. He said, "In this land, there be demons, spirits, and then there be Wajickee. I will only say that Wajickee is incredibly old, and has tutored my family for centuries. I know some of you people don't believe in hocus pocus, but I will show you an anomaly that you will never forget, for he is both a predator and a family member of mine. His name is The Great Saltie, and once you've seen him, you will never want to see him again. In addition to all that I've said, there are gold and diamond mines throughout the village. If you attempt to place a nugget or a stone in your pocket as a souvenir, you will be buried on this land because the stones are for the Aboriginal people. We have had several people attempt to take stones and nuggets, and their deaths were agonizing, to say the least. All stones and nuggets are in the caves. I beg of you, don't be tempted by a bauble. If you have a need for a special gift, then consult me, and I will barter for you."

The Sarge paused for a moment, drank some water, and said, "More than anything else, I want to thank you people from the bottom of my heart. We had no clue as to what the wizard had been up to, but when I got off that bus, and I saw all of you people, I just wanted to cry. I thank all of you. Now, here is another thing you will find hard to believe. From the time that the mercs set foot on our soil, things will begin to happen.

Some will eat tainted fruits and vegetables that our villagers will sell them, that will make them have a runny affair with a make-shift loo. Once they enter the outback, and once they display that they are armed, and prepared to attack us, two very diametrically opposed events will happen. From both sides of the mountain ranges and hills that lead into the village, there will be a whistling sound. That will be the sounds of hundreds of arrows and spears raining down on that group. That will happen in three consecutive sessions. The mercs will fire blindly into the night and will probably not hit a single attacker. They will instinctively set their firing sequences to continue to fire at the rocks. After a reloading session, more spears and arrows will rain down on them. They will instinctively, check on their wounded, and the remaining major forces will venture to our village, and those wounded will be left to protect their retreat."

The Sarge paused again, took a nonchalant sip of his water as if there was nothing to worry about, and said, "The second thing that you will find hard to believe is that a number of predators will smell the blood that the wind will blow to the east, and there will be a feast held by dingoes and wombats, two indigenous animals that have been here since time. If you encounter them, walk away, but keep your weapon in the ready position to fire."

The Sarge continued, "Now, a significant number of their group will cross an area that must be defended by us. Let me announce that this group is hell bent on sending us straight to Hades. We blew a man's house off its stilts in Poughkeepsie, New York, sent his son to prison where he's enjoying the carnal benefits of the place, and we pretty much took a small fortune from him. He had a body-double in his place with rings, dentures, and other identifying markers that would lead the coroner, one of his puppets, to certify that the body was his. Well, we strapped his being to a Victorian era chair, and thought that when we blew the house off its stilts, that we blew him into a new dimension as well. Unfortunately, that was not the case, and he aligned himself with someone else who has a straw up their ass for us as well.

Listen, I have been led to believe that the size of a battalion is coming to conclude all that I know. Now, that could be between three hundred, and up to one thousand or more depending upon whose definition you're using. If it is three hundred, well, I think we can deal successfully with them. If it's a thousand, then I think the animals will finally get their chance to feast upon us. Therefore, I want to start strategically laying this village out in quadrants. Before I take a deeper dive into this problem, are there any questions?"

John Lee stood up, and said, "My name is John Lee Jones Jr., and this here guy next to me is Mr. Jilkes. Now, Sarge, I be thinking, and I know Mr. Jilkes be agreeing because I'm the smarter of the two, that we should be considering at least six parts to this party. A quarter becomes too big and unmanageable, ain't that right Mr. Jilkes?"

Jilkes stood up, and said, "For once I agree with Mr. Jones, and that's all I have to say."

Hutang rose, and said, "Mr. Sarge, I agree with six parts or even larger. Me and my people have been working on a new tactic, and I would like to implement it. It takes us out of the comfort of the village, and leaves us in their formation where we provide swift, deadly, attacks at lightning speed against them. We'll play amongst the bush, the rocks, and decimate a large number of them prior to them entering the village, which gives you three unanticipated attacks prior to your people and my people facing them. We took some actions when we were last here, and developed a deviated strategy that works well, keeps us safe, and those attacking, won't know we were there."

The Sarge looked at him for a few moments, and asked, "Are you preparing a Ninja type exhibition?"

Hutang smiled, and said, "I thought that was child's play."

The Sarge responded, "Let's talk when we finish here, my friend." He looked around and asked, "Are there any other questions?"

Clyde stood up, and said, "Given the right ingredients, we can make cluster bombs that we can fire from up to fifty feet away. We have all of the ingredients, and I have to say that wife of mine is becoming super creative."

The Sarge exclaimed, "Wow Gilda! You are so important to us, and I am so happy you're here. You will work with

Rashida and Juan, and try to develop additional points of impact as well as develop a retreat scenario in case we are overrun. Oh, people, if I give the signal to fall back, don't hesitate. Shortly thereafter, my great, great, great, great, great grandfather and his associates will join the buffet line. Now that's a preliminary and less than a fact-based interpretation of our current condition."

Darryl stood up after finally getting the last word in with Sue Lyn. He said, "Uncle, if it's a thousand individuals, why don't we spread some distracting valuables around the place, and let them fight over something that they will never be able to take from this area. I mean, there are stones and nuggets, why not take a sizeable number from the mines, and lay them around for the taking, knowing full well that if you're not sanctioned to handle or take either one, then your next visit will be to hell."

The Sarge paused, and displayed a huge grin. He said, "Nephew, was that your wife's idea or yours?"

"Uncle, you know that she is smarter, wiser, and more cunning than I am. It was her idea, and I think if it will save lives on both sides of the equation, then why not."

Chakes stood up, who was being badgered by Ms. Viola and Luana, said, "I used to think that I was the man of my hut, but seemingly, these two think they can control my mind, and what I say. I personally like the idea of spreading a distraction around the village. I also believe that two of those mines have different entry and exit points that end right near where that thing, sorry Sarge, your forefather rests, and sunbathe all day. I'm just adding on to what Darryl and Sue Lyn propose, but making sure that it's a one-way trip."

As Chakes started to sit down, Luana rose, and said, "I'm pregnant again, but I can still shoot." There was a quiet that came over the village, when Courtney stood up, and said, "Don't you fools look at me like that. I ain't pregnant, but there are six other new mothers to be, not including the one who made the announcement. Come on ya'll, stand your butts up, and be counted."

Rashida, Mary Alice, Okema, Somara, Yeshida, and Asiram stood up. Zanthius screamed to the top of his lungs, and was joined in by Jilkes, Juan, Chakes, John Lee, Brown, and lastly, Jong. As if they had created a new tribal dance, the men joined in a circle, and danced.

The Sarge yelled, "The blessings of God and the Spirits, we will celebrate tonight with a combination of Middle America and Aborigine dishes being served, Hallelujah!" the Sarge exclaimed.

## CHAPTER ELEVEN

Early the next morning, Wajickee, the Sarge, Asiram, Courtney, and Zanthius sat by the billabong that housed the Great Saltie. Others from the village were in attendance as well. Quietly, they began to assemble as if a text message was sent that directed everyone to that billabong instead of the one where they showered, swam, and enjoyed the freshness of the water. Some people stood, others sat, but there was no talking. Even the children who took front row seats, sat, and watched fearlessly, the emergence of several extremely large amphibian heads rise to the surface. Ben Beckmire stood, and whispered to the group, "These are my relatives, and I promise you if we live through this adventure, I will tell you the story of the beginning of the Beckmire clan, and the person who began it, Andy Beckmire. He is typically shy, but he is aware of the impending confrontation, and has summoned animals from one end of Australia to the other. Listen, do not be afraid for he knows that you're all friends."

Suddenly, there was a huge commotion in the billabong, and all of the huge crocs swam away. Ms. Beatrice said, "They were gigantic, but Pop Pop's, great, great, great, great grandfather is magnanimous." No sooner said, the entire village witnessed the spectacle that is known as the Great Saltie. Its tail seemed to transverse the entire billabong. It disappeared, and its next sighting, was directly in front of all of the children. They gasped, but did not run away. The Sarge said, "My friends, and my family, behold my ancestor and protector, The Great Saltie."

# # #

At dinner that night, everyone reflected on, and were still amazed at what they saw. Clyde stood up, and said, "I'm a man of faith, and now I am a man of faith who believes that there are anomalies in this world that just can't be described. That thing could have swallowed most of us in the first second, but Mr. Beckmire stood there with his back to that beast, and introduced us to him. That Wajickee fellow told the kids that they would not remember what they saw before they went to bed. I don't agree with him because we all need to know the truth about things that are just too unbelievable to acknowledge. I am so happy to be here to help my friends and family. This has been such an awakening for me and my wife, and hopefully, we'll be able to share it with our church community.   I praise God the almighty, but I certainly acknowledge the Spirits, and that Mr. Wajickee, well, he can come and stay with us anytime."

# # #

Anel said to Hood, "Do you know that slutty sister of mine slept with Dempsey?"

"Anel, that is not an uncommon thing amongst humans. That is how they communicate, share passion, desires, and develop eternal, or not, relationships. He has not said a word to me other than the fact that he wants to marry your sister before the incursion."

"You seem to portray that as a final act. Do you think it's wrong?"

"Anel, I think that they should do whatever sits right with them. Too many people are reactive to tradition, and not their individual thoughts and decisions."

"You are oversimplifying their union. They want to get married. Dah!"

"So, the hell do I!" Hood exclaimed.

"To whom?"

"Oh, my goodness. I know you're smarter than that. I want to marry and love you forever my friend."

Anel hysterically began to cry, and yelled at Hood, "You don't know me, you don't know anything about me, why are you toying with my emotions?"

Hood responded, "I am not toying with your emotions. I am only telling you that from the moment I laid eyes on you, each night you were the vision that put me into a mellow place of rest and wanting. I want you so badly, and only wish that I were as smooth as Dempsey, and that I was able to show my swagger this morning rather than watch his."

"Oh, so you two are in a competition?"

Hood stood up, and said, "If and when you want to talk to me about a sustained relationship that is new and exciting, and comes with little baggage, come see me. At this rate, and your unbelievable notions of my feelings, I think that I'm trying to go up a mountain backwards. I have no need to trifle with your emotions because I know that I love you, Anel. It's not about swagger, or conquest, it is about the beginning of a new life with a prefab family. G'nite."

# # #

In the morning, Leonardus was first to arise, and said, "I'm hungry." With Stella draped across her back, Anel asked, "Can someone get my little darling off my back without waking her?"

Leonardus responded, "Watch me." He pulled Stella by the feet until she was lying on the bed instead of on top of Anel.

Stella stated, "I slept like a baby last night."

Anel quickly announced, "I didn't."

"Why not?" Stella asked.

"Oh, I had this beautiful and wonderful little lady lying on me, and snoring most of the night."

"Who was she?" Leonardus yelled, "Dah, it was you silly girl." Stella pulled the cover over her head, and began to cry. Anel thought that she was playing, but when she pulled the cover back, Stella was shedding real tears. Anel got under the covers with her, and asked, "Why are you crying?" Between sniffles, Stella said, "I thought you liked me to be near you."

Anel realizing that there was something else eating at Stella, asked, "I guess you miss your mom and dad?" Stella really began to cry hard until Anel said, "Stella, I don't have any children, and I was hoping that you would allow me to be your new mom. I am so new at this, but I so desperately want to be a mother to you and Leonardus. Angel and I want to adopt you guys, much like Ms. Monica and Mr. Mallory did with their two children. And I have a secret to share with you, but you can't tell anyone."

Stella began to cease crying, and asked, "Are you going to marry Mr. Hood? I like him a lot, and Leonardus likes Mr.

Dempsey a lot as well. Is that what you were going to say to me?"

#

Mr. West called Mr. East, and asked, "Is everything in play?" There was a long pause until Mr. East exclaimed, "I should lead the charge, but that wouldn't be right! We have more people than we need, and we'll pay less because of attrition. As I study the village where I think they are holed up, there is this mountainous range that is perfect for an ambush, and I believe they have used it before. Now, I hear on the other entrance to the village, you can literally just walk in because no one would dare come by that route. If one were to take another approach to entering the village, it would bring you near an interesting billabong that is rumored to have saltwater crocs, the size of whales, if you believe in fairy tales. I'm thinking that our first line of attack will be the drones controlled by us, hundreds of feet away from the incursion."

Mr. West interrupted the session, and stated, "Drones rely on signals. There is no internet in the outback."

"That's where you are absolutely wrong. We will bring our own internet and signal systems, the same one that our government uses," Mr. East stated.

Mr. West asked, "So, if we are going to use drones, then we're going to blast our way in and out of the place, and then send our people in to do the cleanup?"

"That is precisely what we're going to do but, you and I will not be doing anything near that place. We will be monitoring from as far away as Sydney. Only after a body count will we show our faces, and claim the diamond and gold mines, as well as those territories east of the village where stones have been found on the surface. How about that?"

"What's your projection on personnel cost?"

"Mr. West, if we blow the place to hell with drones, then we'll have a helluva contractor bill to pay. No, sir, we're going to blow half the village to hell, and then send our hired people in to mop up, at which point I'm afraid that more than 2/3rds, will be injured or killed. Our hardcore people won't be sent in until everyone that is expendable is disposed of. They will become our new overseers. Listen, Mr. West, we don't go near the fucking place until every one of those people are dead, and I do mean every one of them, and that includes children who grow up to be a pain in your ass. Are we clear, and are we on the same page?" Mr. East asked.

Mr. West responded, "I'm just interested in bringing this long and arduous event to completion. You're right, children grow up, and can become a pain in the ass. Everyone goes, and the only things left to testify in court will be the fucking animals. When will we commence operations?"

"Now that is a great question. On the 16th of the month, the moon will be as full and ripe as it will ever be this year. I have sources providing me with pictures of entrances, valleys, billabongs, and mountainous terrain. In other words, are you busy four days from now? Transportation is dropping people all over the outback, from planes, trains, and buses to Darwin. From there, buses for hire will take our people to where it all will happen. We will invest in buses for hauling our booty out of the villages.

Listen, Mr. West, I've calculated this project and process, over and over again. Our personnel losses will easily reach the 2/3rds level, and we will cull from those remaining, but we have to keep that core group in place to protect us from any unforeseen contingencies. We have been planning this event for a while, and now it's time to implement. Oh, and that property that the lady spy owns in the Northeast, well, my people went over and undid a series of protocols designed to protect the place against crooks. Simply elementary, and we probably took a half- million from the safe. Don't worry, I'm keeping an accounting of all expenditures, income, and everything else. What is so fantastic is the fact that they don't believe that they are exposed in the wilderness. They have a lot of faith in spirits and allegedly, a beast in the billabong. My people have never seen anything other than the little crocs that feast upon each other when times are hard."

"What about the weather? Is there any chance of blistering heat or rain fall that could create a problem for our people?" Mr. West asked.

"Another excellent question my friend. It is forecasted to be in the high eighties during the day, and the mid-forties at night, for the next eight to ten days."

Mallory and Monica were sitting near the safe billabong watching the children swim when a reflection of some sort caught his eyes. He said, "Monica, don't look anywhere, but at me. Did you happen to see a flash or reflection at twelve o'clock?"

"Okay honey, it's been a long time since we played that game. However, I didn't see anything out of the ordinary."

Mallory said, "I'm going to slowly recline, and I'm going to point my right foot in the direction that you should pay attention to." Mallory reclined as if he was stretching tired muscles, and finished by pointing his right foot at what he considered twelve o'clock. As Monica looked in the direction of Mallory's extended leg, she saw exactly what he was referring to. It was two Aboriginal men taking pictures.

Mallory asked, "Honey, do you have a weapon on you?" Monica smiled, and replied, "I do, as a matter of fact."

Mallory said, "I'm going to go to the left, and you head to the right, and when I throw my hand in the air, I want you to fire a single round into the air. They won't come your way because that's the entrance to the billabong."

As the two made their way to the designated spots, Mallory raised his hand, and Monica fired a single round into the air. Two Aboriginal men made their way towards Mallory and were surprised when they saw him waiting with a weapon pointed in their direction.

Mallory said, "Good day mates. What brings you blokes so far into the outback? You're not from this tribe, are you? Oh, I see, the cat got your tongues, eh? Well, we got just the magic for making you talk. Where did you ditch those cameras?" Again, nothing but silence from the two. Mallory said, "I'm done waiting for answers." He screwed a silencer on his weapon, and without warning he shot each man in the foot.

The shots were not bone breakers, but strategic soft tissue wounds that could be easily attended to. He then said, "I bet you I got your attention, now, don't I?"

Of course, the shot fired by Monica sounded the alarm, the entire camp armed up, and the kids were escorted to their hiding place. Dempsey and Hood, along with Darryl and Larry, were first on the scene.

Mallory said to Hood, "Get John Lee, I'm going to need him to cut this fella's tongue out because he ain't talking." Suddenly, both men wanted to discuss being shot. Mallory, halted the nonsense, and said, "That was a warning shot, the next one will be a bone breaker, and it won't be your damn foot mate, it will be your kneecaps, and that way once our friends the dingoes smell that blood and realize that you're in the killing territory, then we'll just watch you scream as you're eaten alive by them and the wombats." In the back of them, sounds could be heard of predators investigating that all enthralling smell, the scent of blood in the air.

Dempsey asked, "What's that sound over there?"

Mallory laughed, and responded, "Probably the dingoes ordering up a live meal."

Hood asked, "Are we beyond the zone where they can attack us?"

Mallory laughed again, and said, "We aren't, but those two bleeders are." The men tried to make their way across the artificial line of demarcation that allows animals to enjoy a meal, especially if there is sanctioned blood involved, when Mallory raised his weapon and pointed it at the two men.

Wajickee appeared, and asked, "Mallory did you shoot these two blokes?"

Mallory exclaimed, "Affirmative!"

Well, the one on the left is the son of the leader of the tribe on the other side of the large mountain range, and his friend is what you guys would call a troublemaker always in and out of trouble with the authorities. Now, the leader is going to want to start a small war because you shot his son. He will come to his senses once I make him aware of what is going on."

Wajickee looked at the man, and instructed him to go and retrieve the equipment he and his friend dumped in the bush. He unfortunately said, "Old man, go fuck yourself, mate." No one really could explain what happened next except their next view of the man was of Wajickee dipping the man's bleeding foot into the billabong where the large crocs liked to play.

Everyone was perplexed about the timing, and how the man got to the billabong where he was being approached by large saltwater crocs. Mallory asked the troublemaker, "Where did you stash the equipment?"

"Mate, we dumped it right over there."

Mallory instructed, "Go and get it, and I'll get that flesh wound of yours attended to by our doctor."

The man asked, what about the animals, will they attack me?" Mallory scratched his head, and said, "How in the hell am I supposed to know what the animals will do to you. I suggest you get the equipment before my man gets here who is a specialist in cutting out tongues."

Mallory looked at Dempsey and Hood, and said, "Escort him to get the equipment they stashed."

Dempsey and Hood knew the deal, and walked alertly behind the man making a lot of noise.

When they returned with the equipment, and the wounded man, Wajickee was there with his captive who screamed, "I'll tell you everything I know. Please, don't let that red eyed devil come near me. He said, he would enter my body, and eat me from the inside out. Please, I'll tell you everything."

Once in the village, the group was met by the Sarge who asked, "What is the nature of this gathering. Who are these people, and what do they want?"

Mallory said, "This one on my left told your family friend from hundreds of years ago, "to go fuck himself."

The Sarge flinched, and asked, "And he's still living?"

"Well, Sarge, I don't know if what happens to him moving forward will be called living. I mean he's already pissed himself."

"Anel, will you fetch Ms. Viola and ask her to come here to attend to a couple of flesh wounds. I sincerely don't think Dr. Beckmire is required to evaluate this. Her liege can handle this. Thanks."

Anel and Angel, in full battle gear, walked over, examined the cameras, and immediately pulled up photos that the two had taken this day, and other recent pictures of the village, the entrances, the billabongs, the mountainous ranges, and every conceivable advantage that the group thought they had. Anel and Angel showed the Sarge and Mallory how to operate the cameras.

# # #

Much later, Hutang, Windom, and Earther were having what seemed like a heated debate. The Sarge, witnessing the encounter, nudged Mallory, and said, "Our support personnel seemingly are getting testy with each other."

The two men walked over to where Hutang, Windom, and Earther were, and asked, "Guys, are we alright?"

Windom replied, "Hutang and Earther realized that everything had been compromised, and were discussing unknown strategies that they hadn't evaluated."

The Sarge asked, "What might that be?" Hutang made a haughty laughing sound, and he and Earther high-fived each other. The Sarge said, "I'm glad to know that there is not going to be an internal war, however, can you help me understand what you're talking about?"

Hutang bowed, to Earther, who bowed lower to Windom, and said, "Brother, will you explain your beliefs?"

Windom said, "I am called Windom because I know and can feel the wind, the flow of air, and most importantly, where and if it has a to and from notion. Years back when the mines were first discovered, you took us all down there to see the diamonds just lying around. Well, I saw the air flow, I saw the volume of the air flow, and it led me to an exit from the mines. I know, you're going to say, that I am mistaken, but I will say that I know what I am saying. I do not want to share any notion of this as long as we have suspicious people in our midst. I will wait, Hutang will wait, and Earther will as well."

The Sarge bowed to the three wise men standing in front of him, and said, "Let me dispatch with these villains, and I will return to you guys promptly."

# # #

It was as though these guys were conducting a podcast. They talked about meeting people on a trip to California, and how they were convinced to take topographical pictures of things in distinct latitude and longitude coordinates.

Mallory asked, "Why did you act so damn smug when I caught you?"

Ms. Viola poured peroxide and alcohol on the flesh wounds, covered them with gauze, and said, "Don't soak your feet in anything other than your own bath water."

"We were told that you people were like gun toting bible salespersons, and that if we encountered you that you would act tough, but for us not to acquiesce to your demands. It was only after you shot us in the foot that we didn't believe that bible toting shit any longer."

Mallory asked, "I'm just curious, what did you see when you were positioned over the billabong?"

The man immediately replied, "I'd rather not talk about it, and you can believe me when I say that I'm on a short and narrow path. I'm done with trying to make a hustle. I saw the devil, and he called my name. He called my name and screamed, "no more, no more!"

As Mallory was about to conclude his interview, the friend said, "Mr., I started feeling freakish about this when I was told that over one thousand reservations on airlines, trains, and buses had been secured to do work in the outback. I asked my friend, "what are they coming to do, and are we helping them to hurt our people? He indicated that we should check our cash app accounts, and then decide if it was worth the aggravation. I told him the slaughter of our people for natural resources was not about aggravation, but more about decimating a country that had already succumbed to tyranny and piracy by the few who conquered the many. What we were doing was continuing the subjugation of our land."

He paused for a few seconds, and then said, "Sorry, to go off like that, however, I heard people mention courthouse, diamonds, and gold. Not sure in what context, but there didn't seem to be a sense of urgency on those issues, rather a critical proclamation of concluding everyone in that village who was not a natural Aboriginal person. There is a hatred of unparalleled proportions for the foreigners in this village. We thought that you were more colonizing people from the east who wanted to take what perhaps we had discovered and enslave us in mines for minimum wages, while you fatten your coffers ten thousand-fold. Now, I realize that someone really hates you people, and I do mean all of you. A final post of last week was that children grow up to be teenagers, and you know what a pain in the ass they can be. Let's clean the place thoroughly and completely."

Mallory asked, "Where did you go to school?"

"UC Berkely," was the response.

"You do know that there are diamonds and gold mines on this property that are certified, parceled out into quadrants, and have the elders and members of this village as the rightful owners? I mean, you being all that fancy with words, I know you know that members of this village, and a few others are going to be rich beyond their wildest imaginations."

The Sarge showed up, and asked Mallory if he had obtained any additional information that would help them prepare for the impending fight.   Mallory responded, "According to this gentleman, everyone is expendable, including our babies."

The Sarge belted out, "That's nothing new. It has always been about complete annihilation of our group. I guess there must exist something that clears the path for our babies to inherit all that there is. Without that notion, why else would they be as expendable as we are?"

The trespasser announced, "They know about your responses in the past when you used your neighbors to lodge spears and arrows at incoming groups from the mountain tops. They will probably capture that first to eliminate that planned event from you peoples' playbook. They were considering using that platform as a sniper's den on both sides of the mountain range. Listen, we were just trying to earn a few extra dollars, we had no clue that it would include the wholesale slaughter of you, your people, and innocent villagers. We are supposed to upload our latest pictures in little over an hour. Of course, we can't do that, but if we don't, it might mean that we've been captured and subsequently compromised. In any event, that could lead to a change in plans on their part, or not."

"If we give them new pictures, they can assess the situation, and decide if they want to alter their plans, hoping that we did this with full fidelity in mind. At least this way, you'll have the same information as them. Listen, I'm just trying to lessen the number of conquerors that come here."

The Sarge looked at the man's foot, and said, "You do know that the wound is superficial, but it needs to be cleaned and cared for. I'm going to let you and your partner go. Where did you leave your transportation?

"Approximately, two kilometers from here."

When the Sarge came upon the three wisemen, he said, "I am now focused, tell me what you guys are feeling so cocky about."

Windom smiled, and said, "Let's take a trip after dark into the mines, I'm not sure if we are being watched from afar."

The Sarge said, "Good point. See you guys just before or after dinner."

After the two men were escorted out of the village, the Sarge began to look for Wajickee. He walked down to the billabong, and sat down. It was quiet, and he decided to sit, and watch the predators slowly make themselves visible. As he watched the over-sized crocs seemingly become aggressive and skittish, he stood up, and walked to the water's edge. To his surprise, there was a strange smell emanating from the billabong. As he stepped into the water, he felt a tingling sensation erupt throughout his body, and before losing consciousness, he saw four figurines surface from the water, and cap his face with a suction-based apparatus. Into the billabong he went, unconscious, and without anyone having a clue as to where he was.

# # #

Later that afternoon when Courtney emerged from her hut looking for her husband, she saw Darryl, and asked, "Have you seen your uncle?"

"Auntie, I have not. Last I saw of him he was with Windom, Hutang, and Earther. I'm sure he hasn't violated his own edicts, and traveled beyond the camp's protective limits. Do you want me to join in your hunt for your husband?" Courtney smiled, and said, "I'm sure he'll show up, if he knows what's best for his butt."

Just before cocktail hour, Earther, Windom, and Hutang, could be seen enjoying an early version of the cocktail hour. Earther saw Courtney, and said to the guys, "Let's check on the boss." Earther said to Courtney, "Dr. Beckmire, hope all is well with you. We are waiting on the Sarge to escort us into the mines to discuss a ventilation issue. Do you know where he is?"

"Earther, I do not, and I am looking for him myself. Let's find Mallory, and see if he has any intel, and if not, then I assume he has been taken by aliens or something." Windom replied, "You do know that we're not the only people on this planet, don't you?"

"Windom, I am a woman of science, and I usually don't indulge in conversations about extraterrestrials. However, if you would like to challenge me, and present me with some new information, then I'm your huckleberry." Windom looking extremely perplexed, asked, "What does that mean, Doctor?"

"Are you asking what does huckleberry mean? If so, it just means that I am the person who will debate you, nothing more."

"Doctor Beckmire, no one is that talented to debate you in this group. You are our lifesaver, healer, and antibiotic. We just trust, respect, and admire you for what you do for all of us."

#

The cocktail hour was over, and no one had seen the Sarge. Mallory placed the camp on full alert, and divided it into halves, John Lee covering the north end and Jilkes covering the south end.

Darryl found his way to the billabong, and looked at the almost fresh indications that someone had been there, and realized that the inhabitants of the billabong were stunned, comatose, and docile. He yelled over and over again, "Full alert, full alert! We have been compromised, and our leader has been kidnapped. Again, I say, full alert, full alert. Take the children to their designated place, and all eligible adults, arm yourselves to the max. This is not a drill. I repeat, this is not a drill."

As Darryl extensively evaluated the billabong, he looked at the impressions in the sand leading from the billabong, and back into it. Wajickee appeared, and announced to Darryl, "Ben Beckmire has been abducted by people who electrified the billabong, captured him, and have taken him in some sort of underwater vehicle that I couldn't track because I don't have access to certain forms of matter. This group is unlike any other we have ever dealt with. They seemingly have a connection to the outback, and they are aware of our culture, spirits, demons, and natural resources. Someone is double dipping, and it's hard to discern who it might be. Ben Beckmire is no longer in striking range. He has been abducted, he's unconscious, and he is on his way to become a bargaining chip.

Word spread around the camp like wildfire. Courtney was in denial, and kept asking that calmness be the attitude demonstrated until all the evidence was examined. Larry appeared on the scene, and begged others not to compromise the area. He and Darryl, from afar discerned that four people were in the water, that two had come on land, and had dragged a body into the water. Near the water's edge was where Larry saw a piece of plastic. He walked over, and fetched it. It was the sterile cover for an individualized breathing mechanism or mask that does not need a tank. He then said to Darryl, "At least this is a good sign that he did not drown in the billabong or become a snack for his relatives." He looked at Darryl, and asked, "What is the breadth, depth, and length of this billabong?"

Darryl responded, "Actually Larry, this is called a billabong, but it is more like a river. If I'm not mistaken, to travel this billabong or river, would take a few days of daylight. There are places where I hear it is as deep as thirty-five to sixty feet, and at some points, you can't see the other side. Whoever did this knew exactly what they were doing. If you're adventurous, we have about two to three hours of daylight left. We could at least try to figure out where they exited the water. Let's go and propose this to Mallory, and see what he says."

Defensive positions had been assumed by all the members of the camp, and people were armed and ready for a conflict. Darryl and Larry saw Mallory, and proposed their plan. He at first didn't want to deplete the village of possible defenders, but Larry said, "If we lose daylight, we will never find out where those people took the Sarge, and how. Listen Mallory, if he was unconscious once, he is going to play that game until he has left a good trail for me to follow. He knows I am going to head this thing because I know how we worked when one or the other had been captured, in Philadelphia. Listen, Mallory, I won't budge unless you sanction it, but we are losing critical time. Let me, Darryl, Dempsey, and Hood, take leave, and we will be back later tonight or first thing in the morning. This is Darryl's hood, he knows what we can and can't do."

Mallory looked saw Courtney wandering around, which motivated his response, and said, "Get those two pirates, load up the skiff, and bring my friend and leader back. Darryl, use those damn drums to communicate with me. I'll keep Wajickee near."

Darryl smiled, and said, "Good luck with that. He is already canvassing the area, and is waiting on me, and the crew."

# # #

As the men slowly made their way down the billabong, Dempsey saw a huge saltwater croc, grabbed Hood's arm, and said, "Look at the size of that thing."

Darryl said, "Mate, that's a small fry. At some point, the Great Saltie is going to rear his head, because he does not take kindly to people trespassing in his billabong, in foreign underwater vehicles, that throw off apparently electrical impulses. Those people are his feast for the month. He wants all four of those characters.

Two hours before dark, eagle-eyed Larry is scanning one side of the billabong, and Darryl the other. Larry whispered to Hood and Dempsey, "Quiet guys, steer the skiff to your right. I think I see where someone beached a boat of sorts."

Larry took an oar to check the softness of the marsh, and as expected, he saw where someone had been dragged. He threw his fist in the air, and everyone fell to their knees. Larry whispered, "Look at my twelve, someone or something was dragged. Let's investigate, but from different vantage points. Hood, you're with me, and Dempsey, you're with Darryl, and Wajickee." Dempsey was about to say something when Darryl placed his hands over his mouth.

Wajickee muttered, "Are you trying to give us away?"

Dempsey asked, "Where did you come from?" Hood was about to announce something when they all heard a noise.

Wajickee said, "There are two Aboriginal people, four African Americans, and six white men. How they got to this part of the outback is a little bewildering, however, I think they flew in a whirly bird. Who saw the tracks that the Sarge left?"

Darryl looked at him, and said, "Larry with his keen eyes, saw the impression on the ground, and knew that someone or something had been dragged from the water."

Wajickee asked, "What took you people so long to get here?" Darryl smiled, and said, "We have a chain of command. We just don't up and go and come, like you do my friend."

Wajickee responded, "I detect a bit of cynicism, in your response my young friend. Do we have a problem?"

Darryl being ever mindful of Wajickee's stature, announced, "I was more focused on helping my uncle, but became sidetracked with the dialogue. Please forgive me for any notion of disrespect."

"I saw, nor felt no level of disrespect. Let's table this until we can free, secure, and return Ben Beckmire to his people. I'll tell you one thing, those who think that they have found a way to neutralize the billabong, have another thing coming their way. It is now impervious to electrical shocks."

As they separated to secure Ben Beckmire, Hood asked, "Are we taking prisoners?"

Larry apologized to Darryl, and said, "If my father is injured in any manner, all bets are off. If they are gentlemen, then we will treat them as such. Is that okay with you Darryl?"

Darryl, appreciating how Larry roped him back in the leadership position, said, "I agree with you 100% Larry. Silencers on your weapons people. Let's keep this quiet, get our man, figure out how they got him, and be gone before the sun sets."

Wajickee announced, "They have him encased in some kind of vest. It appears that one person has a transmitter with him at all times, and it apparently controls, some function of the vest."

Larry looked at Darryl, who said, "If that's the deal, then they are expecting us, and one push of a button, and my uncle, and your dad is no more. How do you want to proceed?"

Larry thought about the new information, and pondered what the Sarge would do. He turned to Wajickee, and asked, "Are you sure that there are only twelve individuals in that camp?"

Wajickee smiled, and said, "You're like your father, always asking for confirmation. Yes Larry, I am sure, my other senses have only located twelve in the entire area. Suppose the one with the alleged transmitter is an imposter, and the real person is hiding somewhere or has a hidden device. I'll be right back." Wajickee, no sooner said, was gone.

#

In the village, Wajickee showed up next to Rashida, and asked, "How far can you block a signal from a common device?"

Rashida jumped, and said, "I respectfully asked you not to show up next to me without some kind of warning." She smiled, and asked, "How far do you want it blocked?" Not being modest, Wajickee simply asked, "How far can you block a signal to protect your father's life?"

Rashida, exclaimed, "I am on it, and all I need is five minutes, and I can block every signal originating within a fifty-mile radius at maximum disruption, and at one hundred miles, with at least sixty five percent interference."

No sooner said, then done, Wajickee once again appeared next to Darryl. He said, "That marvelous young woman, the Sarge's daughter has created a disrupting signal for one hundred miles. Let's go and get our guy, and take those who took him to the billabong, so that those they shocked, can shock them."

#

After freeing the Sarge, he smiled at Larry, and asked, "Did you see my signs?"

Larry exuberantly responded, "Dad, I was on it. Are you okay?"

"Yeah, I'm fine, but I need to know, who in the hell is tracking me with such forward knowledge that they know where I am going, and when. These people showed up at the billabong, as if they were residents. What the hell is going on Wajickee? How can these people negate my ancestors, taser me, slap an apparatus on my face, and submerge me into or on some kind of underwater sled? Who is my Judas, and why now?"

Larry grabbed the Sarge's wrists, and said, "I need you to calm down dad. I need you to relax, and let us figure out how this all happened. Four of the twelve are still alive. I wish I had brought John Lee and Jilkes along to do some serious surgery."

Hood interrupted Larry, and announced, "Oh, we've done some serious surgery on people before, and we have been able to ascertain critical information. It's a bloody mess however, we sort of know how to do it, and get everything there is to obtain."

Darryl said, "We don't have a lot of time to figure this mess out, because there may be a full battalion coming to erase us all. We have an hour or so."

Hood looked at the captives, and announced, "Oh, we only need five to eight minutes, and then we're out of here with full details."

Hood and Dempsey took their captives down to the billabong, randomly sliced both feet of one of the individuals, gagged him tightly, and pushed him into the billabong. Less than a minute later, dozens of big eyes popped up around their location, and the other captives tried to back up. Darryl said to the group, "They're here because you shocked their waters, put them in a coma of sorts, made them miss two meals, and now they want to be fed. We sliced his feet because he was the architect of capturing my uncle, and shocking our water family." The others watched as his body was pulled, and severed by the inhabitants. Darryl looked at the remaining three individuals, and said, "Where is the underwater device that you used to pull my uncle and yourselves with?"

No one immediately said anything until Larry stated to the guy next to him, "You look a little beefy, I think you'll be the next meal." The guy started screaming, "I'll tell you anything you want to know. Please, I beg you, don't throw me in that water."

Larry yelled, "Now you're willing to cooperate. Who hired you to kidnap my father?" The guy dropped his head, and said, "We were told to capture anyone, and that a child would be the perfect bargaining piece."

Darryl asked, "Bargaining for what?" The guy said, "To take over the gold and diamond mines by default."

Darryl responded, "Are you saying this is all about gold and diamonds?"

The guy screamed, "It is, but it's also about our children, and in some cases our wives. We were forced into this action by a guy who used to be a government official, and his thugs. He looked at the guy to his immediate right, and said, "They have his son, daughter, and his wife. They have the daughter of the guy to my left, and they have my wife and son. The guy you fed to the crocs was our bailiff, and he had a check in time and if he missed it, our families would be taken advantage of."

Larry asked, "Where is your underwater vehicle?"

The guy looked at the water, and said, "Your first victim was the operator, and he had the necessary fobs to raise it, lower it, and propel it forward or backwards."

Darryl exclaimed, "Hogwash! We're done with this conversation, we have to head back to our village. Tell me where the unit is or join your friend in a very violent demise."

One of the guys who seemed to be the smallest, and quietest said, "I can raise it, I can operate it, and I can blow it up by uttering a few words. If I surrender it to you, will you let us go to try to find our families, and save them from despicable terror?"

Larry looked at Darryl, and stated, "We were being hoodwinked at first, and now I don't know if I want to release them or kill them. They basically, deceived us."

The guy who allegedly knew how to raise and operate the vehicle proclaimed, "What I said is the truth. They have members of our families, and they have promised to violate them in every conceivable manner if we failed to capture a member of your group. Listen, we're not afraid of dying, but we have seen them abuse a female family member of our group."

Larry, knowing all too well about being abused asked, "How did you get here? Who brought your underwater vehicle to this area, and who is ultimately in charge?"

The quiet guy said, "The man called Stilts. That is the person I think is in charge of this operation along with someone they call the commander."

Darryl asked, "Any other clues"?

"Oh, I heard someone call the name, Lawrence "of Arabia" Humphries, and Simpkins of Howard. I have no idea what those names mean, but that's additional information that caught my attention. Listen, we are not mercenaries and, therefore, we are not in the killing business. We try to help people, not to hurt them. One of our friends who died of a heart attack shortly after watching those animals abuse his wife, over, and over again, cried, "In heaven or hell—I will find you and abuse you."

# # #

As the group headed back to camp on the skiff and a submersible sled with three captives, the Sarge announced to Darryl, "This is deja vu. Hood and Dempsey came here to kill us, and look at them now. Do we kill everyone who is paid to eliminate us, or do we attempt to rehabilitate them by making them work in the mines for the very thing that they will never own? I don't have a clue, but I do like the idea of not killing everyone that attempts to kill us. My problem is whether or not that family hostage notion is for real."

Darryl looked at the three men, and then his uncle, and said, "Whether it is true or not, forgiving souls that are our enemies, earns us credits where we will ultimately find ourselves. Let's have Hood and Dempsey handle this, and see how they evaluate, and/or pardon people who are somewhat like they were with a mission."

The Sarge looked at him, and said, "That's a great idea, nephew. I trust them with my life, but let's understand what they will do in a situation much like theirs, but without the liability that those guy's claim to have at stake. Great idea."

# # #

Back in the village, the Sarge said to Hood, "Gather Dempsey, I want you two to handle a situation for me."

Hood responded, "I'll be right back. He ain't far."

When the two men returned, the Sarge laughed at them, and said, "Just think, not long ago, I was about to do a thumbs down on your asses. I am going to leave those three men in your care. I need you two to figure out the facts concerning their families, and who is controlling the action. Therefore, you will determine if we let them go, kill them, get them back to the states, assist them in obtaining their families, and if so, when."

Dempsey said, "I don't know about Hood, but I would like to work closely with Angel on this matter if it's okay with you."

"I give you an assignment, and the first thing you ask me about is a woman. What's up with that?" The Sarge inquired.

"Sarge, she is much more than a woman to me. I am in love with her, and the children. I need her near because she counter-balances everything that I do in a positive manner. I ask the questions and she gives her perspective, and we discuss it to the void."

Hood said, "Sarge I agree with him. I was going to ask if Anel could help me with this matter. We aren't putting the relationships in front of our priorities, and that is to protect the tribe, we're just saying that we work a helluva lot better and smarter when we're both trying to impress those two beautiful ladies."

The Sarge laughed a little, and said, "I like it when you guys level with me. Take over this assignment, and make sure those guys are on the level. Have your mates assist, but discern the facts and let me know in the morning. Thanks guys."

# # #

After a long and intense debriefing of the three men, it was decided that they would have to do community service, work amongst the spiders and snakes, and extract valuable products from the mines. However, first they were going to be placed on a plane for Sydney, and eventually back to the

states. The three men had served in Desert Storm, and were a
part of the group that ran Saddam out of Kuwait.

Dempsey said to the three men, "You're going to have to
come back here and work in the mines alongside snakes and
spiders if we vote to let you go. Now, let me be clear, you
might get back home and think that you're safe, and that you
don't have to honor any commitments made here. Let me tell
you something about this group, they fund education and
training programs, and support vets who come back home and
found out that someone had penetrated their private domain.
This group has people everywhere you can imagine. We know,
because we came here to rip them off, got caught, and we were
sentenced to the mines. In other words, don't play with this
group. We're going to get you out of here and back home, but
you're going to have to come back here, and pay homage to
all that live here. I'm going to ask the Sarge to take you to see
his great, great, great, great, grandfather. If he agrees, and after
you've seen it, and you want to play games with the lives of
your family and yours, then so be it. This is one unforgiving
place that has tentacles that reach far, far, away."

Hood stated, "When we take you to the Sarge, be ever
mindful that bullshit will get you served to the monsters in the
billabong. By the way, what are your names?"

The soft-spoken guy said, "My name is Al, Al Green, his
name is Mousey, or Gordan Gant, and the guy in the yellow, is
King Arthur or Art King. I can assure you that if you get us
back before the transmitter is discovered inoperable, we'll be
able to locate our families, eliminate their abusers, gather a
few belongings, and be back here to accept any tasks that you
guys prescribe. We don't want to be eaten by crocs, and we
don't want to die for a false cause. We will honor our

commitment, but as I consider our costs, I'm not sure we can afford a trip back here with our families in tow."

Hood astutely stated, "Your choices are limited, and all obstacles need to be presented to the Sarge. Don't, and I can't emphasize it enough, don't play games with the Sarge for you will certainly, and individually or collectively, become the lining of one of those awful crocs in that billabong."

## CHAPTER TWELVE

Earther received an email from the agency that represented the city government in matters relating to properties and eminent domain indicating that the city had received four bids on the parcels of land in question, and that the beginning bid was $30 million guaranteed for thirty-six hours from the posted time on the email. Earther gathered Windom, and they proceeded to find Courtney and subsequently, Monica.

Once they had the two women together, Monica said, "Let's do this systematically and, therefore, I want Luana here. I love Courtney, but she don't know shit about the law. Now, I will trust my body to her as a doctor, but for now, I need Luana, and I also need Sue Lyn." Courtney looked at Monica, and said, "You know Ms. B, you're going to have to pay for this." The two women embraced, and Monica stated, I'll see you at the appointed hour for our cocktails—love you!"

# # #

After reviewing the email over, and over again, Monica said, "Windom, ask the Sarge to join us as well. Someone has gotten to the powers that be, and they're trying to set the bar low and, therefore, sell below the threshold of the potential value. We need to make a trip there, and thwart this attempt by organized individuals to keep the bidding process low and to their advantage."

After hearing the gist of the issue, the Sarge laughed, and said, "Those scoundrels never quit. Okay, the land is titled to the families that hold the deeds. They're trying to smoke you out if I can use that analogy. In thirty-six hours, what are they going to do? They can't say the land has been abandoned. What I propose is that you and Earther, huddle and decide what it is you want for your properties, and the other two that Mysteir has ownership of. Monica, you know what oil is going for in Venezuela, just figure out what the pipeline should net these guys, and then use the crooked version of tabulating the price. First of all, I know you guys aren't going to sell that land. Am I correct?"

Windom stated, "We like the notion of a long-term lease renewable every twenty-five years, subject to inflation, foreign pricing, and the supply chain."

The Sarge smiled, and said, "I think those people are going to pee themselves when you propose an annual lease price for the four pieces of land that you, your daughter, and Earther own. Now Monica, why don't you and Luana prepare an email to the powers that be, and announce that their opening price range is the costs associated with entertaining a conversation. Tell them some crap like the non-refundable $30 million will have to be placed in a secured account, and that will get them invited to the discussions around the leasing cost. Say, some mess like, each organization wanting to invest in this process will have to place $30 million in accounts, to be considered a viable partner. Also, tell them that the $30 million has to be in place within the next thirty-six hours after the receipt of this email. If the funds are not in place, then it is unlikely any further discussions with the groups attached to this email will be held. Sincerely, The Equity Fund for Native Americans, (EFNA)."

Luana looked at the Sarge, and asked, "How do you come up with this mess? I mean for a lack of strategy, that is the perfect one. You are correct, they want to smoke the owners of the land out, and probably have plans for a mass burial. I think if you really want to have some fun with them, how about sending the two crooks, Hood and Dempsey and the women they like. Let them hand deliver your immediate terms and state to them that the bidding for the lease of each parcel of land will begin at $36 million."

Monica said, "I like your proposal, but I think those in attendance should be you, me and the two upstarts. Not sure what the two arrow shooting ladies' backgrounds are, but I also think we need to look at this thing from a legal perspective and make sure that those people haven't found a loophole, especially since they're trying to dictate time and amounts."

Everyone became silent, and considered Monica's input. Luana said, "You're one smart lawyer, and I respect you so much, and I yield to your proposal because it may be a conspiracy of sorts that is being planned to control the land at any cost. What is the young man's name that we met in the belly of that mountain?"

Earther said, "His name is Litefoot. Why do you ask?"

"If the plan is acceptable by the higher ups, then we'll need someone to show us around."

The Sarge looked ominous when he said, "That action will surely place him and his family in an unmarked grave. I think we should personally play this game, fully loaded. We fly to the ranch, get on the best bus in the west, and head to the mountains in the sky with a full contingency of our people. We place the ranch under double protection and, therefore, we make an unannounced visit to those who think that Earther and Windom are operating without legal protection, and let them know that the protection covering them is unforgiving. We can attain additional security in Minnesota by our network of friends in the sewers. However, Windom and Earther, this is your show. We're not going to let you do stupid, and think that the people making the offer are legitimate groups without the ability to bury your entire family."

Windom said, "Sarge, the numbers you so casually throw out are inconceivable to us, we don't know where to begin, and who to trust, other than this group. We yield to the best thinking of the group, and know that in all cases, this tribe has our backs. In other words, we use your playbook."

Windom saw Hood waving his hand in the background, and asked, "What might you add to this conversation, my friend?"

Hood, with Dempsey trying to quell his comments, suggested, "Why don't you send me and him as emissaries, and float those three guys in and around that area. Sending the principals and lawyers back, I agree with you, would be suicidal for them. Those people will never stop their greedy desire to control those lands that the pipeline certainly has to cross. The other places, near those lakes, are totally unacceptable to the entire community."

The Sarge looked long and hard at Hood, smiled at Mallory, and said, "I want Jelani in the middle of this thing. I need to find out what he can do beyond his FBI training." The Sarge looked at Hood and Dempsey, and asked, "Are you sure you don't want to include your lady friends in this matter?"

Dempsey laughed, and said, "We might have to escape to the mountains again, and plus they have family responsibilities to attend to."

Mallory jumped into the conversation and went directly for the jugular, when he said to the captives, "I don't like their benevolence, and if it were up to me, I would feed your asses to the beast in the billabong. If I detect any bullshit from you people, I will personally gut you from the penis to your brain. Am I making myself clear?" The three men began to nod and shake their heads which gave Mallory another opportunity to blast them. He screamed, "I can't hear your empty heads. Am I making myself clear?"

The three men yelled in sync, "Yes Sir!"

Mallory screamed again, and asked, "Do you see silver, gold bars, or stars on my shoulders? No, you don't. Just indicate that you understand what I have said." Each man acknowledged what Mallory had stated.

The next day, a small jet landed at the group's airport in Middle America. Gladstone and McArthur were seniors on this trip, followed by Jelani, Hood, Dempsey, and three former strangers. Clyde flew back with them, and was asked to make the long road trip again, but this time he was instructed to engage two younger men to do the driving.

The three individuals whose lives were spared, happen to be from Omaha, Nebraska, the group's first stop on their itinerary.

Gladstone said to McArthur, "We've kind of been here before. If those people have abused those guy's wives, then these guys are probably going to sink deep into a bottomless pit. We had better be prepared to support them or turn them loose, and give them some cash. Speaking of cash, did you bring any?"

McArthur laughed, and said, "You know there is a shit load of money here at the ranch."

Gladstone laughed, and said, "Do you remember when we didn't have a pot to piss in, a righteous woman to go home to, and not 100 bucks between us? Now, we don't even think in terms of cash, we have debit cards with $100s of thousands loaded on to them. God has been good to us brother."

Hood asked Al Green, "I know you have heard of the singer with that name. Are you related?"

"I wish I were. That relationship would have kept me from doing desperate things to keep my wife and family together." Hood cocked his head to the left, and asked, "What does that mean?"

"Listen, I don't want to be a snitch, or confess to things that were not asked of us. I am alive, those guys are alive, and we're married to three sisters who we knew were players. We met them long ago one night at a bar, hooked up with them, and after eight months, we were standing at the altar about to say I do. When and if you see them, you'll understand why we made that choice. We knew each other long before meeting them, and before enlisting in the military. Our deployment was an eye opener. The damn guy in charge of the recruitment center, was intimately involved with King Arthur's lady. Eventually, she convinced him that he was old dirt, and that she was pregnant by him. They all convinced us of their fidelity. Arthur decided to have a DNA test conducted that came back positive, meaning that the child was 99.99999% likely to be his child. I didn't bother because my child looks exactly like me, so I thought, until I was introduced to another recruiter at our departure site.

To make a long story short, we all received positive DNA test results. When you stop getting letters from home, you begin to wonder if, "ain't no sense in feeling blue, Jodi's screwing your woman too." Anyway, we love our kids, be they ours or theirs, but we love them. Ironically, this opportunity came to us at the same time. It was like, oh, shit, this we can do, and make a shitload of money. And, then we were captured by your people. Gant on the other hand has an ulterior motive for getting back to his woman. His on, and off again lover, saw his wife out with the recruiter that convinced him to enlist, and followed them to a sleazy motel, where they spent the night. He's not interested in freeing her, he wants to place a bullet in her head."

Hood listening to the guy, decided that this conversation was enlightening, and illustrated the kinds of questions that needed to be asked. He knew that they were not going to sanction an assassination and, therefore, he would consult with leadership to figure out their next steps.

# # #

Hood and Dempsey expressed their reservations to Gladstone, McArthur, and Jelani, about Green, Gant, and King. Hood had each man individually appear before the hierarchy to tell them their long-term goals and objectives. He selected Gant to be the first to appear before the group. Dempsey asked, "Mr. Gant, what are your long-term goals and objectives, and can we trust you to not do anything that is detrimental to our group?"

Mr. Gant unequivocally said, "Listen, when we were over there in the outback, I realized that we were not supposed to come back from that mission. The very people that recruited us into the military are the same people that proposed that adventure to us in the outback. It was a win-win for them and our wives. Our insurances would go directly to their benefit, and basic information about the layout of the village would be used for future strategic incursions and control, and the recruiters were key to all of these events. One of them worked with a bigshot from New York that became even more famous when his house was blown up, and he escaped via a tunnel he had in his place."

Gladstone commanded, "Stop right there! How does a military recruiter from Nebraska know about a man's house in New York that was blown up?"

Gant responded, "The recruiter is his nephew, and the cousin to his son who is in jail, who likes what he's able to get consistently, in the rear."

Gladstone placed a call to the Sarge, and expressed the details, associations, and conspiracies that were in place. The Sarge asked him if he felt that they needed to abort the situation, and was told that they were discovering players and relationships that are connected, like the man who had the house on stilts, his son, and now his nephew. The Sarge told him to stay in touch and be careful.

When Al Green was interviewed, he stated that he had nothing new to add to what he had said before. Hood asked, "Are you sure you don't have an ulterior motive, as well?"

There was silence until Al Green sighed, and said, "Listen, I married a real floozy, and so did the rest of the guys. As I think about it, I realize that the people who encouraged us, recruited us, shipped us overseas, probably had fun with our so-called wives while we were in the desert. Listen, we are solid, and we are grateful to be alive. You guys could have capped us over there, fed us to those monsters in the water, and no one would have cared or would have investigated our status. This whole thing is about opportunity, conspiracy, fraud, and unfaithfulness. I'm not saying we're saints of sorts, because while in the desert, we had our steady supply of booty. However, we didn't know that our wives were banging the recruiters, and had taken additional insurance policies out on us. The recruiters also developed the job for us in the outback, with the notion that we would not be returning. They were playing small stakes until the outback came up as an opportunity. The nephew of the man who had the house on the stilts, told us this was a no brainer, and that when all was said and done, we would all be counting billions of dollars before we went to sleep each night. I know, too damn good to be true, and so is the value of snake oil. Hey, here's a question for you. Are those mines really churning out billions of dollars in gold and diamonds?"

Hood vociferously responded, "If I answer that question, I will have to place a round in your head. Is it worth your life?"

Al Green raised his hands in the air, and said, "I don't give a shit about nothing that ain't mine. I got my life back, and I'm hoping like hell we can be given the same considerations as you two brigands, and we can join an outfit that ain't built upon someone else's suffering."

Dempsey smiled, and said, "Looks as though you're well on you way. Keep up that kind of response, and I'm sure the powers that be will open their arms wide and embrace you. However, the downside to that equation is simple; you bring bullshit, and you will die a horrific death."

When King was brought in for his interview, he opened it by saying, "I am happy to be alive and ready to conclude a relationship based upon attrition. So, ask me any questions you like, and I will answer them honestly. Listen we know we've been duped, and I'm sure that they're celebrating thinking that we're dead, and they've probably been to the insurance companies trying to get an advance on their policies on us. I know this, Gant knows this, and so does Green."

Hood asked, "Are we interviewing you, or are you interviewing us?" King said, "I'm just trying to set the stage for our continued existence." McArthur shot back, "This ain't about anybody, but you, my friend." King lowered his head slightly, looked directly at McArthur, and said, "I'm sorry, but this is a package deal for me, unless someone has invoked the "I" as in individual, rather than the "T" as in team." McArthur asked, "Are you a trustworthy person?" King smiled, and said, "My word is my life. If I say it, then so be it."

"Are you always this cocky?" Gladstone asked. King fired back, "If I say my word is my life, then so be it. I will give you all that I stated I will do. I won't cheat, steal, or barter the groups' demise. I am a loyal soul, I became this way after people like my wife and her playmates took complete advantage of my honesty. Now, I will lie to them, and deceive them at every moment. And do you know what, the booty wasn't all that impressive."

Dempsey cleared his throat, and said, "You know you guys have a date in the mines with the snakes and spiders back in the outback. What I suggest that you do on this trip is try to impress Messrs. Gladstone, McArthur, and Jelani, and then negotiate your time in those mines. Trust me, you don't want to get stuck down there for doing stupid."

# # #

When the group entered Omaha, Nebraska, Al Green said, "I hope the next time I come to this place, is to gather my child." His sentiments were echoed by King and Gant. Gant said, "I don't believe it's to our benefit to be seen in this town. I don't believe they're being held, and I suggest, if Mr. McArthur and Gladstone agree, that we just stake out the most likely place the sisters will be."

Gladstone asked, "Where might that be?"

Gant yelled, "The Hilton Hotel with the revolving rooftop bar."

"Clyde get directions and let's head there for a few. We should send our anomalies Dempsey and Hood in to scout for us, and place those new cameras that your wife developed for us in play. Guys I don't want you carrying, but we'll be close if in fact there is some negative noise resulting from you guys just having a drink."

Ten or so minutes later, Hood and Dempsey entered the lounge, and admired the revolving bar. Hood said, "Oh my goodness, I guess if you sit in one place long enough you can see the whole city without moving. How cool is that?"

Dempsey said, "Let's have a drink, chill out for a few, and then head to sleep. We have a long and arduous day ahead of us tomorrow."

Hood replied, "Check out my six. Can you guys in the bus see those ladies?"

A muffled voice cried out, "That's my wife, and her two sisters, with the assholes who sent us to the outback." Gant started towards the door of the bus, and McArthur calmly stated, "If you exit this bus, you will die here and now."

Gant walked up to him, and said, "Dude, I mean Mr. McArthur, those dogs have been sleeping around since we married them." McArthur repeated himself, and said, "If you walk off this bus, I will have to follow you, put a bullet in your head, and leave you on the street. This mission has now been compromised in every direction."

"Listen, I don't want to die in this town, and if I get off this bus, Green, and King are going to follow me and, therefore, all three of us will be dead, and providing those harlots with our insurance monies. Would you really do that?" Gant asked. Gant paused for a moment, smiled, and said, "You people must be crazy. I just want to puff on this unit until I can quit cold turkey. Wow people, get a hold of yourselves. I ain't dying for no cheating ass ex-wife. You hear me, I said ex-wife. My new mission is to figure out how to get my child from her."

Gladstone said, "Our lawyers are working on that as we speak."

"Would you have shot me in the back if I left the bus?" Gladstone lowered his head, smiled, and replied, "Absolutely not. It would have been a bullet in the back of the head."

Gant said, "Guys, I had my moment of weakness concerning that freak, I am now on a mission to rescue my child, get involved with this group, and make sure my brothers are on the same page. We ain't going back for sloppy seconds, we're moving on, and hopefully with this group. Am I right fellas?" King and Green both yelled, "Now that's what we're talking about."

#

In the bar, the three women kissed, touched, fondled, and played with their respective dates. At the table, King's wife slouched in her chair as her date fondled her private zone, removed his fingers, and inserted them in his wife's mouth. He said, "How despicable. Is that camera feed live and recording?"

McArthur responded, "On several different systems."

King announced, "I would like to post that video on Instagram, Tik-Tok, and Facebook. Can you guys send it to me?"

McArthur said, "Once my crew are safely out of there, and that's what you want to do, then brother, go for it. However, I certainly wouldn't let them know that you're still alive. Find a neutral site that doesn't expose you guys or us. However, nothing happens until our people are out of that place. Do all of you agree that you were duped, and that your wives are not under duress, and have not been kidnapped?" There were motions of acknowledgment, from head movements, thumbs up, and an actual verbal agreement.

Hood received a text stating that the bus was leaving in ten minutes. He said to Dempsey, "We have a lot to do, let's get the hell out of here now. He placed a $100 bill on the bar, and asked the barkeep, "Do you get this level of talent in here on most days?"

The barkeep said, "You guys should drop in here on Thursday, Friday, or Saturday, and you might just find your future spouse. I mean the sisters are phenomenal looking people, and the cream of the crop, but what comes after them is not that far from perfection. Guys, sincerely, you come on the nights I mentioned, and you'll not want to ever leave this place. The talent here is clean, unattached, looking for stability, and appreciation. Most of the eligible men in this area, are accidently or intentionally screwing each other in state prison." The two men turned to walk away, and saw the disappointment on the faces of the three women who were with their three intoxicated male associates.

Back on the bus, Hood asked, "What is our mission? Do you want me to go and get one of those women and interrogate her?"

Gladstone looked at Green, King, and Gant, and said, "I don't think so. I think we have a clear picture of what is going on, and what is important to them. Clyde, chart a course to Minnesota."

In the meantime, the three men agreed on posting some of the video on social media platforms. Gant walked up to Gladstone, and asked, "Is it possible to stop somewhere soon so that we can post the video of our remorseful wives?" Gladstone responded, "The last I heard, the bus has its own Wi-Fi connection."

Once Gant received the login and password to the Wi-Fi from Clyde, the three men started posting pictures of their wives mourning them in a bar, with three men who were over-comforting them.

# # #

The long ride from Nebraska to Minnesota was uneventful and full of sights. Gladstone announced, "Listen up people, this bus is our home for the next day or so. Treat the restroom like it was your very own. Hopefully, we'll be out of here by tomorrow."

# # #

Clyde, following his saved coordinates, made the turn at the right place and gave his horn three short blasts. Fifteen minutes later, a weary Litefoot knocked on the side of the bus from the rear to the front door, and when the door was opened, he said, "You people sure know how to time supper." He entered the bus, and showed Clyde where to leave it.

Later during the eating of some unknown meat, Hood asked, "This taste good, what is it?"

Litefoot laughed, and said, "It's chicken my brother, plain old chicken seasoned with native herbs and spices." Litefoot asked Hood what was the response to the proposal that was issued. Hood looked at him, and stated, "That request was in the millions, we are only entertaining numbers that start with a billion and end with billions."

Litefoot looked away, and said, "I smell a rat. I think we should head near town tonight, so that any attempted ambush can only happen in a populous area. From here to town, there are a lot of places to shoot up that old bus of yours and kill everyone in it."

McArthur exclaimed, "I wouldn't diminish that old bus's capabilities. It has a few surprises built in it, and believe it or not, it's armor plated." Litefoot proclaimed, "You make joke about a serious matter. I think this is all a set up."

McArthur proclaimed, "Litefoot, I kid you not! That old blue school bus is armor plated, it has machine guns in the front and in the rear, port holes on the sides, and the windows are bulletproof." Litefoot looked for any signs of 'bs', and when he didn't see any, he asked, "Are you guys messing with me?"

Gladstone replied, "I don't usually swear, but in this case, I will affirm that we are not messing with you, and that the bus is its own armada. In the morning, I will show you the inner workings of that monster."

Litefoot stated, "I would still sleep better if we were on the outskirts of town. Oh, do you people have enough firepower for your group?"

Gladstone replied, "I think we have enough to supply everyone with a weapon or two. Back to your comment about feeling better if we were on the outskirts of town, I think we should load up, and follow your wisdom. This is your hood, we are foreigners, and don't know squat about this area, or the motivation behind what people will do to get an advantage."

As the group gathered their belongings, Litefoot once again repeated, "I smell a rat."

# # #

Fifteen or so minutes from town, Clyde pulled the bus into a lot that was full of yellow buses. He said, "I remember this place from our last visit here."

Litefoot said, "This is exactly what I had in mind, but I wanted to make sure they used this facility this time of the year as opposed to the one clear across town. Good looking out Clyde."

Clyde said, "People, until I lower the window slats, please do not turn on any lights until I have completed that function. In addition, I'm going to run everything off the generator that is super quiet. I will extend that unit ten feet down wind away from the vehicle. I am also going to engage the surveillance system that will capture images of anyone who comes within twenty feet of the bus. Gentlemen, if you want to stretch completely out, use the buttons to turn your seats into a bed. Goodnight, and I'll see you guys when the sun comes out."

Twenty minutes later, one could hear a pin drop. The occupants were sound asleep.

# # #

At the break of day, Clyde hit a button that opened the slats in the windows and another that shifted the direction of the generator. He ran the camera system back, and it showed that there were no unwanted visitors. He said to Litefoot, "Do you think we can go to that restaurant we ate at the last time we were here, and chow down?"

Litefoot yawned, and said, "That sounds like a great idea."

Hood received a text message from Anel and Stella. It read, "We both miss you and want you to come back as soon as possible. Love Anel & Stella!" He smiled, and said, "People let's make this a great day because I have two people that I love so much texting me that they miss and love me. How about you Dempsey, you get any such messages?" Dempsey began to say something when his phone started buzzing. He said, "Hold that thought jerk, let me see who this is." Lo an behold, it was a message from Angel stating that she is in need of constant nighttime spooning with a mysterious man that she met. Oh, and that Leonardus asked, "when can the two of you go fishing? Well, well, well, how about that Mr. Smarty pants."

In the meantime, Gladstone, McArthur, and Jelani were strategizing about how to approach this thing. Mac said, "They know Hood, Dempsey, and Litefoot. Let's not crowd the space, I think we should send those three in alone, armed, and with the front of the bus pointing to the restaurant. Also, Jelani, you can wander in, and take the temperature of the place as well."

Ten or so minutes later, Clyde pulled the bus in front of the restaurant, he and one of his support drivers got out of it, and stretched. Meanwhile, Hood, Dempsey, and Litefoot entered the restaurant. Upon entering it, Hood saw the guy he had rapidly and brutally dispatched of. The guy saw him, dropped his fork, and walked towards the door. Hood said, "I need to speak to you." The guy swelled up, and said, "I don't want no trouble mister, history is history. People are planning to assassinate you. Don't go to the town center building." The guy threw his hands in the air, and hurriedly exited the restaurant.

Hood called McArthur, and told him what the guy had said. McArthur asked, "How dumb are these people? Didn't we rain fire and abuse on them the last time we were here? I have to call the Sarge."

#

After briefing the Sarge, he asked, "Do you need us out there to provide security for you?" McArthur looked at Gladstone, then Jelani, and each man gave him the thumbs down. McArthur replied, "No Sarge, we got this under control, and plus the new guy, Jelani, looks so bureaucratic and official, he might scare them away. I think once they lay eyes on him, they'll realize this thing has graduated from the local to the national level."

#

Jelani walked into the restaurant, found a seat, and ordered scrambled eggs, with chopped ham and cheese. He began to read his newspaper, when from the rear of the restaurant, a man appeared, and asked out of the blue, "So what brings you to our Minnesota Nice city?" Jelani, finished the section he was reading, looked up at the person, and responded, "I'm here on official government business."

The man asked, "What government?" Jelani slowly pushed his chair back, stood up, and said, "Friend, you sure ask a lot of questions that are not your concern. Do you have a purpose for disturbing my breakfast, or are you the town clown?"

The guy looked at Jelani, and mumbled, "We'll see who the clown is."

Jelani said, "I'm from an agency in Washington. Who are you with?" The man shook his head, and hurriedly left from the rear of the restaurant. Jelani sat back down, continued to enjoy his breakfast, and read the newspaper. Hood made his way to the back of the restaurant and saw that the man had left from the rear entrance. Dempsey walked out of the front door, pointed to Gant and King to follow Hood, and for Green to come with him. Jelani never took his eyes off the newspaper.

The manager casually walked back to his office, made a phone call, all of which was being recorded by the systems that Gilda had created. A call was placed to 999-999-9991. The person answering the call asked, "What's the status of the venture?" The manager announced that the FBI was in the house, and having breakfast." The person receiving the call said, "We need to shut this thing down now. I'm off the grid, this number is no longer in service."

#

Fortunately, the Native American population was well represented at City Hall. Hundreds held signs that read, "Once again, the White man is trying to steal our land." TV stations, both local and national, were stationed outside of City Hall.

Jelani, after enjoying his breakfast, caught a cab for the short ride to City Hall. Gant, Green, and King exited the bus several blocks away from City Hall. Clyde gave the men an opportunity to scour the area, and slowly proceeded to City Hall. Once at the semi-circle, McArthur and Gladstone exited the bus. They looked around, and signaled to Hood and Dempsey to exit the vehicle. As the two men made their way towards the entrance to City Hall, reporters and camera persons began to follow, asking them who they were, and whether they were representing the families that owned the property that was under investigation.

Hood uncharacteristically looked at an inquiring reporter, and unequivocally stated, "There are no properties under investigation. The rightful owners, through me, and my colleague, will lay out the temporary terms and conditions that are non-negotiable. Thank you, and that is all that will be said publicly."

#

At the beginning of the preliminary hearing, Hood and Dempsey were positioned in the front, and in the back were McArthur and Gladstone. When Jelani walked in with a cup of coffee in his hand. The administrator asked, "Sir, may I ask your reason for being in this closed meeting?"

Jelani took a sip of his coffee, and said, "I'm just passing through, and decided that I wanted to hear what was happening to my Native American brothers and sisters. Is there a problem with that?"

"Sir, this is a closed meeting, it is open only to those who received an invitation, have an interest, or a controlling position in the area under negotiation."

Jelani took another sip of his coffee, and said, "Oh, don't concern yourself with me, I'm one of several agents assigned to monitor these hearings. You didn't get the email?"

The person in charge replied, "No I didn't."

Jelani smiled, then frowned, and said, "Carry on with your affairs. We are here to make sure that these hearings are transparent and legitimate. Please, continue, and thanks for asking."

Hood was asked to present the beginning quote for the sale of the properties in the stated quadrants on the rendition of the map on the screen behind the person managing the meeting. Hood stood up to make a few clarifications, when a person yelled, "We want to buy those properties, and we're willing to pay as much as $30 million." Hood began to jump up and down with joy, but finally stated, "That bid will not buy you an outhouse on each property. I am only going to say this once, and then I'm out of here. No attention will be paid to anyone who is not serious about the project. Therefore, the opening acceptable bids for a twenty-five-year lease, that's correct, a twenty-five-year lease for the four main properties will start at $36 million per year, per property. Thank you, and good day!" People started screaming, but stopped when Jelani started taking photos with his Iphone.

The person in charge said, "Please, calm down. You people thought you were going to catch this fish with bloodworms. An official representative of the families has spoken, and has listed the terms of the relationship. Please be advised, unless you want to learn to speak another language, then I suggest that you consider the opening bid seriously. This hearing is adjourned."

# # #

Once most of their crew was on the bus, they rendezvoused with Jelani, and when he entered the bus, Gladstone said, "Good job Mr. Agent man. Good job, portraying an FBI agent."

Jelani smiled, and said, "I never said that I was an FBI agent, I merely stated that I was one of several agents assigned to this case. I never said that I was with the FBI." McArthur replied, "You know what, you are absolutely correct, you never said FBI."

# # #

Clyde said to his support drivers, "I'll take the first part of the trip, you guys sit back and listen to that devil worshiping music, you like to play."

On a stretch of road that leads to the interstate, four black SUVs with flashing lights entered the road and negotiated their vehicles between traffic, and ultimately and aggressively, behind the bus. Clyde yelled, "We got company, and lots of it."

The lead vehicle eventually pulled up next to the driver's window, and motioned to Clyde to pull over. Everyone saw that the men in the vehicle were heavily armed. Clyde continued to drive, and yelled, "I need a command."

Gladstone looked at the lead vehicle, and told Clyde to hit
number six, and for everyone to arm up, and for Clyde to
pretend to pull off. The windows are one way—they could see
out, but no one could see in.

Suddenly, the lead vehicle tried to force Clyde off the road
by veering its wheels towards the front of the bus. Clyde
naturally tried to avoid the collision, and that's when the
passenger in the front seat displayed his automatic weapon.
Clyde yelled, "The guy in the front passenger seat has an
automatic weapon with a bump stock on it." Clyde then
engaged the front and rear armor plates. Gladstone yelled,
"Hood and Dempsey, cover the driver's side of the bus, Mac,
take the rear of the bus, and I'll take the front. Jelani, the right
side of the bus is yours with our new recruits. Don't let no
body on this damn bus." He then yelled, "Clyde, run the
motherfucker off the road."

Clyde smiled, looked at the guy, and gave him the bird.
He then proceeded to put the much heavier vehicle in a sports
gear, and banged the SUV causing it to flip over. From the
rear, the passengers in the other vehicles started firing at the
blue school bus that was armor plated and loaded with twin
machine pistols in the front and back. McArthur eased into
place, unlocked the twin machine pistols, took aim, and
blasted two vehicles mercilessly. The second and third
vehicles realized that they were out gunned, and backed off the
chase. On the freeway, Clyde yelled, "Boy that'll get your
adrenaline flowing. I'm beginning to like these high stakes
chases, and watching this old girl do exactly what I wanted her
to do."

McArthur asked him, "Shouldn't you be saying a prayer
or something for them people."

Clyde remorsefully stated, "I ain't praying for no more people who try to kill me. That last bullet I took, well it extracted a lot of my faith with it. I know God is with me, but I also know that you people are here on earth, and that's what makes my life worth living, alongside of that fantastic wife of mine."

After driving for thirty-five minutes on an empty highway, everyone thought that the aggression was over, when lo and behold a helicopter was hovering at the crest of the hill waiting for the bus to breach the valley, and start its rise to the top. Approximately two miles down the road, Gladstone instructed Clyde to floor the accelerator, when two loud bangs hit the windshield. Gladstone slipped into the small tunnel, and began to spray the helicopter to the point that it began to smoke. The helicopter pilot hauled ass out of range of the machine pistols, but had succumbed to several critical hits to its engine. It sputtered until the pilot realized that he had to set the bird down. Gladstone said, "Let's go and see if they all survived, that was a pretty hard landing."

At the crash site, one of the shooters was impaled by his weapon. The pilot was semi-conscious, and Gladstone attempted to extract him when there was a small explosion in the tail section of the bird. Gladstone cut the seatbelt off the pilot, saw an interesting looking logbook, slipped it into his belt, and pulled the pilot out, who sustained serious injuries and succumbed to them. The other shooter's leg was mangled beyond recognition, and Jelani stated, "I can free you or put you out of your misery."

The man said, "They owe me money, I have to collect it to pay my mortgage, or my family is going to be evicted."

Jelani studied the man's condition, and said, "I can help you, but you have to help me. Who hired you?" The man looked long at Jelani, and asked, "What does help look like from your eyes mister. I'm literally bleeding to death. How can you help me?"

Jelani replied, "I can make sure your family does not get evicted, and that they have enough money to live there forever."

The man replied, "You talk shit just like those people that made me do this dumb shit."

Jelani said, "Tell me who they are, and I'll send $50k to your family while you're alive. You don't have a lot of time to negotiate. Give me your wallet, and on my word, I'll make sure they never have to worry about a mortgage again. By the way, how much are we talking about?" The man between almost expiring, sleazily said, "$60k." Jelani called McArthur and stated, this guy is willing to tell us who ordered the hit, if we pay his mortgage, and allow his family to live in the house. My question is, can we help this guy?"

McArthur said, "While he's giving you information, I can transfer funds to any account that they have from here, and in front of him. However, we're not buying any shells, I'll need good information that allows us to get to the head of the snake."

The information began to flow freely, and included the financiers, the organizers, and the operators. Jelani after listening to a slew of information asked, "How were you contacted?"

The man said, "A good friend of mine knows some people who work for one of those underground groups, and turned me on to some off the books kind of work, you know enforcement type jobs. This job, however, was advertised differently, meaning there would be gunplay involved.

When I was told the payment amount for successful kills, well, I just thought about how I could provide for my family in a big way. I never realized that I could be a victim of gunplay. Anyway, before I tell you anything else, tell me how you can help me."

Jelani replied, "Give me your wallet, and does your family use Cash App, Zel or some other kind of money transferring system?"

The wounded man replied, "My wife uses Cash App."

McArthur replied, "Perfect. I will transfer the funds to her while you watch, and you can make sure she receives them. Now tell us who your contacts are."

The man looked at Jelani, and stated, "You look too prissy to have an understanding of the kind of people I'm involved with."

Jelani shot back, "Don't make assumptions or stall for time, tell us who was supposed to pay you."

The man said, "The colonel himself was to meet us at the airfield, and make everything right with the payment, and a bonus if we succeeded in eliminating the threat, which of course is you guys. We kind of figured there might be a bit of treachery entangled with the payment issue."

McArthur after providing the man with fresh bandages, asked, "Why are you stalling? You are going to die, and I mean soon."

The man looked at his legs, and said, "I ain't got nothing else to say until I see that money enter my wife's account."

A few moments later, MacArthur hit the send button, and $50k was entered into the alleged account of the man's wife. The man waited, and said, "I need to ask my wife if she got the money." The man pulled out his cell phone, texted his wife, and inquired if she received the money that he sent, and she texted back, "Oh my goodness, God is good, hurry home." She texted him inquiring about the nature of the money, and he texted back, "I love you and the children." He looked at Jelani, and then McArthur, and said, "The person orchestrating this event is the colonel, the same person that is in charge of the sewer system in D.C."

After a deep sigh, the guy said, "The colonel has been double dipping on you guys for years, selling you inconsequential information, and providing you with strategic timetables of things to happen that you would have figured out in due time."

McArthur asked, "Are you a confidant of the colonel? How did you come by such information."

The man sighed from his pain, and replied, "This job was to get our money. He owed me and the other guys on the copter, for executing his wife years ago. He never paid us, cried broke, and promised that he was good for it. There was a drug deal that went bad in Maryland about a year ago, the colonel was the lead, took the drugs, kept the alleged payment, executed the dealers, the buyers, and four other people. We knew he had scored, and kept the money. He called the pilot and told him that he would double the money he owes us if we did this one last favor for him, and that's where you people come in. The pilot and the other guy adamantly told him no. The colonel told him that if that was their answer, then he was not going to pay them a dime, and that they should keep a sharp lookout for the hitman. Well, that's like getting screwed without any lubricant, we agreed to incapacitate the bus, and send the Native Americans, a message. Didn't know the damn school bus was an armored vehicle with active machine gun turrets mounted in it."

The man winced, looked at his leg, and said, "Leave me my pistol, and one round. I promise not to do a stupid thing and try to hurt one of you guys. I am dead either way from a self-inflicted wound or from one of the colonel's assassins. Oh, one other thing I can tell you, is that you blew up his partner's home, and tried to kill him. He, and his other partner have begun to gather a force beyond reckoning to erase your DNA. They want deeds to the mines, the land here in Minnesota, and literally the head of your tribe on a stick. The colonel and his partners know that you'll figure it out, and come after him, but not before he decimates your group. You got someone who is close assisting them at almost every turn."

McArthur called the Sarge, and reported exactly what the captive had indicated. The Sarge said, "I always felt that he was slimy, but he always was there to help us. Okay, clean that mess up, get on our plane this evening, and get out of dodge. Safe travels, and I'll see you tomorrow."

CHAPTER THIRTEEN

Halfway around the world, people were congregating in Brisbane, Cairns, Sydney, and the Northern Territory. Also, a large contingency of mercs had gathered in snotty Perth, and were preparing to fly to the Northern Territory. All in all, nine hundred ninety men and women were paid a per diem, provided a contract that would endow them with a portion of the natural resources, and they would earn $100k upon completion of the job. To minimize the opposition, it was told to groups of people that the mines were guarded by small tribes, and that the show of force would eliminate the need for mortal combat. Nothing was communicated to the group about the Fab 10+2, and their friends from around the world. No, the picture painted illustrated a cakewalk with untold fortunes awaiting each person who participated in conquering the mines and the small attending tribes.

#

Approximately twenty-four hours later, Clyde, McArthur, Gladstone, Jelani, Hood, Dempsey, and newcomers, Gant, King, and Green entered customs in the outback.

The agent said to Gladstone, "These guys are getting off your plane, and I know that they're with you. The one guy looks like a person of interest on one of our Wanted Posters, take a look, and let me know if you have a problem that I can blindly overlook."

Gladstone looked at the Wanted Poster, looked at King, smiled, and said to the agent, "This guy has a small scar below his left ear. Look at my guy, and plus, that guy looks taller than my guy."

The agent smiled, and said, "Just making sure we pretend like we're doing our job. We have an inspector evaluating our protocols. Thanks, and I'll see you again soon. Oh, there is a lot of noise going around about a large number of people coming to this area in the next few days."

Gladstone looked at him, and said, "Thanks for the heads-up. We heard those rumors as well, and we're trying to make sure that we come out on top."

The agent stamped his passport, and said, "We'll make it difficult for them on this end, and I'll tell the local magistrate that the rumors are true, and that perhaps he and his group can be on standby to assist those in need." Gladstone replied, "Every little bit helps, my friend."

# # #

Once in the village, the group was met by the Sarge, Mallory, Windom, Earther, John Lee, and Jilkes. McArthur announced, "Hood and Dempsey left a beginning number in the amount of $3.6 billion over the twenty-five-year lease, with all interested parties depositing $36 million, non-refundable, in a secured account, within thirty-six hours."

Gladstone indicated the new guys did okay, and followed the rules and mandates without any washback. However, he felt that they still needed to work in the mines to become sensitized to the powers of the outback, the spirits and most of all, the Great Saltie. Gladstone also told the Sarge about the rumors of large numbers of people coming to the outback.

The Sarge looked at him, and said, "We can't do anything except prepare for the inevitable. Those people will massacre our people here if we turn tail and run. Listen, we will prevail, or die trying. Now you guys go and freshen up and get ready for dinner. You new guys, well, you see that ridge about one hundred yards from here, there is a hut there, clean it, prepare to live in it, and make it your home. Develop your own personal loos, and I'll have someone bring dinner to you people. You have to put in your time in the mines, but anyway that's better than the alternative. Welcome aboard."

# # #

The following morning the entire camp, including the children, could be seen developing and marking off firing sequences, distances, possible retreat scenarios, and the use of the mines as a last resort. Windom, with Hutang, Earther, and the Sarge in tow, entered the mines that were clear of snakes and spiders. At the bottom of the diamond mine, there was a small ledge that led to another narrow passageway and eventually, into a larger area that had a tunnel that was at least fifty yards long and well ventilated. Windom said, "No one ever ventured this far on this side because it looked as if all of the precious stones were on the other side. I mean, we all saw stones, but I also saw the airflow. I smelt the fresh air, I saw the wind currents and, therefore, I knew there was another entrance or exit. The airflow was unobstructed which led me to believe that we can perhaps use this area for hiding our children, stocking weapons, and as an escape path if all else fails. Now, Sarge, can you get those new guys down here with shovels, pickaxes, and lanterns?"

The Sarge headed out of the mine, turned around, and humbly said, "I don't know what I would do without you people. Damn I love you guys, and I'm sure as hell glad I didn't terminate you." Hutang exclaimed, "So are we, my Sarge, so are we!"

When the Sarge returned with King, Gant, and Green, he found Hutang, Windom, and Earther, smiling and discussing the fact that Hutang was sitting on a giant diamond. The Sarge said, "Please tell me that's what I think it is."

Hutang smiled, and said, "Mr. Sarge, this rock, forever more, shall be called the "Rock of Hutang."

King asked, "Are these real diamonds or some kind of look alike?"

The Sarge replied, "These stones are as real as those snakes and spiders that are coming out of their hiding places. If you think that you can walk out of here with a stone or two, then you're in for a rude awakening. Never think about it or place them in your pockets. The reptiles will strike you with a vengeance."

As the group explored deeper into the mine, it became apparent that there was an enormous amount of precious stones lying around just for the taking. Hutang said, "Once this information gets out, the entire world is going to try to take these mines away from the Aboriginal people, one way or the other."

The Sarge paused, and said, "We could aways consider flooding this place until such time as we have the proper people, security, and materials to extract them methodically, securely, and safely transport them."

Earther replied, "This place could naturally become a new billabong by just removing several tons of dirt and rock, and during the rainy season, watch the place flood beyond reproach. At some point in time, this was all under water, we just have to find out where to approach the reconstruction if in fact that is a real consideration."

The Sarge said, "Look at the size of some of these stones, people will wipe out this entire continent to get to these stones. Someone knows this, and I bet you that is why close to one thousand mercs are coming here to clean out this area."

After traveling unimpeded over seventy yards, in the distance a glimmer of light could be seen, and Windom announced, "That is a small opening, that is not the one that is bringing us fresh air and a breeze with it. No, my friends, let's keep moving for I am sure that there is an unobstructed entrance into this place."

The appearance of diamonds began to disappear until there was only rocks and an occasional reptile skin. Forty or so feet in front of the group there was an obvious source of air presenting a strong draft. Windom said, "Now that's what I'm talking about. We've traveled approximately two hundred seventy-five yards from where we started, and look at that opening."

After clearing away brush, the Sarge neared the opening with caution, and was amazed at what he saw. He exclaimed, "Well, I'll be blessed, there is a natural dam built by our little friends, twenty feet from this entrance. As the rest of the group reached the opening, they were all in awe at what nature and its inhabitants could do. "Behold, look at what those lively creatures have done over the years. This billabong extends beyond the animal free zone, and appears to have several tributaries that will allow, if necessary, the flooding of mines.

God and the Spirits are great!" Ben Beckmire proclaimed. The Sarge looked at Windom, and confirmed, "Your name is as mighty as the wind that blows, my friend."

# # #

The drums from afar began to beat, and announce the arrival of people who were unfamiliar with the outback. Large scale fires were glowing in the distance that filled the entire outback with fear, because a single airborne ember could decimate millions of acres of land, and many animals. Wajickee appeared on the scene, and indicated to Darryl that he recommended that everyone in the village seek refuge in the mines because an unseasonal storm was going to put those massive fires out before they destroyed all of Australia.

The Sarge asked, when he encountered Wajickee, "Did you know that there is another exit and entrance to the diamond mine?"

Wajickee looked at Ben Beckmire, and responded, "Indeed I did. Why do you ask?"

Ben Beckmire looked at Wajickee, and said, "It would have been good of you to inform me of the other entrance/exit."

Wajickee, snidely remarked, "If you had asked, I would have informed. Not sure you want me trying to read your mind and interpret the mess that it processes."

Beckmire bowed low, and said, "Sometimes I forget who you are and what you are to me. I mean no disrespect, but sometimes I become overwhelmed when the odds are strikingly against me and my team."

After a long pause, Wajickee continued, by asking, "Did you happen to ask Darryl about your newfound exit?"

Being ever mindful that he had pissed off a spirit, Beckmire bowed again, and said, "My liege, I did not. Please temper your anger at me, for I am all consumed with the massive number of individuals who are coming here to end our existence."

Wajickee looked long at Ben Beckmire, and said, "With mounting insults, and the lack of faith, I command you to the billabong and sit for one hour, expressing your reservations to the Great Saltie. If he doesn't eat you whole, then I will put you to sleep, and conduct the battle by myself with the help of your friends, Darryl, the animals, and my faith. Never come at me like that again Ben Beckmire. Pessimism is not the trait of a great leader, and that is what I thought you were until you began to illustrate your lack of faith. You are in the land of your forefathers, those who come here for wealth will witness excessive pain and death.

Some members of your beloved crew might meet their conclusion, however, it all depends upon the amount of faith and courage their leader demonstrates. If you make weak and vacillating decisions, then many of your people will die. You Benjamin Beckmire are from a long list of royal beings and spirits. Act like you know this." Beckmire, for the first time in his life, saw Wajickee disappear before his very eyes.

Later when Ben Beckmire ran across his nephew, he said, "Darryl, I was looking at Wajickee, and I literally watched, and saw him disappear before my eyes, into a vapor of sorts."

Darryl's eyes opened as wide as possible, and he acted as if he had seen a ghost, dropped to his knees, placed his head to the ground, and muttered, "Only a spirit, can see another spirit move between worlds. My uncle, my Spirit, I humbly accept you, praise you, and will be your everlasting servant as long as I breathe life."

Ben Beckmire bellowed, "Get your narrow ass off your knees, and stop this spirit shit. I ain't no damn spirit, I am a mortal man, capable of being injured, dying, and becoming sick. Stop this spirit shit, and don't you dare mention this to anyone."

Darryl said, "My uncle, my Spirit, let me announce once again, only a spirit can see a spirit come and go. I will not debate your demands, but I will also not place my earthly being in jeopardy by acting like you are a normal human being. Uncle, if you saw Wajickee disappear, and a vapor-like trail followed, then I suggest that the next time you're in the presence of Wajickee or the Great Saltie, that you inquire about your ability to watch a spirit come and go. My uncle, I will rise, and I will act as if I am protecting a significant finding with my life. However, I will not create the notion of disrespect when addressing you. Please, and I beg you, confer with Wajickee, the Great Saltie, and your forefathers on Walkabout and Dreamtime."

CHAPTER FOURTEEN

The village was sectioned off into seven parts, with part seven being the escape tunnel through the diamond mines. The notion of spreading stones near the edge of the village gained overwhelming support. Darryl used King, Gant, and Green to distribute the precious stones. Darryl collected the stones by himself, and prayed over them. His prayer was that anyone removing stones from where they were placed, be targeted by spiders, ticks, and snakes, if they are not sanctioned.

King said to Gant, "This is a fortune that we're laying out for people to just pick up. Why don't we each put a stone in our pocket?"

Al Green responded, "I ain't doing stupid over here. Did you see that thing in the water? And you, want to mess around and steal a trinket? Man, distance your ridiculous ass from me. I'm not blowing this chance to live, for a damn stone."

King responded, "I just asked the question. I have no intention of challenging shit that I can't figure out. Okay, leave me be, I'm going to place my stones over there leading from the billabong. You two guys go east and west of here."

# # #

The drums became increasingly louder as the mercs got closer to the village. The children were placed on the school bus, and were driven to the airport where the people who ran the customs office armed themselves and promised that they would die before a single child was injured or captured.

At midnight, the night noises disappeared. Knowing that the plans for using the local tribes to throw spears and shoot arrows from the mountain ranges were discovered, the locals watched as mercs fired cannister after cannister of tear gas towards the tops of both mountain ranges. The recent storm left the mountain sides wet, and they absorbed a lot of the gas. The rest was blown westwardly impacting mercs more so than villagers.

Once in no man's land, where stones had been randomly placed, and where everything on that side of the line was eatable by the animals, a merc stepped on a stone, cut his flashlight on to examine it, and quickly placed it in his pocket. Another merc yelled, "Oh shit, look at the diamonds laying around for the picking. They can't be real," he stated. The men in this section began to fight over the stones, and gunfire erupted as they shot each other over the stones.

When the gunfire ceased, the commander of that division lay dead as well as the next in command. The surviving men abandoned their mission, and began foraging for precious stones. After an hour of digging wildly for stones, they were exhausted, and became easy prey for the animals. Those with stones were bitten by snakes, spiders, or ticks. The outcome was delirium, dehydration, and a painful death. Those who suffered gunshot wounds became the main menu on the buffet for the wombats and dingoes.

#

Hutang and his people were assigned two sections to defend. He and his forty men, made fast and decisive attacks on those nearing their sections by moving speedily through the merc's ranks, swiftly slicing and dicing them, as they disappeared into the night. The second barrage from his group was from their bows and arrows. All in all, fifty-two mercs were dead or injured from Hutang's men, in their initial confrontation. The mercs began firing indiscriminately in the direction that they thought they saw men run. Unfortunately for them, Hutang's men ran straight away, made a hard oblique to the left, and were now in the back of the merc's line, slicing and dicing men to their deaths. When the original group of two hundred mercs approached the no man's land, they were only one hundred and twenty. The leader of this group yelled, "Shoot every damn thing that moves, and things that don't. Let's keep those guys off us, because we can't counter their moves, their numbers, and their commitment."

As men became distracted by diamonds lying on the ground, more confusion erupted as they began to fight over the stones of death. Three men saw an extremely large stone, and began to knife fight over it, until a fourth man pulled out his pistol, and shot the three knife fighters, bent over, picked up the stone, only to be bitten by a Sydney funnel-web spider, the most venomous of its kind in all of Australia. All of the mercs who came in contact with the stones that were randomly thrown about to distract them, became immediately sick from the poisonous ticks and spiders that attached themselves to the diamonds.

In another part of the camp, the women were assigned to guard the entrance to a cave that housed snakes. This entrance was near the no man's land, and the women quickly fired a salvo of rounds, and disappeared behind huge boulders, and into a kill zone where Darryl, his crew along with members from the sewers, and the new guys waited for advancing mercs with lots of automatic weapons fire. As the mercs entered the killing zone, the women began to fire from behind the rocks without exposing themselves. In the meantime, Darryl's group, from another direction, pummeled the mercs unmercifully with automatic weapons fire that seemingly never ended. When this event ended, one hundred fifty mercs laid dead or mortally wounded.

Meanwhile Beckmire and his group, with Clyde and his crew were handling a different kind of warfare. Rashida engaged the signal scrambling device that Bertha developed which caused the mercs to lose control of their drones loaded with explosives. The drones began to crash and explode in merc encampments, leaving death and injury. Once Rashida realized that she could control the drones, she employed them on the mercs in several areas. In addition to exploding drones, Clyde and his crew had developed exploding projectiles, much like grenades being launched, and caused a significant amount of damage to the mercs as well.

Having no working communications, in any areas outside of the village, mercs began to fly the white flag. In other parts of the village, fierce fighting continued between the two groups. Tactical mistakes were made by the mercs when they assumed that firing tear gas cannisters at the mountain ranges would eliminate attacks from the air. The night breezes swept the remnants of the gas towards the mercs, thus freeing the ranges for the throwing of spears and the shooting of arrows. Chaos was abundant as two volleys of spears and arrows rained down on helpless men and women with nowhere to hide. Hundreds of people were slaughtered or mortally injured from the free-flowing volleys of spears and arrows.

There was a breach momentarily of the village boundaries when members from the sewers were temporarily overrun by advancing forces, but were turned back when Bertha and Rashida used the very weapon the mercs developed to inflict death on the group. Yes, the drones were a powerful weapon brought to the fight, but not secured in terms of its codes and internet IP addresses, and were used unmercifully against the aggressors.

The dingoes and wombats stuffed themselves on eatable bodies that were not poisonous. Many of the animals ate so much that they couldn't walk. Where Wajickee and Beckmire were, the battle was fierce, the animals attacked mercs in groups, thus further distracting the attackers, along with the diamonds on the ground.

In two groups, mercs began waving white flags indicating that they were surrendering. However, in the Beckmire led group, fighting continued, and was fierce and terminal. Three members of his contingency were killed, four received various wounds, and one died because he did not believe that the diamonds were for the benefit of the villagers. He knowingly slipped a small token into his pocket, and was eventually bitten by the Sydney funnel-web spider. His passing was enormously painful and hideous.

Hutang's group suffered several wounds, but his men kept fighting, and circled those attacking Beckmire's group from the rear, and eventually forced the mercs into a crossfire. When Hutang met up with the Sarge, he said, "Mr. Sarge, we have them shooting each other in the crossfire. Can you contact that wonderful daughter of yours, and have her send three drones with double the load, and drop the payloads once my people paint the ideal spot?"

The Sarge looked at Hutang, and said, "I would be toast, if you and your men weren't here to help out a friend." Hutang looking a little confused asked, "Mr. Sarge, you hungry?"

The Sarge laughed, and said, "My friend that is a colloquialism, you know just a saying, has nothing to do with the notion of eating. When and if we survive this mayhem, I'll tell you the full meaning."

In the meantime, the Sarge called Rashida, but her phone was answered by Bertha who said, "We could use a little help over here. Seemingly, they have RPGs, and are about to use them."

The Sarge asked, "Where is my daughter?"

"Oh, Mr. Sarge, she took a round in the arm, but she'll be alright if we can hold these vermin off."

The Sarge yelled, "Jilkes, John Lee, Hood, and Dempsey, load up and help my daughter. The people targeting their section are unloading RPGs. Guys, help my little girl and the others out."

When the group commissioned by the Sarge to help Rashida and the others, came across people trying to figure out how to use the RPGs, Jilkes commanded in a whisper, "Silencers, double head shots, and one to the heart. These guys were going to use RPGs against our women folk. No way we let these assholes draw another breath of this precious air."

The group with the RPGs were quickly dispatched of, and the RPGs were confiscated by Hood and Dempsey, two exemplary thieves, who were well aware of how to use the weapon. Dempsey signaled Jilkes, and pointed towards what looked like a field command center. Jilkes, through sign language, instructed Dempsey to place a rocket right in the middle of that compound. Without any delay, he prepared the weapon for firing. He hesitated, looked at Hood, and then said to Jilkes, "He is much more proficient at this mess than I am. I yield the firing scenario to Hood."

Jilkes looked at the man, and said, "I am so glad we didn't dispatch of you two. Give him the damn weapon, and let him do his thing."

Hood took aim at the makeshift command center, murmured fire in the hole, and engaged the firing mechanism on the weapon. The aftermath was incredible, in that the rocket hit the merc's ammo dump, and the ensuing explosions got everyone's attention. That fortuitous strike saved hundreds of lives on both sides of the equation. As the night sky became as bright as day, men and women began to disarm, and lay on the ground with weapons several feet away from their bodies.

Bertha reprogrammed a drone, sent it hovering over the group attacking Beckmire's section, filmed and provided a search light for those who were surrendering. The drone also broadcasted a message, "If a weapon of any nature is found on or near your person, you will be executed without trial or jury. Once again, if a weapon of any kind is found near or on your person, you will be unmercifully dispatched of with a bullet to the head."

# # #

Although many of the mercs had surrendered, succumbed to termination, or were still fighting for stones of death, a significant number of them had been allowed to ease past the billabong where the Great Saltie and other like predators were quietly waiting for the appropriate moment to enjoy a meal. As men passed the billabong, an astute merc asked, "Why wouldn't they protect this direct access into their village? We need to be extremely cautious because those guys aren't first timers, they've been fighting wars all over the damn world."

The squad leader said, "Keep it down and let's make sure that we're the owners of this place once we get into the middle of their camp. This is a life changing event people, and I don't plan on leaving here without a fortune in either gold or diamonds. Get your shit together and let's get this job done and over with. We're the last act. Hopefully and unfortunately, a significant number of our colleagues are no longer. Listen, get this through your heads, I strategically designed this attack, whereby, my group, you people, would be the clean-up team. People, I am not leaving here empty handed. Now, if some of you want to head back to the staging area, go ahead, and be my guest. But realize this, you ain't got a single penny in our benefits when we're successful. Hear me out, not a fucking penny."

As the group walked along the billabong and reached a point of no retreat and definitely no way to advance, the merc suggesting caution said, to the squad leader, "I just saw a monstrous head appear above the water. Did you see it?"

The squad leader looked at him, and said, "Mr. you spook my people, and I will with regret, place a bullet in your head. Are we clear?"

The men proceeded through the rough grass and marsh until they heard movement in front of them. The squad leader, in a low voice, commanded, "First three on my right and left, let's light that area up on the count of three."

The seven men began to randomly fire rounds at an indistinguishable target. However, the ricocheting bullets caught two people in another section. The 'idiot spy' and his wife received superficial wounds from the random firing.

As the first seven men began to reload, monstrous sounds could be heard all over the immediate area. What happened next was as savage, and as terminal as nature could be. Small, medium, large, and giant-sized crocs began to scurry through the marsh to feed on mercs. Screams and gunfire were evident as the mercs began to fire indiscriminately, hitting and killing other members of their squad. Ten or so minutes later, the only sounds heard were of bones being broken, chewed, and bodies of mercs being mercilessly ripped apart and eaten.

Other than a few sporadic weapons being fired, the gunfire began to subside, and more white flags began to be waved in the air. Ben Beckmire instructed his people to tell those waving white flags that they were to disarm, huddle in a circle, use glowsticks, and listen out for predators. He also instructed his people to tell the mercs that no quarters would be given until the rising sun could illuminate their positions, to see if they had weapons. If any person violates the terms of the white flag waving, then that entire section would be dispatched of without hesitation.

# # #

In the morning, the Sarge tended to his wounded. He adamantly stated, "Keep your captives in front of you at all times. Never find yourselves with your backs to the enemy. Also, if a pocketknife is discovered or any other kind of weapon, I want you to immediately kill that person or those persons. I will make a village wide plea to those people, and beg them to not have as much as toothpick on their body. I will sternly announce the consequences that will be irreversible."

The Sarge continued, and said to his people, "We are going to do this thing by the numbers, and we will always have the village behind us, and our people with long guns spotting for those who want to die for stupid. Systematically, we are going to have my main contingency supporting those who will place straps on those mercs. No bunching, no double lines, no talking. If someone steps out of place, execute him or her where they stand. Remember, these people came here to kill us, our children, our friends, the villagers, and to take whatever they wanted. No sir, fuckem, and the pigs they rode in on. No conversations, no question-and-answer sessions, just tell them to keep their mouths shut or receive a round to the head. People, some of us have been here before, and a lot of people were wounded when we were ambushed by a Gatlin gun using a drone to target my people. No, no! This will be done by the numbers. I will speak to Wajickee to have the animals lay low, but I want the snakes and spiders ready to send people to hell who can't follow rules."

John Lee asked, "Who be putting wire ties on them there people?"

The Sarge responded, "I want Angel, Anel, Hood, and Dempsey, with Michael overseeing the process. I don't want anyone to get creative, and try to help a wounded person. Place wire tires on their asses, and if possible, seek help after they are secured. No risk, damn it. We've been here before, and it wasn't pretty at all."

Jilkes stood up, and said, "Sarge what my illiterate friend wanted to ask was why are we doing babysitting work. We know how to secure people."

The Sarge smiled, and said, "I'm just feeling notions of what happened in the mid-west. That shit ain't never going to happen as long as I breathe fresh air."

Zanthius who was screaming and executing people on contact exclaimed, "One of you morons, shot my wife. I'm going to kill every damn soul here."

His father, after tending to his daughter-in-law, corralled his son, and said, "I had this conversation with you several times in the past. If you pull that trigger again without my consent, I will personally beat the living shit out of you. I love my son, but my son needs to have his ass whipped to understand the nature of who we are. I don't want to fight or beat my son, but my son needs to know that when I say, no more, I mean no more. Now, my son, are you prepared to fight your father?" Zanthius fell to his knees, and said, "I would rather end my life than disrespect our love for one another, and fight my father. I love you Benjamin Beckmire, and I will never consider doing battle with my only existing parent. Please dad, forgive me. I promise I will listen and learn your humanity."

Ben Beckmire stared at his son, reached down, and grabbed him by his hands, pulled him to the standing position, and with tears in his eyes, said, "I love you so very, very, much my son. I apologize for challenging you in combat, but I need you to temper that dimension of you that I have cautioned you about." The two men cried, held each other, and in front of the entire village, confirmed who they were and what they meant to the group and the community.

# # #

Later during the day, Asiram, after seeing Courtney, said to Monica, "My husband went ballistic because someone shot me. If this is the extent of a bullet wound, a crease to the arm, then I'll take one for each member of the group."

Monica said, "I'm pissed because these people have interrupted my evening of drinks with my friend and busting on her ass about things in the past."

Courtney said, "The one thing you won't have to worry about girlfriend, is busting on my ass. I have enough sorry stories about you to write three books. What pisses me off is that I haven't had a drink in thirty-six hours. Once we figure out what to do with these people, I'm going to sit, drink, cry, and realize that this is the greatest group on earth, and I love everyone here."

# # #

Angel, Anel, Dempsey, and Hood began to place double wire ties on each individual as Darryl, and Larry watched carefully, and Michael made sure each person was targeted in case of an infraction. Angel approached a woman who was apparently in pain, and who was pleading for mercy. As Angel bent over to help her, the woman raised her hand with a small knife in it. Hood and Dempsey dispatched of her, and three people to the left and right of her. Michael announced, "Try that shit again, and we will blow each of you straight to hell."

Jilkes stated, "Before your people move to a subject, make sure we have two beams on their ass. We almost lost one of ours because she was trying to be compassionate about helping a feigning woman. Listen, if they move the wrong way, or sneeze, then we are going to execute them with two shots to the head."

After securing the mercs in their section, the Sarge instructed Hood, Dempsey, Anel, and Angel to proceed to the area near the billabong, and secure it, but not to get too close because the crocs and other animals were still in a feeding frenzy. The Sarge bellowed out, "Hood, you're senior. Is that clear everyone?"

Once the four members of the group got near the billabong area, the sound of bones being crunched and broken could be heard. Anel asked, "Are we a safe distance away?"

Hood responded, "I really don't know, but I'm thinking we are because we hear noises, but we don't see any crocs or other animals. Dempsey, what say you?"

"Boss, I say, we need to back up another fifty yards or so, and just listen for faint sounds and aggressive movement."

Hood looked at his team, and said, "You heard the man. Let's get the hell out of here. I can't imagine being eaten by one of those critters, let alone being chewed to death by a damn dingo."

The group moved fifty or so yards to the west, closer and almost infringing on the line of demarcation that allows the animals to enjoy whatever or whoever crosses into that territory. Hood said, "I'm not feeling this area. It smells of fresh carrion which makes me feel as though we may be in the eat what crosses the line area. I want to retreat another thirty yards to the east."

As the group made their way towards an artificial point, Wajickee appeared, and cautioned, "You are too close to the eat whatever line. Take your people and move them one hundred yards to the south where you will find people trying to figure out how to operate rocket launchers. Be ever so stealthy because they have lookouts. Head directly towards those sand dunes. Spread your people out, but not too much." Hood started to respond, but Wajickee was long gone. Hood said, "That Wajickee person told me to move one hundred yards south because people are trying to figure out how to use rocket launchers. Let's head out."

Anel said, "We've been here, and close to you all day, and none of us saw Wajickee."

Hood looked at her, and said, "We're in Australia, in the outback, where some crocs are as big as airplanes, and they eat people. I am just relaying what was said to me by the spirit. You may question it, but I don't. And if you do, that means you are questioning my authority that was given to me by the Sarge. Is that correct?"

Dempsey said, "People, I am not going to debate his information or his epiphany, I am going to move with him, one hundred yards south of here. I suggest we all get with the program and make sure that our people are safe."

Anel cozied up to Hood, and stated, "I love your decision-making skills. Lead me on, my future lover and husband."

Hood, hearing this information, broadly smiled, and said, "Saddle up people, be alert, and look out for people spotting for those trying to figure out a complex weapon. No injuries, let's do this mission, and get back to the main force."

#

Approximately, one hundred twenty-five yards from where Hood was directed by Wajickee, Demspey threw his fist in the air, and whispered "I smell cigarette smoke." Hood whispered, "So do I."

The group took up defensive positions, and placed ten to fifteen feet between them. Hood threw his hand in the air, and everyone froze. He pointed to the southeast, and signaled Dempsey and Angel to head in that direction, and that he and Anel would continue due south. As Anel and Hood saw what was going on, a projectile was fired accidently. Someone with authority said, "Didn't I tell you not to mess with that thing until I got the codes? Are you crazy? You could have killed one of us, and not those Abos."

Both ladies had their powerful bows with them, Hood communicated, these guys are still planning to use those things against our people. I count twelve, that's three each. On my mark." Wajickee slid next to Hood, scared the crap out of him and Anel, and said, "There are twelve in sight, and another twenty-four, just around that bend. Call Rashida, and have her send one or two of their drones to the place where I left a bright yellow flag."

Dempsey made the call to Rashida and Bertha, and said, "Send the drone high, and I will search for the marker." Five or so minutes later, Bertha announced, "I see you worthless assholes who kill for money. I be a God-fearing woman, but my tolerance has been exceeded."

Rashida hearing this asked, "Would you like to be directly responsible for the demise of those people who want to kill all of us, Clyde, the children, and all of these wonderful natives?"

"Give me that controller! Bertha exclaimed. If I can't pray you into a better life, then I certainly can end the one that you have." With no further ado, Bertha said, I'm going to crash this drone right in the middle of those evil, non-believing, s-o-bs."

The night sky lit up once again, and the agony and pain could be heard for a few minutes and then the night became silent once again. Hood yelled to the twelve in his group's sight, "Drop the weapons or suffer the same fate as your comrades."

There is always a couple of cowboys in most groups who think they're faster than the people targeting them. In this case, twelve men and women decided to grab their weapons and attempt to spray the nearby vicinity. Prior to them gathering their weapons, four were hit by high powered bows, four were provided head shots, and the four trying to escape, were hit by arrows and gunfire. Not enough to kill them, but the weak, young, and old animals, would have a wonderful meal.

# # #

Back in camp, Darryl said to his uncle, "The safest place for them, and us tonight is in the mines. We know what the snakes and spiders will do, but they don't. We can place them in the lower quadrant and let them look at the very thing that they would kill us for, but they themselves would never touch or enjoy the artificial benefits the stones bring."

Beckmire looked at his nephew, and said "I like your plan, my concern is that we don't know how many others are out there lurking in the dark planning our demise. If we go deep into the mines, then they could conceivably pour gasoline and throw grenades in our captive space."

"Uncle, please forgive me for not completing my thought. We purposefully let them see us descend into the mines, and we leave where Windom exposed a forgotten and hidden entrance/exit."

"Now nephew, I like that thinking. However, once we come out of the other side, we are clearly without provisions, ammunition, medical supplies, and a few other things," Beckmire expressed.

Darryl fell to his knees, and said, "I neglected to tell you that we have stations around the village with all that you have mentioned. We recognized the likelihood that this village, and the others will always be under attack as long as they are the source of stones and nuggets. That is why the opening of the other mines throughout the outback is moving slowly. Until we control the environment, can secure the villages and the mines, it will continue to be us against the world, with them eventually evolving a mechanism that will allow them to take control of the mines, and kill all of the people."

"My nephew, why do you keep falling to your knees when you have something to say, or an omission to acknowledge?" Ben Beckmire asked.

"Because uncle, once again, ordinary people cannot see a spirit come and go. You acknowledged that you saw Wajickee leave, the vapor trail disappear until he was no longer in your space. I, once again state, only a spirit can see another spirit come and go. I know you have not mentioned this to Wajickee because you know that you are his replacement unit. Uncle we all will go to the great beyond, but you will not be going anytime soon. However, you will go, and you will retire your friend, and send him home for the peace and rest that he deserves. Uncle, I know this because I too, can see him come and go, and I also know that Jelani is getting closer to having that vison, but not believing what he thinks he saw. Uncle, I only ask that you not share this information with the fabulous and most acclaimed Dr. Courtney. Unfortunately, when a spirit confesses to a mortal of significance that they can see spirits come and go, well, if the spirit is to remain of this earth, then those who he or she confesses to, will be no more."

Darryl turned away for a moment, and then forcefully stated "Uncle, I know you think I'm smoking some new kind of weed, but I assure you, I am not engaging in any such events, and I am definitely not blowing smoke up your ass as I have often heard you say. Guard the information, and eventually, Wajickee will bow to you, and fall to his knees. His acknowledgment allows him to barter with you to gain favor, and some smidgeon of existence in the here and now world, as he resides in that ever-vaporizing dimension that he is accustomed to. Wajickee will be your guide, and has always been your friend. Heed his messaging, especially since he is now computer literate, and knows the world wide web better than those who constructed it."

"Darryl, get off your knees, stand and talk to me to my face, and never again, and I do mean, never again, shall you, or will you, fall to your knees unless you have clearly screwed up an assignment. Are we clear?" Ben Beckmire inquired.

CHAPTER FIFTEEN

At first light, Beckmire's group began planning how they were going to help those who peacefully surrendered, out of the feasting zone of the animals. Hood said, "Once in the desert, we managed two hundred forty prisoners by stating one important fact."

The Sarge asked, "What was that?" Hood smiled, and said, "We told them if a single person does stupid, we will turn our weapons on them, and not stop firing until everyone was dead."

The Sarge said, "The only difference between the desert and here, is the diamonds and gold. Some of those captives found a precious stone, but I'm doubtful that they are still alive. No sir, the spiders, and snakes, and only God and the Spirits know what drives them, will not let you live with a precious stone on your person, if you're not sanctioned. Anyway, back to the issue, who do you need to make it happen in each section?"

Hood responded, "I'll need the sisters, Dempsey, Jelani, and maybe Larry and his brother."

"Who is Larry's brother?" The Sarge asked.

"You of all people should know that Mr. Beckmire, it's Zanthius."

"I knew, I just didn't know that you knew it. How would you use Larry and his brother?"

"Mr. Beckmire, I would use them as spotters searching for sudden movements, weapons, and anyone with beady eyes," Hood stated. The Sarge looked at him, and said, "I'm afraid to ask you to describe what beady eyes look like. However, I want to know, so please define beady eyes."

"Mr. Beckmire, you remember how you looked at me and Demspey when we let you capture us, well, beady eyes are the eyes you examined us with. You know, they have death as a final solution, no matter the interventions or potential deals."

The Sarge looked at him, and asked, "Do you want to continue to mock me, or do you want to round up our prisoners and prepare them for interrogation?"

"On it Sarge. Dempsey, get the ladies, and I'll ask Zanthius, his brother, and Jelani," Hood said.

# # #

Man after man, woman after woman, and hour after hour, people swore up and down that they did not know who their employers were. They indicated that they responded to an ad, gave a few qualifications and the desire to conclude all that was in the way of the employers gaining their rightful place and assets. Dempsey loudly exclaimed, "Fuckem! Let's kill them all, and move on to the next group." He slid the bolt back on his weapon that sent the 1st bullet from the sleeve of the weapon, into the chamber. Hood made the same move, as well as the two sisters. Dempsey screamed, "On my mark!" As soon as he said that a guy yelled, "The man who owned the house on the stilts."

Everyone backed down, and Dempsey screamed, "We already know that bullshit. Who is his damn partner?"

The same person asked, "If I give you an idea, will you still kill us or get us to the airport?"

Dempsey looked at Hood, and said, "Those cooperating will be given every ounce of compassion and transportation, those handing out bullshit will be wounded, and the animals will be allowed to share your bodies as you are consumed alive."

Another guy yelled, "We don't know who his partner is, we only know about him because of pictures of his house being blown off the stilts, and crashing down the hill in front of his property. The only other thing we heard as a group was that someone in your network was involved in determining the outcome. Obviously, not the outcome they expected."

Hood yelled, "We already know about the colonel, and we'll deal with him in a permanent manner soon."

The man yelled, "I wasn't referring to the colonel. I was talking about someone in your inner sanctum that seemingly knows a lot, and shares a lot about you people. I hear that person is somehow connected to your leader."

Hood proclaimed, "Rubbish! People I need better intel than that or I'm going to hold a massacre right here and now. Don't give me rumors, give facts that can be substantiated. Somebody at some point in time must have heard people speaking about an unknown person with a name." A quiet came over the area, and a woman yelled, "The person of concern is apparently an idiot, or has some kind of mental issues."

Hearing that bit of information, Dempsey summoned Mallory and the Sarge, and when they arrived, Hood repeated, "A woman in this group yelled that the person who may be involved in this matter has some kind of mental issues and some refer to him as an idiot."

The Sarge bellowed out for all to hear, near and far, "Bullshit. My son, Zanthius Beckmire De Lombardo is neither an idiot, nor a conspirator against me or my friends. Get that bullshit out of here."

Demspey, trying to ease the Sarge out of his current mindset, asked, "Can we transport these people to the airport, and be done with them?"

Mallory, realizing that the Sarge was in a funk as a result of the innuendo, responded, "I see no benefit in inflicting further pain on these mercs. Secure them, and take pictures of each one of them."

Mallory looked at the captives, and said, "If you ever attempt to come up against us again, God have mercy on any relatives you have. We will contract with some very thorough friends of ours in Northern Africa, and have them slay, cousins, nephews, nieces, daughters, grandmothers, grandfathers, and every fricken body else associated with your lineage until your DNA has been erased."

# # #

Later at the airport, the slightly wounded woman who spoke of the idiot, said to Hood, "Listen, I have nothing to gain by saying this, but I distinctly heard on two occasions, references to the word idiot and mental illness. Just saying, and thanks for the parley from all of us. Not sure we would have given you guys the same acknowledgement."

Hood, without a basis for his actions, asked, "What will you do when you get back? Why on earth did you sign up for this kind of work."

The woman teared up, and said, "My husband, who I love to death, convinced me that the world was purple, and his way was the only way or the highway, told me to get hard or get lost. I loved this man without limits, until I found out that this man was another man's bitch. I wanted more than a wound. I wanted to be in that bronze box."

The woman began to limp up the steps when Hood asked, "You want to try something different, that is people oriented, and pays well?"

The woman turned around, and said, "That's the same "bs" that my husband sold me, as he beat me during sex, and suggested that I should like it."

Hood, almost tearing, asked again, "Would you like to try something different that helps people help themselves?"

The woman turned around again, and asked, "Tell me who first coined that saying and belief?"

Hood smiled, and replied, "The Lion of Zion, the Reverend Leon Howard Sullivan."

The woman's eyes opened as wide as apples, and she asked, "What do you know about Rev. Sullivan?"

Hood responded, "He had an OIC in Omaha that I attended prior to enlisting in the military."

The woman asked, "Is this a sincere offer, or are you in need of someone to exploit?"

Hood smiled, and said, "I am taken, but I feel that you can be of help to yourself and others if you're honest, sincere, and you are willing to dedicate your life to helping people help themselves."

Hearing this exchange, Demspey acknowledged, "I am so enormously proud of you, my friend. You just edged up another level in my book of humanity. I forgot about how we met, and it was at that OIC in Omaha, and the leader was named Dr. Dodd. Damn, you never forgot what got us to where we are, where we almost ended up, and how we changed to become better human beings." He looked at the woman Hood was talking to, and stated, "This is an opportunity of a lifetime. He is staking his life, reputation, and everything else on converting you to the mindset of Dr. Sullivan. One time offer, now or never."

The woman paused, looked at the steps, turned around and said, "I have faith in what you say. Please help me to help people help themselves."

# # #

The wounded were loaded on the transport plane first, those who surrendered were next, and finally, a bronze 12 x 12 x 12 box was carried on the plane. It had the identification tags of those who died in their adventure to gain power and wealth, at the cost of anyone who stood in their way. They paid the ultimate price.

# # #

The following morning, the weapons, and munitions that each dead person had on or near them was confiscated by the natives, and the group. Darryl was responsible for collecting the stones from those who picked them off the ground. At one place, the bodies that were consumed by the dingoes and wombats were a bit much to comprehend. People who had bullet proof vests on were torn out of the protection and consumed until nothing relating to a human being, was present. Anel said to Angel, "I can't do this. This is too much for me to stomach."

Angel replied, "Just be thankful that someone isn't picking up our weapons and looking at what remained of us."

Individuals attacked by spiders and snakes became the guests of a huge fire held in a cave to guard against embers blowing into the environment and starting a fire. After a full day of loading weapons, and in some cases, toxic human remains, the group was bushed, and ready to spend, hopefully, a peaceful night.

# # #

The next day, Hutang and his group prepared to load a bunch of weapons, and smuggled them aboard his ship. The Sarge, openly said to the customs agent, "My friend who came from afar to help us in our moment of crisis, has loaded useless weapons aboard his ship. Is that going to be a problem?" The agent turned around, and said, "I can't hear or see you for the next twenty minutes because I am looking for a file that I can't find."

Hutang and his people expeditiously loaded the contraband aboard the ship, and when the Sarge saw the name of the ship, tears came to his eyes. The ship was named "The Sarge". Beckmire hugged the man, and said, "I love you and hope to see you again, but not with so much drama and death near. Maybe it's time for me and my people to come to your village. Think about it, and let me know when would be a good time. Love you Hutang."

# # #

Later at the airport, Clyde and his crew boarded the plane along with members of the ex-colonel's group. One of the men said to the Sarge, "The colonel is dead, and doesn't know it. We'll try to bleed info from him first, but he is already dead.

We appreciate what you have done for us, and if this sort of mess shows up again, make a call to the sewers, and we'll be ready to lend a hand."

# # #

That afternoon, John Lee said to Jilkes, "Oh boy, we had better stay away from the Sarge today?'

Jilkes, nonchalantly asked, "Why is that my country friend?"

"Boy you be as dumb as my dumbest piglet. That there wizard fellow is on his knees, and not the boss. He must have really fucked something up because he be kowtowing to the Sarge in a fierce manner. Ain't it supposed to be the other way around?"

Jilkes looking long and hard at the scene announced, "Big Country, I agree with you on this one. He must have really screwed up. Listen, let's not go that way, why don't we double back to our huts until we're summoned. This looks awfully bad, the conjurer bowing low and avoiding eye contact with the Sarge. I'm going to my hut, and I am not coming out until someone beckons me."

As the two men turned around, a booming voice could be heard all over the village, saying, "Jilkes and John Lee, I need to talk to you. Now!"

Jilkes said, "Oh boy, we were at the wrong place, at the wrong fricken time. Please don't say or do anything that will stimulate his rage."

When the two men walked up to the Sarge, he said, "I am having a difficult time with those who I see as my brain trust when I am here. I told Darryl that I saw Wajickee disappear, and leave a vapor trail, and the kid fell to his knees. Just now,

Wajickee came to me, announced that I was his replacement unit, fell to his knees, and asked, "When would you like to assume my role?" I told him in a million years, I might consider challenging his position, but right now, I am with my crew until the day I die. I also told him to tell the entire spirit world, even at my demise, I could never replace the greatest teacher on earth, and that as long as I am of this earth, he is never to descend to his knees to me. I told him that I will always be on my knees because he has continuously mentioned that I was a challenge. You two are the only ones who are sanctioned for this information. Do not, repeat."

The Sarge sighed, and announced, "Guys, we need to head back stateside, and sort out our issues. Here, the game is getting too complex. I can't compete with people who are beside you one minute, and the next, who knows where the hell they are. Anyway, tell no one of these issues, and I want to be out of here in the next forty-eight hours, I want to be on our plane heading to *The Sanctuary*. Let's leave Jelani in charge and assign King, Gant, and Green, as his first tier if he so accepts. I would also like to leave the sisters, Hood, and Dempsey, but we need to keep all of the children together. I would like to begin excavations from the new areas that everyone knows about except those who have to mine them, protect them, and secure them."

John Lee responded, "Sarge, before you be making that assignment with those new fellas, I would like to have a short conversation with them to make sure that they are on the same page as our group. And of course, I would have my minority representative present as well."

Jilkes looked at him, and responded, "Sarge, he has been like that for damn near over fifty years. Do I get pissed and offended by his racist statements? Naw, Sarge. I realize that he is a mental midget trying to operate in the big boy's air space. I'll continue to help his dumb ass."

"You two, seemingly, are unable to find a happy medium, yet you are always together and if not, you're seeking information on the other's whereabouts. I learned long ago to never cross the road on you two, but I have to admit it sometimes troubles me how you people interact. I'm just saying, sometimes it doesn't appear to be healthy."

John Lee exclaimed, "Why is everyone always trying to be our psychologist or therapist. He ain't mad about anything I've said today, and I ain't pissed at him for calling me dumb all the time. We be in a good place. Ain't that right Jilkes?"

"You called me Jilkes."

John Lee hastily responded, "No I didn't. I ain't said no dumb shit like that."

"Sarge, didn't you hear him call me Jilkes?" Jilkes inquired.

The Sarge replied, "I am not going to get caught up as a witness for the defense or the plaintiff. Call me Wes, and keep me out of that mess."

John Lee walked over to Jilkes, and asked, "Do you be feeling offended or something?"

"John Lee, I just love and respect you no matter how much you try to belittle me," Jilkes stated. He looked at John Lee and saw that he was about to flood the area with teardrops. Jilkes said, "Everything is good my country friend. I ain't got no beef with you, and you be who you be, the dumbest country pig farmer that I have ever met and loved. We good brother, draw them tears back into that well. Let's go and talk to them three suspicious, but potential team members."

# # #

John Lee and Jilkes summoned Jelani to discuss the potential direction that the Sarge was planning for the next few months. They told him that it was definite that he would be stationed in the outback, lending assistance to Darryl, Sue Lynn, and coordinating the excavation or flooding of the various outlier mines and access points. John Lee, cutting through the chase, asked, "What you be thinking about them there new people that you went to Nebraska with. Do you think you can trust them?"

Jelani looked at John Lee, and asked, "What do you mean trust them? I mean if you do stupid here, you die here, unless you're sanctioned. I'm just trying to figure out exactly what you mean before I delve into the essence of your question."

John Lee looked at Jelani long and hard, and announced, "I didn't understand a damn thing you just said. Can you put that in English?"

Jilkes touched John Lee, and said, "Brother, let me give it a try."

Jilkes after comforting John Lee, said to Jelani, "The Sarge is not sure about the fabric of those three guys, and wants to know if you can handle them?"

Jelani looked at Jilkes, laughed, and said, "Collectively or individually, they are not a threat to me on this continent. As a matter of fact, I want them here, I want them to do sweat equity in the mines. I want them to account for those precious stones in the midst of snakes and spiders, and I want them to try to do stupid. Doing stupid here is a death sentence guys. And let me say, I have the utmost respect for you two pirates. I have heard a lot about how you two saved the lives of the group on many occasions. I honor and respect you both, although I don't understand some of the characterizations that you two throw at each other, but I do know to stay in my lane because obviously, this has been going on way before I was born."

John Lee walked quickly towards Jelani, grabbed him, hugged him, and said, "You be the first damn spirit that knows what's happening, but be smart enough to stay in his lane. I be at your beck and call. If you need me, and I will bring him along, just don't hesitate. I be done had you all wrong, and I'm glad I had this chat with you. I will convince my not too smart friend that you're good people. Don't worry, I'll manage his ass."

Thirty minutes later, Gant, Green, and King walked near the billabong where Jelani, Jilkes, and John Lee were sitting. Once again cutting through the chase, John Lee asked, "How many times did you people consider putting one or two of those stones in your pockets?"

Green and Gant looked at King, who announced, "I considered it more than once. I have also come to realize that this is not your ordinary place. I have seen animals that I didn't know exist, I have seen things in the water that reminded me of the movie Jurassic Park, and I have seen a merc reach down, pick up a stone, place it in his pocket, and seconds later, watch spiders and snakes bite the shit out of him. Yes, I thought about it, but I am truly clear about the fact that this ain't your ordinary place."

John Lee said, "Damn boy, that be a mouthful. How about you other people, you got anything to add to that equation?"

Green said, "Listen, I was spreading the things around as if they were candy for children at a Halloween party. I'm a simple man looking for the good life like everyone else. I know that sometimes, things ain't what they seem to be. It's unlikely that I'll be able to get my child from under the clutches of his mother because that's her paycheck until she finds a new scam to participate in. The mother uses him for her welfare checks, and has not mentioned to him that I may still be among the living. Sir, I just want to do what's right, earn a ticket home, and collect my child. I have no interest in acquiring something that I am not entitled to."

Gant said, "I saw them and knew from the jump, shit laying around ain't for the picking. I therefore knew that there was a death knell somewhere near. I just want a steady job to present to the court and hopefully have the court remand my child to me."

Jilkes after considering what each man had said, responded, "I am going to give you guys a chance to do the right thing. If you want employment that guarantees you benefits, a steady income, and an investment strategy, then we can make that happen. Insofar as your children are concerned, once you get through our artificial probationary period, our lawyers will hire lawyers indigenous to where your children are, and if they want to be with you instead of their mothers, then so be it. We can make that happen. Your tasks will be ominous in that you're going to be left here to provide security, advice as to how to secure other mines, help in the transport of all stones and nuggets, and you will earn more money than you can count. Here's the thing with our group, we don't do stupid things, and we don't buy stupid. If you need a Rolls, or a Benz, then you might want to find another job. This opportunity is an adventure, and like any adventure, there is hardly a need for those kinds of wheels. Now that's just a subtle statement of fact. We also don't condone gaudy rings and chains weighing down the neck as well."

Al Green raised his hand, and when acknowledged he said, "Guys, you don't understand where we're coming from. We are trying to leave the 'hood', begin an adventure that is life sustaining, and that takes us far away from the shithole we've been living in. I dedicate my life to proving that I will be a worthy hire, will be obedient, trustworthy, and faithful to the mission of this group. See, we learned a lot about you people when those hundreds of men probably focused on your age, and how few you were. Their problem was that they should have focused on your character and determination, not the numbers in your group. That's all I have to say, I ain't speaking for nobody, but me. I'm going to talk out of school for a moment, and say that I chased King away from me because he was considering putting a trinket in his pocket. I mean we all couldn't believe our eyes, but I also couldn't believe my eyes when I saw that thing in the billabong. I say all that to say, I know that he has changed, but I can only speak for myself."

Before being asked, King said, "That snitching ass Al Green. Yes sir, I was spreading them stones around like candy, and wanted so desperately to place one in my pocket. I mentioned it to the guys, and they ostracized me. I made my amends, and I too have learned an important lesson, and that is if you're spreading them around like fertilizer, then you'd better not try to eat them or take them."

Gant empathically stated, "We all had that avarice look in our eyes, but again we defended where we were assigned, and we saw how the animals dispatched of those mercs without any mercy. A couple of those stones would go a long way where we're from, but not far enough. We all had that look, but we all overcame it individually and collectively. That's all I have to say."

Jilkes said, "The truth shall set you free. Okay, you will all report to Jelani, who is younger, smarter, and a former FBI field agent. Now, we are going to have to make you complete the following background checks: child abuse, criminal background, and FBI clearances.

Now, depending on what comes back, we will make you a full fledge member of our group. Now guys, don't make me waste my time, have any of you done major time for any crime or abuse?" All three men responded that they had not been involved with the real law. John Lee asked, "What other kind of law you be knowing about?"

Gant paused for a moment, and said, "That asshole over there damn near caused a riot in the desert. Some guy kept looking at him in a strange way, and they finally got it on, and his friends and our friends had a free for all. We spent three days in the brig until there was a need for our services."

"What be them there services that you people be special at?" John Lee inquired.

King responded, "Much like the things you do to people."

"Oh, I see," John Lee responded.

Jilkes looked at Jelani, and asked, "What do you think?" Jelani motioned for Jilkes and John Lee to walk with him out of the hearing range of the three men he interviewed. Once a fair distance away from the three men, Jelani started moving his hands in an absolute negative manner, all while verbally articulating that he liked the three men, and felt that he could handle them individually as well as collectively. Jelani even clearly articulated the words "Under no circumstances." Jelani watched each man's reaction to his orchestrated negative attitude, and he knew he had them concerned with his antics. He said to Jilkes, "I want you to admonish me, and tell me that they are mine to kill or keep." When the three men heard this, their hearts collectively fell to their feet.

Jelani looked at the three men, and said, "You will be loyal, respectful, trustworthy, and not a pain in my ass. Am I crystal clear?"

The three men shook their heads, and that is when Jelani screamed, "I can't hear your heads speak. Verbalization is a must in a relationship with me, am I clear again?"

The three shouted, "Crystal clear, and we agree." Jelani smiled, walked over to each man, and gave them a surprisingly strong handshake, and welcomed them aboard. He then said, "Many wonderful things can happen if you listen, be loyal, be trustworthy, and place the group first. I am staking a lot on you guys, please do not let me down."

As the men thanked him, and began to walk away, Jelani asked, "Gentlemen, do you know what you are going to be doing? Do you know what you're going to earn? Do you know what benefits you'll have? I have a couple of other questions that I would ask before signing on to this group, if I were you."

Each man stared at Jelani, and Al Green asked, "Is it possible for us to discuss those things later, we're just happy to be alive and well at the moment?"

Jelani said, "Sure, go and have some piss, and maybe I'll join you for one or two."

CHAPTER SIXTEEN

Mr. West called Mr. East, and screamed, "We wasted a lot of money, and we don't have shit to show for it."

Mr. East calmly stated, "I wouldn't totally agree with that. We know where the mines are, we know that snakes and spiders protect them, we know that those who came from afar to provide additional protection will be leaving sooner than later, and I know that I have twenty experienced snipers placed around that village. So, I wouldn't totally agree with you. Insofar as money is concerned, the project wasn't successfully completed, and if any of those signing the contract read the small print, it clearly indicates that payment is contingent on the successful completion of all terms of the agreement. Therefore, if I were you, I would shut the website down, drop the 800 numbers, and remove all possible indicators that reference our group. It was done online, you nor I ever signed a damn thing, we just paid the fee, and the service company made all of the arrangements. As I see it, we paid nothing, but airfare and a per diem. Am I correct?"

After a long pause, Mr. West agreed, and said, "I guess you're correct, we only lost a couple hundred grand in transportation and per diems. It's so smart of you to know how to structure contracts, and arrange shit online without any connections. I guess that education of yours is paying off. By the way, do we have a body count for them and us?"

Mr. East responded, "I heard that several of them received wounds, but to what extent, I can't attest. However, in forty-eight hours, the people who read the small print and know where to find me will begin to pick off the main characters."

# # #

Activities in the camp proceeded as normal without any indication that the group was planning to leave the outback in four hours. In exactly four hours prior to when the assassins were to begin their work. The Sarge gave the word, and people picked up their fanny packs, backpacks, and proceeded to the school bus. It was early in the morning, and before the assassins could coordinate a response, the group had boarded the school bus, and were on their way to the airport.

Rashida with her scrambler still in active mode, noticed that someone was trying to make a call near the village using a satellite phone. She allowed the call to connect, and the caller asked, "Are you prepared to execute our alternative plan?"

"The group left early, and are heading to the airport." The receiving voice exclaimed.

"What the fuck! Were you able to begin the mission?" The caller inquired. The receiving person said, "You gave explicit directions insofar when to execute the plan." The person making the call disconnected it.

Rashida made her way to where her dad was sitting, and said, "You need to hear this conversation that I just intercepted from a Sat phone near the village." She proceeded to play back the recording, and the Sarge asked, "When did you record this?"

Rashida responded, "Literally, three minutes ago, and what I'm thinking isn't nice." The Sarge continued to play the conversation over and over again. He then asked Rashida, "Can you reach Darryl and Jelani? I think we left some assassins near the village who might be the alternative solution if and when the others failed?"

Rashida called Darryl on the Sat phone, and when he answered, he announced, "I believe there are, no, I know there are people hiding in the mountain ranges, and other places as well. I saw two places come alive with movement, and Jelani indicated to me that he saw one."

Rashida said, "Hold on, here's my dad."

The Sarge took the phone, and said, "Nephew, if you had to guess, what's the range of where you believe people are hiding?"

"Uncle, I would say, four hundred to six hundred yards away."

Wajickee appeared, and said, "Those people dug holes, and are hiding in the ground with long guns. Master, I mean Mr. Beckmire, give me the okay, and I'll have them people provide lunch for my animal friends."

The Sarge asked, "Do you think it's possible that two or three of them could be taken alive, and I definitely want the Sat phone that they used to communicate with someone across the water. Wajickee, please don't call me Mr. Beckmire or Master, ever again. I beg of you."

"I hear and I obey. I will seek out the instrument first, thus crippling any chances of them communicating with each other." The Sarge paused for a moment, and then said, "I want to send the new guys on this mission, Darryl are you listening?"

"I am, Uncle. I'll send them with Michael as the lead," Darryl responded.

The Sarge stated, "Excellent."

# # #

With an old battery-operated bullhorn, Michael began to announce, "We know exactly where you are. Your mission is busted. Come out of your holes, place your weapons in front of you, and no harm will befall you. If there is as much as a toothpick found on your possession, you will be summarily dispatched of, or fed to those growling sounds that you're hearing near each of your hiding places." He repeated the exact message three times. As he stood in the middle of the village, a shot rang out, and landed a few feet from his foot. Michael looked down at the hole in the ground, turned around, and casually walked to safety. The person firing the shot, also one of the individuals with a Sat phone, found his hole being dug up by dingoes. He attempted to turn around, but one of the animals found his boot, and began to pull on it until others had an opportunity to get to his legs. The man screamed for ten minutes or better before he was consumed alive.

Michael behind cover yelled, "Any further stupidity, and the animals will feast on the nineteen of you that are left." The men realizing that Michael knew their exact number began to shed their weapons, and vacate the holes they had dug. Once seeing the animals, a few of the men tried to negotiate a departure however, at every move they made, the dingoes showed their massive jaws and teeth in a menacing manner. Nineteen individuals heard the eerie sound of a comrade being devoured by a bunch of dog-like looking animals, and decided that the outcome wasn't worth the agony.

Jelani knew who had the Sat phones, and decided to see if the persons would come forward. He asked, "Who was in charge of communicating with the people who hired you?" There was a long pause, and a single hand was raised, followed by two others. Jelani said, "I am happy you people realize that deception at this point in time is unwarranted, and also deadly." As soon as he made that comment, four dingoes attacked one of their comrades, and began to devour him in front of the others. As the others sought refuge behind Jelani and his people, King said to a captive, "If you think that's something, wait until you see that thing in the billabong."

Many turned their heads, and began to heave up all that was in their stomachs. Jelani said to the other three, "It is a good thing you guys didn't try to deceive us because that would have been your fate as well."

The men began to watch the dingoes fight each other over scraps, and knew that the ending for them was not picturesque. Darryl asked the three holders of the Sat phones, "Who were you communicating with on those phones.

The first guy said, "My function was logistics, and I talked to one of my buddies from the sewers that worked with the colonel that was in charge."

Darryl asked, "Are you saying the colonel was involved in this whole thing? I mean, are we talking about the same man? I am referencing the man in DC that handles almost all of the outposts, and their activities."

The guy acknowledged, "One in the same. We were told that this job was a one day, in and out, adventure that could net us a percentage of gold and diamond mines."

Jelani asked, "How long have you been buried up on the range?" The man responded, "three days."

Darryl looked at the other two men, and asked, "What were your functions beyond shooting innocent women and children?"

The first man said, "We were told that everyone was expendable when we made our way to mountain ranges, and that children grow up to become adults so, therefore, everyone was disposable. We were also told that if that was a problem, then we could leave immediately, but without the weapons that were supplied to us."

The third guy indicated that he was told the same thing, and was given a Sat phone to report about the village. The person I spoke to sounded young, and seemingly acted as if he had been in the outback before. He asked me on several occasions, "Do you have the big guy in your sights yet?" I would say, we have his entire team in view, and he would exclaim, "Not yet! All of the other issues are out of sync. Not yet."

Darryl looked at Gant, and said, "I need you to take a picture of these guys. I need to send them to our friends in Northern Africa."

Jelani lined the men up, and said, "Here's the deal. The pictures that were taken of you people will be provided to some incredibly special friends of ours that we pay to handle the families of those who go against us. Whereas your employer talks about children growing up, our friends kill every person in your lineage until your DNA has been erased from the book. Listen, don't fuck with us, and never go up against us in the future because you will write the epitaph of your entire blood line. We're going to have you escorted to the airport, and, oh, King, get all identifying information from them, dog tags, pictures of licenses, passports, and anything else that will help us track them if they do stupid."

One of the mercs said, "They only gave us a one-way ticket."

Darryl looked at him, and said, "Oh, we'll get you home, but when you get a call that says 'outback', put your man-size drawls on because you owe us. Is that clear?"

# # #

Later that evening, Darryl called the plane, and asked to speak to the Sarge. After going through an identity process, the Sarge was linked to him. He told the Sarge that they put eighteen men on a plane back to the US. He told him that one of the men fired a shot at Michael, another lied, and the dingoes feasted on both men.

The Sarge said, "Wow, that must have been ugly to watch. Once things settle down, leave King, Gant, and Green behind, and take our plane to *The Sanctuary.* Tell Michael to accompany you, Sue Lynn, and pick a few others to stay to work with Jelani, and the new guys. By the way, I want everyone to scour that place looking for discarded weapons. I certainly don't want any of the children or curious natives to pick up a loaded weapon and fire it."

As the Sarge concluded the call, he looked towards the galley, and saw Jilkes and John Lee going at it about something. He walked past Mallory and touched him on the shoulder. When he and Mallory entered the galley, Jilkes and John Lee became extremely quiet. The Sarge stated, "I show up with Mallory, and you two look as if you've seen a couple of ghosts. What's the deal?" Both men shrugged their shoulders, and acted as if everything was copacetic. The Sarge replied, "I guess you two want to be alone. Anyway, we'll catch you later if you want to discuss anything."

The two men turned to walk away, when John Lee asked, "Can we go into the belly, and be having a private conversation?"

The Sarge replied, "Only if you're going to be honest about what's on your minds."

In the belly of the plane, the men unfolded their assigned tables and chairs. Jilkes said, "Sarge, we want to have an honest and frank conversation without you going off the handle, and wanting to break our backs."

The Sarge smiled at the them, and replied, "Boy, I guess I really fucked up this time."

John Lee interjected, "Naw, boss you be upstanding, and spot on. What we be arguing about is that every time we get a high valued target, Zanthius blows their heads off as if he be trying to cover up some shit. I mean he evens shoots them after they have been shot."

The Sarge looked at both men, and shook his head. It would be a full minute before the Sarge responded. He said to the group, "Now I know you're going to think I'm talking shit, but I was in my seat thinking about all of the times he has pulled that trigger without regard and/or information. Why I shook my head, and took so long to respond is because those of you who were in the Nam, know that our thoughts are never that far apart."

The Sarge looked at each man, and said, "I've been trying to figure out the benefit equation. Listen, Zanthius, as a result of his mother's death, is fully loaded, and could never spend all of his assets in five lifetimes. However, I keep seeing him pull that trigger time and time again. I love my son, and God please forgive me for having any doubt about his loyalty, but damn, I keep coming up with the same scenario. Hell, he even shoots you in the head after you've been shot in the head, and you're dead. Guys, I am where you are because we've all seen him do that thing, time after time, and now it's beginning to haunt me to figure out what's the end game. He's rich, loyal to Asiram and the kids, no longer philandering around, and just a great husband."

John Lee asked, "What that there big word be meaning?"

Jilkes said, "Fucking around."

"I didn't ask you smarty pants. I be asking the Sarge since he said it."

The Sarge responded, "Fucking around."

John Lee replied, "Oh, I see."

Mallory said, "Listen when more than one person gets the same feeling, it usually has some yeast in it. How do we investigate this issue, I mean this is as serious and as sensitive as it can be."

A few seconds later, the elevator rose to the top, and someone entered it. Beckmire uttered, "Not a word until we can figure this mess out."

When the door opened, it was little Ben, and his father. Zanthius said, "You people act as if you saw a poltergeist, or something. Are we interrupting something important?"

The Sarge stepped all over his tongue, and yelled, "Son, we have a problem with some of your antics, and we're wondering if you have some sort of alternate plan that you're trying to implement?"

Zanthius stood in place, staring straight at his father. After a few seconds, Zanthius placed a headset on his son's head, and told him to watch tv for a few minutes. He returned to where his dad and the others were uncomfortably sitting, looked around at each person, making them feel guilty, and exclaimed, "I was DOA! I was dead on arrival, until my mother saved me from myself. For a while, I hated her because she denied me a father because she wanted to be both mother and father. I met you and your motley crew, and thought what an existence I could have experienced had you been in my life. Ava, my mother, saved me for you, introduced me to you, and I have loved you ever since. I didn't know your crew was as ruthless as I learned they could be, or as compassionate, as I realized they are. I executed people because I was trying to impress my father, and let him know that I am a lot like him."

Zanthius looked to make sure little Ben was okay, and said, "This group is all that I have besides my wonderful wife and children. I have more money than I could spend in ten lifetimes. I have the world by a string, I have people who genuinely love and respect me, and I have some who consider some of my actions as treasonous. Guys, I get it. Every time someone wants to confess, they point to an inside plant. Let me say, and not hold it against anyone here, I am not a plant, a part of a tontine, anxious to inherit a fortune, or a killer of those who have saved me, my children, my mother, and my wife. I love everyone who makes up this rag tag group. I agree, I have impetuously assassinated a couple people in the midst of interrogation, and I promised my dad that I wouldn't do it again. I'm holding true to that pledge, and I don't want to see anyone in this group die. My mother, Carlos, Mike, Franco, and Carla, oh, and the attempted slaughter at the Star Bucks, no guys, I know it's been said, that there is someone near and dear, but I ain't that someone. I came down here because I knew this was about me, and my quick draws. I apologize, but

I ain't the snitch, or the plant. I will die with this group when it's my time."

Zanthius paused for a moment to attend to Ben, and when he finished, he said, "This family is all I have, I mean every person in this group. I ain't it, and nor do I want all that we have amassed. What else could I possibly want, or any of us for that matter? No, Dad, I ain't your Judas, and you are the father that I have always needed and wanted. Love you guys, and please, don't think that I'm pissed at you. Wajickee told me that you people would have a discussion about me, and that I should go and curse each one of you out. No, he didn't suggest that I just adlibbed that part."

Beckmire stood, and beckoned his son to him. When Zanthius came to him, the Sarge gave him a man-size hug. Mallory, Jilkes, and John Lee also gave him massive hugs. John Lee, said, "I told my African American friend that you were innocent."

Jilkes looked at him, and responded, "Country man, why you go and dirty up a good ending?"

John Lee then exclaimed, "Zanthius, that be my creation. He be innocent on that allegation. Love you."

# # #

The co-captain came on the radio, announced the weather, when they should be touching down, and for people to begin to prepare the plane for arrival. The sun shined extremely brightly, and the blue water appeared as pristine as it could be. Ben Beckmire said to his bride, "Baby, it will be great to get some sun, those silly umbrella drinks, and rest."

Courtney grabbed his hand, and responded, "I'm getting a bit weary of all this galivanting, aren't you?"

Beckmire seemed to slip into a funk, but then smiled, and announced, "I will do whatever Mrs. Beckmire demands of me. If she wants to call it quits, then I will respectfully submit my resignation."

Courtney looked at him, and said, "You're so full of it, man. I guess that's why I love you so much because you at least consider my feelings. Thanks, big guy, and I would like to continue the conversation on that topic at some point in time while we're here."

Mrs. Carter and Ayesha waited patiently for the group to exit customs, and both were aware that Michael would be delayed for a few days. Ben Beckmire was the first to exit customs. When he saw Mrs. Carter and Ayesha, he said to them, "This will never happen again. Where I go, your son, and your fiancée, will be right behind me. I needed him in the outback for a few more days. Please don't be mad at me, but all is well, and he will be here in two or three days, I promise you."

Mrs. Carter replied, "He had better get here soon because his fiancée has missed two cycles, and is beginning to show signs of pregnancy."

The Sarge exclaimed, "Oh, Boy!" He turned to Jong, and asked him to call the village, and tell Michael that you have a plane waiting on him. The Sarge said, "If he asks about the sudden change of direction, tell him to take it up with the Sarge when he gets here."

The Sarge gently bent over and kissed Ayesha on the cheek, and poorly signed, "You're one beautiful little lady, and we all love you. Tell me, any idea how we do all that we do, and operate a home for the hearing impaired? I need you to come up with a plan because I'm sure Michael is going to want you with him every second. We have a dedicated group of people that we can place in the home to provide, care, guidance, education, and everything else that the kids need. We sent the group that oversees our airport in Miami, handbooks on signing, and by now they should be proficient at it. We also had child abuse, criminal background, and FBI clearances done on each person. Listen, I'm giving you a heads up, let Michael remember the group he befriended, and suggest those guys initially, and let them interview for the positions. Now one of them has a MBA, and another guy has his Ph.D., I forget what they are in, but they come with credentials, and they need another job beside waiting on a plane to land at our airstrip."

Ayesha, surprised at the amount of information the Sarge had garnered about things she had been considering, signed, "Are you a seer of sorts? I have been thinking about my home, Michael, Mrs. Carter, and the group in general. A while ago he mentioned the fact that he had guys that were wasting away watching an airstrip when they could be watching and providing for my kids. Mr. Beckmire, things have happened so fast that I haven't had a chance to figure anything out. However, you seemingly have placed an objective in front of me that only I can figure out, and I appreciate your innuendos without literally saying, girl you had better get a plan in order."

Ayesha reached up and kissed him on the cheek. Courtney seeing this bellowed out, "Okay girl, don't be messing with my man!" Everyone laughed. Courtney then went on to sign asking how she was feeling, and that she would accompany her to town and have everything checked out.

The Sarge asked, "You knew she was pregnant?" Courtney replied, "Monica and I knew, but we didn't share the information because it wasn't ours to share."

#

Once in *The Sanctuary*, the other members of their association requested a meeting with the Sarge, and his brain trust. The Sarge replied, "I have a lot of people who are my brain trust. My entire group, including you guys are a part of my brain trust, so, do you want to be a little more specific?"

Mrs. Carter laughed, and said, "I would like to wait a few days until my son gets here if it's alright with you guys." The guys aren't stupid, and knew better than to go against the wishes of the matriarch.

Monica upon seeing Mrs. Carter, walked over to Courtney, and said, "Girl, I don't like the way Mrs. Carter looks. She is breathing hard, and sweating like a pig. I think you should have a talk with her and escort her into town to have blood work and other things evaluated."

Courtney looked at her, and said, "Nurse Monica, when I got off the plane, I saw everything that you're presenting to me. I can't just run up to her, and scare the crap out of her. I was picking my time, and as a matter of fact, I'm going to use Ayesha to help get her to the hospital. She looks almost like she's waiting on a stroke. However, I will say this, you're one smart lawyer, not a doctor, but in this case, I totally agree with your prognosis. Can you subtlety get Ayesha in a place where we can stage our getaway?"

Monica smiled, and said, "You're a great doctor, but you don't know shit about conspiracy." The two women laughed, and off Monica went to secure Ayesha.

In the meantime, Courtney made a call to the hospital, and told them exactly what was going on to elicit their cooperation. Less than fifteen minutes later, Ayesha signed to Mrs. Carter, "Something is not right. I need to get to the hospital."

Mrs. Carter yelled for Courtney who happened to be suspiciously nearby, and said, "Ayesha is having issues and wants to go to the hospital."

Courtney calmly responded, "Mrs. Carter get me a van to take us to the hospital. I need you to come with me to help sign to the doctors."

Mrs. Carter quickly replied, "I am on it, and will have a driver in the next five minutes, but I need you to get the security thing arranged quickly."

Exactly seven minutes later, a van raced towards the hospital with a front and rear protection team. Twenty-two minutes later, the group was pulling in front of the emergency entrance. A doctor walked out of the hospital, and said to Mrs. Carter, "Oh, my goodness, you came here just in time. You look as if you're going to have a stroke.

Ayesha grabbed her stomach, and Courtney said, "She's not the patient, this little lady is pregnant and communicates through signing. Mrs. Carter is here to help with the translation."

The doctor vehemently stated, "If Mrs. Carter wants to live to see tomorrow, she had better sit in this chair, and let me take her in for an examination."

Two hours and forty-nine minutes later, it was determined that Mrs. Carter was in stroke territory, with her blood pressure exceeding 220-140. The doctors medicated her, providing her with blockers to reduce her blood pressure readings. The nurse that helped the team on many previous occasions saw the group, and said, "Your less than luxurious living space is ready if you so desire it.

Courtney called the Sarge, and gave him the news. He told her that he was going to rotate security, and send a replacement group. Ayesha unquestionably signed, "I am without debate, staying with Mrs. Carter."

# # #

The following morning at 0800 hours when Courtney, Monica, Luana, and their protection team showed up at the hospital and entered Mrs. Carter's room, no one was there, and the room was in somewhat of a disarray. Courtney exclaimed, "Oh my!" She called the Sarge and told him what they found, and he told her to hold tight until he got more support to her.

Courtney replied, "Minutes is what makes the difference. Honey, we got this, or we'll die trying. We can't sit here and wait until you send people. I think this is all fresh, and I don't want to lose an opportunity." The Sarge commiserated and agreed with her.

Courtney said, "I want people to fan out in twos. She looked at Luana, and asked, "Do you have a weapon?" Luana smiled, and said, "I actually have two."

As the group began to scour the hospital from one end to the other, Luana and Monica heard noise coming from a storage closet, and summoned Courtney. When Courtney arrived and listened to the disturbing sounds, she motioned, "Luana, you cover everything to the left, and Monica, you cover all things to the right, and I will blast everything in front of me."

Courtney said, "On my mark." Monica smiled, breathed deep, and whispered, "I hope we get to play this game again."

Courtney recognizing the apprehension on Monica's face asked, "Are you with me?" She then looked at Luana, and asked, "Are you with me?" Both women gave a thumbs up.

Courtney placed her hand on the door handle, and realized that the door was not locked. She methodically, and slowly, lowered the handle towards the floor, and it moved ever so slowly until the door opened. Once the door handle clicked, the group didn't hesitate. Each women covered their assigned area, and to their surprise, they were pointing their weapons at Mrs. Carter, who had tubes connected to her arm, Ayesha, two nurses, and one orderly. They were in the closet gambling. Mrs. Carter, after Courtney opened the door asked, "Why the guns?"

Courtney, after assessing the situation said, "Your room is a mess, what happened?"

"I told these feisty women that I was leaving and that there was no way in hell they were going to keep me here. Ayesha, seeing my determination, suggested that we play cards to see who gets their way. Anyway, we've only been in here for a few hours, and I owe these hussies a lot of money."

Monica suggested that they vacate the premises, that Mrs. Carter pay her losses, and that everyone pretend that this illicit party never happened. Courtney said, "Mrs. Carter, I need you back in your bed resting. You have a triple threat going against you young lady. You have high blood pressure, high cholesterol levels, and the potential for a massive stroke/heart attack. I wouldn't be so casual about approaching this stage, young lady."

Courtney left the room, called the Sarge, and told him what was going on. He laughed, and said, "You gotta have fun, because you just don't know when it's your time."

# # #

Michael arrived in St. Thomas, was met by his sister, and they were rushed to the hospital in a van driven by Hood, and riding shotgun was Dempsey. No one was aware of the shenanigans of Mrs. Carter the night before.

Arriving at the hospital, Michael and his sister were ushered to their mother's room, found her sitting up in the bed laughing, and signing with Ayesha. After the normal greetings, Michael and his sister asked questions about the status of her health, what triggered the incident, and what would prevent it from happening again.

When Courtney entered the room, she stated, "Your young mother is taking the situation that she finds herself in, far too lightly, and I am extremely concerned about her health. She doesn't realize that she was banging on death's door, and tried to leave the hospital in the middle of the night, with tubes in her arms. I need you guys to stress upon her the significance of high blood pressure, high cholesterol levels, pre-diabetes indicators, and the strong possibility of a concluding event. She is a train about to wreck, and doesn't realize it."

An hour later, Michael and his sister emerged from the room with Ayesha, who told them that their mother was willing to fight the nurses to leave the hospital last night, and the only way she got her to stay was by suggesting that she gamble with the nurses to see if she could just walk out of the hospital. She signed, I know what you're thinking, but she told me there was no way, and no one who was going to keep her in that place overnight.

# # #

Later that evening, and back at *The Sanctuary*, Michael received a copy of a text message that was allegedly initiated by the Sarge. It was addressed to the colonel, the ex-leader of the sewer command. It said, "There is no place you can hide, and you can trust your command that I am coming for you. We didn't mind you pilfering the coffers, but to turn against us, and join those who would see us dead, well, that's a little much. See you sooner than later." Michael thought about the message, and decided to get someone else to join him in presenting it. He saw Zanthius playing with Ben Jr., and asked him if he could spare a minute to look at a text message. Zanthius paused play with Ben, looked at the text message, and responded, "My dad, as you well know, does not telegraph his moves. As long as I've known him, he has never announced his moves, and besides, have you ever seen him text anyone?"

Michael replied, "That is exactly what I'm talking about. He barely knows how to use the phone that he has. Someone is trying to involve him in some shit. It's greater than the colonel, this is leading to somewhere else."

A little while later, the two men saw the Sarge lounging around the beach with this bride, and decided that they didn't want to enjoy the Sarge's wonderful personality.

Michael saw Jilkes and John Lee exiting the water, and decided to ask them how he should proceed. John Lee after reading the text exclaimed, "No damn way this here be sent by the Sarge. First of all, he ain't that smart to know how to send a text because he ain't never sent one before."

Jilkes announced, "I will be sure to tell him your exact sentiments."

John Lee responded, "You always be interested in starting some shit for me. Why you be like that? Is that because you just be mean spirited?"

Jilkes looked at him, and replied, "Yes, sir. I always like to keep a foot up your country ass."

Michael asked, "Do you think this is significant enough for me to go and disturb him and Courtney? Jilkes said, "Give me five minutes to disappear, and you go for it."

John Lee said, "I be right behind him. When the Sarge be with the Doc, and they be holding hands, I ain't got nothing to say to him because he'll hold it against you if you mess up their mood. If I be you, I'd wait until they started leaving the beach, and then I'd show him what he be done sent while he was asleep."

Michael looked at his watch, and knew that he would have to leave soon for the hospital to relieve his sister and Ayesha. He started for the Sarge, and at that precise moment, Courtney and the Sarge wrapped themselves in towels. The Sarge saw Michael and wondered why he was acting a little weird.

Michael walked up to the Sarge, and said, "I know your time with your bride is precious, but I have to head to the hospital, and I wanted to show you a text message that I received, that allegedly emanated from you." The Sarge asked Courtney if he could borrow her reading glasses.

The Sarge asked, "How long have you had this message?"

Michael stuttered, and replied, "At least one hour plus."

The Sarge looked at him, and asked, "Why didn't you interrupt me?"

Michael responded, "Sarge, everyone told me not to bother you, and I listened to them."

The Sarge hugged him, and said, "You, my son, have an open door to me. I know you are about business, and I know if you have an issue, it's important. Now, this email thing, I didn't send this."

Michael responded, "Sarge, it's a text message, there are differences."

The Sarge laughed, and said, "Okay, son. I didn't send that text message. I don't think my phone is capable of sending messages. Anyway, we need to get the guys together to figure out what is going on."

Michael responded, "Sarge, you know those people in the sewers love the colonel, and he can do no wrong. I'm wondering if this is a rallying call to have people to independently attempt to place a hit on you."

The Sarge stopped smiling, and considered how this could be used to gain alliances to go against a benefactor. He said, "I need to somehow reach out to Rheingold. Do you think you can send him a subtle message that I need to talk to him?"

# # #

Approximately twenty-two minutes later, Michael received a call, and was told the alternative contact number for the Sarge to use. He raced to the Sarge's room, knocked lightly on the door, and stated that he had a contact number for Rheingold. The Sarge opened the door, and invited him in. The two men wasted no time, and called the alternative number that was provided. The captain picked up the phone, and then hung it up. The Sarge was aware of this antic, and waited thirty-five seconds, and placed the call again. Rheingold answered the call, and said, "Be deliberate. This place is crawling with good and bad factions."

The Sarge asked, "Where is the colonel?" Rheingold responded, "MIA." The Sarge told him about the text message, and Rheingold said, "They are looking for support to take care of a problem, and it's you."

The Sarge replied, "I can clean up that sewer, and place an honest soldier in charge. Give me the word, and I'll come, sanitize, and refinance that network."

Rheingold replied, "Appreciate that, but this toilet is self-cleaning. Keep an eye on the horizon, until I've taken care of all the stains. Appreciate all you do, and I'll keep you informed of what's going on here. Michael, I like. Wish I had him here. Later warrior!"

The Sarge and Michael discussed what had been relayed to them, and decided that *The Sanctuary*, was too open, and the group needed to move to Virginia or the mid-west until they could get a full understanding of the impending individual strikes against the Sarge. Michael made his way to Mallory and told him about the message, the text, and the follow-up call with Rheingold. Mallory's immediate response was, "Wheels up in an hour. I need everyone fully dressed, with an eye towards snipers."

Like a well-oiled machine, all the parts worked. The members of *The Sanctuary* placed a veil around Mrs. Carter. Michael approached the Sarge, and said, "I can't leave my mother in the hospital, and fly off to avoid a maybe attack against you and the group."

The Sarge asked Courtney, "Is Mrs. Carter movable?"

Courtney replied, "If her levels have begun to decrease, and if we can medicate and monitor her, then absolutely."

The Sarge looked at Michael, and asked, "Does your mother have a passport or other identifying documents that will get her through customs?"

Michael replied, "Sarge I don't know. I know where she keeps important papers. Can you give me a few minutes to search for documents?"

The Sarge responded, "Son, take your time, and be reminded that we will not leave you or your mother. We all go, or we all stay."

Michael began to tear up, and the Sarge commanded, "Go, do your thing, and let's see where we are."

Michael said, "I need a hug. Those close to me are in more jeopardy than I could imagine. Losing my sister, my dad, now my mother is in disrepair, and is being as stubborn as ever, I need all of the support possible to help those who have been my lifeline. Sarge, I thank God and the Spirits for you, and this group."

# # #

Courtney made the call to the hospital, talked to the head physician, explained that the group was under attack once again, that Michael was hesitant to leave his mother and his sister. The doctor explained that they had minimized some of the previous threats, and with medications it was conceivable that she could continue to progress.

The head physician said, "You're a doctor, give her what we prescribe, and make sure she is monitored to take the medicine. She's a feisty little thing, and believes that she doesn't need all of the stuff we're providing and prescribing for her to have a normal life. She discounts the fact that she was banging on death's door. I showed the numbers representing her health, and those of normalcy. She refuted them, and I told her, if she wanted to die, then just don't take the fucking medicine. I got pissed at her, and began to deal with her selfishness. She finally began to take heed and admitted that she was afraid, and felt alone. Please take her with you, but monitor her ingesting the medicine. I'll have her ready and enough medicine for a week, but after that, you'll have to prescribe and acquire. Thanks, Doc, and stay safe."

## CHAPTER SEVENTEEN

The group decided to make an interim stop in Virginia to check on the property as well as the horses. The ride from the airport in Maryland to the ranch was boring as usual until they came upon a tractor trailer collision that involved several smaller vehicles. The men got out of their vans and began to risk injury from the fire, and potential explosions. Trapped in the back seat of a burning vehicle were twins. The mother was screaming, and trying to open the door. Hood sent Dempsey to the other side, and at the count of three, the two men smashed the windows, cut the seat belts, and yanked the two children out. The children, Hood, and Dempsey received superficial burns, but would be alright.

On the other side of the median, Zanthius, the Sarge, Chakes, Gladstone, Montomie, McArthur, Bernstein, Brown, Jong, and Whitmore, were desperately trying to free the driver of one of the trucks. Once John Lee and Jilkes leant their strength to the equation, the group was able to free the trucker.

Later at the nearest hospital, Hood and Dempsey were treated, and released into the care of Dr. Beckmire. The mother of the twins begged the men for contact information so that she could properly thank them. Hood responded, "We are thankful that we happened upon the scene when we did. No additional thanks is needed. Take care of those beautiful children of yours."

#

At the ranch, Stella and Leonardus helped Hood and Dempsey as much as they possibly could. They were assisted by the sisters, Anel, and Angel, who really helped the two pirates through the night.

Mrs. Carter signed to Ayesha, "They've only been here a couple of hours, and look what they have been involved in. And my goodness, if this is just the farm, then what the heck does the ranch look like? These people be living large, and I am so glad my son found a home with them, and enjoys working for them. I mean, look at this place, and did you see those horses running around like they be in control?" Ayesha smiled, and signed, "God is good!"

#

The weapons system had not been attended to for some time, and Rashida assigned teams to dismount each one, clean, oil, reload them with fresh ammunition, and lock them back into place. Mrs. Carter was awed, and cautious about what she was witnessing. She asked Luana, "Are things that bad here that you need automated fire power?"

Luana looked at Mrs. Carter, smiled, and replied, "Some of the enemies that have come to terminate us have shown up with rocket launchers, and other deadly weapons. Seemingly, the list of enemies continues to grow as the group attempts to settle down."

Mrs. Carter seemed saddened by the information, and when questioned, she asked, "Is this group good or bad?" Luana without hesitation responded, "This group is both good and bad. If you come for one of them, then you have to deal with all of them. We have done some bad things, but always in response to an action against our group, our friends, our country, and our beliefs."

# # #

The following morning as the maintenance crews continued working on the defensive systems, Hood and Dempsey were excused from all duties until their bandages were removed. The two men saw the benefits of their conditions, and decided to work it for every penny. From breakfast, lunch, and dinner, in bed, to having their backs lotioned, their feet, scalps, necks, shoulders, and legs massaged, yes those two guys played that harmonica all the way home. When they happened upon Courtney, she reminded them, "Hey guys, I am a doctor, and I hope you're enjoying your little charade. The attending physician indicated that fresh air was better than bandages for your blisters. How about tomorrow, you guys come back to earth. What about that?"

Both men smiled, and Hood asked, "I'm planning on proposing tomorrow, and these bandages might help my cause, do you think I can keep them for two more days?" Courtney made noises with her teeth, and asked, "Are you two nuts? Those women would have you if you had one eye, one leg, no teeth, and bad breath. They are absolutely enamored with you two nuts."

Dempsey asked, "How do you know that?"

Courtney said, "Gee, I just happen to be a woman, and I know what other women think and like. Plus, you two aren't hard on the eyes. One more day of playing cripple, and then off with the bandages."

#

Mr. East called Mr. West, and said, "I know exactly where they are going to be for the next few days. They are in Virginia, and will probably be making their way to the mid-west. Is there any way we can get a crew in both places to perform a little attrition until there is no one left?"

Mr. West quickly reminded Mr. East that people are still seeking the buyers of that last adventure who never paid one red cent. We might have to consider paying partial up front and completing payment on the rear end. This time no chicanery, just pay the people if the work is satisfactorily completed."

Mr. East responded, "You're such a goody two shoes, much like the people we're trying to eliminate. I say, if you don't read the small print, then you are still bound by the tenets of the agreement. Don't just look at the asking price, and sign, but look at every aspect of the contract. Anyway, good luck to those people trying to find out who the purchaser was on that last event. I locked that mess up so tight that a witch couldn't sneak her ass in there. By the way, what are we going to do with the colonel? He has exposed us to a degree, or shall I say, he has exposed you to a large degree. I'm still an anomaly, and good luck with tracking me down and my source of information. Speaking of my sources, the naivety of some people. They think that I'm going to come forward, and have a grand séance with all who I want to terminate. Maybe at the repass, but not until then. Anyway, see if you can find a couple of shooters to cull that herd. Remember, two days near here, and then on to the mid-west. Keep the faith, this thing is going to work out to our advantage, I promise you that. Later."

#

Stella accompanied Hood to have his bandages removed by Dr. Beckmire. Dr. Beckmire appeared to be in some sort of funk to Hood. He asked, "Doc, are you okay? You seem to be preoccupied with something, and you're not your bubbly self." Courtney smiled at Stella, and asked her to sit in the chair facing the door so that she could keep an eye on her. Once Stella was out of hearing range, Courtney said to Hood, "So I look like I'm preoccupied, eh? Well to tell the truth, I am concerned about someone dear to me that I have not been able to reach for a couple of weeks."

"Well listen Doc, if there is anything that I can do, don't hesitate to ask me. Lord knows, you do enough for everyone else, and rarely are you in need of an ear, or a conversation except from your girlfriends."

Courtney, after removing the bandages, stated, "Let me think about that young fella, and maybe I will call on you to do me a favor."

Hood made the mistake of responding, "Yes Ma'am."

Courtney announced, "You were doing simply fine until you pulled that "Yes Ma'am" shit on me."

#

Later during the day, Stella said to Hood, "I think I would like you as my new dad. Do you think you would like me as your daughter?"

This caught Hood completely by surprise. He said, "Nothing would make me happier than to be your dad, and you my daughter. How do we make it work?"

Stella said, "Well you know legally, Anel and Angel are in charge of us. Now, if you were to marry Anel, then we would be a family, but then if Mr. Dempsey doesn't marry Angel, then Leonardus will not have a mother and a father." Stella began to cry, and Hood, for the first time, hugged her dearly, and assured her that everything is going to work out.

Anel, who was looking for the duo, saw Hood hugging Stella, backed up around the house so as not to be seen, and began to ball her eyes out. Angel saw her, and asked, "What on earth is going on with you?"

Anel replied between sniffles, "Hood was comforting Stella, and it made her realize that she had to get with him or get rid of him."

Angel responded, "Maybe we should have a double wedding. What do you think of that?"

Anel asked, "He asked you to marry him?"

Angel replied, "No, idiot, I asked him to marry me." The two sisters hugged, and walked to the front of the ranch where Hood and Stella were.

Stella walked over to Anel, and said, "He wants to be my dad, but I'm worried about Leonardus. Can he be his dad too?"

Anel bent down, and replied, "You're having a lot of grown folk conversations today. Do you think we can discuss this later when we are all on the same page?"

Stella looked at her, and asked, "What book are we reading?"

Anel smiled, and said, "That's just a saying that means some things take time, and require a lot of discussion. Let the grown folks think and talk about it, and I'll let you know soon. How about that?"

#

The Sarge knew that something was troubling his wife, and every time he inquired, she would state that she was tired. He asked Courtney, "Is this gallivanting and globetrotting getting to you?"

Courtney responded, "No more than anyone else. I think we're all tired of living in the alert zone, and carrying damn guns everywhere we go. It gets to you after a while, but I'll be okay."

The Sarge looked at her, and said, "I promise you that in six months, we will be watching kids, and not our backs. How about that?"

Courtney half-smiled, and said, "Ben Beckmire, you need that adrenaline rush, and so do I, on occasion. Don't promise me something that events control, and not you. Make me a reasonable proposal, and let me stew over it for at least a year. However, at years end, I expect you to make a decision, and turn the reins of this group over to those young people that we've been grooming. Now, I feel that's a reasonable, manageable, and doable arrangement. So, in your words, "how about that?"

The Sarge hugged her, and said, "You're my lifeline. If you give me a full year, then I promise, come hell or high water, I am going to walk away from this unless someone is holding a gun at one of my boy's head. I mean stuff comes up, but if we're not being hunted, then I will marry you again, and retire from this life permanently, and you can take that to the bank."

#

Courtney saw Hood, and beckoned him over. She said, "Since you want to use that "Ma'am shit with me, I have a job I need you to figure out how to accomplish without a lot of people knowing that you and I are in cahoots. I want to investigate someone, but I only want you to figure out how to do it, and how reliable the sources are that you select to answer my burning questions."

Hood looked at her, and asked, "Can you tell me who it is that I am going to place under the microscope?"

Courtney replied, "At this point, it's not your business. When and if I want to continue with certain thoughts of mine, I'll clue you in. However, let me be crystal clear, if you murmur a single word about this liaison to anyone, I will have you dismissed, and shot by friends of mine in Northern Africa. Are we clear? I mean, not your bride to be, nor your new ward or wards, not Dempsey, not no fucking body. Am I more than crystal clear?"

Hood replied, "Dr. Beckmire, do I have the right to decline this mission?"

Courtney laughed, and said, "Actually, you do, but then you'll die from a strange poison. Son, don't fuck with me on this matter. It's a matter of life and death, and since you asked and volunteered indirectly, I am now accepting your services."

In the interim, Courtney wrote her cell number down, and told Hood to call it so that she could record his number. Courtney's final words were, "Discretion is so important in this matter. The Sarge would break your back if he thought you were trying some dumb shit with me. Are we clear, and do you understand that until I want to make a disclosure about someone, it is you and me, my brother. Nice chatting with you, catch you later."

Hood caught up with Anel, and she asked him if everything was okay. He shrugged the comment off, and said, "I need some time alone. I'm going to go and meet some horses, think about all that has happened to me, and where I want to go moving forward. Before you ask the question, let me answer it. I intend on marrying you if you will have me, and the question I have is when and where. My need for solace is all about me, nothing to do with you, my love."

Stella saw Hood going into the field where the horses were, and yelled, "Can I come with you?" Hood took a deep breath, exhaled, and said, "Sure my love, but you must do exactly as I say."

Hood had snacks in his pockets, and the horses were really interested in meeting this new guy with snacks. He said to Stella, "I want you to stay really close to me, and watch exactly what I do. I'm going to let you feed them snacks, but you must do it exactly the way I show you."

Two horses came up near them, and backed off. Hood said to Stella, "When you offer them snacks, I want you to extend your hand all the way out so that they can't bite your little fingers. Watch me."

After a successful outing with the horses, and no one lost a finger, Stella acknowledged, "That was really cool." She also requested that the next time they bring Leonardus.

Later that evening, Courtney said to the Sarge, "You never talk about him, do you miss him at all?"

Knowing full well that this conversation was going to go sideways, the Sarge responded, "Of course I think of him, and miss him every day. I'm just sorry that at an early age, he felt that we weren't good parents and, therefore, decided to divorce us. Although we support him, it's not easy having a child say that you are horrible parents, and that there is no love lost from either side."

Courtney realizing the truth in his words, said, "Honey, I don't want to place fault, I want to try to reconcile our differences with him. I know he still thinks that we are poor, and that his friend's parents are rich, and are intellectuals. I think he came under the influence of a giant stupid spit ball, and the residue is still clogging his mind. Honey, he came out of me, and from you. How can we turn our backs on him?"

The Sarge wanted to have this conversation like he wanted to shoot himself in the foot. He reminded Courtney, "Sweetheart, we didn't turn our backs on him. We got a notice from the courthouse indicating that our child was essentially filing for emancipation from his parents because they do not live up to his expectations of what parents should be, and what they should do. He went so far as to get a restraining order placed on us. It is the most troublesome thing that I have ever had to deal with. My own child becoming legally detached from us, and then on top of that, being granted a monthly subsidy allowance from us that also included that expensive military school. I mean, come on now, tuition, room and board, books, and living allowance of $3,500 per month. Shit, that's a lot of money for his poor old parents who don't make what his friends parents make."

Courtney began to cry, and Ben tried to console her. She said, "I want you to promise me one thing, that is we will go and see our son before something happens to one of us. I need you to promise me that." Ben realizing that his wife was way past stop, with the crying, said, "Honey, I don't even know how to find the child."

Courtney smiled, and said, "I do, because I force him to talk to me before I send him additional dollars. We usually just talk about the weather, and on occasion, he asks what we do and where we do it, and when my five minutes are up, the alarm sounds, and he says the same old stuff, "Nice hearing from you, talk to you soon."

The Sarge looking furious asked, "Are you saying that little motherfucker times your conversations."

Courtney responded, "Sarge, I don't mind. At least I get to hear him breathe, and occasionally, he'll ask about you, and what you're doing."

"Courtney, how much do you send him, and how do you send it to him when he asks for funds?"

Courtney's head dropped, and she whispered, "No more that $25 to $50."

The Sarge sighed a sound of relief, but immediately asked, "$25 to $50 what?"

Courtney looked away, and announced, "$25 to $50k, and the most I have ever sent him at one time was $150k."

The Sarge looked at her, and said, "Baby, let's have a drink before dinner. I would like to hear what else you two talk about."

# # #

Later that evening, Ben fixed he and Courtney a couple of drinks with Cruzan and Coke. Courtney asked Ben if he was mad about her reaching out to their son, and he told her unequivocally, no. He told her that he had often thought about it, but realized that the two always seem combative because he was once a peace officer. He hated the fact that I was just a cop, but accepted you because you were at least a doctor. I thought I was much more than a cop, but he wouldn't listen, and at first I thought he was blowing smoke up our asses, but when the letter from the courthouse came, I backed all the way up, and realized that my son was out of his fucking mind. Anyway Honey, back to your promise, I will set a time when we will go and find this character, and at least gather conclusive information that he is a weirdo and a sicko, but that he's still our son."

Courtney looked at Ben, and asked, "When? I don't want this thing drawn out. I have been feeling strange, and I'm having terrible night sweats."

Ben looked at her, and said, "Let's take a vehicle, and head to the hospital down the road. Those guys treat presidents and their children, so let's at least let them draw blood, and begin the analysis trip at that point."

Courtney pondered the notion for a moment, and said to Ben, "I think that's a great idea because I can't help the masses if I'm not well. Okay, give me thirty minutes, I'll take a quick shower, and then we can head down there."

In the interim, Ben secured a security team, and told Rashida to place the farm on moderate alert, meaning all adults were minimally armed with a sidearm, and the mechanized weapons system was on standby. The Sarge assured everyone that Courtney was feeling fine, but needed to investigate a personal issue.

Thirty minutes later, and no Courtney. The Sarge decided to go to his room, and see what was taking her so long. When he opened his door, he found his wife stuck behind the door in an unconscious form. He called for help, and people began to show up. He pushed the door slowly until he could squeeze past it. Once in the room, he saw that Courtney was bleeding from the mouth. He astutely opened her mouth, and realized that she had not fallen and hit her face, but that the blood was from internal bleeding. He gathered her up in his arms, and made his way to the van.

Jilkes was standing on the outside of the van, and John Lee was in the driver's seat, and the Sarge handed Courtney off to Jilkes, who entered the vehicle, and off they raced to the local hospital. John Lee enroute to the hospital made a call to the hospital indicating that he was enroute with Dr. Courtney Beckmire who was found in her room bleeding from the mouth.

The nurse asked, "Is this my benefactor from up the road?" John Lee responded, "This here be me, and I be bringing the Doc, and we ain't got a lot of time to be waiting in the lobby with an unconscious doctor."

The nurse asked, "What's your ETA?"

John Lee looked at the navigation system, and said, "We be getting there in ten minutes."

The nurse said, "We'll be waiting with a gurney, doctors, and myself. See you soon my friend, and be careful driving."

At the emergency entrance at the hospital, one would have thought that the President of the United States of America, was arriving. There was a beehive of activity going on, and several specialists from various fields were on duty. Once on the gurney, Courtney was hooked up to blood pressure, heart monitoring, pulse measuring, oxygen in blood level, and a few other machines. A vein was found, and blood was immediately extracted from her arm for analysis, and an IV was installed in her arm. By the time she got to the nearby observation room, blood samples were being handed off to the lab, and doctors were poking, and viewing every aspect of her body.

A nurse began to query Ben Beckmire about the last thing that he knew that she ate, any previous symptoms or knowledge of her not feeling well, and on, and on. Ben replied, "We were on our way here to have blood work done so that she could at least begin to self-diagnose. My only indication that something was wrong with my wife was when she noted that she had been having night sweats. It was at that point that I suggested that we take a ride down the road to the hospital. She went to take a shower. After the agreed upon time for her to show up at the van had elapsed, I went to the room to see what was taking her so long. Apparently, she was trying to leave the room when she passed out. I had to push the door open with her body providing resistance. I searched her for an obvious injury, didn't see any, opened her mouth, and saw blood, and decided that we were out of there, and on our way here."

The nurse asked, does she take any medicine?" Ben thought for a moment, and said, "She believes in those baby aspirin, is always self-medicating so it would be hard to announce any medical considerations that she may have been dealing with. Today was the first day I saw my wife feeling and announcing that she was basically lethargic.

Meanwhile, the team of doctors were examining every inch of Courtney's body when a nurse asked a doctor to take a look at the early CT scan images. The astute doctor loudly exclaimed, "There is blockage in her frontal lobe. I need the specialist to confirm my rudimentary evaluation. In any event, we need to prepare Dr. Beckmire for surgery, just in case I'm correct."

The same doctor asked a nurse to summon Mr. Beckmire, and when he arrived in the room, the doctor asked, "Has your wife had any falls lately or banged her head on anything substantial?" Before he could answer, the doctor asked, "Has her speech been fine, her mind functioning well, and any notions of paranoia."

Beckmire responded, "The only fall, was when I found her behind the door, and it didn't look as though she had hit her head, I mean I didn't see any bruises, swelling or cuts. Insofar as her speech and mind are concerned, no slurring of words, her mind was as sharp as ever, and she didn't seem to be concerned about any demons or issues confronting her or our group."

The doctor asked, "What's this group like, a fraternity?"

The Sarge looked at him, and replied, "No, not like a fraternity, more like a family that shares the same values, and have as their main objective, to help people help themselves."

The doctor responded, "How noble, but how can you do that?"

The Sarge responded, "After you attend to my wife, I'll be glad to give you a lesson in helping people help themselves."

Two hours and forty-five minutes later, Courtney exited the operating room. Apparently, she had fallen, hit her head, as well as banged it in the same spot on an open cabinet door at the farm, but did not tell the Sarge or anyone else.

In the interim, the Sarge made several calls to the only number that he had for his son in Maryland. There was no response to the calls or the messages that were left by the Sarge. He said to himself, "I promised my wife that I would go and see this useless emancipated adult, but if he doesn't call and inquire about his mother, then I'm fucking completely done with that little shit."

# # #

Five days later, Courtney was released from the hospital with specific instructions to not do anything strenuous, not to engage in debilitating discussions, and to watch no more than two hours of TV per day. It was also recommended that she not enjoy any alcoholic beverages, and that the sun was not going to be kind to her eyes and, therefore, she would be prone to headaches if she stayed in the sun. She was also given the standard instructions concerning unnatural suicidal thoughts, and notions of unprovoked anger, should be reported, and she should be immediately returned to the hospital for observation and evaluation.

# # #

Hood and Dempsey, proposed to Anel and Angel, and wanted to wed in the middle of the field with the horses coming and going during the ceremony. Stella and Leonardus were so happy that they were going to have new parents that they both liked and loved. One evening, when they were in the outback, and down by the billabong, Stella asked Hood, "So, when you marry Anel, will that automatically make you my father?"

Hood looked at Stella, and replied, "As soon as I say I do to Anel, the very next day, we're going to proceed to the county courthouse, and file papers for your adoption. After they check to make sure that we're good enough for you, they will bless us with you as our daughter." Stella looked a little sad, and began to cry. Hood asked, "Are those tears of joy or sadness?"

Stella began to cry harder, and Hood gathered her up and pleaded with her to tell him what was wrong. Stella was sniffling and crying, asked, "What will happen to my brother, Leonardus?"

Hood smiled, and said, "I neglected to tell you that on that same day, Dempsey and Angel will accompany us to the courthouse to ask the court to grant them custody of Leonardus." Stella stopped crying, and said, "I love you guys so much, and I promise you'll never want to give us back."

Hood looking a little perplexed stated unequivocally, "Stella, you will be ours until the day we go to the great void."

Stella asked, "Where is that?"

Hood responded, "Ask your mother to be that question."

CHAPTER EIGHTEEN

It was mid-April when the farm was decorated for the marriage of those who initially appeared to the group as a source of harm. On this day, two pirates and two archers would join together to enter the institution of marriage. Unbeknownst to anyone, on this day, Stella and Leonardus would be officially listed as adoptees respectively, of Hood and Anel, and Angel and Dempsey. Somehow also on this date, Stella, Leonardus, and the caretaker would lavishly decorate the horses for the wedding. Also, two days prior to the wedding, Courtney was given a clean bill of health, and was told she could resume her duties as the doctor and mentor. Clyde was there to officiate the ceremony, and Gilda was present to enjoy the wedding, and to introduce a few new toys for the protection of the group.

Speaking of Gilda, she and Rashida developed a sophisticated blocking device that impacted phone, internet, Bluetooth, and every other type of digital signal. It was demonstrated to the CIA, and the prototype was purchased by that agency for $100 million. Unfortunately for agency, they also needed to purchase the source codes that operated the signal blocking device. The codes were provided to the agency for free. However, training, and technical assistance were provided at cost. Rashida and Gilda announced that they were near the completion of a system that could intercept coded messages from above water as well as under water, and the Sarge agreed that he would provide the system to the agency at no cost.

# # #

Hood said to Dempsey, with tears in his eyes, "Together we've come a long way. From the entry lobby to hell, to in a few moments, standing in the middle of a field to marry two dynamic and beautiful young ladies, who happen to be sisters. Do you remember when we didn't have $20 between us? I checked my account yesterday, and was scared to repeat the amount out loud for fear of someone taking it back. I mean look at us, from that first job in Minnesota, to that junket on the island, and they continue to rely on us with a certain expectation that we will make it happen. I've never had someone to trust me like that, except you."

Dempsey replied, "I know my friend, it has been unreal, and what I'm so proud of is despite our initial traumatic relationship, we came together, and began to act as one. We have saved each other, and this group as well. I am so happy the Sarge didn't oblige us, and place a round in each of our heads. Remember how he kept asking, "What am I going to do with you two." Also, do you remember Dr. Beckmire empathically stating, "If my guys haven't terminated you yet, then more than likely, they're not going to."

# # #

In the middle of the field, with horses prancing around and decorated like flower maidens, Hood and Anel, Dempsey, and Angel, repeated their vows to each other. What was spectacular was the announcement that Stella and Leonardus would be officially adopted by Hood and Anel, and Dempsey and Angel, respectively. It was a great day at the farm. The mood was festive, rewarding, and sacred as two children whose parents were assassinated, were adopted by two pirates and two bow toting sisters.

Leave it to Stella to ask the hard questions. She cozied up to Hood, and asked, "Before I call you dad, are you sure you want to be my dad?"

This too, caught Hood completely off guard. He looked at Stella, cocked his head to the side, and said, "You are the most courageous person that I know. You always ask questions of substance. I just married Anel, and I love her so much. Even if I hadn't married Anel, Stella, I would have been honored to be your dad. However, I married Anel, and we are in the process of adopting you, and I can say without question, I love my new little lady." Stella began to cry, and Hood asked, "What's wrong, you don't believe me?"

Stella began to ball her eyes out, and asked, "Will Leonardus and me be separated?"

Hood sighed, and looked her straight on, and said, "As long as we are with this group, then we will always be together. Also, remember that Mr. Dempsey is my best friend, and where he goes I go, and where I go, he goes. This is all new to everyone Stella, but if you give us time, we will figure it out. The last thing we want to do is separate you and your brother. I promise you, the adults will work this thing out."

Still crying, Stella ran to Hood, hugged him, and said, "I am happy now, and Leonardus will be too."

Anel showed up by the billabong, and saw the two embracing, and asked, "Is there a hug or two left for me?"

Stella ran to her, jumped into her arms, and said, "My new dad has promised me that Leonardus and me won't be separated."

Anel said, "Baby, that was never a thought. Give us time, and we will become a real family, and besides little lady, this is my wedding night, and I should be spending it with my new husband. But since we both love you so much, we're going to spend it together, and talk about things, like what does my little lady expect from her new parents. How about that?"

Stella smiled, and replied, "I need my new parents, and I need my brother because we saw what happened to our other parents. I see it every night I try to sleep. The bang, my mom's hand landing on the front window of the car." Stella opened the gates to the dam, and literally cried herself to sleep.

Hood said to Anel, "The first thing we have to do is find out what happened to their parents, what they saw, what they understand, and how do we transform them." Anel looked at her new husband cradling their new daughter, and she too began to cry. Hood said, "Baby, one resolve at a time. I need that calculating mind of yours right now to save our new baby from drifting into a world of hurt."

Anel walked over to Hood, and said, "Man, never in my life have I ever felt a blessing, but I am blessed that you chose me, and I will honor and protect you until the day I die. Your handling of this situation is absolutely, heavenly."

The following day, Hood and Dempsey walked up to Dr. Beckmire, and asked her for an audience. After the normal niceties, Hood said, "Doc, my Stella is experiencing memories of what happened to her parents including her mother's hand landing on the window of the limo before it sped away. We come to you because we don't have a clue as to what happened, and we need to know the details in order to help our babies. Can you direct us to the appropriate party to gain full knowledge of what happened, and what our kids are dealing with mentally." Courtney suggested that they obtain a few medallions for identification purposes, a thermos full of fresh coffee, a couple bottles of water, and some Kleenex. She also requested that the two men bring their brides along for the ride.

Forty-five minutes later, two off-road vehicles left the immediate area of the farm, and headed deeper into the fields with mechanized mayhem watching over them, and Rashida and Gilda at the helm of the automated system. Once the group found a shaded area, Courtney began to tell the sordid story of how their parents were assassinated, as well as Zanthius's mother and her husband.

Two hours later, the group returned to the farmhouse without a dry eye visible. Dempsey announced, "We will provide those kids with our never-ending love, and we will under no circumstances separate them. On this I swear!" He exclaimed. Hood repeated the same information, and he too swore to the conditions.

The Sarge came over to where the group was, and asked his wife, "Baby, are you okay?"

Courtney said, "I am going to take a nap. These two pirates, and those two bow-toting ladies have tired me out. People, I am here to help. Catch you later."

#

Later in the early afternoon, Courtney asked the Sarge, "Did my baby call to check on me, or better still, did you try to reach him, and tell him that I was hospitalized?"

The Sarge replied, "I called several times, left messages on each number that I have, and decided that before I go to hell, I am going to kill my own seed for placing a tremendous hurt on the woman that birthed his ass, whose breast he suckled for food and familiarity."

Courtney looked at Ben, and screamed, "Never say such a thing to me about our blessing, even though he may seem like a curse. You will never touch our child in a disdainful manner Ben Beckmire for I will hate you beyond the hell we all will experience. Promise me if we or you ever see our child, you will love him, express words of love, and never the violent turpitude you just expressed. Promise me Ben, or I will exit this life knowing that I had no life when the father kills the son."

Ben Beckmire with tears in his eyes, said, "Please forgive my outburst. I could never hurt our son, no matter how debilitating he has been. I just know that if he needed money, he would have called you. I would never hurt my own, but he is so selfish, and could give a shit about you or me until his ass is broke."

"I know this Ben, but he is still our baby, and we must protect and provide for him as long as we live."

Ben Beckmire said, "Baby, I made you a promise, and I will never raise a finger in violence to our son. I need you to get some rest, and we'll have a private dinner tonight if you like."

Courtney said, "Man, I know about your private dinners. You're trying to isolate me so that you can do the nasty to me, aren't you?"

Beckmire responded, "Naw, baby, I just don't want to share you with anyone tonight. Listen, we can play scrabble, chess, or checkers until we fall asleep. I just don't want to share my wife with a single soul tonight."

That evening, while the two played an assortment of table games, Courtney announced that a few weeks ago, she had talked to their son, and that she had received a call from him while they were in the outback. The Sarge focused on his next move, basically ignored the information, and just assumed that his wife had sent him a lot of money this time. After two small drinks, Courtney told her husband that she needed to rest, and for him to cease all notions of trying to seduce her with his wicked notions and proposals. He laughed, and replied, "I am only interested in my wife's health at this point. I can wait until tomorrow to make sure the rest of you works okay."

# # #

Meanwhile, the 'idiot spy' is being bothered with night sweats, dreams of mayhem, strangers, and his own death. He woke Asiram up, and she asked Zanthius, "Is this the same dream that you have been having of late?"

He paused, and slowly replied, "Honey, it gets more real each time. It's much like what happened to John Lee, but I am not getting any suggestions of hurting anyone, no the hurt is the various ways in which I die each night, and they are all different, unique, and sadistic. I can't figure it out. Maybe I should ask Courtney for a low-dose sedative to help me sleep, and to stop interrupting your sleep state. Baby, this time I was gutted from my crotch to my brain before I died. Something is going on, and I don't know what, or why now. It just doesn't make sense. You know I sleep like a log, anywhere, and at any time. Now, I am witnessing my own destruction, and each time it becomes more sinister." Asiram hugged him, and suggested that he attempt to go back to sleep.

#

About 2 in the morning, the Sarge began to yell in his sleep, and Courtney had a difficult time waking him up. Once semi-conscious, he began to pant as if he was having issues breathing. Courtney calmed him down to where he could speak, and he announced, "I just met the fucking devil, and he cut my heart out and fed it to stray dogs."

Courtney insisting that he calm down, asked, "Do you want me to give you something to calm your nerves?"

Ben proclaimed, "No, no drugs! I have to stay awake, and wait for this demon. He's coming expressly for me."

The balance of the night, the Sarge walked aimlessly around the room, looking in each closet, opening the bathroom door, and peeking under the bed. Courtney begged him to come to bed, but the Sarge was on a mission. Someone or something scared the big guy beyond anyone's wildest imagination.

#

In the morning at breakfast, everyone noticed how tired the Sarge looked, and when they saw Zanthius, they assumed that the two played cards all night long. At the table, Asiram announced that her husband dreamt that he was gutted from his crotch to his brains, much like the what John Lee has become an expert at.

Courtney proclaimed that her husband met the cacodemon, he cut his heart out, and fed it to stray dogs. Asiram stated, "I think we're under attack again, but why these two. I mean neither is a religious individual, and they probably have never been to church except to enforce some kind of statement that the group needed to make."

The Sarge, who was still on edge, stated, "I have had lots of dreams, good and bad, but this dream was foreboding and evil throughout. It awakened me, proclaimed that my heart was tainted, and that it needed to be purged from my body. As I watched without the ability to respond or move, that thing dug its claws into my chest, and yanked my heart out as I watched. I mean I have had nightmares about the things that we did for our country that has been trying to terminate us from the beginning. I have committed some horrific acts, but this thing scared the shit out of me. I am afraid to go to sleep."

John Lee and Jilkes walked in the breakfast area, and appeared to be arguing about something, as usual. John Lee looked over to the table where the Sarge and his family were, and announced to Jilkes, "Oh, boy, something be done stirred that pot again. Look at how the Sarge looks, and how them there people at that table be looking as well." Jilkes took notice of the Sarge as well as the others at the table, and concurred with John Lee. He said, "Perhaps we need to go over there, and see what's going on."

The two men approached the table, and dead reckoned on Courtney. They both realized that she had lost weight, pigmentation, and her eyes looked empty.

John Lee said, "Good morning people, I just can't help seeing that down look on ya'll faces. Ya'll be done caught something that we should stay away from?" John Lee then looked at Dr. Beckmire, and asked, "Doc, you be feeling alright? You kind of be looking challenged. There be anything that I can help you with?"

Courtney smiled at John Lee, and said, "I am still in recovery. I'll be alright in a couple of days."

John Lee said, "Doc, you be looking like it be more than a couple of days before you be feeling better."

The Sarge cleared his throat, and asked, "Did you come over here to annoy my wife or to speak to us, and then have some breakfast?"

Jilkes motioned for John Lee to stand down, but John Lee said, "There be something going on at this table, and it don't be healthy. Somebody needs to tell us what's going on." There was a long silence, and John Lee said, "I be apologizing for thinking that how you people be feeling is my business."

Asiram proclaimed, "The Sarge had a terrible nightmare last night, and so did the 'idiot spy'."

John Lee asked, "Did they die in them there dreams?"

Jilkes yelled, "What is wrong with you? Let's leave these people alone."

John Lee said, "Somebody needs to tell me what in the hell happened. I need to know did you people see yourselves being killed. Listen, that there 'idiot spy' is from your loins Sarge. Dr. Beckmire has been sick for a few days, and that ain't like her. Look at her eyes, they be empty of life. Now ya'll better listen, and pay real attention to what I be saying. When that there holy father got a hold of me, well you all know what he wanted me to do so that he could distract us from his real conscription. I be thinking that the Doc's sickness was a message telling the Sarge and Zanthius that there is another demon waiting to unfold. Now I know ya'll don't believe in all this shit, but I be knowing the signs."

The Sarge stared at John Lee in disbelief, and then said, "You are such a strange and wonderful human being. Last night, someone or something woke me up, stuck its claws into my chest, pulled out my heart, and fed it to some stray dogs while I watched.   Zanthius, tell John Lee about your horrendous experience."

Zanthius took a gulp of his coffee, sat his cup down, and said, "Someone is better than you at gutting people from their crotch to their brain. This guy or this thing made me watch him with a small blade or fingernail, gently stab me, and then methodically ran it from my penis to my brain. It was so real and believable."

John Lee thought for a minute, and then yelled, "Somebody fetch Ms. Viola. She be the only one who can help me funnel this thing out of the right faucet. People, look at me. The Doc be sick as a dog, the 'idiot spy' be watching him ass get gutted, and the Sarge be watching something, or somebody cut his heart out with claws. This here be some powerful witchcraft guided by a powerful overlord. It took me three days to climb out of my hell. I be believing that if we catch this thing from the start, we can figure out who it's trying to conscript, and who be the main distractions. So far, and I ain't no saint, because I considered doing despicable things to my family, I know that this stuff be from the center of hell a place where that fellow who tried to conscript Ms. Beatrice, and use me as the distraction by instructing me to do ungodly things to my family. This here thing needs to be considered, and figured out now, not after ya'll be done with them there eggs."

# # #

Ms. Viola appeared on the scene with Ms. Beatrice, Chakes, Luana, and the baby. They were totally unaware of the issues that were being discussed at the Sarge's table. When

Ms. Viola walked into the dining area, John Lee loudly stated, "Ms. Viola, I be needing you over here in a hurry."

When she approached the Sarge's table she spoke to everyone, and then asked, "What's going on?"

John Lee said, "Ms. Viola, we be having a demon kind of involvement with them there people sitting around this here table. The Sarge dreamt that someone or something stuck its claws in his chest, pulled out his heart, and fed it to some dogs. Now, hold your horses, the 'idiot spy' hallucinated that someone or something gutted him from his crotch to his brain, and made him watch. Now, add that there stuff, and throw in that the Doc is not feeling well, and her eyes be looking like an empty glass of water, I be saying that there be a demon somewhere connected to this formula."

Ms. Viola looked at Courtney, then at the Sarge, casually at Asiram, and then fully at the 'idiot spy'. She quietly asked, "When did these things that John Lee talked about happen?"

Asiram spoke up, and said, "Last night the 'idiot spy' began to scream in the middle of the night about what John Lee described."

Courtney announced that the Sarge saw something insert its claws into his chest, remove his heart, and feed it to stray dogs, last night as well."

Ms. Viola asked the Sarge, "Is there any way we can leave the farm and head to the outback. Someone or something is sending you a powerful message. Zanthius is yours, the Doc is pure as fresh snow on the Alps, you are, and have been a magnificent leader focusing on the whole, and not the individual. I so respectfully request that you pull up stakes, and we head for the outback. Listen, these three in one are signs of the cacodemon. Select a source, you and the 'idiot spy', design the attention by an infliction, Dr. Beckmire, inflict trauma on two, you and the 'idiot spy', and let the demon in to assume Dr. Beckmire, unless there is another Beckmire that is in his sights. Larry and Rashida are not blood, but are very much Beckmires from the core. Is there another?"

Courtney yelled, "Yes, our son, who does not acknowledge us as parents because we don't meet the standards of his pretentious friends from school."

Ms. Viola fell to her knees, and said, "Mr. Man, if all that you value and love be here, then I suggest that you have people gather those fanny packs, and be out of here in the next hour in order to be in the outback in the morning at the break of day. I am no bruja, but I came to this table, saw what I saw, and all that I know says, that we need to be out of here, now."

CHAPTER NINETEEN

In the outback, Wajickee patiently waited for the group to arrive from the airport. Once they were in the village, he immediately recognized that all was not right. He looked at Dr. Beckmire, and said, "My healer, I have a drink being prepared for you as we speak. It has an awful taste, but it will clear that brilliant mind of yours of anxiety, and it will help you focus on this new potentially dangerous demon that is circling around all Beckmires. Come my healer, indulge me. While we are in private, I need to ask you about your son, the one who does not wish to recognize you as appropriate parents. His aura has been blowing my way in turbulence for the past few weeks. I cannot propose or suggest resolutions, but I can solicit from you and Ben your real feelings about your offspring. He is under tremendous convictions that have led him to a place of no return."

Courtney asked, "What does that mean in plain old English?" Wajickee replied, "Please wait until Ben catches up with us, and I will give you the torment inflicted on me by him in my protection of Ben Beckmire. Ms. Viola and that John Lee are correct in their base analysis of the three in one approach. Ah, here comes my conscript."

Ben Beckmire appeared on the scene, and asked Wajickee what he was prescribing for his wife?

Wajickee replied, "I am giving her native ingredients that will help her fight the battle that is yours, hers, Zanthius, and your other naturally born son. There are some things that I am prohibited from trying to dissect, and I can only draw inferences. Please forgive me, but this limitation is provided for the protection of all who are involved. However, I will say this much, I will probably be relieved of my lifetime duty as your liege once I make certain admissions."

Ben Beckmire exclaimed, "Whoa, my friend! I don't want you looking into the future and providing me with ways to avoid certain outcomes including the death of my family, and members of my group. I forbid you to tell me the source of these new maladies that are facing me and my family. I absolutely forbid you from informing me of real life, natural occasions that will occur in the future."

Courtney after consuming the awful tasting concoction, announced, "I am tired from the long trip, and I just want to sleep in my hut and with nature."

Wajickee looked at Beckmire, and said, "I suggest that you pick your lovely bride up, and take her to your hut. She will not be able to walk on her own."

# # #

Eighteen hours later, Courtney woke up from an invigorating sleep, and said to her husband, "I am hungry as hell. Man, let's go and eat."

The Sarge replied, "Don't you think you should take a shower first, and then we'll go and eat?"

Courtney replied, "Ben Beckmire, "Are you suggesting that there is an odor about me that is offensive?"

Beckmire replied, "Honey, ever since I met you, I have never smelled anything about you other than an intoxicating scent of love and desire."

Courtney exclaimed, "You're so full of stuff, and that's why I love you to the moon and back."

Courtney and the Sarge exited their hut, and it seemed as though the entire village was there waiting to accept her back into life. She started out of the entrance, turned around and headed back in with tears in her eyes. She asked Ben, "Why are those people out there with flowers and gifts for me?"

Ben said, "Baby, you've been sick for a few days, both physically and mentally. I've had horrendous nightmares, as did 'the idiot spy'. That is pure love out there, please go and accept the appreciation that is due you. We all love you, and I thank God my love is supreme."

Courtney exited their hut, and the first person in line was Monica who said, "Girl, I've been on the wagon since you've been missing. Can you give me an idea when I can start drinking again with my best friend?"

Courtney whispered, "You're such a wicked bruja. How about this evening?" Other members of the group welcomed her back and everyone indicated that her wisdom, smile, and love were missed.

Mr. West called Mr. East, and asked why he hadn't heard from him in the last four days. Mr. East told Mr. West that he had been sick as a dog, and was having dastardly dreams about death. The two talked about their failed missions against the group, and the ultimate loss of scarce funds. Mr. East said that he convinced some really close friends to assist in this matter, and to strategically plan and execute a cost-free event that is based upon a code, superior intelligence, which supersedes brute strength, and unwieldy numbers of egos looking for an advantage. My associates are in this for the challenge, and the most creative plan with the least amount of personnel will allow the winner to be anointed leader of our cult.

Mr. West asked, "How will this adventure be financed?" Mr. East responded, "My associates are terribly rich and bored. We decided that we needed to beat the system, and what better way of accomplishing this than by eliminating one of the most feared and revered groups. A group of people led by old people, whose ranks are essentially old people as well, who are sitting on billions, and perhaps trillions of dollars, in assets to match. Now that is what I'm talking about, and the beauty of this new plan is that these people are proven, brilliant, and are doing it because it is a challenge."

Mr. West stated, "This is the same hyperbole that you fed me on the last two attempts on those old people who are led by other old people, who seemingly beat the shit out of us at each turn. Listen, no more stories of smart people terminating obtuse people. I've lost a shitload of money in this scheme of yours, and rightfully I must admit that it was driven by my hatred and detestation of those fucking people who blew my house up. I lived another day, and all of my days are dedicated to the destruction of every last one of those old people. I want to piss down Ben Beckmire's head after cutting his wife in half, and mutilating all that is dear to that bastard. So, Mr. East, no more fucking games or I might have to consider you in that equation. Talk to you later."

# # #

Later that afternoon, Courtney found Monica, and asked her if she was ready for a drink. Asiram who was nearby inquired, "Am I not worthy of having a cocktail with you two ladies?"

Monica looked at her, and stated, "Asiram, you have never been interested in drinking with us before. Why now?" Asiram took a deep breath, and burst into tears. She immediately started hyperventilating, coughing, sneezing, and turning colors. She announced, "I need to be hugged and loved by the only mother that I know. I am hurting so much inside that I can no longer hide what is going on in my home."

Courtney grabbed her, and said, "Baby, you know I love you even though you can be a cantankerous ass at times. You've given that 'idiot spy' a strong family of boys, and a girl. I told Ben that you needed to step away, and have some Asiram time, but no one listens to me. I have told you on many occasions that I needed you to focus on you sometimes because your total center is your family. Come now, tell me what's going on."

Asiram between double breathing stated, "Oh, you want me to tell you what's going on without offering to buy me a drink. You are such a cheap bruja, but I need your help and advice. I need advice from both of you who I respect and love."

The three ladies made their way to the billabong that the Great Saltie occupied, with containers full of a wonderful and stimulating native drink. As they sat down and watched the calmness of the billabong, Asiram took a deep breath, and said, "I think that my husband is involved in some sordid scheme to take control of the finances of the group."

Monica said, "Asiram, that's incredulous. Why on earth would he need to do that, he's already filthy rich. I can't believe that the man you love from Jupiter to the earth and back, could be caught up in some nonsense like that."

Asiram took a drink, looked at Monica, and said, "You know how the captives kept saying that there was someone on the inside who was feeding them information. Well, during the past two weeks, Zanthius, in his sleep, has been laying out elaborate plans to succeed to the throne. The first night I heard him speak in his sleep, I just blew it off. Each succeeding night, the plan became more elaborate, and the actions more descriptive. I distinctively heard him say in the first week of his announcements that he had to sever the head of the snake first, and then his eleven disciples. I ignored it initially, but then I started adding up his dad's buddies, they totaled eleven. What really freaked me out was when he said, "I am being counseled to annihilate my father in order to succeed to the throne. The throne is mine and my families way to eternal life. This is a thing that I must do. I must ascend to the throne, eliminate the eleven apostles, bring the Holy Father out of hiding, and restore him to his rightful place—Supreme Ruler of the World."

After a moment of disbelief, Courtney said, "I must bring my husband in on this conversation. This is incredible and places us all in jeopardy."

Asiram exclaimed, "Not a wise move! There is more to his sinister plot." She broke into tears again, and it would be two minutes or so before she was rational enough to announce the more diabolical conversations that the 'idiot spy' held during his sleep.

Finally calming down, Asiram stated, the 'idiot spy', as if answering to someone asked, "What level of sacrifice would thou have me offer?" As if someone was talking with him, he said, "I will do as thou has exacted. It will be done by the first night of the full moon. My current family will be no longer after that point in time." Again, as if he were having a conversation with someone, he said, "On a regular basis I provided the alleged enemy with strategic information, timetables, positions of the mechanized weapons systems, weak points in the structure of the facilities, and ranges from incursions to targets, and in most cases the battles were lost because they did not control their men, and thought that mass was might, when less was best."

Both women listened intently, and Courtney asked, "Why did you wait so long to inform us."

Asiram exclaimed, "Because he's my husband, and I love him dearly. I had a hard time convincing myself that I was hearing a diabolical plot to inform the enemies of the group as well as to sacrifice members of his family. I am having a hard time reckoning with the fact that I heard what I heard."

# # #

When the Sarge showed up, and after looking at the less than festive group, he said, "This looks really serious."

Courtney responded, "Sarge, this is as serious as it can get. Our daughter-in-law has confided in me and Monica who the inside person that former captives kept alluding to is. Sarge, according to Asiram, it is 'the idiot spy', your son, better known as Zanthius Beckmire De Lombardo." The Sarge looked at the three ladies, and announced, "That is a sick joke. What on earth has gotten into you people?"

Courtney exclaimed, "Listen to Asiram, and then you let us know if it's a sick joke or a cause of concern."

Forty-five minutes later, a weakened Ben Beckmire rhetorically asked, "How can so many be affected by the same chicanery? Who is the conductor of these mind-boggling events? My son is being targeted by a serious demon because no ordinary fiend can penetrate a Beckmire with all of the Spirits that support all of the good work that we do. My wife is plagued, my son is now in cahoots with a cacodemon, and I think we should reach out to our supernova of a son to see if he too is tormented. How can this all be happening at the same time?"

Courtney interrupted Ben, and asked, "Have you consulted with Wajickee?"

Ben replied, "If I use him in this manner, knowing that he would have to be completely honest with me, then he would be relegated to history, and would no longer be in service to me."

Monica interjected, "Someone is playing for all of the sand, meaning that they know that any information coming from the shaman would relegate him to a final resting place. At least one son is under the control of someone, and the other one is missing in action, but presumably is unavailable for such trivia because he and his friends are probably enjoying a yacht ride somewhere in the Mediterranean. My two cents say, try to find the missing child, and see if he sees no Alps."

Beckmire looked at her, and asked, "What's that see no Alps stuff?"

Monica replied, "It was an old saying of that Philadelphia preacher, Leon Sullivan meaning, nothing can stop us from crossing the mountain top."

Ben Beckmire gave Courtney the Sat phone, and said, "He is more likely to respond to you than to me. He hates me for some odd reason."

Courtney screamed, "That's not true, we just didn't meet his expectations of what parents should be."

Beckmire vociferously exclaimed, ***"Then we should have aborted the motherfucker!"***

# # #

That night, Asiram and the children stayed in the hut with Ben and Courtney. Gant, Green, and King were stationed in the nearby area. Jelani, Dempsey, Hood, Anel, and Angel were positioned near 'the idiot spy' and Asiram's hut. Anel and Angel also had non-lethal darts that were provided by the locals that would put a person to sleep in a matter of seconds.

At 10 pm, Zanthius emerged from his hut looking like Rambo with sleeves of bullets crisscrossing his body, two automatic rifles, two knives, three pistols, smoke grenades draping his torso, a bandana on his head, and black paint running down both sides of his face. Anel announced, "Too much fire power, let's put him down."

The two ladies placed darts in his neck, and the 'idiot spy' fell to his knees giving everyone in front of him the bird. The ladies placed wire-ties on him, and secured him in his hut. Anel and Hood had first watch which meant that Dempsey and Angel would stay with the kids.

The Sarge walked in, saw his son in restraints, and began to cry. Courtney assured him that he would be alright. He looked at her and said, "I'm without the wisdom of Wajickee, I don't know who else can bring him out of the clutches of the demon or demons that are working his mind and body."

Courtney smiled, grabbed the Sarge's hand, and said, "I made a call to Minnesota, they were airborne sixty minutes ago."

The Sarge's eyes, appearing big as apples, looked at Courtney, and said, "Oh my God! You are my heartbeat, my love, my air, my breath, and my mind. Oh, baby, you are always in front of my primitive mindset. Thanks for being smarter than me on every front, except one."

He smiled, and Courtney asked, "Don't you even think about trying to debate that one, because brother, I got you covered."

# # #

The next day late in the afternoon, Windom, Earther, Daniel, Mysteir, Litefoot, and a few others entered the village. It had been a long and arduous flight, but the group was more than happy to extend help to their new family and friends.

Windom and Earther met with the Sarge and his family, talked extensively to Asiram, and then decided to start their ritual outside of the hut since it was obvious that the 'idiot spy' was confined in a space that was completely covered, and that the negative energy from his occupying force could wreak havoc on those entering the enclosed confines without an invite.

Without any indication or knowledge of what was about to happen, Mysteir walked towards the hut housing the 'idiot spy'. Her father saw her out of the corner of his eye, and yelled, "Do not break that plane."

Mysteir smiled at her father, and entered the confines of the hut. With a small pocketknife, she cut the restraints off Zanthius, and said, "You will do nothing except sit here, and tell me who occupies your mind and body. I have never done this before, but I was told to do this in order to save you, your family, and your friends."

For five minutes, Zanthius sat there, said nothing, and neither did Mysteir. As her father, the Sarge, and other members of their tribe stared into the hut, they could see them sitting there with nothing being said. She said to Zanthius, "Obviously, we have company trying to figure out what's going on. Tell me Zanthius, who has entered your mind and what things are you being instructed to do."

Zanthius responded, "I can't tell you that, it's a secret."

Mysteir asked, "Do you love your wife and children?" As though he had been transported into someone else's body, a deep and demonic voice, announced, "Child get out of here before you become a memory." Her father started to enter the hut, and his daughter yelled, "Father, do not cross the plane. The voice you hear is only a manifestation of a demon that is trying to gain control over Zanthius, and now me. It is weak because it has no heart or soul, and cannot make decisions unless they are approved by its overlord."

She looked at Zanthius, and said, "I too have had dreams of destruction, and my target was you, Zanthius. I also know who is driving these unprecedented thoughts, and feelings in you. It is another like you, but from a different mother. You are one in the same, and the one who was replaced as the Holy Father is still trying to distract, confuse, and take complete control over all who are of this world."

The temporary voice inside of Zanthius, screamed, "Bitch, stay a bitch, or your runts will remain where they are throughout all of time."

Mysteir looked at Zanthius, and said, "Please tell your master that he has no leverage over me or mine. What he should be concerned about is that it is I, and not my father and his friends that have come for this conference. Also, tell your temporary overlord that in this land night is day, and day is night and, therefore, his tenure with you is rapidly diminishing. Also, tell him that the real forces for engagement are waiting for him outside of this hut. He has no home, he has no rights, and I demand that he stop hiding behind an innocent victim and display who he is. I demand that he come forth in his natural state. He has no time, he has no home, and here night is day, and day is night. I demand that he show us, those of us who are among the living, who this serpent is and who it serves."

Clearly the occupant was neither of this land, nor of this time, and sought a victim that had victims lined up waiting on his arrival in hell. When Mysteir made her final demand, that which was never seen, made its exit from the body and mind of Zanthius Beckmire De Lombardo.

Beckmire said, "I am going in there to see what the hell is going on." Windom said, "My friend, my leader, and our savior, please do not enter a place that I didn't know my own daughter was privy to. Please acknowledge her presence was summoned by someone other than me and mine to intervene in this matter. May I ask, where is that Wajickee fellow?"

# # #

Mysteir walked out of the hut with Zanthius in tow, and said, "People, say hello to Zanthius Beckmire De Lombardo."

Zanthius, a little slow to respond asked, "Why are you people hanging around my hut, and where is my wife and children?"

The Sarge asked, "Son, do you remember anything?"

Zanthius replied, "Like what Dad. All I know is that I was thinking about Rambo and the next thing I know, those two brujas shot darts into my neck."

The Sarge said, "Those two ladies are Anel and Angel, and you will respect them for saving your life in the long run."

Zanthius looked at Mysteir, then at his father, and announced, "Dad, I feel like I've been on a bad LSD trip. I can't make heads nor tails of anything that has been going on. And by the way, where is my brother?"

The Sarge looked at him, and asked, "Which brother?"

That evening, Asiram approached Zanthius with a look of suspicion and apprehension. She said to him, "Honey, do you know what you talked about in your sleep? Are you aware of the dastardly outcomes you had prescribed for me and your children?"

Zanthius said, "Whoa, wait a minute, what on earth are you talking about? What the heck is going on with you? I would never hurt you or my children."

Asiram stated, "You agreed to terminate me and our children for whoever was occupying your mind. You even indicated that you would, without reservation, eliminate your dad." Zanthius looked at her, and said nothing.

An hour or so later, Zanthius ran across his dad, and asked if the two of them could take a walk. Ben asked, "Do I need protection?"

Zanthius looked at him, and asked, "Why on earth would you need protection? And from what or whom?"

The two men walked by the billabong that housed the Great Saltie. The crocs seemed agitated, but it did not phase either man as they sat at the water's edge. Zanthius said, "My wife indicated that I promised someone that I would kill her, my children, and also you. Do you believe I could do such a thing?"

"Son, when apparently your mind and body are controlled by a foreign presence, anything might be possible. I think that by the mere fact you are a Beckmire, you would have come to your senses and refute any command such as that. You remember how John Lee was on the verge of doing terrible things to his family, and then his coup de grace was to sever his best friend's head from his body. Well, he sought help, you came out in your Rambo outfit ready for Freddy," Beckmire stated.

"Dad, there is no way I could hurt Asiram, our children, and you. You people are all that I have on this side of the grass. My mother is gone, and the rest of my family are only interested in what will happen to my fortune once I am no longer," Zanthius reported.

"Son, I have learned that when someone or something possesses a person, there are no boundaries that are sacred, no lives that are not expendable, and no manner of deceit and chicanery that wouldn't be used. Listen, I'm not like Earther, Windom, and now Mysteir. I mean she, from out of nowhere, broke the plane to your hut, cut you out of bondage, had words with you, denounced the occupying demon, and made it flee. This is all too mysterious for my little brain. Then to watch my son being restrained, well that was over the top for me. Again, I don't understand none of this, but for all of our sakes, I am going to summon Wajickee and ask him if you and we are free of the demon that was within," Beckmire stated.

CHAPTER TWENTY

The following day, Wajickee appeared in the village and greeted everyone. Ben Beckmire said, "You have been markedly missing my friend, and I understand your reasons. You followed my request, and I will hopefully, never have to speak to you in that manner again. I am sure you are aware of the happenings in the village over the past few days. Walk with me for a few, would you?" Beckmire requested.

"Indeed, I am, and I am so proud of Mysteir, what a shamanka she is. When I first shook her hand, her entire aura passed through me like a lightning bolt. She is, and will be the high priestess when she returns home. Her force is compassionate, but she uses the old school adages when dealing with demons. Believe it or not, this was her first confrontation or conversation with a cacodemon. Inside of that hut, it threw slurs of insults at her, but she maintained her lady like demeanor. She is as powerful as I am, and that means she is not to be trifled with. I'm probably going to be retired for saying this—Beckmire yelled, "Don't go there. Do not cross that threshold. I command you. What are you trying to do, leave my side as my liege?"

"No, my son."

"Wait a minute, you called me son. Am I missing something?" Beckmire asked.

"Mr. Beckmire, Sarge, Ben, and a few other names, please forgive my feelings of familiarity when addressing you. I felt so comfortable addressing you like that because I feel that you are my son. If it offends you, I will make sure it never happens again," Wajickee stated.

Beckmire announced, "I just need you around, and I don't want you to violate any rules that would extract you from being my ultra ego. I need you, not some new upstart."

As the men walked back towards the village, Beckmire said, "I'm going to ask you a question, if it borders, on crossing that plane of no return, I respectfully request that you immediately go on Walkabout and then Dreamtime. My question is simple, is my son safe from further possessions?" Wajickee was gone before he could put the 's' on possessions. Beckmire screamed, "Is Zanthius free of demons?"

Wajickee reappeared, and stated, "It is important to be precise, and I will take a hit on this one, and say, he is demon free, but he is also a Beckmire. Goodbye, Mr. Beckmire."

# # #

The Sarge knew that his Minnesota family was preparing to leave the village and return home. He walked over to Mysteir, and asked, "Will you walk with me?"

Ben Beckmire said, "I would like to introduce you to a relative of mine. He's a little frightening in appearance, but no harm will befall you. Is that something you're up to?"

Mysteir announced, "This visit has been bizarre, and I need to know who or what is calling me into action. I mean, Mr. Beckmire, I got off the plane, refreshed a little in the village, and countermanded my father's demand of crossing the plane to that hut. I'm really scared about what I did, but I just didn't wake up and say to myself that I'm going to free Zanthius from his restraints. Mr. Beckmire, I'm getting conflicting messages from the village, and they are all leading me to a place where everyone is faceless. I am confused," Mysteir admitted.

Ben Beckmire said, "If you're confused, then I don't have a clue. When you meet my ancestor, perhaps it will give us guidance as to why you, why now, and who is opposing this relationship?"

# # #

Ten or so minutes later, Mysteir and the Sarge sat near the water's edge, she asked, "Are we waiting on something to surface from the deep. I've heard about the oversized monsters that reside in these waters, but I really don't believe in monsters."

The Sarge looked at her, and said, "You just bested a monster, how can you say that?"

Mysteir smiled, and said, "Let me restate. I know that crocs can grow big, and, therefore, they are still an aquatic reptiles of sorts. What I consider a monster would be the likes of a prehistoric dinosaur rising from the deep with a taste for human meat."

The Sarge said, "Oh, I see. What would you call that which is looking at us on your left?" Not a single word was spoken until Mysteir was revived after fainting from seeing the anomaly called the Great Saltie.

Once back in the village, the Sarge said to Windom, Earther, and Litefoot, "I have it from high places that we have witnessed the orientation and inauguration of a new high priestess. She will need guidance from you three, but she will only act when requested. You guys remember how you dealt with the John Lee situation deep in the belly of that mountain, well, Mysteir uses a more modern approach to relate to demons and spirits. Learn to acknowledge her ways, but insist that she engages in the ways of the elders also. As we mature, as I prefer to call it, the entire nature of how things are done is going to be technologically challenging for us old folks. I cannot thank you enough for your immediate response to my wife's call. I cried a billabong full of tears after seeing my son in restraints. And when Courtney told me that you people were airborne, I cried for the friendship that we have and will have throughout our lifetimes. You my friends are like everyone in this village is to me, special, truthful, honest, reliable, and I love you with all my heart. Oh, here comes Mysteir," the Sarge stated.

When Mysteir approached, she dead reckoned on the Sarge, and asked, "Why is the missing Beckmire not in communication with his parents?" Mysteir paused for a moment, and said, "I sincerely beg your pardon Mr. Beckmire. Of late, I am not in control of my thoughts, and the verbal acknowledgements that come from my mouth. I have no idea why that might be relevant to me. However, I must state a premise, Mr. Beckmire, if you will allow me."

Mysteir acknowledged Daniel, and said, "Honey, I may sound strange, but since coming here, a new set of experiences have encompassed me, and I don't know really how to control what comes out of my mouth. My approach apparently is not politically correct, my resolve is intended to get expeditiously to the answers, rather than take a long arduous trip. So, Mr. Beckmire, I've been commanded to figure out what is going on with transgressions within your family and the group. My analysis keeps me close to the locus of control, and that is the group's immediate location.   However, something keeps saying to me that a Beckmire nearby, is responsible for the trials and tribulations of the group.   However, I then get a reading that there is a Beckmire who does not communicate unless there is a request for support, is that true, or am I being a bit intrusive?"

After a pause in the rapid inquisition by Mysteir, Windom said, "You must learn that each inquiry causes a certain amount of pain to the one you are inquiring with. Your rapid-fire approach is harmful to our relationship with our friend and host."

Mysteir fired back, "Sorry to cut you off, but people are planning to kill all of our friends, and I was anointed by someone to find out in a hurry, who is trying to take all that the group has acquired."

The Sarge cleared his throat, and said, "Mysteir, do you remember the first time we met? Anyway, I do. It was on our plane after we figured out that people were trying to take what belonged to your family. I remember Daniel standing up, and saying to his father, "I'm in love with Mysteir, and we want to be together. His father harshly told him to sit down and shut up. Daniel replied, "I will not. I'm in love with Mysteir, and we want to be together." Anyway, I say all of that to say, I welcome your curt and to the point questions, and I do not have a problem with their impact. I need to know why several of my friends were assassinated. So, Windom, Daniel, Earther, and Litefoot, please let her be as aggressive in questioning me as possible without any backlash. I don't need a song and a dance, I need answers, and her approach is getting me closer to both the name of the song, and the specific dance."

#

At the airport the Sarge, said to Windom and Earther, "Mysteir is a God send. Please don't try to manage her approach, let her be as free as the wind and as expansive as the earth." Both men looked at Beckmire, and fell to their knees. Beckmire yelled, "What the heck are you guys doing? Get the hell off your knees, and look me in the eyes. We don't kneel and kowtow, there is no superior person in this group."

Windom stood first, and said, "It has been written that those words would come from the individual who would make our land prosperous, and our people respected and admired." Earther stood tall, and said, "Those words were spoken many years ago to the two of us, Mr. Beckmire before we went off into that police action in the Nam. There is no way you could have just made those words up, at this moment in time, after conjured and distorted truths, dealing with marco, marco polo, helping friends & chasing diablo, mechanized mayhem, *The Sanctuary*, deific intermediation, treachery, carbon factor unleashed, between heaven & hell, and primarily coming together as group to support your mission—hell, hell, the gangs all here. Mr. Beckmire, we salute you, pray for you, and will always be at your beck and call when and if we're needed. *us against the world*, we feel will be costly, and mentally painful for all who enter this new era. We pray that you and your people will live long, prosperous, giving, and thankful lives."

The Sarge, in tears, said, "I think one of my own, who is near, is going to cause me more pain than I think my little heart can endure."

Earther replied, "What stands you apart from most, my friend, is that you forgive people, you help them help themselves, you even appoint known assassins to critical and sensitive positions in your group. This is unheard of Mr. Beckmire. No matter the attempts, or the revelations, you will always be the head of the pack because of your compassionate nature. Look at the two of us. We were hired to find ways to kill you. Look at Dempsey, Hood, Anel, Angel, King, Green, and Gant, they all make up critical positions in your defense/offense and they are committed members of your family. Yes, perhaps you will ultimately be betrayed by one who you love, but the love that you have spread across this land and the world will provide you with more than enough expressions of friendship.

# # #

As the group boarded the plane, Mysteir deplaned and announced that she would be needed and, therefore, she would join her family on another day. Daniel said, "Honey, I do believe that you must seek permission from Mr. Beckmire. What has gotten into you? You are all over the place, going against your meek and demure nature to commanding the attention of everyone around you. What is going on my love?"

Mysteir looked at Daniel, and asked, "Can you come with me for a minute?"

Ten minutes later, Daniel walked over to his father-in-law, Windom, and requested, "I need you and Nanna to take care of the babies until we return. My wife, your daughter, is on a mission, and I have to support her, and make sure she does not get in over her head. From what I have gleaned from her, this mission is important to everyone involved, and may end in a lot of pain for some."

Windom looked at Daniel, and said, "At first I didn't respect or like you, I guess a lot of it was because of your father. I have grown to love you because you protect and secure my daughter. I just want you to know something that I have selfishly kept from you because of my ego, I guess. Son, please take care of my daughter, your wife, my grandbabies' mother, and now a mother of the Earth and Wind."

# # #

The Sarge saw Mysteir and Daniel, and asked, "Is there a problem?" Mysteir replied, "As a matter of fact, yes there is my friend. I am not sure of all who are involved in it, but yes there is a problem, and since Wajickee is being reprimanded about providing you with future oriented events, he quietly suggested that I should hang around, and that he would greatly appreciate it. What makes me really happy is that my one and only true love, is remaining here to support me."

The Sarge started to speak his mind, and say, "I think we got this under control...." Wajickee showed up, and announced, "Ben Beckmire, Mysteir has gotten her wings in another dimension, she is able to do and assist in matters that I can't. Please welcome her and Daniel, and treat them better than you treat me, your servant." Beckmire started to say something, but Wajickee was long gone.

# # #

Back in the village, Courtney and Monica saw Mysteir and Daniel, and approached them. Monica asked, "Is everything alright? Why didn't you two go back with the others?"

Mysteir replied, "Monica, hi Dr. Beckmire, I do not know what draws me to this land, this place, at this time. I do know that the very fabric of the group is under scrutiny, and is in danger. As I entered the plane to head for home, I received several visceral messages that stated that all had not been resolved, and that the focus leads directly to the 'idiot spy'. Why is he called the 'idiot spy', and why does he warrant that title?"

Courtney smiled at Mysteir, and asked, "Would you like to join Monica and I for a cocktail?"

Mysteir replied, "I'm not really a drinker, but I would love to be in the company of you two royals."

Forty-five minutes later, Mysteir was laughing, touching, swearing, revealing, and having a grand old time. She and the ladies tore into that local drink, and before you knew it, Mysteir had over consumed. All that she had eaten became obvious to the other ladies, as well as all that she had not eaten. She went straight for the lining of her stomach.

# # #

The next morning before the village came to life, surprisingly, Mysteir was up and out doing calisthenics. When Monica walked over to her, she politely said, "I don't think I'll ever hang with you two veterans again. It was fun, but I paid a terrible price."

Monica smiled, and said, "Honey, but you had one hell of a good time. You were dancing, prancing, touching, laughing, and on occasion, swearing. Not the kind of behavior I would expect from a person who is here to save us from Armageddon."

Mysteir stared at Monica, and asked, "Why the use of that word?"

Monica responded, "Because last night you mentioned it at least on five different occasions."

Mysteir asked, "Do you think you can mobilize Dr. Beckmire, I'm going to need you two ladies to help me with the 'idiot spy' and his wife. It's the bloodline that is contaminated, and someone near and related is the cause."

#

A few hours later, Mysteir saw Asiram, and asked, "Do you think I could have a conversation with you and the 'idiot spy'? Somehow, there is a force that leads to him that's blaming him for all that is wrong with Dr. Beckmire and Mr. Beckmire." Asiram looked at Mysteir as if she had just landed from Mars, but decided to engage her until it was time to diss her. From out of nowhere, the sage appeared, and said, "Ladies what a beautiful day to discuss the current issues of the village, and the group. I sanction this meeting, and I know that everyone will cooperate with my visiting friend." Asiram didn't see him come or go, but tried to respond to no avail.

Asiram suggested that they have breakfast first, then meet near the billabong so that she could watch her kids play, and discuss the matters that are of concern to Mysteir. Mysteir asked her which billabong, and Asiram pointed to the one which housed the Great Saltie, and a few of his associates. As Mysteir thanked her, and turned to walk away, Asiram, feeling guilty, decided to correct the information, and yelled, "Oh, Mysteir, I lost my bearings, it's not that billabong, it is the one over this way." Mysteir was aware of the deceit, and thanked her for the corrective information.

Later when Zanthius appeared with Asiram, Courtney pulled them aside, and said, "Listen you two, this child is trying to find out who is attacking us from so many fronts, I need you guys to be hospitable, frank, and easy with her. Wajickee can't intermediate, because if he does, this would be his last assignment. Therefore, after realizing that this young lady is from his realm, he in order to continue service to my husband and the group, has asked her to look into this matter."

Zanthius asked, "Mom, why is everyone looking at me like I'm trying to pull a coup?"

Courtney touched him on the shoulder, and replied, "Son, the consistent information coming from those who were captured, those who bargained for continued life, and even some spirits, is that the charlatan is a member of our group, and is closely tied to a Beckmire. You've heard people say, "someone close to you is feeding your enemies, information. Then when you think about the notion of a tontine, everyone begins to look closer at each other. Now what bothers me is that other than Hood, Dempsey, Gant, Green, King, Anel, and Angel, we are all rich beyond our wildest imaginations. Even the kids are fricking millionaires. So, I say all that to say that you're the only seed of Ben Beckmire that is nearby and somehow, rumors keep circulating that it's you. I know Larry and Rashida are here as well, but from the loins of Ben Beckmire, you are the only one within smiling distance."

Zanthius reflected on the information for a minute, and asked, "Mom, you and dad have another son. Where is he, and why isn't he under scrutiny?"

Courtney looked at him, and said, "He is so stuck on imagery that he could care less about what happens to me or his dad. I was sick, your father reached out to him, but never reached him nor did he return his calls. I mean no card, no flowers, no nothing, but a few days after I was up and around, that little bugger informed me that he and his pretentious friends were heading to Greece for an extended amount of time, and that he needed some spending money. I sent him $100k, and was admonished by your dad for doing so."

Asiram astutely asked, "Is there any way he could be a part of a conspiracy? Courtney, being the mother that she is, said, "Oh no. He thinks that we are poor because his father was a cop, and that he knew that I had saved $500k for him that he could have at any time."

Asiram asked, "Where is he heading on his junket?" Courtney responded, "Thessaloniki."

Asiram asked, "Do you think it's time that the group met him? I mean is he a part of your will? Courtney, we're talking a lot of billion dollars between you and the Sarge, insurance, investment, cash accounts, and other assets. Could he be the Lone Ranger?"

Courtney looked at Asiram, and emphatically stated, "Our money and assets, don't meet his standards. He feels that his dad was a cop, I am a doctor, there is no old money in the pipeline and, therefore, we don't qualify as meaningful parents. He once, in the midst of asking me for money, announced, "Thank you for having me, but there is no need for a mother-son, or father-son, relationship. I know this seems hard, but your pipeline is unacceptable to my goals and objectives in life. Thanks again, but no thanks to those touchy-feely events that people celebrate."

Courtney began to cry, and that is when Asiram embraced her, and cried with her. Asiram verbally stumbled, and said, "I've told you more than once Ms. Lady, that you are the closest person to being a mother to me. I cry because I was a throw-away until you and that cantankerous Monica rescued me from the abyss. I love you both so much, and I have often wanted to just take you and Monica away for a girls' trip. I need you in my life so much Ms. Lady. Excuse my expression, but fuck that overly self-appointed son of yours. I'll replace him and pay homage to you on a daily basis, if you will agree to sit in for those people who were alleged to be my parents, but did everything in their power to break me, torment me, bully me, abuse me, and literally sink me into servitude."

All three women were crying their hearts out when Mysteir announced, "What a scintillating display of emotions, friendship, and love." With tears in her eyes, Mysteir asked, "If you can manifest that trip, do you think I could come along as well. However, I will not let you people trick me into over imbibing."

# # #

Mysteir looked at Zanthius, and asked, "Why are you called the 'idiot spy'?" Zanthius looked at her, and responded, "Why are you named, "Mysteir?"

After a few seconds, Mysteir asked, "Can we take a walk, just the two of us because I need you to have a blunt and honest conversation with me? Somehow your blood, or bloodline is connected to this never-ending assault against the group.

As they began to walk away from the others, Mysteir said, "I know your history prior to your meeting your father. I am aware of all of your shenanigans, going all the way back to when you worked on the Islands. I am aware of your many pleasurable, but sordid affairs. I am aware of everything that is Zanthius. So, are you prepared to engage me on the most honest level that you have ever played on?"

Zanthius stared at her, and inquired, "If you know so much, give me a few names?"

Mysteir laughed, and said, "Why don't we start with Brenda. Oh yeah, you met her in Arizona. Then let's move to Caroline, Amsura, Tiffany, her sister, your secretaries that you promised a meaningful relationship, your first wife Pamela, and the most famous person of all, the multiple named bruja, Helga Spengatsenburg, or depending upon the day, Sister Mary. Is that good enough, or do you want me to provide you with details of the encounters."

Zanthius looked towards Asiram to make sure she couldn't hear about his litany of lovers, and Mysteir asked, "Would you like to include Asiram in our conversation? Of course not, even though she has some idea of who you were, I know exactly who you were and who you are, and I must say, you would make any women proud the way you love, and are dedicated to your wife and children. In my world there are no leaks. None of this will be disclosed. I just need you to help me figure out the dynamics of those who are constantly trying to terminate the group."

Zanthius stood in awe of Mysteir, and asked, "How could you know this information? Who are you? What kind of witch are you, to be able to go back in time and identify my former associates? Please, give me a clue before I bare my soul to you."

Mysteir looked at Zanthius, and inquired, "Do you believe that there can be good witches who mediate between the bad ones? I need you to realize that I am here because someone wants everyone in this village dead. A strong sense of direction leads me to you, and that stupid notion of a tontine."

Zanthius started to say something, and Mysteir stated, "Wait Zanthius, let me finish my thought." Mysteir paused for a few seconds before continuing, and stated, "I am convinced that it is a member of the Beckmire clan who is involved in this underhandedness. As the witch, that you called me, there is some information that is off limits to my level of being. However, here is my first real question. Zanthius, could you have possibly fathered another child that is under the radar?"

Zanthius looked at her, and calmly stated, "Not to my knowledge, but it's possible that such a thing could have happened."

Mysteir smiled, and said, "That was an appropriate response. Never tightly close the lid on a bottle if you don't want all of the contents to remain inside. Have you ever met your half-brother who was fathered by your father and your stepmother?"

Zanthius replied, "Mysteir how much deeper are you going to dive into this well. My father does not speak about him, my stepmother aches because she mothered him, and he feels that she and my father are not representative of the kind of people he wants his friends to meet."

Mysteir asked, "Do you ever have dreams about a person whose face is never presented?"

Zanthius flinched, looked at Mysteir, and asked, "What fucking kind of witchcraft are you performing. I am done with this inquisition."

As he started to walk away, Wajickee appeared, and said, "Zanthius my friend, I need you to complete the session with Mysteir. She is truly on our side, and has to ask uncomfortable questions to gain information on who the villain is that's creating so much turmoil at this late stage of the game."

Zanthius turned around, and replied, "Mysteir, I see this image at least two to three times a week, and he's always faceless."

Mysteir asked, "Does he always appear in the same place and under the same circumstances?"

Zanthius once again flinched, and said, "This is too much for me to digest. Is it possible for us to continue this after sundown?"

# # #

Mr. East called Mr. West, and began the conversation by stating it was highly disturbing to hear him directly threaten his partner. Mr. East said, "I know you've invested a lot, and so have I, but we can't commit to ending each other's lives at each turn when we fail to accomplish our mission. It is totally unprofessional to act in that manner, it mirrors the barbarians, not socialized, intelligent human beings such as you and I."

Mr. West considered the information, and replied, "You have lost some funds, but not nearly the amount I have invested in this hare-brained scheme. Your people are resilient, and are not easy targets. I just need closure, as do you, so that we can move to the next level of our plan."

Mr. East said, "I was feeling terrible about the outcomes of the last two events. I called my broker, and sold some of my Tesla, Amazon, Apple, Meta, and Alphabet stocks. I wanted it to be a surprise to you, in order to let you know that I know that you have invested a lot in this project, and in me. It was one-third of my portfolio, and it was FedExed to you yesterday morning, and should be arriving today before 2 pm. Hey, I need to call you back. I am in need of a little carnal satisfaction, and she is attempting to gain entrance to my place. Let me call the desk and okay her entrance. I will call you back soon. Give me thirty or so minutes, and we'll continue our conversation." The two men agreed, and disengaged the phone lines.

Mr. East made a call to a number, and said, "He's there, make it messy and obvious. I'll show this asshole who's in charge. The nerve of him threatening me."

Mr. West thought about the conversation with Mr. East, and decided to have one of his henchmen preside over the event. The package required a signature. Mr. West had his man go down to the lobby, sign for the package, and bring it to him after it was opened and secured.

Less than five minutes later, gunfire broke out in the lobby, and the person who was considered Mr. West was shot twenty-two times, and was decapitated.

After the dust had settled, and the true meaning of the event was defined, Mr. West sent a concluding message to Mr. East, saying, "Family and ex-friends. Good luck with solving the equation and achieving a successful out. Keep your eyes on your rear!"

Mr. East made a call to his associate, and asked, "How did we blow a simple fucking extermination?" The person on the other end said, "We responded to who picked up the package. Apparently, that was not the target. A photo would have helped identify the target. Sorry boss, but we need to work on our communication skills. You indicated that he would pick up the package, and sign for it. That didn't happen. You see where I'm going with this one."

Mr. East said, "We now have to find his ass before he finds me. He's pretty precise, and if I know him, he has already made a few calls to have me hit. I guess I thought it would be a simple operation. I should not have acted in haste. I should have thought about it, to make sure if we attempted to whack him that there would be no slip-ups. I screwed this one up. Get out of dodge, drop your weapons in the water and catch the next flight this way. Thanks, and I accept total blame for this hitch!"

# # #

Daniel asked his wife, "What is going on with you these days. I know you woke up changed from being my wife and lover into being a high priestess of some kind. I'm just trying to figure out how this happened, and how it will impact our marriage?"

Mysteir looked at her husband, and responded, "Nothing on earth will interfere with our marriage. I don't know what's happening, and why at this time, but apparently I am being called into service. I suggest that we act as we normally do, and always place our relationship ahead of the issues, where possible. How about that?"

Daniel smiled, and asked, "Does that mean that I can try to seduce my wife, the high priestess, whenever I have the need to?" Mysteir threw her hands in the air, and asked, "How about right now. I would love to make love to you in the middle of the day without having the children press us into action to support whatever they are into at that moment." Daniel smiled, and the rest is history or the beginning of a new future.

# # #

Zanthius asked Asiram if she would walk with him to discuss some troubling feelings that he was having, and she agreed. As they approached the limits of the village, Zanthius announced, "I am feeling terrible about things that I did, prior to meeting you. Honey, I have had multiple relationships with multiple women, loved many, and married you. I have had them separate, together, and I have not been honest about my past to you. I know that you've never asked me about my past, but you told me about the abuse you experienced at the hands of those who should have protected and loved you."

Asiram exclaimed, "Wait! Are you having an affair?" Zanthius dropped his head, paused, and said, "Of course not."

Asiram, with daggers in her eyes, asked, "Have you been screwing around since we've been married?"

Zanthius proclaimed, "Absolutely not!"

Asiram asked, "Then what is your 'idiot spy' ass talking about?"

Zanthius smiled, and said, "My session with Mysteir was informative because she delved into my past with specific names, places, and times. That's the Zanthius that you don't know, and I was feeling that I was not leveling with you."

Asiram said, "Your past, my past, are things that can't be changed. I am only concerned about our now, and tomorrow. I can't throw stones at a glass window, when my past is cloudy, dirty, incestuous, and painful. Honey, remember, I killed my abusive family, and burned them beyond recognition. I'm only concerned about our today and tomorrow. Your past and my past are not even a part of the equation. All I hope is that you, my babies' daddy, and I are in this marriage until truly death do us part."

Zanthius with a smile on his face, said, "I love you more than life. You're always in my corner protecting me." He gave her a seductive kiss, and perhaps began a new era.

#

After all of the magnificent, suggestive kissing, and ultimately supercharged love making with their partners, Mysteir and Zanthius met near the fire pit in the village. Mysteir stated, "I feel compelled to ask you this question again. In all of your travels and transgressions, is it possible that you could have created another life, not that it would matter because they would be too young to implement the kind of activities that have been pointed at this group?"

Zanthius looked at her, sighed, and said, "As I said before, anything is possible. You're so particular in your inquiry, why don't you tell me if in fact there is another Beckmire from my loins."

After a long pause, Mysteir asked, "May I hold your hands?" Zanthius replied, "If you must, then by all means." Mysteir took in some deep breaths, and expelled them. She slowly reached out for Zanthius's hands, and after caressing them, the faceless person appeared before her. She immediately let go of his hands, and backed away. Zanthius demanded, "What did you see, who did you see?" Mysteir did not reply. Zanthius raised his voice, and insisted on an answer. Mysteir said nothing, but looked at Zanthius straight on. Zanthius grabbed Mysteir's hands, and commanded her to tell him what or who she saw.

Mysteir finally replied, "I saw your father."

#

Mallory told Monica that he was going to take the kids for a hike. She replied, "Give me fifteen minutes, and I will accompany you guys."

By the time Monica got prepared, every kid in camp wanted to go. Each was given a survival package that included water, band aids, and bug spray. Most of the adults internally reluctantly agreed to go along, but realized that they needed to provide security for that many children. Wajickee showed up, and whispered to Mallory, "Take the kids Northeast of here, don't head Southwest. There is trouble in that area that I need to investigate."

When the Sarge came out of his hut, and saw all of the activities that was happening, he asked, "Whose bright idea is this?" Mallory raised his hand, and said, "These children are in need of exercise and exposure to what surrounds them."

The Sarge replied, "I like that idea. Do you think I can come as well?"

Courtney hearing his request, yelled, "I'm coming as well."

Mallory said, "Well, we're leaving in ten." The Sarge asked, "Do we have enough firepower to cover the fringes?" Mallory saw Jelani and summoned him over. He told him that he needed him and his crew to provide security for a hike that the children wanted to take.

Jelani responded, "Mallory, give me five minutes, and I'll take the lead, have dual coverage on both sides, the front, and the back." Mallory thanked him.

Three minutes later, Gant, Green, King, Hood, Dempsey, Anel, and Angel, were loaded for bear. Jelani assigned Hood and Dempsey to the front, Anel, and Angel to the rear near their wards, Gant, and Green to the East, and he and King to the west. The Sarge said, "It's unfortunate that we have to prepare in this manner to just exercise our children, but we all know the consequences of not covering every position. Okay, let's go exploring and hopefully have some fun, see other

Aborigines, and make peace and friends with them. The kids need this exercise because hopefully, they will take up the mantra when we are all looking down from heaven or up from hell, more likely the latter position, at our progression."

The front security types, with a couple of warriors from the village struck out first, and headed due northeast. All of the adults were wired, and had in their possession the small device developed by Bertha and refined by Rashida.

###

Wajickee and several villagers encountered a group of fortune hunters who were from the west coast. They drew weapons on Wajickee and his group, and demanded that they lead them to their village. The villagers knew that Wajickee was able to be there one minute, and gone the next.

One of the blokes asked, "Where you darkies be heading in this direction if'n your village be that away?" One of the men started to say something, and was hit with the butt of a weapon in the head for addressing the white man while looking at him at the same time. This action caught Wajickee off guard, he fell to his knees, and while looking at the ground, replied, "Sir, we came out here because we heard some beastly noises last night that scared everyone in our village. It sounded like the devil himself was abusing someone."

One of the men said, "You expect us to believe that dumb shit? Where is your village, and is that the place where you darkies found a lot of gold?"

Wajickee, who was churning inside, responded, "Yes Sir. Our village is where the gold was found." The men looked at each other, and started to give each other high-fives. Wajickee asked, "How did you people get out here without transportation?"

One of the men replied, "Darkie, when I ask you a question, you answer it. You don't get to ask me any damn questions. Now get your ass up, and lead us to your village."

Rashida, in charge of security, placed the village on alert as a result of the children and many members of the group going on the expedition. John Lee started sniffing around as if he was searching for something in the air. Jilkes asked, "What is your dumb ass doing?"

John Lee replied, "Can you smell that there cigarette smoke?"

Jilkes stated, "I don't smell anything other than you, my friend."

John Lee insisted, "Listen, African American, I smell cigarette smoke, and no one around here smokes."

Jilkes saw Rashida, and flashed a closed fist in the air. In turn she sounded the low-level alarm, that consisted of erratic drumbeats. The remaining women grabbed their weapons, and body armor, and made their way to the main entrance of the diamond mine.

Jilkes sent Montomie and Jong to the east, McArthur, and Gladstone to the north, Chakes and Whitmore to the west, and Bernstein, and Brown to the south. He and John Lee hung out near Brown and Bernstein. Somara, Asiram, Zanthius, Yeshida, and Okema, made their way to the high ground, where they had a spectacular view of the interior of the village.

Fifteen minutes later, drums began to beat at a rapid cadence to indicate the distance the predators were from the village. Darryl and Sue Lyn were at the entrance to the village, and everyone was in a down range shooting position. Suddenly, the drums ceased to beat, and everyone knew that in ten to fifteen minutes, strangers would be entering the village.

Fourteen minutes later, Wajickee entered the village with armed strangers scouting the area. One of the men asked, "Where are the rest of the darkies?"

Wajickee responded, "They took the children for a hike this morning."

Twenty-two armed men began to move about the village. Wajickee announced, "If you don't drop your weapons, you will be slain where you stand."

One of the men put his weapon to Wajickee's head, and proclaimed, "You die first darkie!"

Wajickee exclaimed, "I highly doubt if that will be the outcome!" And before the man could respond, Wajickee was gone. He appeared next to Rashida, and asked, "What do you want to do?"

Rashida, startled of course stated, "I asked you not to do that to me. Anyhow, I will see if I can spare their lives. She got on her bullhorn, and announced to the visitors that they were completely surrounded, and that if they didn't put their weapons down in the next ten seconds, then they would be mercilessly terminated. The men began to bunch up, and back out of the village with two villagers in front of them with weapons pointed at their heads. Rashida announced, "Since you have taken hostages, there is no room for parley." She then yelled, "On my mark." Seconds later, twenty men were systematically terminated, and the two mouthpieces, were wounded, but would live to provide the group with information.

Wajickee appeared, and said to the man that used the butt of his weapon to humiliate one of the villagers, "You seemingly like inflicting pain when you have the upper hand." He turned to the villager, and said, "I want you to give him the same treatment that he gave you."

The villager picked up the man's weapon, and asked, "Where did you people come from?" The guy was about to say something, when the villager slammed the butt of the weapon to the man's face, breaking his nose on impact, and yelled, "How dare you speak to me, and look directly at me at the same time."

Wajickee said to the other person who addressed him as 'darkie', "I want you to place your face so close to the ground, that the ticks in front of you can crawl up your nose, and decide where they want to lay their eggs."

After waking the guy who was hit by the butt of his own weapon, John Lee asked, "Are there any more of you people?"

The guy smiled, and said, "I guess you'll have to wait and see, won't you."

John Lee smiled, and said, "Well, there be plenty more of us." He and his crew gathered the weapons, and realized that most of them were Kalashnikov rifles. Jilkes said to one of the captives, "These are the real deal. Where did you get them from?"

The guy quietly, exclaimed, "Go fuck yourself, Nigger!" John Lee hearing this, pulled out his knife, and stabbed the man in the foot. He then withdrew the weapon from the man's foot, and in front of everyone who wanted to watch, forcefully stabbed the man in his groin area, and began to yank his big knife upwards cracking, and breaking bones as he ventured towards the man's brain. He cut the man's heart out, and threw it into the fire. A sign of disrespect as he did not attempt to take a bite out of the heart before the man died.

John Lee exclaimed, "You call my friend the 'N' word, expect to die a horrible death." Covered in blood, and everyone else in shock, John Lee said, "I'm going to fetch some water and wash this tainted blood off me. We need to clean the village up before our kids come back. Let that other vermin find his way out of here. I be believing the animals will want to enjoy his fat ass."

## CHAPTER TWENTY-ONE

Later, as the group gathered for pre-dinner cocktails, Mysteir said to Mr. Beckmire, "You are the faceless person in your son's dreams. I do not know what that means in the outback. However, a short and simple definition from back home is that the person who witnesses the faceless person is the person who is the betrayer."

Beckmire studied her mannerisms, and decided to push the edge of acknowledgement. He asked, "So, Mysteir, are you accusing my son, Zanthius Beckmire De Lombardo of being the source of treachery against me, and our group?"

Mysteir looked at him for a long time in silence. When she decided to speak, Beckmire cautioned her about breaching the bounds of conjecture and reality. Mysteir paused again, but this time she flatly stated, "I don't even know why I was chosen for this mission, however, I am not manufacturing information, I am stating what it means in a land far, far away from here. Can I without ambiguity testify that Zanthius is the center of deceit, treachery, and is playing a tontine with your lives, not at all. What I can say is that this issue is much like how a demon uses a slew of deceptions to redirect the attention of those who it is trying to mislead. It selects a medium, in this case perhaps Zanthius, it presents a ruse, perhaps dreams, suspicions, hints of deceit, and many other false accusations, all designed to keep the real target free, and easy to conscript.

He is called a demon because what he does is demonic in nature."

The Sarge immediately jumped in, and said, "Much like it tried to do with John Lee. It tried to make him kill his family, and his best friend, which was the ruse and focus, all while it had its sights on one of our children." Mysteir responded, "That is exactly what I am trying to state. So, in my analysis, there is a 50-50 chance that Zanthius is the culprit or the ruse."

As Mysteir continued, she asked, "By the way Mr. Beckmire, in your travels, is it possible that you may have fathered another?"

The Sarge reared back, and declared off the cuff, "Mysteir, anything is possible. However, I don't think that I have fathered another child, but again, I can't stake my life on that information. I can unequivocally state that since I have been married to Dr. Beckmire, there is no way under the sun because I've been as faithful as any human could possibly be."

Mysteir smiled, and said, "That I sincerely know about you and your wife, Mr. Beckmire. The love that you two share is as radiant and effervescing as the rising and setting sun. Mr. Beckmire, I feel my work is nearing an end here, and I thank you for such a transparent and direct dialogue about facts that are neither my business nor my concern. I now know why they call you the "Mountain", in my home. It is not your stature, it is your honesty, benevolence, and loyalty to those who had adverse missions towards you, and your need to help people help themselves. I thank and adore your leadership, Mr. Beckmire. Again, thanks for a straightforward discussion."

# # #

An urgent message was filtered for the Sarge through the sewers. It stated that a former adversary had conclusive information about who was the brains behind the recent assassinations, attempted murders, and the reason for the targeted and direct actions to end the group's existence. The message also stated that the person wanted to meet in person, because he wanted to make sure that there is an agreement of no further hostilities from you or him. He also wants to meet in an extremely high-profile place to discuss the information as well as provide factual data. Michael received the message from his guys who previously worked at the airport in Florida, who were now tutors, mentors, friends, disciplinarians, and managers of the home for children who are hard of hearing and sight challenged, and who were in many instances, abandoned.

Michael announced to the Sarge that a former adversary wanted to meet with him in Sydney, Australia, at the airport, and in front of hundreds of people. After presenting the information to the Sarge, he asked Michael to take a walk with him. As the two men approached the boundaries of the village, the Sarge asked, "Michael, do you think that a member of our current family could develop a tontine or an outright plan to eliminate the rest of us to acquire all of the group's assets, both personally and organizationally?"

Michael asked, "Sarge, you're fooling with me, aren't you?"

The Sarge continued to walk, and finally stated, "Mysteir believes that Zanthius is the person who is anxious to have it all."

Michael screamed, "Horseshit!" After taking a few steps, he said, "All that I have learned to believe in, appreciate, admire, love, and praise is in that village back there. Zanthius is more like a brother than just a member of the group, to me. Much like Jilkes and John Lee, not as strong as their bond, but it is built on faith and your teachings. Your son, my friend, is not capable of being the toxic pill that would kill us all. Zanthius is you, Mr. Beckmire, a little impetuous at times, but he is you, and he strives at every turn to be representative of you, and gain your favor. He used to be envious of the relationship that you have with Larry and Rashida, but realized that you loved everyone, and that he is your very own child. He got over that, and even once stated that he owes Larry and Rashida a lot for filling a huge gap in the lives of your wife and yourself. I once again say, "horseshit!"

The Sarge continued, and stated, "Thanks for that vote of confidence. Mysteir announced that my son had repeated dreams of a faceless person. When she unmasked the faceless person, it was me. In her village, the person who dreams of the faceless person, and once it is unmasked, and it is a ranking family member, then it becomes a formal accusation. Once Mysteir unmasked the face, and saw that it was me, then the obvious in her world is that the person dreaming is the source of deceit."

Michael once again yelled, "Horseshit!" He paused, and said, "I will not accept this conversation as fact, Mr. Beckmire. I am dutifully announcing that I don't believe that the woman is correct."

The Sarge said, "I'm going to need a security detail to accompany me to the meeting in Sydney. I want you to take the lead, but I want Hood, Dempsey, Anel, Angel, Gant, Green, and King as sleepers." Michael inquired, "When is this going to go down?"

The Sarge announced, "Just have everyone in a ready position to leave on the minute. And Michael, thanks for your honest and direct comments about my son. Do you remember when I said, "I am not your father, but I'm here for you? Anyway, as you can see, it works both ways, my son. Thanks. Oh, one more thing, assign permanent seats on the plane for Anel, Angel, Gant, Green, and King."

# # #

Mr. West knew not to try to engage Mr. East in a game of treachery because he was aware of exactly how dangerous and shifty Mr. East could be. No, he decided to solicit the assistance of a person who he hated, the one and only Benjamin Beckmire. Yes, Ben Beckmire would become his saving grace even though Beckmire allegedly took money from his son in a California drug deal, blew his house up with him supposedly in it, and sent his son to prison where he became the queen of the balls. Yes, Mr. West hated Mr. Beckmire, but wanted to come clean about who he was collaborating with to exterminate his group.

The meeting was set for a Wednesday, which was exactly three days from the point of sending a message through the sewers requesting a conference. Mr. West was extremely paranoid because he knew that if a Beckmire was out to kill other Beckmires and their associates, then his life was as insignificant as swatting a fly on the wall. Mr. West requested that the confab be held at the Sydney International Airport, and stipulated that no immediate family members should be in attendance.

Everyone was aware that only a suicidal person would bring a weapon into an international airport, let alone be a part of a conspiracy to commit murder. Mr. West felt that his safety and anonymity was the most critical issue facing him since his ex-partner attempted to kill him for just thinking about the notion of revenge. He didn't want to go into the lion's den smelling like fresh meat, so he asked for the meeting at the airport, knowing full well that certain members of Beckmire's contingency would not be a part of the parley.

#

Mr. East reached out to his associates in the sewers, and found out that Mr. West had made plans to go to Sydney Australia. Mr. East called a fringe group in Sydney, and asked the going price for remediation at or near an airport. He was told $100k. He casually agreed to the amount, but indicated that failure would be at the price of those people in Northern Africa paying a visit to Sydney. The person responding said, "We will attempt to deliver the results, but we reserve the right to abort this mission since it is in or near an airport, which is heavily fortified, and with cameras everywhere."

Mr. East replied, "When I say failure, I mean if there is a clear opportunity, the outcome is in your favor, and you do not succeed. I do not expect you to walk into the airport, and take out the trash in front of hundreds of people and cameras. However, if there is an unobstructed occasion, then I expect a report card with 100% scores."

The person on the other end of the telephone announced, "For a cool $million, I'll send people into the fucking airport to clean the carpet."

Mr. East responded, "I hadn't anticipated expending that kind of paper for that dirty work. I'm staying with the low-ball, $100k."

The person on the other end asked, "If we have an understanding, can you send me descriptive information, times, and the full Monty on the activity. Do not send me money until the carpet is cleaned. And as you may not know, I too have contacts with those in Northern Africa, two cousins and one brother-in -law."

Mr. East paused for a moment to reflect, and responded, "Touché, my friend, touché!"

# # #

The sewer exists because it receives and sells information where possible. Mr. West's advances about a meeting with Mr. Beckmire was sold online for $20k. Not a paltry amount, but eight to ten of those a day, well, that's a significant amount of net new income. The only group that was held in sanctuary, was, and is, the Beckmire group because of their incredible financial backing to the sewers. No information of any kind is permitted to be bartered with regards to the group.

The potential contractor said, "I have two days to get ready. I'll need everything in view by tomorrow this time. Placement is delicate, and this game is for the outside, unless there is a window snapshot from long distance. I have people who can make long shots with specialized equipment. I suggest we conclude the threats, and see if it can be done, and then no harm—no foul if it doesn't work. That's the only way I'm going to proceed. Too many obstacles, and of all places, the fucking airport. Get me the intel, and I'll let you know the probability of it happening by us. Thanks for inquiring. Catch you later."

Mr. East commanded, "Hold on a minute. There may be a high value target with the initial person of interest that could net you up to $3 million."

The person on the other end of the phone asked, "Who the hell is worth $3 million, the Pope, the President, who?"

Mr. East responded, "A man named Beckmire." The person on the other end of the phone asked, "Ben Beckmire?"

Mr. East stated, "The one and only."

The person on the phone replied, "You must be fucking crazy. Where would I go to spend the money, and who wouldn't be looking for my ass. No way my friend. As a matter of fact, take me off of the job at the airport. Later!" Mr. East continued to talk and finally realized that the person he was talking to was no longer on the phone. He attempted to call back and a recording stated, "The number you have dialed, is no longer in service."

Mr. East realizing the magnitude of respect that the Beckmire group garnered, found himself slipping into a depressive state of mind. He asked himself, "how can those old fucking people from Viet Nam command so much loyalty from places full of scum, chicanery, and death. Perhaps, I should have approached this thing from another point of view. As he was sulking about his inappropriate request to have Ben Beckmire hit, his phone rang, and the person on the other end commanded, "Never use that name to me. If you're in conflict with him, then keep it between the two of you. I will take care of that other person because his son's lover, sliced my nephew beyond recognition. Ben Beckmire is off limits to me and most of the people doing this kind of work. If you have an alternative, then I say exercise your options. However, if asked, I will absolutely tell the truth about the inquiry. Are we clear?"

Mr. East feeling humbled, responded, "Crystal clear, and thanks for giving me a second consideration."

# # #

Courtney turned her phone on to see if she had received any messages in the past few days. As she scanned the incoming messages, her heart felt at ease when she initially saw a message from her son, but after reading the entire thread, he had seemingly succumbed to a fall in the Swiss Alps while skiing, and was confined to a hospital bed. As usual, he needed funds to pay for the hospital stay and incidentals. He informed her of the fact that his friends received a monthly stipend or an allowance, and wondered if she and his father could manage that proposal on any level. Courtney told him that his only being available when he was in a pinch had to stop, and that she would attempt to manage such an arrangement if he would visit, call his father, and stop acting like a jerk. Her son's response was that he was tired, and that the pain medicine made him sleepy. Her son did not say goodbye, rather he just hung the phone up.

Courtney, considering the matter, and weighing the pros and cons, realized that if this arrangement created constant communications, then so be it. She called her banker and arranged for him to send her son $150k. After the completion of the transfer, Courtney rationalized that money was a thing, but love was a commitment and feeling. She began to cry with joy that this was hopefully a small beginning to reconstituting her family.

When Courtney saw the Sarge, she joyfully exclaimed, "I talked to our son earlier, he was in a skiing accident, but only suffered a broken arm, and a sore back. He'll be alright and has promised to work towards a more stable relationship with us!"

The Sarge, looked curiously at her, and asked, "Baby, how much did that cost you?"

Courtney's joy turned to spite, and she vehemently stated, "As much as we have been through with this group, and its adventures, don't you dare ask me a question about money when I am trying to gain a relationship with our son. Don't you dare, Ben Beckmire."

## CHAPTER TWENTY-TWO

At the Sydney Kingsford Smith Airport, Hood, Anel, Dempsey, and Angel entered the airport as if they were travelers. Gant and Green hung outside, both scouring the area as if they were looking for someone. Ben Beckmire walked into the airport with Michael and King at his side. Ben Beckmire saw a bench that was near a window, and proceeded to walk towards it. He checked the marquee to make sure he was in the Quantas departure area. He sat down on the bench, and no sooner had he assumed the sitting position, a person appeared, and asked him, "Are you Ben Beckmire?"

Michael quickly moved in front of the person, and demanded, "Back the fuck up! You appear to be a little too aggressive!"

The person whispered, "I guess I'm a little scared of the man who allegedly took my son's drug money, blew my house up with me in it, and sent my son to a place where people line up to have an affair with him. Just a wee bit nervous and cautious."

Ben Beckmire said, "Have a seat, and let's make this as comfortable as possible for each other, and by the way, I didn't take anything from anyone."

The man addressing Beckmire said, "I don't like sitting in a place with windows behind me. The person who I casually mentioned the word revenge to, put a hit out on my ass.

Please, can we move to where that column is, fifteen or so feet away from here?"

Ben Beckmire said, "There are windows everywhere. I came here in good faith, unarmed, my people are without weapons, and I'm now trusting a person who tried to erase me and my friends from this existence. Please don't do stupid."

A few minutes later, as the two men made their way towards the pillar, the man known as Mr. West said, "We have been at odds for a long time, and for the wrong reasons. I realize that the game I was in was wrong, and fortified with people who are unscrupulous. I hated you because of that event at the Bonaventure Hotel in LA. I was all wrong, and I let my son talk me into helping him to become his own person. He accused me for everything negatively that happened in his life, including the death of his mother. I thought I could use my clout to help hide his business, but I was wrong to react when you and your people were asked to intermediate. Anyway, fast forward, I made another deal with a devil to take over your entire enterprise. Many years ago, I was skiing in the Swiss Alps, and met an American who was loquacious, smart, and determined to become the richest man on earth. His entree into this mindset was by way of a person by the name of Ben Beckmire, who controlled billions of dollars in bearer bonds from Venezuela, as well as prime property, assets, investments, and cash on hand that totaled in the hundreds of billions of dollars, if not trillions.

Initially, I thought that the fifty-year-old Grand Marnier he constantly drank was impacting his brain. He then began to speak in distinct terms about properties, and your loose ownership relationship to each one. He even mocked that in a court of law, he was the rightful owner of those properties, if all who were a part of the group, were dead. As I listened more intently, he spoke of the amount of cash you had in semi-secured places. It seemed like a fantasy at first until he spoke about the millions of dollars in a home owned by one of the members of the group in the Philadelphia area. He also stated that there was at least $120 million in cash in a vault in Virginia. He then spoke of the mid-west, and said, "In that place there are diamonds, gold, and so much cash that it would take a month to count."

Ben Beckmire stared at him, and exclaimed, "Pure fantasy! He must be an aspiring fiction writer."

After a brief pause, Beckmire continued, and asked, "Can you describe this fiction writer?" Mr. West replied, "I can do one better than that. I have pictures of him and I in a bar in Switzerland. As Mr. West began to activate his telephone, a splash hit the window leaving a small hole in it, drawing everyone's attention, but it left a bigger hole in Mr. West's head. He was dead before he hit the floor. Michael, recognizing what had happened, tackled Ben Beckmire, and covered him with his body. Beckmire after staring at the lifeless body lying on the floor beside him, stated, "I'm sure the shooter is gone. Get that phone, and let's seek a safer area." Michael picked the phone up, and placed it in his pocket.

# # #

Later, after giving a statement to the constables, Beckmire gave them his contact information. He turned to Michael, and said, "Every time I think I am getting closer to finding out who is the treacherous party in our group, we receive another setback."

Michael replied, "Sarge, if we can get into his phone, then all may not be lost."

The Sarge looked at him, and asked, "How can this person know where to hit us? How can I leave my village, come to Sydney to meet a foe, and just before he shows me who is trying to kill me and my people, he gets his head blown open. This is not happening by chance. The problem is trying to discern who is the leak. Was it my camp or his connections? I mean you have got to be gutsy to shoot someone in an airport from afar. What was even more troubling to Beckmire was when the constable asked him if he knew of any kin of the deceased. Beckmire thought to himself, "what a terrible way to die, not that being dead in itself isn't terrible, but your only kin is in a prison servicing random inmates."

On the flight back to the Northern Territory, Michael began to play with the deceased man's phone, and eventually was locked out. He indicated to the Sarge that he was unable to gain access to the phone.

# # #

Back in the village, Courtney asked her husband, "How did it go? Did you find out any useful information about who is trying to undermine us at every turn?"

The Sarge smiled, and asked, "Honey, before I become inundated with group stuff, can you take a walk with me?"

The Sarge, untypically, walked towards the boundaries of the village rather than towards a billabong, and showed Courtney a view of the mountain ranges that was spectacular. He asked, "My love, have you ever seen anything in nature that is so perfect, beautiful, and welcoming? Before you answer that question, let me make a statement. Whenever I see you, or I am near you, I feel as majestic as that mountain range. My love for you is like an addiction that keeps me in love with life, people, and you. You know my past, you know my now, and you are my future. I will not live forever, and nor will you my love. I want you to never let anything or anybody come between our love."

He paused for a moment, and then said, "I know you want to establish a meaningful relationship with our wayward son, but he has other lofty goals and objectives, and they don't include us. You remember the day he told us that we did not represent who he would like to introduce to his friends as his parents? Of course, you do. I will let no one come between us. No child, no mammon, no lust shall ever come between my love for you. I say all of this to let you know that I am not on board with your trying to buy love, communications, and visitations from our son. I also know better than to ask you what you paid for a modicum of satisfaction from our fractious son. I, however, will not stand by and let him burden you with false guilt. I hope that the day never comes when I have to become the anti-parent. If payment is your saving grace, then by all means, support our child. However, this I promise, if he begins to noticeably weigh on your psyche, or our relationship, I will find a way to conclude all that is."

Courtney after listening patiently, inquired, "What does find a way to conclude all that is, mean, Ben Beckmire?"

Ben Beckmire stood tall, and said, "I will my love do whatever you require me to do, and that I will never address the notion of our son again, for he is what I consider, less than a faithful child whose parents gave him everything possible to succeed, and now, he wants to measure us against his friend's parents. I will be with you until the day I die. I will turn my back on he who says we are his parents, if you begin to weaken to his continuous need for your financial assistance, and ignore your human need and aspirations to communicate with him."

At this point Courtney is crying her heart out. Ben Beckmire said, "I am sorry to be so crass, but this is how I feel at this moment. I love you, and I will not let an inconsiderate child cause you or I any degree of anguish because of his blind ambitions and misguided sense of self-worth."

Courtney deep in Ben's arms, admitted that she sent their son $150k, and she also informed Ben of his son's request to receive a stipend or advance each month of a to be determined amount. Ben Beckmire looked at Courtney, and replied, "Honey, your money is your money, and I will never try to tell you how to spend it. If you think that will buy you into your son's heart, then so be it. Insofar as the stipend or advance is concerned, from my point of view, I don't see me participating in that madness."

Courtney looked at him, and declared, "Ben Beckmire, I don't see me partaking in that event either! I sometimes get really lonely for our son, but I also realize that he is a piece of shit. Do you think he has a hand in trying to terminate us?"

The Sarge announced, "Honey, I have had him followed, wiretapped, filmed, set-up with lucrative schemes, and every other nefarious machination that you might imagine. He has no information about what we do, or where the money you send him comes from. He knew you were once a doctor, and probably thinks that the money you send him is from your retirement account. I can't figure out who the culprit is that is causing us so much trouble. Zanthius is right under our fingernails, so that eliminates him. By the way, Mysteir asked me a puzzling question when she was here. She asked me if during my travels, might I have had a transgression, and from

my loins created another Beckmire who is unannounced."
Courtney astutely asked, "What was your answer?"

Ben Beckmire smiling, replied, "I have been married to
the world's most beautiful and wonderful woman for a long
time, and during those magnificent years with that beauty, I
have never once crossed the street on her or even considered
such a thing."

Rashida played around with the deceased Mr. West's
phone, and gained entry to his settings. As though magic was
in play, the entire system shut down, and erased every bit of
information housed in the phone. When Rashida saw her dad,
she informed him of what had happened, and he politely
stated, "Some people will go to great lengths to protect the
integrity of their phone information."

"Good try, baby!" He exclaimed.

Michael received a message from the sewers asking him
about the transfer of $150k by a member of the Beckmire
group to an account that belonged to a person who was
deceased, and one that a foe had previously used to transfer
money into. After further inquiry, it appeared that the funds
sent by Courtney to her son, were entered into an account
belonging to a deceased navy captain. The account was the
same one that received funds on several occasions belonging
to the recent collaborator with Beckmire. The person in the
sewer indicated that their interest was purely financial, in that
the former foe, now dead collaborators account was being

programmed for a con. Michael sent a text indicating "all hands off that account until the $150k is tracked".

Michael saw the Sarge, Mallory, Gladstone, Jong, and Montomie having a pint of piss. He walked over, and asked, "Sarge, can you indulge me, and read this message I received from the sewers?"

The Sarge, after reading the message, excused himself from the group, and instructed Michael to come with him. Once he caught up with Courtney, he asked her to excuse herself from her drinking duties because he wanted to show her something.

After Courtney read the message, she, as expected, stated, "There must be a mistake. This communique suggests that the money I sent our son, is tied to an account of the man who lived in Poughkeepsie, New York. How can this be? Ben are you suggesting that our son is in cahoots with people like him, and more importantly, is planning a travesty to kill us for the fortune we have amassed? Ben, please, don't bring me any more shit like this. Our son is in a hospital in Switzerland with broken bones from a skiing accident."

Ben quickly asked, "What hospital, and where in Switzerland?"

Courtney asked, "Why, Ben? What are you planning to do?"

Ben replied, "Honey, I am going to reach out to him, and see if he needs anything. However, Honey, can't you see the obvious connection between what has been happening to us, and the distinct collaboration of our son, and a person who has tried on many occasions to terminate us. I just want to talk to him, and make sure he's okay."

Courtney shouted, "Stop lying, Ben Beckmire. You want to make our baby a co-conspirator no matter how thin the facts are. I won't have it Ben Beckmire. You hear me, I won't have any inquiry into perhaps this happenstance, and further alienate our son from us. I advise you to tread lightly, and from afar, Ben Beckmire, or I will truly leave my back to the sun."

As Courtney stormed away from Michael and Ben Beckmire, Michael said, "Sarge, she gave you exact marching orders that you must follow. Your wife didn't say a word about your people checking on your child. Sir, I recommend you engage Hood and Dempsey, and dispatch them to every place your son is supposed to be." The Sarge looked at Michael as if he were expecting something else, grunted and mentally entered his own world.

The wonderful world of coding. Gilda and Rashida discussed how data is gathered, transported, stored, and assimilated. The two women, through zoom discussions, diagnosed the development of the Apple product, its protocols for encryption, and how to get around those protective procedures. Two days later, Rashida, with the help of Gilda, entered the private messages of Mr. West including his photo gallery. Rashida, having never met her stepbrother, saw the Sarge, and confessed, "Gilda and I broke every law conceivable, but I don't know what we did it for. I don't know who you're looking for, Dad."

The Sarge hugged Rashida, and said, "I am afraid to look baby. If my wife finds out that I'm trying to find negative information about our son, I believe she will leave me."

Rashida said, "Dad, what parent would go looking for negative information about their child unless something was amiss. I don't blame mom, but it's clear that whoever this person or group is, they are playing for keeps, just ask, Ava, Juan, Mike, Carla, and Franco."

# # #

The following morning, the Sarge met Michael for breakfast, and asked, "Do you think Hood and Dempsey are enough?" Michael smiled, and indicated that they were more than enough, but it would be prudent to send some back-up with them." The Sarge after filling his plate full of grits, crushed sausage, ham, and cheese asked, "What are your thoughts about King, Gant, and Green?"

Michael, with a huge smile on his face, announced, "Excellent selection, my liege. I really believe that great minds find the opportunity to coalesce, and develop worthwhile strategies for the good of the group."

The Sarge proclaimed, "You are so full of it, Michael, but I like it. How do we deploy them without my wife noticing that they are missing."

Michael laughed, and said, "Oh Sarge, we're not deceiving anyone. They have duties in Minnesota that I am recommending based upon a subtle threat that was conveyed to me via Litefoot."

The Sarge stared at Michael, and stated, "You, I am glad I didn't feed to the fish. Michael, you are so important to this group, *The Sanctuary*, and your Mother."

# # #

Two days later, Hood, who was made senior, and Dempsey entered the local hospital and asked the head nurse if she was available to make a few extra Swiss francs. She responded, "Absolutely not. This is a place of healing, and our staff are not here to earn extra francs. No sir, we are here to serve the people who need our assistance."

Dempsey pulled a stack of francs out of his pocket, and said, "We are missing a family member who is extracting funds from his parents, and we think there may be a switch in play or, perhaps, he is deceased. Now we know you don't need this stack of francs, but we would be incredibly grateful if you would assist us with locating our family member or acknowledging that there is a body double in play."

The nurse knew where they were standing and talking there were no cameras. She said to Hood, "I need my job, but I also need some extra money for an emergency however, I am not for sale. If you are legitimate, then I will help you free of charge."

In her office, Hood pulled out a picture of Beckmire's son, and presented it to the nurse. Her face turned into a massive scowl, and she asked the men to leave her office. Dempsey said, "He is a pretentious person, but his parents would be very appreciative of any information that you can provide us about him."

After a few moments of shaking her head violently, the nurse exclaimed, "That sonofabitch, pursued one of our new nurses like a demon, seduced her, impregnated her, left her with a hefty hotel bill, other expenses, and slipped out of town! That was little over a year ago, and since that time, our nurse committed suicide, and the baby is in an orphanage. He is truly dirt, and is the most despicable asshole on earth.

Both men displayed absolute surprise, and Hood said to the nurse, "Our leader is going to be extremely annoyed at his son, but even more astounding, wherever that baby is, it won't be there for long. I need you to listen to me very carefully. Once I make the call to our leader, a plane full of people, good people, are going to come here to get that child out of the orphanage. We didn't try to hustle you, and we recognize that you didn't take our funds. Again, when my people come here, they are going to need a liaison to help them navigate the Swiss system. We can do this by contract, and be completely above board, but in return, all we want is your honest opinions, and directions."

Dempsey said, "Our group is a caring group, but people who are not who they say they are, go missing. Now, is this something you can do, and swear upon your life, and everyone who you care about that you will do the right thing?"

The nurse replied, "How do I know that you people are honorable people?"

Dempsey replied, "If you do this thing on the up and up, my people will be obliged, and in debt to you for your guidance through this foreign system."

The nurse stared long at Hood, and stated, "If this is in any way against the law, then I shall publicly announce my involvement, and inform the powers that be that this is about a child in our system."

Dempsey exclaimed, "Fair enough! I guarantee you that this is a great opportunity for all, and we are terribly sorry that our leader's son is a real asshole. We've never met him, and I pray to God that under no circumstances we ever do."

Hood stated, "We were told by his father that he had an injury skiing here recently."

The nurse exclaimed, "I can assure you, a visit here, at this hospital by him, would not be to his advantage!"

Hood responded, "That sounds like a threat." The nurse proclaimed, "That was not a threat, that was a promise! He swayed her away from a true suitor who had character and spirit."

Dempsey stated, "I would like to move this conversation towards the child. Did the father know about the child? Did he make any attempt to see, acquire, or do anything that a father should do?"

The nurse began to cry, and said, "He told her to get rid of it because he would not be available mentally, physically, or financially to support it. He referred to the child on every occasion as it."

Hood reached for her hand, and said, "I pray to God that I don't meet this person."

Dempsey asked, "Do you think that when you get off, you can take us to the orphanage, and show us the child?"

The nurse said, "I pray to God that you are honorable people, and that this is no scam."

Hood asked, "Can I tell you a story about how we came to be?"

Ten minutes later after telling the story about their salvation, escalation, and promotion to a level of trust, Hood stated, "In the name of our Savior, Lord Jesus Christ, I promise you that we are not disciples of the devil, but that we are, and our group are servants of our Lord Jesus Christ."

The nurse said, "My name is nurse Mathews, Earline to be exact. If any of this is full of deception, then I will curse you and your master, the loser, the devil. Please, don't mess with me, and my faith.

# # #

An hour or so later, Dempsey, Hood, Gant, Green, and King arrived with nurse Mathews at an old, dilapidated facility that was full of love, but was not fit for human occupation. Hood said to Dempsey, "The boss is not going to like this place, and will probably gut it, and rebuild it once he sees it."

Nurse Mathews said, "In this area, we don't have many people dropping kids off in the middle of the night. This is the only such facility within a 300-mile radius. However, as you can see, there is much love and attention here, despite the condition of the facility."

# # #

Hood called the Sarge and told him what they had discovered, and that it was highly unlikely that his son was still in Switzerland. He announced to the Sarge, that after the picture of his son was shown to the head nurse, her response upon seeing it, was exponentially deleterious. The Sarge asked, "Why was that?"

Hood replied, "We don't have empirical information, but it seems that your son befriended a young woman who was a nurse, impregnated her, left her with a substantial hotel bill, and told her to rid herself of his seed. The child was eventually born, the mother was faceless within her community, and subsequently committed suicide. I asked the head nurse if she was certain of the identity of the person in the picture, and she stated that she was. Now Sarge, me, and the boys along with the nurse went to the orphanage, and on our first viewing of it, the place appears to be unfit for human habitation. However, there is a lot of attention, and love being given to the children who are there."

The Sarge asked, "Did you see the child? What does he look like? Could he truly be a Beckmire?"

Hood hesitantly replied, "Sarge, we saw a lot of children, and they look like babies, and of course one of them could be a Beckmire, a Dempsey, or even a Hood. I'm not trying to be humorous, I am trying to give you facts."

After a long period of silence, the Sarge said, "I'll call you back in a few. Keep an eye on the child, and ask the owners of the place if they are there, what are their needs to bring the place up to standard. Just keep them engaged, and promise them anything, but make sure you guys keep an eye on that child. I'll call you back."

The Sarge hung up the phone, walked down to the billabong, and submerged his entire body into the water. After coming up for air, he noticed that he was surrounded by huge eyes. He asked, "Could there be another Beckmire in an orphanage?" The eyes disappeared.

# # #

Once back in the village, Beckmire saw his bride, and said to her, "I need you to come with me right now. We have a decision to make!"

A curious Courtney whispered to Monica, "Oh shit, what the hell have I done?"

A few minutes later, Ben asked Courtney to sit at the edge of the water, and to place her feet in it. He then said, "What I am about to tell you, is going to create a lot of anxiety within you, and subsequently your reactions are going to unsettle me. The water will help calm you."

Beckmire told Courtney about the sanctioned trip he commissioned to Switzerland. Courtney stood up, and said, "I told you to not investigate our son." Before she could say another word, Ben Beckmire loudly announced, "I need you to listen to me, and not issue idle threats."

He initially focused on their son, and finally said, "There was a woman who was purportedly impregnated by our son, who subsequently committed suicide."

Courtney yelled, "I don't want to hear negative things about my son. I am going to leave you, and you will never see me again if you continue down this road."

At an ear-piercing level, Ben Beckmire yelled, "Damn it woman, listen to me or leave me. It is your choice, I am tired of how this child from hell manipulates our marriage to the dysfunctional."

Courtney yelled, "I told you once that I did not want to hear anything negative about my child, and that you were not to go investigating what he was up to. I warned you, Ben Beckmire."

Beckmire yelled, "Courtney, now I am warning you! Listen to me or leave me for I will no longer be a part of this silent, three-party marriage, controlled by a child who could give a shit about whether we lived or died. I need you to calm down, and listen to the full story before you castigate me."

After a few moments of quiet, Ben said, "As I was saying, there is a lot of raw negative energy against our son in St. Moritz. The woman before committing suicide, conceived a male child who is in an appalling orphanage, according to Hood."

Courtney stood up, walked into the billabong, and began to cry. She came out of the water, and said, "I want to be on my way to Switzerland in the next two hours. Can you make that happen? If this child is from the seed of our cantankerous son, then an orphanage is no place for a Beckmire. I want to be in the air soon."

## CHAPTER TWENTY-THREE

On the plane ride to Switzerland, Courtney said to the Sarge, "Now is the perfect opportunity to share with me what your people discovered. I want to know everything that Hood said to you. If there is a child that is from our son's loins, then I want to employ every resource to extract that child from the orphanage. I don't want a lot of conversation about process and procedures from you my husband, I want you to do this for me, and make it seamless. If the child is a Beckmire, I want it on board this plane heading for our home in the South, in three days, not four, but three days. Okay, I'm tired, and I want to be fresh when we land. G'nite my love. Oh, by the way, your strident warning to me was nuclear, and got my undivided attention.

The Sarge looked at Courtney as if she were possessed. He said to himself, "All of a sudden, our son's activities and embarrassing events have consumed my wife. Somewhere in this equation, I feel that mammon and false prophets are at play in this matter. I fear the outcome of this trip to the mountains."

#

The group's plane landed in Zurich Switzerland, and they immediately caught a train to the top of the mountains. When they arrived in St. Moritz, Mallory took a group by bus to the hotel that they were staying in. King, Green, and Gant, were waiting to escort Mr. Beckmire, Mrs. Beckmire, Chakes, Luana, and Monica to the orphanage. In the bus they hired, Courtney asked, "Who among you is qualified to answer questions about why we are here?"

Green responded, "Mrs. Beckmire, we are not knowledgeable enough to provide near perfect information about what was discovered, and what the senior on this mission has concluded. In a matter of forty or so minutes, we should be arriving at the orphanage, and there the appropriate people charged with this mission can respond."

Courtney smiled, and stated, "That is the answer I was hoping you would share with me. Sometimes, people try to upstage those given the control function, but I am proud that you insisted that I wait and talk to the mission leaders. Mr. Green, where possible, I will champion any issue you have. Thanks for not trying to interpret information that you are not privy to."

# # #

The Sarge looked at the three men, and announced, "We are in a foreign land, and we are naked. Has there been any conversation about clothing?"

Green looked at King, and nodded his head. The Sarge said, "Hold up a minute. Did I just see you nod your head to him, indicating that he can speak?"

Green lowered his head, and said, "Sarge, we have inner managers on missions. Green was elected for this mission because he is a smooth talker. He deciphers things much more quickly than we do and, therefore, he is it. The nodding of the head basically addresses what each of us is charged with. Listen, I have security, King has procurement, and Green has everything else. We value our relationship with this group, and we decided that our salvation and longevity depends on our ability to assign each other tasks based upon our individual strengths. We're not the smartest chips in the bag, but we know where our bread is buttered."

The Sarge smiled, and said, "I like all that I have heard, but I suggest that when another leads the mission, you let them know how you people work together. My wife pulled that seat from under you, now you need to make sure that when it comes to the group, everyone is on board with how you assign tasks. I'm simply happy we didn't feed you to the Crocs."

# # #

At the orphanage, Nurse Matthews, Hood, and Dempsey, were discussing the politics of adopting/extracting a child from the Swiss system with the head administrator. Hood stated that the alleged child's grandparents were on their way here with their lawyers, and it would be greatly appreciated if all could remain here until they arrived. He suggested that once they see the orphanage, they will certainly want to contribute to the renovation or a complete rebuild of the institution. The administrator smiled, and asked, "Is that a serious comment or one that is made to get my attention."

Hood responded, "Our leader, Mr. Ben Beckmire, and his wife, Dr. Beckmire will most definitely want to discuss a possible quid pro quo relationship. Let me be frank, your facility is not where children should be kept. It is crumbling in places, it has its own peculiar stench, wires are tied unsafely, exposed pipes that relay something that looks like water, but has other chemicals in them from old, and rusting conduits. There is a lot to be done here, and I'm just suggesting that if you can help them, then they will help you beyond your wildest imagination, including gutting and rebuilding this place in record time."

#

When the bus arrived, Courtney and Ben Beckmire were first to alight from it, followed by Monica, Chakes, and Luana. Hood met the group, and beckoned them to walk with him for a few minutes. He explained the entire situation to them, and stated that the only empirical information that he can attest to, is that their son was identified by multiple individuals who would like to liquidate him. Hood stated, "As I indicated, the mother of the child was looked upon as if she were a person with leprosy or something, and I guess the disdain was too much for her to accept. She, therefore, after dropping the alleged child of your son off at this institution, she forthwith committed suicide."

Courtney asked, "What is that stench I smell."

Hood replied, "It is coming from within the confines of the orphanage."

Monica looked at Courtney, and asked, "Do you think you're too old to embark down this road?"

Courtney smiled, and said, "Doing this again will be the greatest gift that I could bestow on any child. However, before we start having baby showers, buying cribs, and bassinets, let's see how we can negotiate this system without a lot of fanfare. Are you with me Luana?"

Luana stated, "Girl, I am right behind and beside you on this one."

Once inside, Hood introduced the group to the administrator, and Nurse Matthews. He also indicated that it was Nurse Matthews who got them from home plate to second base. He looked at Ben Beckmire, then at Courtney, and confessed, that he had made some notions of support to the orphanage, based upon an earlier conversation with Mr. Beckmire, about the conditions of the facility, and that he had told the administrator that you people would not tolerate this place for the keeping of children. Hood also told them about some of their deeds. I did not ask to see the child because that is a thing that I reserved for you and Mrs. Beckmire."

Courtney asked, "Do you remember when I told you to stop breathing so hard before you hyperventilated, and that my husband and his crew were not going to hurt you? Do you remember that day?"

Hood lowered his head, and softly replied, "That day changed my life, and Dempsey's for good. I will never forget that day."

Courtney responded, "Neither will I. Now, let me and my ladies talk to Nurse Matthews and the administrator. I think we'll be alright. You men type, just hang out and see what is going on with this building."

# # #

The administrator talked about the process for adoption, and suggested a protracted course to make sure that everything was above board including DNA testing to confirm the information that had been alleged. Monica asked, "Can I speak frankly without this ever being mentioned outside of this room?" The administrator and Nurse Matthews both agreed. Monica said, "Let me tell you something about us, and orphanages. We closed one down in the DC Metropolitan area because the people in charge were mistreating, and in some cases grooming children for sexual favors, and other sordid activities. My husband and I, adopted a brother and a sister from that facility. Most of the people involved in those activities died suspiciously. We petitioned for the facility, received permission, had it demolished, had a new one built in its place, hired people that we trust, endowed the place, and an inspection is conducted each year for everything concerning the facility. We are a wholesome group, and children are particularly important to us. We have lots of children in our group, and the child in question would be loved immeasurably. Now, I say all of that to say this, your place is not fit for human dwelling or development. We can fix that in a hurry, but for such an undertaking we would like some considerations in wading through the Swiss adoption system, immediately. A protracted approach would not benefit anyone."

The administrator looked at Monica, and said, "I am named Joan Nuehergun, my friends call me Joan of Love because of my commitment to the children, and this dilapidated facility. Most of what is here is from donations from friends, family, and the guilty people that drop children off in the middle of the night, and leave guilt-ridden francs. I am pretty much impoverished because I have sold all that was mine, mortgaged my home, this facility to the hilt, and I have to close it due to its condition. I am afraid those so-called friends, some who are unscrupulous in nature, are trying to take over the place, and build a fancy ski chalet. My problem is, I have nowhere to take the children that are here."

Luana asked, "How many children are under your care?" Joan lowered her head, and replied, there are thirty-six children between the ages of three months and eleven."

Courtney asked, "Would it be inappropriate to ask to see the alleged Beckmire child, and how old is he?"

Joan replied, "He's our youngest, three months old. And to your other question, I can make that happen." She paused, and asked, "May I offer you some water?" Everyone politely declined her offer.

Joan continued, "You guys have asked me poignant questions, and I am desperate for I fear if the building doesn't fall in on us, then the thieves will come in the night, and force us out."

Monica replied, "We can help you in so many ways, and all we want in return is some modicum of consideration in adopting the Beckmire child."

Joan announced, "It is that kind of pledge that got those thieves in the door, who are now about to force us out with the help of local people, and the greedy politicians. No one wants an orphanage in this town, especially one that is about to fall in. They won't say it, but they really don't want these children here either. And if you look out of the window, the slope are perfect for cultivating for skiing."

Monica said, "Listen Joan, we have many options for you and your children. We have a hotel in St. Thomas, we have a farm in Virginia, we have a ranch in the mid-west, we have a new facility for hearing and sight impaired children in Florida, and much more. We are not thieves, we are honorable people who can change the course of your life, and the lives of the children that are in your care. You do your best in getting the Beckmire child legally adopted by Mr. & Mrs. Beckmire, and I assure you before the week is out, we will have people here to assess the property, design a three-shift construction plan, hire the best local craftsmen and women, and have a new furnished facility in place in record time. This will cost you not a single Swiss franc. We will also endow the facility with an amount to be determined by Mr. Beckmire and his associates."

Joan, at this time is crying her heart out, as was Nurse Matthews, who announced, "However I can help, count me in."

Twenty or so minutes later, an older lady appeared with the alleged Beckmire grandchild. The child was given to Courtney wrapped in a slightly tattered blanket. Courtney gazed upon the child, and burst into tears. The child was smiling at her, and she announced to Ben, whether it is our son's or not, I want to keep this bubbly little guy. Please make it happen, honey." Courtney, Monica, Luana, and the woman who presented the child, sat, and played with the baby.

## CHAPTER TWENTY-FOUR

Jong spoke with the people from the sewers, and traced over two years of transactions between Courtney, and purportedly her son. Jong saw that once the funds were transferred, someone would enter the bank and make withdrawals using the Beckmire name and identification, and/or forward them to yet another account. Michael requested his contacts in the sewers to breach the banks' camera systems for the last six months.

At the approximate time, and on each day a withdrawal or an in-person transfer was made, and an image of the person making those transactions was provided to him. Jong announced, "Unless you guys got this all wrong, there were three different people entering the bank and making withdrawals from the designated account."

One of his comrades in the sewer replied, "That's why we made contact with you guys. We also considered that perhaps the teller was in cahoots as well, but the camera footage from when the withdrawals were made, showed different tellers." Jong thanked the man for his help and told him that he would present the images to the Sarge, and that he would get back to him.

#

The Sarge was busy trying to slow down the minds at work about Courtney becoming a new mother. Nurse Matthews said to Courtney, "If half of what you people say is possible, then I know another way to make the adoption process happen in a maximum of three days. Joan is a cautious woman who owes a lot of money to some unscrupulous people. She has committed or threatened acts that are frowned upon to delay the seizure of the facility."

Courtney asked, "Suppose I deposited $1 million in a bank today, would that show our commitment?"

Nurse Matthews asked, "Is such a thing really possible? I mean, can you really do that?"

Courtney responded, "I can do that, and I will do that. I just need to know that we are not going to have to be Swiss citizens to adopt and extract our grandson out of here."

Nurse Matthews looked at Courtney long and hard, and said, "I know of a way to get around the system, but I will need you to swear that this is no scam, and that you will honor your articulated commitments to the children and the facility."

Courtney asked Nurse Matthews to excuse her for a minute while she summoned her husband.

When Courtney returned, Ben Beckmire announced, "In no uncertain terms, if this is what my wife wants to do for our grandson, the other children, and the facility, then so be it. After certain milestones have been accomplished on both sides, I will deposit $2 million into a secure account with you, Nurse Matthews, and you Ms. Joan, as co-signers, in conjunction with our fiscal manager, and the banks."

Nurse Matthews asked, "Why are you so committed to this child? It has not been proven that he is your grandson."

Ben Beckmire smiled, and said, "We are a feeling group of people. I know that this child is from our son, and we want to take care of him, get the others out of this place, and rebuild it."

Nurse Matthews asked, "Where would the children stay while all the work is being done?"

Ben Beckmire said, "We have places in the states that will accommodate large numbers of people. We also could find shelter here in Switzerland if that is more comfortable for everyone. It would be much more palatable for us if we could keep them on the ranch or the farm. Plus, exposure to another country would be good for their growth and understanding of how the world works. All we have to do is figure out how to get our grandson legitimately out of here with our names."

Nurse Matthews smiled, and said, "The mother is deceased, her remaining family wants nothing to do with a mixed-race child. They have not seen the child, and would prefer not to as a matter of fact. The father is not attentive or active in the child's life, and is heard to have told the mother to get rid of it. All I'm saying is that no one wants the child that is family, the mother is deceased, and the father is not interested in being a parent, and the community does not want to support another baby fathered by a foreigner. This can be simply easy, but you must do your proposed part, and figure out how all this can work."

Jong saw John Lee, and said, "I think someone is holding the Sarge's son for ransom of a gentle nature."

John Lee scowled at him, and asked, "How can ransom be gentle, unless the kid is somehow involved."

Jong exclaimed, "That's precisely what I'm thinking! He is either being forced or he is a part of this scam."

John Lee paused, and proclaimed, "Him could also be dead!"

Jong and John Lee entered the facility, and saw the Sarge looking out of a window. Jong said, "Answer not out there, answer in here."

The Sarge turned around, and asked, "What the hell are you talking about?"

Jong replied, "What were you hoping to discover looking through the window?"

The Sarge said, "You're trying to piss me off, aren't you. However, I'm not going to be bated by your senseless comments."

Jong replied, "I told you he didn't love me anymore."

The Sarge said, "Cut the bullshit, what's going on?"

Jong looked at John Lee, who said, "There be many people showing up to that there bank to withdraw funds that your misses be sending your son. Our problem be, we don't know what your son be looking like. Come on Jong, show him the pictures from the bank, and let the boss ID his boy."

A few minutes later, after Jong downloaded the files, he showed the images to the Sarge who responded, "None of those characters are my son. Are you telling me that these bandits extracted money from my boy's account on several different occasions?"

Jong responded, "Sarge, this is the information that I received from the sewers."

The Sarge yelled, "Bullshit!"

John Lee responded, "Sarge, we be just carrying the message, we ain't got no hand in the content. This here be information gathering, and we ain't made no analysis other than the fact that your boy be held hostage, he be a part of this here ruse, or even worse, him could be dead."

Jong gently punched John Lee, and said, "Sarge forgive him, his brain is deteriorating by the minute. Since the same person never retrieved funds from the account, we surmised that he was being held hostage, is a party to the scam, or is in serious trouble if not deceased."

The Sarge looked at both men, and sternly stated, "Not a word of this information is to be presented to my wife under any circumstances. Am I clear?"

# # #

When Jong, Monica, Luana, Hood, and Dempsey entered the local bank, Monica said to Jong, "Deja vu, my friend. Deja vu."

Ms. Nuehergun seemed a bit unsettled and intimidated. Luana said to her, "Joan, if you show weakness, this process is going to take forever to convince these people that we don't play games. We need you to operate from a position of strength. This is your deal, your terms, your funding, and your decisions. Don't retreat from these people, tell them you're tired of being fucked and fucked over. That should set the tone."

The head banker greeted the group, acknowledged Ms. Nuehergun, and asked, "What brings you into the bank today? Have you finally decided to rid yourself morally and personally of that albatross? As I have always stated, the bank will find suitable homes for those kids that have been the bane of your existence."

Joan initially stuttered, and mixed her words, but after a couple of sentences that lacked clarity, she said, "I'm sorry, I guess I'm still feeling a little bit under the weather, and subservient to you thieves. No, Mr. Jerkemister, I am not here to sell anything. However, I am here to pay off my mortgage, deposit $2.5 million in that competitive bank across the street, and to tell you and your cronies that they can kiss my old, voluptuous, round ass. What is my payoff balance, bring the mortgage papers and deeds, and let me hurry up and get out of this crooked fucking institution."

Mr. Jerkemister said, "Come now Ms. Nuehergun, you can't afford to pay off the balance, and all of the interest that you owe for late payments or no payments. The bank essentially, owns your property, and as a matter of fact, in two days, you should receive an eviction notice."

"Hi, my name is Mrs. Mallory, and this is Mrs. Chakes. We are both lawyers, and although we can't represent the orphanage, or Ms. Nuehergun in this situation, we can certainly hire the best lawyers in Switzerland to sue you for all kinds of issues. To me, it would be in your best interest to hear what Joan wants to accomplish today, and then make your decision. However, she has the capital to meet any and all expenses, as well as to hire the best institutions to conduct an analysis, and then pursue recourse against your bank. Our initial proposal for the lawsuit would be $2.5."

Mr. Jerkemister said, "That's a miniscule amount for our institution, and besides, our lawyers are the best in Switzerland."

Luana asked, "Are you saying that CHF 2.5 billion is a small amount?" Mr. Jerkemister coughed for a few moments, and pretended to feel faint.

#

Realizing that the bank had a lot of exposure to many sordid deals, after leaving the bank that night, Mr. Jerkemister felt that it was time to disappear. Once home, he packed lightly, transferred funds from different accounts, refreshed his cash app, and funded several Mac cards with deceased clients assets. He looked in the mirror, and smiled at what he saw. As he turned to leave, he announced to himself, "This has been a wonderful hustle, it's time to move on and start anew. I think those foreign women were spawned from the loins of Lucifer, too smart just to be women."

#

Later at the hotel, Michael received another message from the sewers that indicated that another account with the Beckmire name potentially could have been the source of payments for some recent activity aimed against the group, was discovered. The person making the statement also said that the signature was as different from the others as night and day. In addition, he said that it had been surmised that the Beckmire name was associated with several suspicious and under review accounts. Michael thought, "I don't want to be the one who tells the boss that his son may be connected to, or is the source of our concerns."

Michael saw Jong and told him that he needed to meet with him, Jilkes and John Lee as soon as possible. Thirty or so minutes later, the three men huddled, and Michael began to give them the information that was coming out of the sewers. John Lee stated, "You know I don't be trusting some of them fellas from the sewers. We be done uncovered plots involving two of them not too many years ago. So, I be taking that there information with a grain of salt."

Michael replied, "I'm just the messenger and my reasons for drawing you guys in is because there are a lot of connections between the purported Beckmire boy, and groups that have attempted to conclude our existence. The people below say the account that Dr. Beckmire sent funds to were further forwarded to accounts that have direct relationships to groups that have attempted our termination. Jong, what did you learn from your interaction with the sewer?"

Jong responded, "I can only concur with what Michael has said. The information given me about accounts, have a relationship with Dr. Beckmire, her son, and purportedly, mercs. I can't make heads or tails out of the information because I'm getting it third hand. That makes me think it could be massaged, watered down, or there is a bigger plot that has yet to be unfolded. I can't dismiss the information, and I don't think it's strong enough to go to the Sarge, but with the new stuff Michael is talking, he had better make the decision to inform the Sarge."

Michael asked, "Why can't we all go to him?"

Jilkes said, "This is the first time I've heard about these findings, I don't think John Lee and I have anything to offer to the discussion."

Michael responded, "So, you guys are going to leave this up to me, and me alone?"

John Lee replied, "Naw, we be kidding. We'll go with you.

# # #

Michael saw the Sarge and Courtney, and decided to get this thing off his back immediately. He approached them, and said, "Sorry to bother you, but I need to speak to the two of you, once I round up Jong, Jilkes, and John Lee. Where are you heading, and is that okay with you guys?"

Courtney smiled, and said, "We'll be in the lounge, just come over to us."

# # #

Jilkes was first to show up in the lounge followed by Jong who asked, "Where is your girlfriend?"

The Sarge asked, "Are you looking to get your neck broke?"

Jong responded, "No I'm looking to get this matter settled. He knows I only call them out when we need to be together."

Jilkes, said, "Sarge, when John Lee gets here, I will inform him that he is now my girlfriend according to Jong." The Sarge said, "Cut the bullshit. Where is Michael?"

# # #

When Michael and John Lee walked into the lounge, they saw the Sarge, and the selected members of the group. Michael walked over to them, looked directly at Courtney, and was about to say something when Monica walked in, and asked, "Girl, what is your problem? You know it's our time to commune."

Courtney instead of making an excuse replied, "I feel I am going to need you here more than ever with me."

Michael, still staring at Courtney said, "I am sorry, Dr. Beckmire, but I, as well as Jong, have received information from the sewers that is troubling and confusing." Michael sneezed, and everyone issued a bless you. Michael looked at Jong, who nodded at him, and announced, "It is what it is."

The Sarge loudly asked, "What in the hell is going on?"

Michael responded, "I am over my head in dealing with this responsibility, and I have not rested since the information came to me from the sewers." Michael paused for a few moments, and then announced, "The stress related to the information that I received, is greater than anyone could ever imagine. I received confounding information that indirectly and directly may bring your son to the center of our concerns. Jong and I both received information from separate sources in the sewer in relationship to the funds that you sent to your son, Dr. Beckmire. Seemingly, on various occasions, these photos are three people who have withdrawn money from the designated account.

More perplexing is the fact that money from other accounts that were tracked, and were used to send money back and forth to groups who have attempted to terminate us, utilized the same accounts. The person that you met with in Sydney, Sarge, had previously sent money to that same account that Dr. Beckmire consistently sent funds to. Now, I'm just going to say it like I see it, either your son is part of the group that has attacked us in the past, or he is being held against his will, is being forced to make the requests, and then approve the subsequent withdrawals, or perhaps a more sinister situation is in play."

Jong stood up, and loudly stated, "I can corroborate his story from a different source from the sewers that asked me about the accounts that were under review."

Meanwhile, Courtney is holding Monica's hand tightly, and is crying her heart out. The Sarge asked, "How credible is the information that you both received?"

Jong noted, "As trustworthy as the colonel that used to run that operation. What is consistent is that the account has been used by our adversaries to fund various groups to kill us. That in itself is strong information to me."

The Sarge looked at Michael, and asked, "Is there anything else that you want to speak about?"

Michael paused, looked at Courtney, and said, "I feel so bad bringing this unsubstantiated information to you and causing you stress. I beg your forgiveness, and plead that you'll understand that when I get a message, I have to relay it to the person in charge. I asked the source on numerous occasions, are you sure that the account number belongs to Dr. Beckmire? On each occasion he stated that he was certain. He provided me with the number, and I prayed to God that he was incorrect. Here is the account number."

Michael handed Courtney a piece of paper with an account number written on it, she looked at it, shook her head, and screamed at the top of her lungs. The Sarge gathered her up, and led her to their room.

Monica looked at Michael, and he knew she was about to light into his ass. However, Monica said, as she embraced him, "Sometimes there is no easy way to tell the facts. You did a good job, and you showed empathy and consideration for our leaders. Good job my friend, and you handled it with dignity."

#

Luana returned from the orphanage with Mary Alice, Yeshida, Somara, and Okema. The ladies went directly to the bar, and ten minutes later, Joan and Nurse Matthews entered it. Okema waved her hands in the air, and the two ladies walked towards them. Joan stated that she had heard that the banker, Mr. Jerkemister, had been apprehended and arrested for extracting funds from several deceased individual's accounts, and for transferring large amounts of money to his personal accounts.

Luana announced, "We made a call to our banker, and gave him the heads up, and he got the law involved in the process. Anyway, ladies, we invited you here to have a drink, and to figure out who does what, when, and next. Also, our bank representative should be showing up in a few moments, with paperwork for the transfer of 2.5 million CHF. Our banker will guide you through the process, we will have our people from Spain on a plane heading this way to advise and design the construction phase. The banker and her assistants will handle the financial part, our guys will handle the construction part, and you guys will work on the displacement of the children in the home. Now, we can send them to Florida, Minnesota, St. Thomas, Virginia, the mid-west, or Australia. Each place is a 5-star adventure with friends who love and care for children. I can propose to Courtney and the Sarge that perhaps we expose them to each place. What about that idea?"

Somara exclaimed, "Now, you're talking! I like that idea because it shows a lot of different venues." Okema interrupted Somara, and said, "I too like the idea of exposing them to other areas and cultures. However, I have another concern. Is it your intent to continue to offer this service to this area, or are you trying to get out of the business?"

Joan said, "I am getting older, the need for this facility is greater now than it has ever been, and I have people who have the right credentials, but I was unable to pay them. To directly answer your question, yes, I am staying and running the home."

Okema, replied, "Then we also need a recruiting arm to this event, and a business plan to make sure that the home is self-sustaining. I mean that if the government doesn't support it, then an endowment from us will sustain it through time. Ownership details will be discussed by Monica, Luana, the banker, and you guys. I suggest a 501c3 or whatever is comparative to it in Switzerland."

Joan, crying her heart out, asked, "Are you people for real, or am I dreaming? Why are you doing this for children you don't know?"

Yeshida responded, "It is rumored that one such child is from the loins of our leader's child. This in itself is enough to make us want to help every child. Our motto is, 'we help people help themselves.'

# # #

The children thought that they were going to be separated, and sent off to work for people in order to pay for their existence. Just prior to the departure of Beckmire and his group, Courtney got wind of those feelings from Nurse Matthews, and told the Sarge that she needed to head to the orphanage prior to departing with their new grandson/son.

Joan was surprised when she saw the line of trucks heading towards the orphanage. Nurse Matthews, said to her,

"I told Dr. Beckmire that the children were feeling a little angst about leaving the home, and therefore, she, hopefully will address their fears, and allay some of the adults' fears as well.

Courtney and Monica apologized for coming to the home without being officially invited, but assured everyone that they needed to address all who worked and volunteered at the facility. Once the children were led to the dining hall, they greeted each one.

When it was apparent that all staff and children were in place, Courtney said, "I am one blessed woman. I have people who love me, who respect me, who trust me, and I love them. Monica is my dearest friend in the world, but even we have our moments. I say that to say, we were on our plane about to leave Switzerland when I received a text from Nurse Matthews. I told my husband that I was not prepared to leave this country because I had not completely explained our position, and what would happen next."

Courtney paused, took a sip of water from a bottle, and said, "Next, is that I am going to have this place demolished, torn down. We are also going to have our friends from Spain to oversee the building of a new home for you guys. Then we are going to have a plane take all of you to one of our places in the United States. Do not worry, you will always be together, we are not going to separate you, and Nurse Matthews, and Joan of Love will be with you as well. Now, we are going to orchestrate a shopping event for you guys, because when you land in America, you will not need heavy coats and boots, but you'll want tennis shoes, shorts, and T-shirts."

As Courtney was about to continue, a frail little boy asked, "Why would you do that for us? You don't even know us."

Courtney walked over to him, and said, "I am doing this because I can, and I want to. My son met a lady, had a baby, and left her and their baby. The baby was cared for by Joan of Love and Nurse Matthews. That baby is now aboard our plane, and me and my husband are going to be parents again. In a way, I am going to be like your fairy Godmother, and you will not want for anything, including love. When it is time for you to go to the university or to a trade school, the only thing that will keep you from succeeding will be you. All of the necessary stuff, books, money, and other things will be provided by my group. All I ask of you guys, is that you trust us, and learn to love like we love each other, and now you guys. By the way, that was a tough and necessary question. Are there any other concerns that you guys have? Don't be shy, I am here, and I want you to be comfortable talking with us and making sure that we are addressing your needs."

As Courtney and Monica were preparing to leave, an older girl whispered to Monica, "We have heard this before. Why should we believe this time is going to be different?"

Monica asked, "May I give you a hug?" The child said yes, and Monica gave her a wonderful hug. Monica asked, "What is your name, and how old are you?"

The child said, "I am called Christin, and I am 11 years old."

Monica asked, "Could you hold that question for later, after you're on a plane in the next few days for America, and after you've had a marvelous shopping spree. I want you to ask me that question again in a few days. Will you promise?"

Christin said, "I won't forget."

CHAPTER TWENTY-FIVE

Two months later!

Courtney and the Sarge had not heard a word or a request from their son. The Sarge feared that his son was dead, but kept telling Courtney that he was probably being pretentious and didn't want to be bothered with poor people like them. She would laugh in the interim, but deep in her heart, she was a mother that was hurting with an enormous amount of pain. She said to Ben Beckmire, "You know I am sad about how our son has hurt us, and denied that we even exist. I am also sad that conceivably he is a part of a group that was dedicated to terminating us and our friends for the fortunes of the group. The one thing that I thank God for, is this baby, Marcelus Benjamin Beckmire. He's ours Ben, can you believe that at our age, we are parents once again? You know as I see it, our son is a real asshole, but I thank him for abandoning his baby that is now ours."

Ben Beckmire said, "Hold up there woman. Are you saying that you've accepted the fact that our child is who he is, an asshole?"

Courtney screamed, "Our child is a royal asshole, and may I never see him again. As a parent, I did, or we did all that we could plus more. That Naval Academy was fully paid by parents that he thought were poor. So, in other words, fuck my son and the pig he rode in on. This baby, our baby, will be his legacy, and his bane if he is still alive."

Ben Beckmire said, "Honey, those are words that a parent should never use about their child."

Courtney yelled, "Ben, fuck him, and may he rot in hell. He used me to finance his efforts to terminate us. Fuck him, fuck him, and may he die from his own venom."

# # #

Benito, and his crew, followed the blueprint that was developed and implemented by their deceased friend Franco in the construction of *The Sanctuary*, *The View*, and other projects. Initially, some of the potential workers presented notions why that model wouldn't work in a European environment, but it was immediately accepted when Benito spoke of benefits, rates of pay, and the long-term potential relationship with the crew to undertake other opportunities like the orphanage.

# # #

Two of the individuals who were photographed withdrawing funds from the Beckmire account were apprehended by members of the sewers, and were held in a secure spot. Two days later, John Lee, Jilkes, Jong, Hood, and Dempsey showed up at a house on Kenyon Street in Northwest, Washington, DC. The men were chained and handcuffed to torture units. When Jong walked in, he said, "They've been prepared for the utmost in torture."

John Lee asked, "Why you be saying such a thing?"

Jilkes interrupted the acknowledgement, and said, "Let's do what we have to do to them, and be out of here. I'm looking forward to a two-pound steak cooked with the blood running out of it."

John Lee said to the captives, "I got pictures of you extracting money from an account that belongs to the son of my boss. However, you ain't related to my boss, and he be wondering why and how you can do that?"

One of the guys looked at John Lee, and stated, "Damn you sound country. Where you be from?"

John Lee astutely replied, "It ain't about me buddy, I ain't the one chained to that torture ring. However, I think you be needing to know who I am since you asked. I be the motherfucker that will make your mother regret that she had sex to have a loser like you. So, don't talk because I was going to choose your cellmate first, but now that you need to know certain things, I can assure you my final answer will leave you with decapitated body parts."

The guy proclaimed, "Fuck you farmer! Take these chains off, and I will beat your country ass to a pulp."

Jilkes said to John Lee, "We're not here to have a fight contest, stick to the plan."

Jong, said, "I would like to see that guy beat John Lee's ass, he's always bullying me."

Jilkes once again said, "People we must stick to the plan."

The other guy in chains announced, "My money is on my friend."

Jilkes paused for a few seconds, and continued by saying, "Since your money is on your friend, when he is declared the loser, you will be our first interviewee." Jilkes looked at one of the members from the sewers, and commanded, "Please, release him."

When the man stood up, he was slightly taller and broader than John Lee. John Lee gave Jilkes his favorite knife, and whispered, "You got any advice for me?"

Jilkes smiled, and said, "He called me the "N" word under his breath."

John Lee asked the guy, "Did you call my friend the "N" word?" The guy aggressively stated, "Yeah I did, and I know he's punking your sissy white ass."

The guy looked around at the rest of the group as if he were going to take on everyone, and somehow escape. Hood said, "I know that look anywhere. You think you're going to take on all of us, and walk out of here. Let me remind you, the completion of your task only gets you a less than invasive interview."

The guy responded, "Fuck you too, lady."

John Lee exclaimed, "Enough talk, it's time to meet your daddy, boy!"

The two men squared off, and the captive threw a thundering blow to John Lee's side that made him wince, and back off. After briefly regaining his composure, John Lee blocked a second blow with his arm that was left tingling. The guy danced around and attempted to slip in a roundhouse kick to John Lee's head that he dodged, but his aggressor followed-up with a grazing right hook to John Lee's head. Jilkes thought to himself, "I had better stop this before this guy hurts my man." As he approached the area, John Lee ordered Jilkes not to interfere under any circumstances.

John Lee watched as the guy began to tire from dancing around as if he were Mohammed Ali, and purposely allowed the man to punch himself out. John Lee pushed the guy off, and said, "You have a thunderous right hand, but now I'm going to show you what an old man can do without all that there fancy dancing and shit." John Lee faked with his left hand to the man's head, followed up with a crashing right hand to his temple, followed by an unorthodox left hand upper cut, and finished him off with a booming and jaw breaking right hand. The blow knocked teeth out, broke implants, and rendered the captive unconscious.

Jilkes looked at the fallen man's associate, and said, "You are about to experience the most sadistic torture that you could ever imagine. My friend is the expert at gutting people from their groin to their brain, and taking a bite out of their heart before it stops beating."

There was a momentary quiet, until the guy screamed, "The Beckmire kid maybe dead I think. I think he may have been decapitated, ground up, and was used for chum for a night fishing expedition with his so-called friends. He bet he could deliver his already rich and entitled associates in excess of a trillion dollars in assets, and failed on any number of occasions to do so, while, as they call it, "conning them and not delivering" on the promise to execute, as I heard."

Hood said, "You seem to hear, and know a lot. Are you one of the people who allegedly saw to his demise?"

The guy's head dropped low, and he said, "I'm not buying a bullet for anyone else. Wake that bully up, and grill him. He is the cousin of one of the perpetrators, and he is the one who snared the Beckmire kid, or what may have been a body double, and took him to the inevitable."

Jilkes asked, "What does that mean? Is the kid dead or alive?"

The guy looked at the knife Jilkes had in his hand, and said, "According to my not too smart associate, he and his crew followed the target for two days, identified him, and saw him leaving his place at 9 pm one night. According to his family member, he was only supposed to track, and follow. My brutish associate acknowledged that he saw the person go into his flat, and twenty minutes later leave. The person had the same clothes on, but once again, no one could confirm his identity because my associate essentially blew his head off with a shotgun. The body fragments and parts were gathered, bagged, and taken for a final boat ride."

Jilkes asked, "Why do you have reservations about who was ground-up?"

The man said, "Having heard about this guy, and knowing some of his proclivities, it just all appeared too laid-back, and easy."

Jilkes, John Lee, Jong, Hood, and Dempsey convened in a corner, and John Lee announced, "I am not going to be the one to tell the Sarge that it has been alleged that his son may be dead, and that he was used as chum. Hell no. Not me."

Jong stated, "I am in the minority, and I will not be the one to tell the Sarge the information that was gleamed from this guy."

Hood said, "Hold on a minute. You guys are senior, and we follow your instructions on missions."

Jilkes cut him off, and said, "You will follow our guidance on this one as well, and craft a conversation that you will collectively have with the Sarge. You will not tell Dr. Beckmire, but you will express your sentiments and information only to the Sarge. Am I making myself crystal clear?"

Dempsey looked at Hood, and then at Jilkes, and said, "We comprehend what is at play here, and only wish that one day we will have that kind of status to relegate others to do tasks that are emotionally corrosive."

Jilkes looked at Dempsey long and hard, and said, "I really understand the underlying principles of your message, Mr. Dempsey. I also must reconcile the fact that even though you people are new, you are emotionally still developing the ethos of the group, and it is with that in mind that I realize that the job in front of us must be completed by one of us seniors. Sorry to misalign your mission with our desire to not be the ones to inform our friend and leader that his son was a co-conspirator to many of the belligerent events that were designed to conclude our existence. The way you stated your premise reminded me of our commitment to each other. This task is one that only members of the Fab 10 + 2 can and should oversee. I thank you for making me and my friends realize our responsibilities to each other, no matter the degree of uncomfortableness."

CHAPTER TWENTY-SIX

Jilkes, John Lee, Jong, Hood, and Dempsey scheduled a time with the Sarge so that they could go over their findings. The Sarge suggested that they meet prior to cocktail hour.

In the interim, the Sarge could be seen playing with his new son/grandson. Courtney stood near the door and watched him having as many laughs as the new baby. Her eyes watered as she thought of their age, and the baby. She asked the Sarge, "Honey, have we bitten off more than we can chew?"

The Sarge laughed, and said, "I don't know about you, but I am up for the challenge. Listen Courtney, we live in a community of love and friendship. If something were to happen to one, or both of us, it's not as though we're poor, no baby, our group will continue on with our mission, God willing. The only thing that concerns me is, if our son attempts to become a parent after we're gone, to access our fortune, how can we prevent that from happening?"

Courtney said, we should talk to Monica and Luana, and let them figure that out. Courtney then hugged Ben, and gave him a salacious kiss, just as Monica crossed the threshold to their room. She exclaimed, "Oh, no! You people are about to do it again, aren't you?"

the end

also in the 'idiot spy' series

Available at Amazon and BarnesandNoble.com